SHADOWS OF THE DRAGON

BOOK ONE OF THE ASHBOURNE SAGA

SAGA

MATT MEMEMARO

To the undying love of everything that we find beautiful in this world

ALSO BY MATT MEMEMARO

The Toldar Series
Voyages of the Kaliban's Cradle Series
The Four Worlds Series
The Kai Flint Series
The Pursuit Series
St. Nick

The Obelisk
The Garden of Chilijo
Zenender's Ranch
Dragontooth Forest
The Seminary of Fire

PROLOGUE

Ayr's muscles tensed as he raised his sword in a defensive stance; steel clashed against steel as he attempted to block the incoming strike. The curved blades met with a loud clang, just as Ayr had predicted, but he still felt the force of the impact jolt through his body. With a swift motion, Ayr pushed back against the enemy sword, feeling the resistance before successfully thrusting it away from his body. He took a step back, catching his breath, and held his sword high in front of him as he grinned fiercely at his opponent.

Standing tall and formidable in the sandy arena was a dark-haired, broad-shouldered man. His fierce gaze locked onto Ayr, his sword hanging loosely by his side, ready to strike at a moment's notice. The intense heat radiating off his body caused beads of sweat to cascade down his bare chest, glistening in the sunlight. Ayr's eyes were drawn to the intricate dragon tattoo coiled over the man's left pectoral, now damp with sweat. It seemed to writhe and slither as the man shifted his weight, poised to continue the fight. He beckoned at Ayr with two fingers.

"Come on, what's the hold up?"

"Nothing, father, I just thought you'd need a moment to catch your breath."

Ayr's father let out a booming laugh, raising his arms high in the air as if beckoning to an invisible audience. He raised his sword and pointed it at Ayr. "That is a bold claim if you think that Dalton

Ashbourne is in need of a break. Need I remind you of my feats against the Commonwealth, without a dragon of my own?"

"What? That you had them on their knees, and if it wasn't for your brother betraying you, you would have had them?" Ayr had heard the story a hundred times before.

"Exactly. Now come on, are we sparring or not? I would not expect your opponent to exchange pleasantries with you when your life is on the line."

His deep, guttural yell echoed through the arena as he charged at Ayr once more. Ayr, anticipating the attack, raised his guard once again. The sharp clang of metal against metal reverberated in his ears as Dalton's sword swung perilously close to Ayr's head. Once the steel had stopped moving, Ayr ducked below the blade and launched a counterattack.

Despite his age, Dalton moved with the same agility and speed as he had twenty years ago. Ayr could not help but shudder at the thought of what kind of fighter Dalton must have been in his prime. His muscles bulged beneath his taut skin, powered by a lifetime of training and battle experience.

Even after all these years, Dalton remained his greatest foe, surpassing him in every aspect of swordsmanship. Dalton, always one step ahead, could anticipate Ayr's every move and easily counter it. With anyone else, Ayr would have been wary and on guard, expecting to beat them. However, despite how well his father had trained him, it was like Ayr was fighting a mirrored image of himself. It was a constant battle against his own reflection, pushing him to be better and never giving him a moment's rest, even if Dalton was stronger and faster.

As they continued their dance, a blur of movement over Dalton's shoulder caught Ayr's eye. He turned his head slightly, trying to get a glimpse of who it was, but Dalton's relentless attacks kept him occupied. The clashing of swords and grunts of exertion filled the arena, drowning out any other sounds. Ayr could not shake the feeling that something was off.

He slipped as his feet fell out from underneath him in the sand, nearly dropping his sword in the process. As he struggled to regain his balance, Dalton took advantage of the opening and lunged forward with his sword aimed directly at Ayr's throat. Acting quickly, Ayr pulled back just enough to avoid a fatal blow but felt the cold steel graze the skin of his neck. It wasn't the first time that a distraction had cost him a piece of flesh.

With a grunt, Ayr fell backwards as Dalton's sword whizzed past his ear. The force of the impact knocked the wind out of him, and he struggled to regain his breath. Dalton regained his footing with the grace and agility of a much younger man, ready to continue the fight. Ayr lay on the ground, gasping for air after having Dalton's knee land squarely in his sternum. He rolled over, groaning in pain as he finally caught sight of their unexpected spectator who had entered the arena.

Dalton was furious. "Come on, boy! I taught you better than that! You can't take your eyes off your opponent!"

The low, mocking laughter grew louder, and Ayr groaned in annoyance. He knew there was only one other person who would have dared to come down to the training pit with him - his younger brother, Byrne. The sunlight filtered through the wooden slats above, casting a warm glow on the sand floor. It was a familiar place for the brothers, where they had spent countless hours honing their skills against each other. Ayr would often be the victor, but Byrne was just as hungry to prove himself.

"Good one, Ayr. Thought you'd be more careful."

"Maybe when I'm duelling you." Ayr tried to not take his eyes off Dalton. "There's no shame in losing to father."

Dalton wasn't distracted by the arrival of Byrne either. He kept his eyes trained on Ayr. "You can keep telling yourself that, boy. But one day that may be the difference between life or death. How are you going to complete your training if you can't beat a man who stopped fighting for his life years ago?"

"I've had enough!"

"Why? Are you ready for your big day tomorrow? Are you getting nervous?" A wicked smile came over Dalton's face as he taunted Ayr.

"No, but I know that this will only ever happen once in my life. I need to make the best impression possible. I won't be able to do that battered and bruised."

Dalton laughed again. "You're the son of Dalton Ashbourne, the infamous rebel king. What more of an impression do you need to make?"

Ayr felt ashamed. "I don't want them to kill me. I'd actually like to get through my training in one piece. Do you not remember what happened to me at the battle academy?"

Dalton deftly tucked his sharp, gleaming sword under his arm and extended a hand towards Ayr. With a heavy scowl, Ayr reluctantly accepted Dalton's help and clambered back to his feet. As they stood together, Dalton's imposing figure towered over Ayr. His dark green eyes held an intense emptiness that made Ayr feel small and insignificant. It was as if he were staring into the depths of a bottomless pit, unable to look away or escape its grip.

"My son, you are an Ashbourne."

Ayr bowed his head. "Yes, father."

"You know what you need to do at the Seminary. If you are concerned about how they will receive you, say that you are Anton's son." Dalton's tone was flat and measured.

Ayr grumbled, looking for a way out of the uncomfortable conversation. "And when Uncle Anton sees me at the Obelisk? What then, father? I will be exposed."

"You will have a dragon by then. Anton is far too busy to meddle in the day-to-day activities of the Seminary and the Obelisk. Prove yourself worthy of it and they won't remove you like they did to me. Allow me to handle Anton."

Despite Dalton's words, Ayr couldn't help but feel on edge. "Your words don't reassure me. I remember what they did to you and how they lied. I won't let them do that to me."

"Good! You are an Ashbourne. You are beholden to no man; not even to one that shares our blood." Dalton took a breath and leaned forward, pressing his lips against Ayr's forehead. "Ayr do not fall victim to the Commonwealth's lies. They will betray you. I am sending you because I believe you can survive there. Now, go and prepare yourself to see it done."

Ayr bowed his head as a sign of respect. "Yes, father."

"May your dragon always breathe fire, and may his wings carry you forward." Dalton raised his hand and placed it over the dragon tattoo that was still shimmering on his chest.

ONE

May your dragon always breathe fire and may his wings carry you forward.

"Attention!"

A sudden, guttural shout ripped through the air; its source hidden from Ayr's view. The bodies of the recruits on either side of him tensed with fear and anticipation. Ayr dared not turn his head to see where the sound had come from; he knew the consequences would be severe if he broke rank. The steward at the black iron gate had made it perfectly clear. Do not move under any circumstances. The voice had been terrifying, sudden and loud. Where had it come from?

Ayr remained on edge as silence filled the air around him. Rather than continuing to think about the voice, he locked his eyes onto the recruit ten paces directly in front of him. Every muscle in his body was coiled like a spring, ready to react at any moment. The atmosphere crackled with tension as they waited for their next command. The other recruit stood tall, his sturdy frame a perfect match for Ayr's own. Every muscle in his body seemed to be chiselled and ready for action, just like Ayr had been when he left his room that morning. Apart from the uniform he'd been given in his room at the inn in the township, Ayr had no idea what to expect. It was clear the other recruits had been given the same outfit.

Dressed in a sleek jet-black vest and tight white riding pants, the other recruits were an intimidating sight. The snug fit of their pants only emphasized their lean physique, while the knee-high riding boots added a touch of formality to their attire. Despite standing for what felt like hours, the comfort of the boots was a small blessing amidst the rigorous ordeal they were likely to endure.

The Seminary was a tranquil haven; the gentle autumn breeze brushed against Ayr's cheek and rustled his blonde locks. He resisted the urge to adjust his hair, heeding the steward's warning. Ayr took in the myriad of sights and sounds that surrounded the Seminary. The vibrant colours of the changing leaves danced in the sunlight, while birds sang their songs in perfect harmony. The faint scent of wood smoke from nearby chimneys wafted into his nostrils. Still there was no sign of who had shouted at him and the other recruits.

In total, twenty other recruits had joined Ayr since he had been standing in his allocated spot. The twenty were split into two rows, each recruit standing on a blackened-out circle that was no wider than the average man's shoulder width. The circles were a stark contrast to the otherwise lighter toned cobblestone path that Ayr had taken to reach the cornered off courtyard that he now stood in. All that Ayr could see to his right was a high green hedge that blocked out anything hidden behind it.

"Attention!"

Ayr went to stiffen again but stopped himself from moving. The other recruit standing opposite him flinched ever so slightly. The differences in their ages could have been days, the other recruit somewhere between eighteen and twenty-one summers. He looked increasingly nervous as the minutes ticked by, more sweat continuing to fester on his brow. Every few minutes, the other recruit would wipe his brow clear, only for it to start soon after once again. Ayr smirked to himself, full well knowing that he would not be faring much better. The uniforms were not breathable, even if they did look exceptionally sleek. With the amount of money that Dalton had spent on his training to this point, he had to succeed. Failure was not an option. His father had warned him of the Seminary and their harsh punishments.

"Attention!"

They were being tested. Ayr kept his head straight, now focusing on nothing but the other recruit in front of him. The more he stared, the more he felt his pulse quicken. Now was not the time to panic. More time trickled by without any more noise coming from the strange, loud voice. How much longer would they stand here? An hour? A day? A week? An itch started to creep up Ayr's index finger. He tried rubbing his thumb against it, giving away as little movement as possible. As he did, another strange sound filled the air.

Whoom! Whoom! Whoom!

A steady beating was growing louder by the second. Unable to contain his curiosity any longer, Ayr turned his head, following the sound. The beating grew louder until an ear-splitting roar broke the sky. Ayr flinched, unable to raise his hands to his ears to block some of the noise. The beating sound was masked by the roar, and before Ayr had time to process what was happening, a shadow, larger than a house shot overhead. It blotted out the sun for only a moment. A gust of wind almost knocked Ayr to his knees, but he gritted his teeth and willed himself to stand. The roar ripped through the sky again, and now Ayr could confirm what it was as it came into view. A dragon. The very thing that he and all the other recruits were here for.

Ayr stood defiantly in the face of the monstrous creature circling above him. The dragon's colossal wings beat relentlessly at the ground, stirring up gusts of wind with each pass that threatened to knock Ayr off his feet. As it descended lower, Ayr's heart raced and he recoiled instinctively, fighting to maintain his balance amidst the chaos. Then came an earth-shattering crash, sending shockwaves through the ground and causing Ayr's legs to tremble beneath him. He could feel the heat emanating from the dragon's fiery breath as it stood overhead.

"You're out! You're out!"

Ayr raised his eyes, confounded. It wasn't the dragon speaking. The sharp, commanding voice of a woman cut through the air, drowning out the heavy breaths of the dragon somewhere above Ayr and to his left. He could see the ominous shadow of its long neck stretching out on the floor, but he dared not move. This was the closest he had ever been to a dragon, and the deep rumbling in its chest sent shivers down his spine. It was a powerful creature, untamed and wild, but its true strength lay in the rider perched upon its back. Without her guidance, it was nothing more than a fearsome beast, ready to tear him to pieces. Not knowing the true size of the creature unnerved Ayr, but he was unwavering, waiting until the moment that he would be addressed. This was all part of the test.

Slowly, the dragon's head came into view. The dragon's black scales shone in the sunlight, brighter than they had any right to be. Ayr wanted to move his head but willed himself to remain still. It was not worth an early elimination from the Seminary process. Out of the corner of his eye, Ayr could make out another recruit that was standing within arm's reach of the dragon's head. The recruit took a step back, and the woman yelled out again.

"Get out!"

A gasp escaped the recruit's lips, and he pointed at himself. "Who are you talking to? Me?"

"Yes! Now get out! You heard the rules!"

The dragon's massive head snapped around with a thunderous crack, causing Ayr to mentally shrink back in fear. He found himself staring directly into the creature's face, his reflection perfectly mirrored in its enormous yellow eyes, each one almost as large as his entire body.

Ayr stood frozen, unable to tear his gaze away from the fearsome beast. His mind raced with thoughts of being devoured whole, all his training and efforts leading up to this moment rendered meaningless.

He had come so far to get in the front door of the Seminary. To not even progress to being paired with a dragon would be considered a failure. Sweat dripped down his forehead as he braced himself for the inevitable.

"Recruits! You may relax and move around. Those remaining have passed your first test!" It was the voice that had been calling them to attention.

Finally, after a moment of confusion and uncertainty, Ayr's senses were able to pinpoint the source of the voice. He turned towards the tall hedge looming to his right, and in the same instant, a sharp clang of steel on steel rang out. As if by magic, a hidden metal gate swung open in the center of the hedges, revealing a path beyond. The sound of footsteps steadily grew louder as someone made their way towards Ayr and the other recruits, their heavy boots echoing off the pavement with each step.

Ayr could not tear his gaze away from the magnificent dragon above him. Its deep, rumbling growls bellowed like a mighty lion, sending shivers down Ayr's spine. Thin streams of smoke snaked out from between sharp teeth as the beast glared menacingly at Ayr and the group of recruits. The air around them was thick with the scent of sulfur. Could the dragon smell the fear radiating from the recruits? The dragon lowered its head, and at last, Ayr could make out the rider.

The rider's attire mirrored that of the recruits, donning a black vest and crisp white riding pants. Their high leather boots were polished to perfection. But it was the rider's vest that set them apart. Unlike the smooth, form-fitting vests of the others, this one was rigid and coarse, mimicking the sharp scales of a dragon as it blended seamlessly with their mount.

The rider's face remained a mystery, veiled by a full-face helmet that was black as night. A fierce, white skull was painted upon it, its hollow eyes seeming to glare at anyone who dared to look. A long, red plume jutted out from the back of the helmet, mirroring the dragon's fiery scales that ran along its spine. The rider paused for a moment, taking in their surroundings before gracefully dismounting from the dragon as it lowered itself to the ground. With a steady hand placed against the dragon's scales, the rider descended with ease and landed on the ground below.

Ayr could not help but raise his hands together, clapping softly at first, then more enthusiastically as the remaining recruits joined in. Their claps became a unified beat. The rider stood up to their full height and moved away from the dragon, its scales glinting in the sunlight. The dragon lifted its head again and the rider reached out a hand to scratch underneath its chin. With a gentle sigh, the dragon lowered its head in contentment.

If the dragon had been any other creature, the sight would have been beautiful - a harmonious bond between two powerful beings. Despite this, Ayr could not shake off the sense of unease around the jet-black creature, knowing it could easily dismember or disintegrate him without warning.

The applause of the recruits was quickly cut off by the appearance of an elderly man passing through the gate. He too wore a black uniform like the recruits, but with a hooded collar and a white pin adorned with a yellow star on his right shoulder. Flecks of silver were sprinkled throughout his thick, full beard, giving him a distinguished look and placing him close to sixty years old. He stood tall and proud, with broad shoulders and a strong jawline, only a few years older than Dalton.

"Gentlemen, welcome to the Seminary of Fire. My name is Lucas Kaiser, and I will be your host whilst you train here."

The name sent a jolt of recognition through Ayr's body. His father had spoken it countless times, usually with a tinge of bitterness and resentment. This was the man who had been responsible for his defeat at the Lord's Pulpit, the legendary battle that changed the course of the war. Now, in the years since, Lucas was reduced to merely administrative duties at the prestigious school for dragon riders. Ayr let out a mirthless laugh, attempting to mask his emotions behind a neutral facade. He knew he had failed as his face betrayed his true feelings - a mix of anger, disappointment, and disdain towards the man who had caused his family so much pain. Did he still have a dragon?

Lucas spotted Ayr and limped towards him. "Is there something funny, recruit?"

Ayr quickly returned to a stoic expression as the eyes of all recruits and the dragon fell upon him. "No, sir. Not at all."

"Pull that expression again whilst I'm talking and I'll have you flogged, boy." Lucas was stern.

Ayr bowed his head. "Yes, sir. I understand."

Lucas scowled at him before turning his attention back to the other recruits still in line. He tucked his arms behind his back and began pacing in front of the recruits. The sneer on his face made Ayr want to punch him, to repay some of the pain that the Kaisers had brought upon his family. Instead, Ayr swallowed his pride.

"Some of you here may think that the Seminary of Fire will be easy, but I can assure you it will not be. Those of you who fail will not be granted permission to step inside the Obelisk. Twenty-one of you began here today. Three of you have already gone home." Lucas stopped pacing and glared at the nearest recruit. "Those were the lucky ones. From here on out, those of you who fail, will be going home in pieces, or not at all." Lucas raised his hand towards the rider who had remained motionless until this point. "I'll hand you over to the Lady Elanor Sunfire and her dragon Evor to explain your first task!"

The rider lifted a gloved hand to her face, the material silent as she tugged at it. Ayr watched on, but instead of the helmet being hard to remove, it seemed to bend and morph like a piece of fabric, sliding off her face with fluid grace. As she shook out her long auburn locks, they cascaded down past her shoulders in a shimmering waterfall. The strands caught the light, reflecting hues of honey and sunshine. Ayr wondered where she had been hiding all that beautiful hair all this time. It seemed to radiate a warmth and vitality that matched her own fiery spirit.

With practiced ease, Elanor folded the helmet into her palm and discreetly tucked it into the hidden pocket of her vest. Ayr froze as he took in the woman in front of him. Whilst Evor was powerful and majestic in his own right, the aura that radiated from Elanor was just as ferocious. She had not taken her blue eyes off Ayr, who felt as though she was staring into his soul.

"What is beneath your feet?" Elanor's question was pointed, but her tone was softer than her yelling had been before.

Ayr took his eyes off Elanor and glanced around at the other recruits. They looked just as perplexed as he felt. Was it a question just for him? He felt naked and exposed. Elanor stood with her hands on her hips, waiting for an answer.

"Cobblestone and dirt!" Whichever recruit had spoken sounded confident.

Elanor's striking blue eyes snapped towards the recruit that had spoken, her gaze sharp and fierce. Evor's long, serpent-like neck coiled through the air as he made his way down the line of recruits. His head hovered over the one who had spoken, his mouth slightly ajar revealing his sharp fangs as long as Ayr's forearm and a forked tongue that was longer than Ayr's body. The scent of earth and musk emanated from his scaly skin as he surveyed the group with a sinister grin on his face.

"Do you fear death, worm?" Evor's voice boomed like thunder, its rumbling echo seeming to emanate from the very mountains in the distance before crashing down upon Ayr. Each word was delivered with such force and power that it felt as though the ground beneath them trembled in response. Ayr felt small and insignificant in the presence of Evor's commanding voice, like a mere mortal standing before a god.

The recruit's response was shaky. "No! No, I do not."

A deep rumble radiated from Evor, a plume of smoke escaping his nostrils. The recruit's eyes widened in fear, and he let out a shrill scream, only to be met with chuckles from Elanor and Lucas.

"Could have fooled me." A childish grin spread across Lucas' face.

"Kaiser!" Elanor's voice shot across the courtyard like a whip. "Can I continue?"

Lucas bowed his head. "Of course, my Lady."

"Dragons. Dragons are beneath your feet. Dragons are the essence of this world and their influence touches everything. They are powerful, magical creatures that are not to be tricked, disrespected or otherwise trifled with. Am I understood?" Ayr began nodding his head as Elanor's eyes passed over him. If Evor didn't turn his attention to him, everything would be fine. "Am I understood!"

"Yes!" Ayr and the other recruits all agreed.

Elanor's eyes worked along the line of recruits, scowling at each one of them. Evor retracted his head from over the recruits and stood back up to his full height. He cast an ominous shadow over the recruits as they waited for what would happen next. Ayr could feel sweat beginning to pool on his palms.

Having finished her inspection, Elanor nodded with approval. "Very well. Now that you understand the essence of dragons, perhaps it's time that you met your potential companions. Kaiser, if you would be so kind as to introduce them, please."

TWO

Dragons? Already? Dalton hadn't informed him that they would be meeting their match this early on in the process.

An anticipatory murmur rippled through the group of recruits, their voices hushed with excitement and nervous energy. Ayr stood apart from the rest, his sceptical gaze scanning over his fellow trainees. They were about to be paired with their dragons, or so they had been told. The thought seemed absurd to Ayr - surely such an honour and responsibility would require more rigorous trials and training. But as he watched, a small roar broke through the chatter, more akin to an excited dog's bark than the fierce cry of a dragon. Ayr's heart pounded in his chest, both apprehensive and eager to meet his companion and prove himself worthy of the Commonwealth's highest honour. It was happening.

The gate that Lucas walked out of was still open, and Ayr could make out fresh movement beyond it. Evor let out a thunderous roar overhead and the movement behind the hedge became apparent. One by one, dragons stepped out from behind the hedge, through the gate and into the courtyard. These were not the colossal beasts Ayr had expected; instead, they were no larger than medium-sized dogs.

As the dragons approached Ayr and the recruits, he was met with a wall of vivid colour, each dragon representing a different hue of the rainbow. One in particular caught his eye, standing out amongst the rest. This dragon was smaller than the others, its body reaching only up to their shoulders, but its presence was undeniable. Against the backdrop of vibrant colours, its scales glimmered pure white, almost blinding in its brilliance. It seemed to radiate purity and grace amidst the chaos of the other dragons. As Ayr got closer, he could not help feeling drawn to this magnificent creature, curious about its story and purpose within the world of the Commonwealth. It had to be a female.

Despite her height being almost on par with the other dragons, she appeared petite and delicate in comparison. Her soft sapphire eyes scanned over the assembled group of recruits, each one eager to prove themselves worthy of being chosen. Ayr's heart raced as the magnificent creature's gaze passed over the recruits. As it passed over him, the dragon paused and turned its head, fixing her piercing blue gaze on Ayr. In that moment, he felt as though he was laid bare before her, his every thought and emotion visible to her. The dragon stood before him with an air of regality, unmoving and unyielding, even as the others continued on their way. It was as if time stood still in her presence.

Another dragon spoke up, its voice little more than a harsh hissing sound. "There's not a lot to choose from, very disappointing."

The creature possessed a vibrant red crest that adorned its forehead, a striking colour contrasting against the mesmerizing violet hue of the rest of its body. The deep shades of purple seemed to shimmer and shift under the light, giving off an otherworldly aura as if it were plucked from a dream. Its presence was both captivating and enchanting, drawing the eye towards its unique and beautiful features. Yet it still didn't draw Ayr's attention as much as the little white dragon.

"I'm sure that we will find our riders. We may just need to be patient." Now it was the little white dragon that spoke up.

The deep, resonant voice that echoed from the dragon's mouth was unmistakably feminine. Ayr blinked, wondering if he was hallucinating. Hearing Evor speak with venom and ferocity was one thing, hearing the regality and innocence of this small dragon was another. He knew that dragons were said to be intelligent beings, but he never expected to hear one speak aloud like this. The stories he had heard about their communication seemed almost mythical in comparison to the reality before him. Each word rolled off the creature's tongue with a hiss, yet there was a soothing undertone that calmed Ayr's nerves. Despite her otherworldly nature, the dragon spoke with surprising clarity and precision, unlike Evor and the red dragon.

The female dragon slowly thawed from her frozen state and continued on, turning to catch one last glimpse of Ayr before joining the rest of her majestic kind in a single file line behind Evor. The larger dragon turned his massive head to survey his smaller kin, with a particular focus on the pure white one amongst them.

"Azura, you don't have to do this again. These recruits will not be worth your time."

So, that was her name. The beautiful white dragon shook her body as she sat down beside Evor. Her piercing eyes scanned over the group of recruits again, taking in each one with a calculating gaze. Ayr felt a shiver run down his spine as those eyes briefly landed on him once more before moving on. There was something otherworldly about this dragon, something that commanded respect and fear in equal measure.

"Maybe one recruit will stand above the rest. I can feel in my bones that it will happen one day." Azura seemed hopeful.

Unlike the other dragons, Ayr's eyes were immediately drawn to her slender, angled face. He noticed that her neck was more refined and graceful compared to the bulky builds of the others. While their scales were dark and dull against the multi-coloured backdrop, hers shimmered and sparkled in the sunlight. What was it about her that captivated him? Despite not being the largest or swiftest dragon, there was something alluring and unique about her that he could not quite pinpoint.

Another deep rumble resonated from Evor. "Hmm. Unlikely, but I wish you luck once again."

"Recruits!" Lucas stood between them with his hands tucked neatly behind his back. "When I call upon you, you will pass by the dragons one at a time. If one bows their head towards you, they have chosen you to join them in life. But be warned, if you pass by the dragons and one does not bow, then you have failed, and you must return home."

The tension in the courtyard was palpable as the recruits exchanged glances, unsure if they were ready for this daunting task. The dragons were small, but if they could breathe fire they could still burn the flesh from a person's body. Lucas' piercing gaze seemed to bore into each of them, daring them to question his instructions. With a deep breath, he asked one final time. "Any questions?"

A lone recruit, positioned across from Ayr, timidly raised his hand into the air. Lucas noticed the gesture and immediately pointed to him. The recruit's youthful appearance was evident in his freckled face and fiery red hair. He looked no older than Ayr himself, but the determination in his eyes showed maturity beyond his years, even if he looked like he had never raised a sword.

"What do you want, recruit?"

"What if more than one dragon bows before us?"

Lucas chortled softly. "Well, that's not going to happen. A dragon knows not to overstep another's boundaries. No rider has ever been that powerful. You get one dragon for life. No second chances, even if it dies."

With a deliberate movement, he reached into his pocket and retrieved a piece of parchment, its surface crumpled from being folded repeatedly. As he unfolded it, the parchment let out a slight rustle, like whispers among friends. Lucas cleared his throat loudly, drawing attention to himself as he peered intently at the first name on the list. He studied it with intensity, his brow furrowed in concentration.

"Recruit Bradley Owens. Step forward!"

With a determined nod, the freckled recruit stepped towards the line of majestic dragons. Owens measured each step as he carefully placed each foot on the ground, as if every step could be his last. The dog-sized creatures all sat on their hindquarters with their wings tucked neatly against their backs. The air was thick with anticipation, and not a single being besides Owens dared to move as they waited for him to approach the first dragon. Its scales shimmered a deep emerald green, its head wider and more commanding than the others in the lineup. As Owens approached, it did not bow but instead held its ground with an air of confidence. Undeterred, he moved on to the next dragon, his determination unwavering.

The yellow dragon, a fierce and regal creature, stood slightly small-er than its green counterpart. Its grey eyes bore into Owens with an air of superiority and condescension. Despite this, Owens humbly bowed before it but received no reciprocation. Owens then moved onto the midnight blue dragon beside it. Ayr was growing anxious; would one of the dragons eat him, or would he be sent home? Much to Ayr's surprise, the blue dragon returned Owens' bow. Letting out a heavy sigh of relief, Owens was beckoned towards Elanor by her gentle hand gestures. As he moved to stand beside her and Evor, the colour slowly returned to his pale complexion.

Lucas was already looking down at the list at the next name. "Re-cruit Logan Evers, step forward!"

One of the smallest recruits, with ebony hair that matched Evor's scales, nervously approached the dragons. He barely reached Ayr's shoulder in height, but his determination burned bright in his dark eyes. Ayr watched as Evers continued down the line, each dragon re-maining unmoved by his presence. Not a single one had acknowledged him. As Evers grew nearer to the end of the line, each new dragon only began to look less impressed with him. Frustration and disappointment etched across his features as he turned to look at Lucas, who could only shake his head in sympathy. Lucas waited until Evers had reached the end of the line and the final dragon shook its own head in disappointment.

"Get out." Without skipping a beat, Lucas picked up his parchment and read the next name. "Stephen Gable."

Stephen took a while to be paired with a dragon. After trying almost all dragons in the line, a large red beast bowed before him. The process continued, one by one, until Ayr stood alone without a dragon by his side. The other recruits had either successfully bonded with a dragon or failed and been dismissed, their hearts heavy with disappointment. With each recruit, Lucas had carefully crossed their names off his list with the precise strokes of his quill. He peered over the parchment at Ayr.

"There's nobody left on this list. Who are you, recruit?"

"Ayr."

"Ayr what?" Lucas' question was pointed. He had no time for games. "How did you even get up here?"

Ayr pointed at the black gate that guarded the entrance to the courtyard. "The steward had me on his list and let me in. I'm sure there's been a mistake."

Lucas scanned up and down the list again, shaking his head. "You're not on the list. We do not make mistakes here. How did you get in here?"

"There won't be a mistake," Elanor cut across the courtyard. She had moved away from Evor and was walking towards Lucas and Ayr. "He'll be on the list. What's your name, boy?"

"Ayr Ashbourne."

"Ashbourne?"

With a swift, fluid motion, Elanor unsheathed her sword and pointed it towards Ayr, the tip glinting in the sunlight. A low growl came from Evor above and he shifted his stance, muscles tense as he glared down at Ayr. There was nothing that Ayr could do. He had a sword on his hip, just as Elanor did, but what? He could fight her and win, only to be incinerated by her dragon. Lucas visibly recoiled as Elanor marched towards him, covering the gap between them in only a handful of steps. He squinted at the list.

The sound of Lucas' shuddering breath filled the air as he anxiously checked the list once again. His eyes darted back and forth, scanning each line with a furrowed brow. A brief glance was exchanged between him and Elanor, causing Lucas to quickly change his demeanour. He straightened his posture and took on a more confident tone, determined to hide any trace of worry or doubt.

"This can't be!"

Ayr stuck his chin out, hearing whispers from both the recruits and the dragons, all waiting nearby. "You heard me."

"Whose child are you?" Elanor rounded on the list in Lucas' hands.

Lucas glared at her. "Does it matter? He's a *fucking* Ashbourne. They're all mad. Even Anton!"

Elanor glared back at Lucas, matching his intensity before she refocused on Ayr. Ayr couldn't decide who he was more intimidated by. "It matters. Are you Dalton's or Anton's spawn?"

"Dalton's." Ayr was unprepared to deny his lineage.

A collective gasp escaped the dragons, including Evor. The other recruits also visibly recoiled at the shocking news. In a fit of anger, Lucas threw the list onto the ground and stomped on it with his foot, taking a threatening step towards Ayr. His hand trembled uncontrollably, betraying his inner rage. "Your father has sent you here to die! Evor!"

Evor raised his head with a grumble. "I am not yours to command, Kaiser. Elanor does not wish to kill this Ashbourne."

"What?" Lucas glanced over his shoulder at Elanor. "You can't be serious. Evor isn't reading your mind correctly. You've gone mad."

Elanor shook her head. "We're not seeing something at play here. He's clearly here for a reason. If he got past the steward, something's happened. He could be lying."

"Nobody would lie about being an Ashbourne." Lucas drew his sword from its sheath.

"Kaiser!"

"I'm going to end the Ashbourne threat once and for all." Lucas started walking towards Ayr with the blade extended.

Ayr had no weapons drawn, but for the first time in a long while, he felt strong and capable. He smirked, waiting for Lucas to swing at him. His muscles tensed as he prepared for a possible attack from the old man, ready to defend himself.

"Kaiser!"

Ayr stumbled backwards, his feet slipping on the slick cobblestones. His eyes caught a streak of light as the back of his head collided with the unforgiving stones. The impact sent a jolt through his body, causing him to see stars and feel the dull throb of pain in his skull. Ayr blinked and looked up, expecting to see Lucas standing over him with his sword raised. Instead of a sword there was a thin white tail flickering in its place. Ayr heard a snarling and saw Lucas backing away.

"Azura! What in Galared's name are you doing?"

"You will not touch him!"

"Why not? The Ashbourne's almost ended your family line!"

"I will claim him." The small white dragon was defiant.

"Azura..." Evor took a step forward. "Do not do this."

"It is done." Azura turned away from him. "This is my choice and my choice alone to make. You will not change my mind. Ayr Ashbourne will be my rider."

"Bow to him if you wish to make this claim."

Azura's sharp hiss pierced the air, directed fiercely at Lucas. Her long, stark tail curled around her body as she turned to face him. Ayr lifted himself off the ground with slow, deliberate movements, never once breaking his gaze from her intense stare. As he rose to his feet, he noticed the other recruits who were all watching with rapt attention, their eyes fixed on the tense interaction unfolding before them.

The white dragon cocked her head slightly. Ayr felt a calming presence wash over him. He was enchanted by her. She started to move like a snake, rising up towards him. As she drew up to his height, standing on her back legs, Azura entered a low bow. She kept her blue eyes locked on him at all times and the wave washed over Ayr once again. It sent shivers down his spine as she continued to stare at him.

Ayr felt a sudden shift in the air, as if a current of energy had passed between him and the white dragon. In an instant, his mind was flooded with new knowledge and understanding that he had never possessed before. He stood transfixed, unable to tear his gaze away from the dragon's piercing eyes. As he tried to reach out and touch her, he realised that his entire body was frozen in place, only able to move his eyes. Time seemed to stand still as Ayr was lost in the depths of the dragon's gaze. A sharp voice cut through the silence like a whip, bringing Ayr back to reality.

"Recruit! Your dragon has selected you! Line up with the others!"

Ayr's exhausted legs stumbled, their heavy muscles burning with each step. It felt like he had been walking for hours without rest. Lucas was engrossed in his list once again, his nose buried in the words as Elanor stood over his shoulder, her delicate frame casting a shadow on the pages in front of him.

Ayr was forthcoming in his apology. "Sorry. I don't know what came over me."

Lucas shook his head and glared at him. "Don't be sorry to me. Be sorry to the rest of your cohort. You're just cutting into their recovery time the longer you're out here. Now move!"

Ayr strode confidently towards the gathering of recruits, his boots crunching against the rocky ground with each step. As he passed by Elanor and Lucas, their voices carried to him in a hushed murmur. They were softly spoken, but still plenty loud enough for Ayr to make out every word. He passed them without comment, listening intently as he glanced back.

Incensed, Lucas rounded on Elanor. "You knew he was coming! Why didn't you tell me?"

"The Overlord only told me this morning before we arrived. I was still surprised that he showed up."

"Anton? Why the fuck would he allow his brother's son to enter the Seminary? Especially after everything that Dalton did to us. Why is the Overlord meddling in Seminary affairs?"

"Do you expect me to be able to pry reason from his brain? I can only do the best with the hand I'm dealt."

"Well, you're the instructor. What are you going to do with them?"

"I knew he'd bond with a dragon, but now we need to put him through the real test." Elanor frowned and glanced at the recruits. "Get them ready, Lucas. I want to have these recruits in the air sooner rather than later."

Lucas drew closer to Elanor. "What are you saying? Do you want them to proceed to the final test already?"

"Absolutely. No lodgings. This intake we're doing in reverse. I'm not wasting any time if there's an Ashbourne in the mix."

"What if he's not Dalton's? What if he is legitimately Anton's?"

Elanor shook her head. "The Overlord is just as deranged. I know he is an authority within the Commonwealth, but I don't trust him as far as I can throw him. Maybe we can change his fate. If he dies now, we'll know he's not up to the cut."

Lucas puffed out his lips and put his hands on his hips. "I hope you know what you're doing. I don't want to face the wrath of Anton Ashbourne."

THREE

"Recruits!" Lucas had finished speaking to Elanor and was now facing the mixed line of recruits and dragons. "Now that everyone has either been selected by a dragon or has failed the first test, your real trials will begin."

"You will come with me to the Hungering. There we will assess your physical and mental fortitude. Just remember, should you fail any task you'll be sent home. Or worse."

Owens stepped up to be the voice for the recruits. "What could worse be?"

Elanor just smiled at him. "There's always at least one that finds out. Now come with me."

The recruits around Ayr looked hesitant. Nobody wanted to move unless they were directed. The direction came from Evor seconds later.

"Move."

The commanding voice of the black dragon rumbled through the recruits, urging them forward. Ayr could sense the apprehension emanating from the others, but he felt determined and ready for whatever lay ahead. The Hungering sounded daunting, but if the other recruits had trained like Ayr, they would be ready for it.

Though he could not see beyond the looming mountains before them, Ayr refused to let fear hold him back. As if sensing his resolve, Azura, who reminded him of his childhood dog, appeared at his side. She tilted her head up at him with big, trusting eyes, and in that moment, Ayr felt a strong connection to her. With a smile of determination, he took a deep breath and stepped forward into the unknown with Azura by his side.

Elanor and Lucas glided effortlessly on the balls of their feet, moving towards the towering gate that loomed ahead. Ayr could feel the cool caress of the breeze against his skin, carrying with it the sweet perfume of newly cut grass and vibrant flowers. As they drew closer, he could hear the faint but steady creaking of the gate's hinges, as if welcoming them inside. The intricately carved designs etched into the metal gate seemed to watch over him and the other recruits, their eyes following their every move. With unwavering determination, Ayr stepped through the threshold, bracing himself for whatever challenges lay beyond the hedges.

Ayr's eyes scanned the towering hedges on either side of him, their thickness seeming to exceed his own height. As he stepped through the gate, a sense of being closed in enveloped him. The walls of green were as tall as Evor, creating a wide pathway that allowed the enormous black dragon to walk through without brushing against the leaves. Elanor and Lucas strode ahead confidently, with Elanor occasionally turning back to check on the new recruits trailing behind. Their footsteps echoed loudly against the silent, dense foliage, adding an eerie atmosphere to their journey. Once all the recruits were inside the hedges, Elanor turned back and stopped.

"Hurry up, you lot! Welcome to the Garden of Chilijo."

Amidst the chorus of gasps and whispers from his fellow recruits, Ayr could not help but feel a sense of awe himself as he gazed upon the breathtaking sight before him. Chilijo, the legendary dragon, was one that Ayr had only heard of in stories - he never could have imagined that there would be a whole garden dedicated to him. As he cautiously stepped deeper into the flora, Ayr could hear the reassuring sound of Azura's footsteps behind him.

Ayr continued to follow Elanor and Lucas into the garden. The walk was brief, with two passages cutting out, one on either side of the main path. The garden began to open quickly, no more than a few hundred meters away. Here on this side, the hedges were growing shorter and thinner, revealing glimpses of what lay beyond.

As Ayr emerged on the other side of the towering barriers, he came to an abrupt halt. Before him spread a vast and breathtaking valley, bursting with vibrant hues of emerald and jade. The rich earth was covered in a lush carpet of diverse vegetation, from delicate wildflowers that swayed in the gentle breeze to towering trees whose branches reached towards the distant mountains like outstretched arms. The air was thick with the heady scents of blooming flowers and damp soil, filling Ayr's senses with wonder and awe.

The rich flora wasn't the only thing that caught Ayr's eye. In every direction, majestic dragons of all sizes and colours could be seen, creating a vibrant display against the lush, green landscape. Some glided gracefully through the sky with their riders nestled on their backs, while others perched atop rocky outcroppings or playfully chased each other through the clouds. Down below, a winding river painted in shades of blue snaked its way through the valley floor, adding a tranquil element to the bustling scene before him. The air was filled with the sounds of dragon roars and wings beating against the wind. It felt like he had stepped into a fantastical world beyond his wildest dreams.

"Wow. What is this place? I've never seen anything like it."

Lucas thrust his arms out, gesturing to the open space. "Welcome to the Hungering. This is going to be where you're going to be doing all of your training until you become a rider. There are plenty of resources here for your dragons to grow and prosper. You're expected to be self-sufficient within this area."

"What was down the other paths?"

Lucas smirked at him. "Don't you worry about that yet."

"Aren't you going to give us shelter?" A recruit standing next to a bright yellow dragon raised his head.

"Didn't you hear me? You need to be self-sufficient. There is plenty of food and water for you. You'll need to work with your dragons in order to survive. This is one of your first tests. If you survive the Hungering, you will be one step closer to becoming a rider!" Lucas smiled at them curling his lips up before starting to walk back into the garden. "Good luck, gentlemen."

"Wait!" Owens threw his arm up in a panic. "How long will we have to be here for?"

"As long as it takes." Lucas grinned at him.

"We'll be back once you're settled in. Evor!"

The dragon's massive neck swooped down in a graceful arc, coming to rest just inches away from Elanor. His reptilian eye glinted with intelligence and curiosity as he observed her. With steady steps, Elanor approached the towering beast and nimbly climbed onto its broad neck. Without warning, Evor launched into the air, his powerful wings beating against the wind with a thunderous roar. The other dragons below let out a deafening cheer, their voices blending together in an exhilarating symphony.

One dragon barked with excitement. "I wish I could do that."

"Soon." Azura rolled a soft glance over to one of the smaller purple dragons. "Bond with your riders and we'll all be able to do that."

"What would you know, Azura? You've been without a rider for the last thirty years."

Ayr felt a pit of rage building in his stomach, but he was not the only one to react. Azura let out a fierce growl, her long fangs gleaming in the sunlight. She lunged towards the smaller purple dragon, its scales shimmering with iridescent hues. The purple dragon hissed and backed away, clearly intimidated by Azura's ferocity. Ayr took a step back, intending to watch from a safe distance, unsure of how to intervene in this clash of mighty beasts. Suddenly, a larger red dragon appeared between them, standing tall and powerful, its ruby-red scales reflecting the fiery determination in its eyes. Ayr could feel the tension in the air as the two dragons faced off, their primal instincts taking over.

"We don't have time for this, Brevor! Any moment you waste here is a moment that you waste in the Hungering. Solve your petty argument later if you have to. If you don't, I'll call Evor."

"I think you need to remember who Evor is promised to." Azura flicked her tongue in and out of her mouth with a menacing growl. "Who do you think it will end badly for? It won't be me."

Brevor didn't take kindly to the growl, reacting with one of his own. "Promised or not, you'll make a fine meal once some of us grow a little more. You'll remain a runt."

"Don't assume that you will grow faster than me." Azura extended her neck, so she reached her full height. She was still shorter than Brevor, but just as intimidating. "The Hungering is all about exploiting your bond with your rider. Who's to say that I won't grow faster than you?"

Brevor drew back, hissing at Azura. His tongue lashed out at her. Azura snapped at him and Brevor took another further step back. The mighty purple dragon's scorching breath steamed through his razor-sharp teeth, hissing with a menacing intensity. Slowly, he retreated to the side of his recruit. Ayr stared at him as they backed away. Ayr could feel the tension dissipating as he watched Azura follow suit. She turned and nudged Ayr.

"Rider. Come with me. The challenge begins now."

Obeying her request, Ayr strode away from the group, his feet sinking slightly into the soft dirt path that led deeper into the valley. The lush greenery surrounded him in a comforting embrace, but there was an underlying sense of unease. This place was meant to test them. As they walked, Ayr noticed a distinct lack of civilization in any direction. He realised that they would be completely alone here, with only each other for company.

As they made their way further into the valley, Ayr's eyes caught small shelters scattered throughout the landscape. They blended seamlessly with the natural surroundings, as if they had been carefully placed there by an artist's hand. The vibrant greens and earthy browns of the valley were like a canvas, with these shelters acting as tiny pockets of colourful life within.

With every step they took down the slope, Ayr's longing for Azura to be big enough to ride grew stronger. It would have spared them both the physical strain of trudging down the steep and winding pathway. Ayr felt a sense of grounding and connection to the land. Despite the weight of his journey, he found solace in being tethered to the earth alongside Azura.

"Do you see anywhere you want to go? There's plenty of game in the garden for us to hunt if you're hungry. I'd advise making shelter first, however."

Having been thrown straight into the challenge, Ayr hadn't stopped to consider the next step in their plan. "You're the expert here. I'm happy to go wherever you think is best."

Azura paused for a moment, thinking about their next steps. "I know somewhere we can go. It's as far away as we can go, however."

"How far? What's there?"

Azura's big blue eyes looked up at him. "Safety. This test is often the last one. It appears that they don't want to waste any time with this intake. It seems to be that your presence here has forced their hand. If you can survive here for a month without getting murdered by another recruit or their dragon, you'll become a rider. Usually at the beginning of the Hungering there are only a handful of recruits, so your chances are low that you'll run into one. With an almost full intake, that won't be the case."

"What are those shelters out in the open for?"

"I didn't say that all the recruits survived." Azura still hadn't taken her eyes off him. "Those shelters were made by recruits that wanted the fight to come to them. I'd assume you'd be one such recruit, but if that was the case, I'm not sure what brought us together."

"I'm a survivor. I want to make it through this test. I'm not going to do that by fighting everyone, now am I?"

Azura shook her head. "No. This is a marathon, not a sprint. I also can't fight any dragons on your behalf. I am too small."

He needed to know what her limitations were. "So, what *can* you do?"

"I can provide you with guidance. Kill recruits if the opportunity presents itself. We need to make it to the final five or survive the month."

Ayr furrowed his brow. "So, what's the plan? Do we need to build a fortress?"

"You won't have time. Don't worry, there is only a sanctioned window for recruits to fight each other. All other time is an amnesty. Lucas will alert us with a signal from the Obelisk."

"Why are they making us do this?" Ayr was curious. "I would have thought it would have been better to have as many recruits as possible to survive."

"Rider, what do you know about the Seminary? I was under the assumption that everyone that came through the gates knew what they were signing up for. They've always ever only wanted the best."

"That would mean lots of dragons would die in the fighting, would it not?"

Azura shook her magnificent head. "No, since most dragons won't be rideable for some time, the chances of both rider and dragon dying at the same time are slim."

Ayr laughed softly. "Well, that's reassuring."

"Nothing about this process should be reassuring, rider. This is the Seminary of Fire."

"Well, I didn't think we'd be getting our dragons straight away, nor did I think we'd be getting thrown in here straight away. You could say that my expectations have been subverted.

Azura nodded, understanding him. "Things change. What are you going to do when we're out there and something happens? Riders need to be adaptable."

"So, we need to thrive here, do we? That should not be that hard, should it?"

"I don't think so. Recruits have been completing this task for longer than I have been alive. However, they'd bonded with their dragons a little before they were thrown out into the garden."

"Then we need to bond quickly. You chose me. Why?" Ayr paused, wanting to see her reaction.

"I'm not sure." Azura stopped alongside him. "If anyone knows it's likely to be Evor. That dragon has been alive longer than most. His bond with Elanor is unmatched and he knows how the magic works. He is directly linked with his rider, like we all are after the Bonding. Since I'm only promised to him, I can't share his thoughts."

Ayr clapped his hands together. "Then we need to find out."

Azura laughed towards him, a strange hissing and coughing sound escaping her throat. "If Evor and his rider want to keep things from me, they will. We're best off passing this test and making it out in one piece."

"Alright, well how are we going to do that? Is this place you're taking me to going to have something special about it?"

"It's a hidden place. If I'm right, there will be no other recruit within a reasonable distance that will be able to attack us in that time frame. It will have everything you need there."

"Where is it?"

"In that forest." Azura stood, transfixed on a point in the distance.

Ayr followed her eyeline towards the distance, searching for what had caught her attention. Beyond the row of rolling hills, he could see a vast expanse of forest stretching out before them. The majestic pines towered towards the sky, their deep green needles creating a blanket of colour against the blue horizon. Ayr wondered what secrets and wonders lay hidden within those trees, tucked away in the mountains that seemed to rise up from their midst like ancient guardians.

"A forest?" Ayr laughed. "You can't be serious, can you? If any dragon can breathe fire we'll be chased out of there."

"Dragons are not wild beasts. No recruit's dragon will willingly burn that forest down. That will be your only lodgings for now. It's not meant to be comfortable. You haven't earnt that right."

"When do I earn that right? When we pass the Hungering?"

"I'd assume so." Azura nodded again. "Do you have any more questions, or can we continue this journey in peace?"

"I just can't see that place being viable."

Azura flashed her teeth at him. "Just like with us dragons, there's more than meets the eye. Do you trust me, Ayr?"

It was hard to resist her. The piercing eyes touched his soul again. Ayr nodded in response. "I do. With all my heart."

"Then come with me. You're going to survive."

Ayr's curiosity piqued; he followed the small white dragon down the winding path. Looking back up the hill, he could see the other recruits, deep in conversation with their own dragons as they made their way across the rugged terrain. With every step, Ayr's boots crunched against the sharp gravel beneath him. Despite her substantial size, Azura's footsteps were silent and graceful. The air was thick with the scent of pine and earth, and Ayr felt a sense of wonder wash over him as he continued on this mysterious journey with his newfound dragon companion.

As the sun ascended higher in the sky, its rays beat down relentlessly upon Ayr and Azura as they trudged on foot. The oppressive heat drenched Ayr's clothes with sweat, their journey taking a toll on both of them. Finally, they stumbled upon the outskirts of the dense forest, its towering trees providing a welcome respite from the blistering sun. Ayr paused to catch his breath and take in their surroundings, searching for any sign of the other recruits in the vast expanse of wilderness before them. But there was no trace of them, their figures mere specks on the distant horizon. Undeterred by the daunting odds and weary from their long trek, Ayr and Azura pressed on towards their destination.

Azura tasted the air with her tongue. "We're here!"

"Where is here? Home for the next month?"

Azura nodded with affirmation. "Precisely. Come on, I want to show you something."

The majestic, pearl-white dragon unfurled her massive wings and took off into the dense forest, with Ayr struggling to keep up. As he raced after her, he noticed the sunlight filtered through the dense canopy above, creating a dappled effect on the forest floor. The once lively calls of birds and animals were now replaced by a symphony of chirping insects and rustling leaves. However, Ayr's sole focus was on chasing after Azura, his pounding footsteps echoing against the damp, moss-covered ground as he weaved through a labyrinth of towering trees and tangled vines.

It didn't take long for him to catch up with her, Azura coming to a sudden and complete stop. Up ahead, Ayr could see the soft glow of light filtering down through the trees, creating a dappled effect as it landed on the forest floor. As he drew closer, he noticed that the light seemed to be focused on one particular spot in the forest. With curiosity piqued, he approached cautiously and was met with a sight that took his breath away. This place had everything he needed.

With the abundance of sunlight, the pit was like a magical portal into another world. There was a small rocky outcrop that rose into a point above the ground, with a flowing stream beneath it. It was protected from the elements. The water looked drinkable. On the strip of land that sat next to the creek, Ayr could also make out a handful of berry bushes. The only thing he had any reason to leave it for would be meat, but it looked like there were fish in the stream. Azura would be able to help with those. If he wanted more, there was always the forest around them. They would be happy here.

"This looks fantastic."

Azura turned her head and nuzzled into Ayr's hand. "Thought you might like it. This is a safe place that we can call home whilst the challenge is completed."

"Sounds like a plan to me. Let's get down there."

FOUR

Filled with newfound determination, Ayr took slow, measured steps as he circled the pit, his eyes scanning every inch of the terrain. The pit itself was no larger than a small village, nestled between a gentle stream and a cluster of vibrant bushes. However, within the seemingly compact space, there were endless possibilities for Ayr and Azura to face the Hungering. Azura walked with him until they returned to the spot where they had started, marked by a thick pine tree. The slope was significant, but there was a pile of rocks, that appeared to have been strategically placed to allow easier access into the pit.

Azura's youthful energy bubbled to the surface as she leapt gracefully down into the pit, extending her wings that allowed her to glide effortlessly through the air. Ayr watched in awe as the sunlight caught her iridescent scales, causing them to sparkle and shimmer like precious gems.

He made his way carefully down the jagged rocks, feeling small and insignificant compared to Azura's powerful and mobile presence. The walls of the pit seemed to grow taller and steeper the further he descended, but as long as he had a solid path to follow, he felt confident that he could make it out safely.

"Come on, Ayr, what's taking so long?"

Ayr grunted as he descended down the rocks. "Some of us don't have wings."

"I'm very much looking forward to the day we can fly together."

With his legs red hot underneath, him, Ayr grinned at the thought. "I feel the same way."

"Maybe our month here would be best served bonding together. Then when time is up, we can fly out of here together."

Ayr smiled again. "That would be nice. I thought the whole point of being a rider was to be able to ride you."

Azura hummed gently. "You're funny, rider."

Ayr finally hit the ground, dropping the last few feet with a thud. It echoed around the pit, and he looked back up at where he had just come from. "Do you think that you're going to grow that quickly?"

Azura's eyes sparkled at him. "Anything is possible. There was more than one reason why I brought you here."

Ayr's lips curved into another content smile as he looked around at their new surroundings, taking in the vastness of the landscape. The towering walls seemed to stretch on for miles, their rocky outcrop looming over the ground below. The idea of getting caught in rain and getting soaked now seemed far-fetched, with the immense distance between him and the walls. As Ayr stood on the solid ground, he felt small in comparison to the expansive scenery.

He noticed an abundance of wood nearby, neatly stacked as if it had been left there by a human. It would provide enough fuel for him to cook with and keep warm during the chilly nights that were surely on the way. He already had a fire starter, and now all he needed was food. Ayr felt hungry from the long journey. He was relieved that the nearby berry bushes would provide him with something to snack on immediately.

Azura put her head under Ayr's hand. "What do you want to do first?"

Ayr shrugged in response. "I don't know. Shelter has been sorted for us already. I hate to think what the other recruits are doing."

"The walk was long, but I'd like to think that it was well worth it. Sometimes, the harder path is worth it. Depending on where they've ended up, I think the other recruits will still be setting up their shelters."

Ayr glanced up at the sky. "When does the fighting begin?"

"We won't need to worry about it yet. But when we hear a particular dragon's roar, then we need to be on alert. Usually, they'll let the recruits start killing each other immediately. This is survival of the fittest. In recent times they've let the recruits settle in and let the dragons grow a little more."

"Wouldn't they rather have everything over and done with quickly?"

"Sometimes." Azura coiled around Ayr like a snake before breaking away, dashing towards the water. "You only need to worry about two things, rider: surviving the month and making it to the final five."

Ayr puffed his lips out. "Great, so we've got a whole lot of sitting around and doing nothing."

"A bored mind will only hinder our venture. We will survive, we will hunt together, and I will grow. The bigger and more powerful I get, the easier the rest of your tasks will be."

"Right, so where do we start?" Focused on the task at hand until now, Ayr had not realised how far they had come. Nor had he considered what else needed to be done.

Azura must have sensed his lack of energy. "Are you tired, rider? Do you need to rest?"

"Yeah, come on, what better way to pass the time than to sleep? Who knows when we're going to get a chance to again."

"We shouldn't be disturbed here, but I like how you think, rider."

A small, sly smirk spread across Azura's face, her sharp fangs glinting in the sunlight as she darted away from Ayr, effortlessly crossing the gushing stream. The speed and grace with which she moved left him breathless, and he wondered how much faster she would be when fully grown. He followed her up the rugged, rocky outcrop that would soon become his new home, marvelling at the stunning view of the surrounding landscape that stretched out before them.

Whilst the covered area of the rocks was not anywhere near as big as his parent's home, it would still shelter both Ayr and Azura for some time. There would be no way that she would outgrow this and reach the size of Evor within the month. Azura disappeared into the darkness that enveloped the rocks, and Ayr quickly followed after her. Whilst it was dark inside, there was still enough light from outside for Ayr to see everything. Azura was nothing more than a shadow at the back as Ayr entered.

"So, this is home, huh?"

Azura nodded. "Easily defensible, warm and dry."

"I can see the first point, but we'll have to find out about the other two. Any room for me back there?"

"Plenty." Her voice was faint considering the distance between them.

With no other resources nearby, Ayr removed the black vest from his body and folded it into a small square. He placed it on the ground near Azura at the very back of the cave in the darkest corner. Ayr sat down slowly, placing his hand against the rock that would now serve as his bed. It was bleak, but maybe something he would be able to change in the coming days. A month of sleeping rough like this would eventually take its toll on him.

"Well, this is alright." Ayr placed his head down on his makeshift pillow.

"Speak for yourself. Don't mind me whilst I get comfortable."

Azura stretched out beside Ayr, her lithe body moving like a graceful cat. As she settled down next to him, she curled up into a small ball. She was still as round as Ayr was long. A few moments passed before Ayr heard her shifting restlessly. It was clear that she wasn't comfortable. Azura shuffled closer, and her warm body pressed against his side, her head nestled against his ribs. Ayr froze at the unexpected contact, but he could not deny the comfort of her body heat radiating through him like a blazing fire. He closed his eyes and allowed himself to relax in her embrace, feeling grateful for her presence.

"Are you ok?"

"I am now, rider."

Ayr laughed and as he closed his eyes, raised his hand and put it on Azura's head. The dragon grumbled happily and shook briefly again. Ayr felt a surge of energy radiate through his hand, sending tingles up his spine. It faded as quickly as it had come on, and Ayr lay there pondering what he had just felt. Azura's next movements was her breathing; the gentle rise and fall of her chest. Ayr lay awake for a moment longer before finally closing his eyes and drifting off to sleep.

Only moments had passed since Ayr had closed his eyes in exhaustion when a sudden and deafening roar jolted him awake. His heart raced as he sprang to his feet, his hand automatically reaching for the sword at his hip. Was this the telltale roar signalling that the killing time had begun? Or was it something else entirely, something even more terrifying? The echoes of the sound still reverberated in his ears, causing an uneasy chill to run down his spine. He strained to listen for any other noises or signs of danger.

The heavy weight on his chest was a reminder that he had another weapon at his disposal. Ayr nudged Azura gently. "Azura! Wake up! I need you!"

As the white dragon stuttered in her slumber, another earth-shattering roar shook the air around them. With a jolt, Azura snapped awake and squinted up at Ayr. He could feel her heart pounding in her chest as she struggled to make sense of their surroundings. The smell of sulphur lingered in the damp air, and the distant sound of rushing water from the creek echoed through the cavern.

"What's wrong?"

Ayr kept listening for any sounds in the distance. "Didn't you hear that? Is it time?"

"No, not yet. This is something else. Let's go see, shall we?"

A dagger of fear found its way digging into Ayr's stomach. "I don't really want to. I think we're much safer in here than out there."

"Do you trust me?"

Ayr bit his lip. She had chosen him, and she would not willingly put his life in danger, would she? "I suppose so."

"Was that hesitation, rider? Come on. I'll go first if you want."

Ayr's muscles tensed as he tightened his grip on his sword, ready to draw it at a moment's notice. With bated breath, he followed Azura out into the blinding light, prepared for whatever awaited them. The ground trembled beneath their feet, a massive thud echoing through the air. Azura seemed unperturbed, stretching out with a contented growl. Confused but trusting in his companion's instincts, Ayr cautiously approached her and peered from their hiding spot.

Ayr's heart caught in his chest as a shadow was cast over the pit. Ayr's eyes adjusted to the light and as he squinted into the sun, he made out a massive, looming figure. Azura let out an excited bark. The figure came into focus and Ayr loosened his grip on his sword. Evor stood at the far end of the pit, staring down at them. Being higher on the walls, made the jet-black dragon look even larger than he already was.

As Ayr's eyes scanned the horizon, he caught sight of a familiar figure atop the giant behemoth. Elanor sat confidently on its back, her striking red plume on her mask, a stark contrast against the ebony scales of Evor. A sense of relief washed over Ayr as he realised there was no imminent danger. Slowly, he sheathed his sword, feeling the tension in his body loosen.

"Hello little one."

As soon as Azura caught sight of Evor, her tail began to wag uncontrollably, like a puppy excitedly greeting its owner after a long day. Evor slowly lowered his head towards the entrance of the cave, and Elanor effortlessly slid down his neck, as if it was a routine they had practiced countless times before. She landed with grace and poise on both feet, her movements fluid and confident. As she stood face to face with Ayr, her emerald eyes sparkled with wonder and curiosity.

"I thought I'd find you here."

Ayr tried to remain cool and leant back against the cave wall. "Oh really, what gave it away?"

Elanor stretched out and touched the same wall in front of Ayr. "Evor put the thought in Azura's mind. I came here myself during my own Hungering. It's smart, but it's only one way in and one way out. Not ideal if a recruit knows you're here and comes after you."

"They wouldn't have enough time to get down here. We're too far away from everyone else."

Elanor eyes twinkled in the sunlight. "You're right, however, we could adjust time to make it more challenging for you. I don't think I will, however."

Ayr frowned. "Why not? I thought this place was meant to be a challenge."

Elanor nodded and smirked. "It is."

Ayr glanced at Azura who was nodding her head slowly. She still hadn't taken her eyes off Evor. "How long ago did you do it? You don't look that much older than me."

"It's only been about a decade." Elanor shrugged.

"A decade?" Ayr's mouth fell open. "You don't look a day older than me, and you've already achieved so much within the Seminary. What did you do to earn that?"

Elanor smirked at him. "A story for another time. I came to see what our newest recruit was up to."

"Just trying to survive. You actually interrupted my sleep."

"Your *sleep*?" Elanor laughed. "Did you look at the sun and think it was the moon?"

"No, I just wanted to rest."

Elanor's eyes narrowed as she eyed him up and down. "What's your goal here?"

Ayr raised an eyebrow. "I'm sorry?"

"Ayr Ashbourne, what is your goal here at the Seminary? Answer me or I will rip your tongue out. Don't lie to me either."

"I'm here to become a rider."

"Horseshite!" Elanor charged at Ayr, as she drew her sword and thrust it towards him. Ayr didn't have time to react as her plate covered arm smashed into his chest, driving him backwards against the wall. Ayr was pinned, between a rock and a hard place. Evor's head came down, hovering mere feet over Elanor's head. He glared into Ayr's eyes, smoke spilling from his nostrils as his long white fangs threatened to lacerate Ayr. Ayr took a deep breath as he tried to maintain eye contact between the two.

"So, *that's* what it means to be a rider. Complete and utter synchronization with your dragon. That's interesting. That's very interesting."

Elanor looked up at him. If looks could kill, Ayr would have had two daggers in his brain. Her sword was still dangerously close to his throat. If Ayr poked his tongue out, he would have been able to taste the steel. "Typical, Ashbourne, I honestly don't expect anything else from your family. Just like your father before you, you'll never become a rider."

Ayr remained defiant, even with the blade at his throat. "I'm different. If you knew anything about me, you'd know that already. Besides, if you didn't want me to become a rider, you could have failed me at any moment before Azura chose me."

Evor continued to snarl overhead. Azura stood beside Ayr, frightened, almost curling up into a ball. She wasn't equipped to deal with this. If only she had been larger, she might have been able to help Ayr escape. Elanor pulled back slightly. At last, Ayr could breathe properly again. He started to raise his hand to his throat, but one more look from Elanor told him that any kind of movement would be unwise. Her sword was still very much in his face and her tone was as sharp as the blade.

"If I *didn't* let you in, then there's every chance that you would have repeated your father's story. He was denied entry to the Obelisk and look what happened. He stole a dragon and started a war. I think the world could do without another generation of dragon wars."

"My father wasn't a thief; he was a good man!"

"History is written by the victor." Elanor leaned in gently, correcting him. "Unless you're calling my father and everyone else who fought in the war a liar, I would suggest retracting your statement."

Ayr stuck his neck out. "Even with your sword at my throat and your dragon ready to eat me, I think you need to hear my side of the story. I was chosen by a dragon that hasn't chosen anyone in over thirty years. I don't think that's something we should overlook."

Elanor scoffed. "You got lucky. Nobody knows what draws dragons to us."

"Well now I'm here, so what are you going to do about it?"

There was a grumbling from overhead and suddenly, Evor pulled back. He was still closer than Ayr would have liked, but at least now he could not feel the direct smoke against his skin. Elanor withdrew her blade as well, turning her head back to look at him. Ayr could just make out the confused expression on her face. Evor started to nod slowly, and Elanor turned to face Azura.

"Really?"

Azura nodded. "Really. I need both of you to trust me on this."

"Are you sure about this, Azura? You've never had a rider before."

Azura nodded again. "I lived through the war. If I wasn't aware of what an Ashbourne is capable of, I would not have chosen him."

"Hmm, if you think you can tame this Ashbourne, then who am I to question your wisdom?"

"As a lesser dragon I exist to serve the Commonwealth. You have every right to question me, Elanor. I can still make mistakes like any rider." Azura bowed her head, submitting to both Elanor and Evor.

Evor chuckled behind Elanor. "Only for now, little one. You still have much to learn."

"I won't forgo my oath to the Obelisk."

Elanor tutted gently. "Every dragon says that at one point in their life. That all changes when dragon and rider become one. You will do anything for your rider, regardless of what the Obelisk decrees."

"Just like my father's dragon did before it got taken from him."

Elanor turned again, glaring daggers at Ayr. "That's *not* what happened."

Ayr shrugged and just laughed. "Whatever you say, rider."

"Elanor, didn't you come here for a reason?" Evor's voice boomed over the pit once again. "I didn't bring you here to be dragged into petty politics and stories of the past."

Elanor smiled. "Quite right, Evor. Ashbourne, would you like to see the secrets of the Garden of Chilijo? Think of it like a private tour."

It was strange that out of all the recruits she was offering him a tour. It would have been better received by one of the other recruits. Ayr didn't want to appear rude. Returning a smile of his own, Ayr gazed deep into Elanor's piercing eyes. "I'd like nothing more. Lead on."

FIVE

"There's plenty to show you here. Especially considering I don't think this place has been touched since Evor and I set foot in it. Every recruit except for a select few just wants to fight in the Hungering. They think that having their dragons grow to be the largest will make them a rider. Walk with me."

Elanor extended her hand out towards Ayr, her delicate fingers grasping his rough, calloused ones. She pulled him towards her with a force that surprised him, their bodies almost colliding as she drew him closer. Ayr's heart raced with anticipation, unsure of what was to come. Instead of a kiss or something similar, Elanor simply released his hand and spun away from him. Her long hair caught the sunlight, and she started down the rock path towards the babbling stream below. Ayr followed after her eagerly, not wanting to be left behind in this moment of adventure.

Ayr shot a glance back at Evor and Azura. They stood together, watching with expressions of curiosity and envy as Ayr and Elanor embarked on their own private journey. A small smile tugged at the corners of Ayr's mouth as he turned back towards Elanor, grateful for the unexpected turn their day had taken.

"So, Evor wasn't the largest?" Ayr found that extremely difficult to believe due to the size of the black behemoth.

Elanor nodded affirmatively. "Yeah, when I met Evor for the first time, he was no bigger than Azura."

"Are the dragons coming with us?"

"I think they're occupied, don't you?" Elanor glanced back over her shoulder.

Ayr followed her eyeline. The two dragons were completely absorbed in each other's company, their scales glistening in the sunlight. The smaller Azura, was nuzzling into Evor's nose while he responded with gentle nudges of his own. Ayr watched on, intrigued by the non-verbal communication between the two creatures. Their bond seemed unbreakable. The earth-shattering roar of Evor could not be heard at this moment, as he was lost in the peaceful exchange with his companion. Ayr raised an eyebrow in curious wonder at this rare display of affection between dragons.

"What's going on there?"

Elanor smirked at him. "You should ask her about it when you have the chance. It will be another opportunity to bring you two closer together. The more you learn about each other, the stronger your connection will be."

"She'll grow more that way?"

"Possibly." Elanor shrugged with an indifference. "Every dragon is different. Anything in this place is possible. Maybe by the time you leave here she'll be big enough to ride."

"You think so?"

Elanor shrugged at him again and looked up at the forest around them. Ayr's eyes followed the path of her gaze, shifting his weight from one foot to the other as he felt a growing sense of unease. The once open pit now seemed to be closing in on them, the towering trees surrounding it casting dark shadows that made it feel smaller than Ayr remembered. He became acutely aware of his own smallness in comparison to the vastness of nature around him.

"I *know* so. I spent my Hungering here remember. Without needing to hunt any other recruits, Evor and I spent every moment in here bonding. He'd hunt for me, and all I did was ensure that our needs were met. We were in a large induction. We actually had to last the entire month; they didn't necessarily want us whittling down a hundred recruits to just five. Now that we've got a decent number of riders, they want the best of the best."

"Who is *they*? Lucas?"

Elanor scoffed. "Lucas is only the curator. He's taken a step back from the turmoil that is the day-to-day operations of the Obelisk. No, my father, Crassus, is now the head of the Obelisk."

"Ah, so nepotism got you to where you are."

Ayr laughed gently until the sting of bare skin against skin echoed through the room as the slap landed hard and fast on his left cheek. His face burned with both pain and shame; tears threatened to spill from his eyes. He turned away from Elanor, unable to meet her gaze as he battled the flurry of emotions within him. Anger, betrayal, and hurt all mingled together, creating a storm inside him that threatened to boil over. With a deep breath, he clenched his fists and forced himself to remain still, hoping to quell the rising tide of emotions before it consumed him completely.

"What was that for?"

"You're an Ashbourne! You don't have the right to insult me or my family again!"

With a low, guttural growl, Evor turned away from Azura and stormed over towards Ayr and Elanor. His massive, black-scaled form seemed to throb with anger as he approached the two figures. Elanor stood her ground, holding her hand up in a calming gesture, while Ayr instinctively took a step back, wary of drawing the ire of the powerful dragon.

There was a tense moment as Evor and Elanor locked eyes, before the dragon finally relented and turned back towards Azura once more. The pair resumed their playful antics, snuggling against each other as if nothing had happened. Still, the tension in the air lingered, a reminder of the fierce emotions beneath the surface of these mythical creatures.

Elanor raised a pointed finger at him. "That was your last warning! Evor was ready to rip you limb from limb."

"You didn't say a word to him. How did you stop him?"

"One day, if you make it, you'll be able to do that with Azura."

"Amazing!" Ayr wanted to change the subject quickly. The less time with Evor breathing down his neck the better. "So, then who is my uncle, Anton? My father never told me much about him. What does he do as the Overlord?"

Elanor glanced sideways at Ayr and took in a deep breath. "That's for another time. I will tell you if you survive the Hungering."

"Great, so what did you want to show me?"

"Come with me, Ashbourne."

With each step, the cool water of the creek splashed playfully against their boots, sending droplets flying in every direction. Elanor and Ayr continued along the shallow bed, moving further away from their starting point towards the towering southern wall. As they drew closer, Ayr's eyes widened in surprise as he noticed a small opening in the base of the wall - a secret passage that allowed the water to flow freely out of the pit. He realised that this was another way out, one that did not require scaling the imposing walls.

"Is this what you wanted to show me?"

Elanor nodded as she examined the opening. "Yes, there's more to this place than meets the eye."

"And we've got to go underwater to get there?"

"Yeah." Elanor smirked at him. "Are you afraid to get a little wet?"

"No! I'm here to be a dragon rider. What would possibly scare me?"

Elanor put her hand out towards him. "I can lead you there if you like. It's not that scary, I promise."

"I'll take your word for it."

"Give me your hand, Ashbourne."

Ayr gently grasped Elanor's hand and led her towards the deeper part of the stream. The cool, clear water rushed against their feet, sending tiny ripples across the surface. As they walked, Ayr could feel his boots slowly becoming submerged, the weight of the water pulling him down with each step.

Soon, the water reached his knee, and he could feel the current tugging at his legs. Elanor, only slightly shorter than Ayr, was already up to her hip in the water. They continued on, the water now reaching their chests. Elanor turned to look at Ayr, her eyes reflecting the light dancing on the water's surface.

"This is the part where we go down. Hold your breath."

"How far is it?"

Elanor shrugged. "Far enough."

Ayr sank down beneath the surface of the water, feeling the cool, weightless embrace of the creek. He opened his eyes, squinting against the blurry images around him. Despite the distortion, he could still make out the faint outline of Elanor swimming beside him. He released her hand, not concerned about losing her in the crystal-clear water. Ahead, Ayr could see a glimmer of light, beckoning them forward. With steady kicks, they swam towards it and soon found themselves passing under what remained of a crumbling stone wall. As they emerged on the other side, Ayr was the first to lift his head above the surface, taking in a deep breath of clean air.

Ayr was greeted by a whole new world - an entire subtropical biome hidden only meters away from where he had chosen to stake out the next month. Sunlight filtered in from above through numerous cracks in the walls on all sides.

Peering out from the shore of what seemed to be a neighbouring island, Ayr spotted several graceful deer standing motionless at the edge of the tree line. Their sleek bodies were perfectly silhouetted against the verdant backdrop of the forest. Despite the looming presence of a dragon, the deer seemed unfazed.

In this compact environment, Ayr knew that they would make for easy prey for Azura. The serene atmosphere was deceiving in its peacefulness, masking the potential danger that lurked within the tranquil landscape. Elanor was already half out of the water, wiping her eyes clear. Ayr followed her, soon finding himself upon the soft sandy beach.

The lush landscape was a sight to behold - palm trees reaching not only towards the sky but also hanging overhead from the ceiling of the dense foliage. Nestled among the swaying palms were clusters of coconuts, providing a potential source of sustenance should Azura's hunting efforts fail.

Somewhere in the distance, a chorus of birds blended their melodies together, creating a symphony of chirps and tweets as the gentle hum of insects added to the natural orchestra. Thankfully, aside from the occasional rustling of deer in the underbrush, there were no signs of any larger creatures nearby. He reminded himself that he had a fierce dragon nearby, so why should he worry?

"Where do we begin?"

Elanor pointed off into the distance in the direction of the deer. "I can show you whatever you want. Come this way."

With Elanor as his guide, Ayr plunged deeper into the island's dense forest. The trees towered above them, their leaves rustling and whispering secrets as they passed. As they moved further in, Ayr felt a sense of unease. He had no idea where Elanor was leading him, and every area of the forest seemed identical to the next. Ayr had lost the path of the deer that had disappeared into this labyrinth of green. Ayr knew that if he were a new recruit on a hunting mission, he would easily fall prey to any traps that Elanor may have set along the way. Every step felt like treading through a maze with no end in sight.

The dense forest began to give way, revealing scattered structures among the trees. Ayr picked out three distinct buildings. The first was a small cabin, barely larger than his own room back home. Its walls were constructed from rough-hewn logs and its roof was a patchwork of leaves and branches. The second looked like an outhouse, with a crescent moon cut into the door. The third structure caught Ayr's attention the most - a compact freezer made from sturdy wood and topped with heavy stones to keep its contents chilled. Despite their crude construction, they all seemed strangely intact in this wild and unforgiving place. As he took in the scene, Ayr stared in bewilderment and awe.

"Who built all this?"

Elanor put her hands on her hips, looking unimpressed. "Come on, Ashbourne. That's a stupid question. Who do you think? This was my escape away from the world when some recruits had bigger and faster dragons than Evor. A hundred recruits also meant that we were more densely packed into the Hungering. They found us early on and we both managed to slip into here. If a recruit wanted to get inside, they'd have to face being torched alive by Evor without their dragons for protection."

"Smart, but why are you helping me? You seem to have a heavy resentment towards my father, yet you're showing me this out of the goodness of your heart?"

Elanor scowled at Ayr. "It's not my heart that I'm doing this for."

"What? You're doing this for Evor?"

Elanor nodded. "I'm not saying anything else. Now come on."

"Why did you bring me here. Surely it wasn't just so you could show me what you had built?"

"No, it wasn't. I wanted to give the dragons time alone."

"Do they need time alone?"

"Yes, yes, they do. Those two are promised to each other. They need to form a bond like you will have with Azura. Do you need time alone with a girl that found her way to your bed?" Elanor smirked and raised an eyebrow at him. Ayr felt his cheeks warming uncontrollably. "Now hurry up, Ashbourne."

Approaching the quaint hut, Elanor reached out and pressed on the door. With a creak, it swung open, unhindered by any lock or key. She gestured for Ayr to follow her inside. Ducking his head to avoid hitting it on the low wooden cross beam, he stepped through the threshold into the cozy space. Taking in his surroundings, he noticed a makeshift bed tucked into one corner and a similar makeshift fire pit in the other. The room exuded a rustic charm, with rough-hewn walls and simple furnishings made from materials found in nature. It felt like a peaceful retreat tucked away from the rest of the world.

Elanor stretched her arms out, almost allowing her to reach wall to wall. "Welcome to my humble abode. Sometimes I come out here if I need time to myself."

Ayr nodded approvingly as he completed his second look around the room. "It's nice. Thank you for showing me this."

"You're welcome. What did you say you wanted to do before? Sleep? Evor and Azura won't be done for some time and it's not like you have anything better to do. Correct?"

Ayr shrugged nonchalantly, trying to hide the butterfly-like flutters in his stomach. He had been with women at his father's home before, but this was something entirely new and exciting. Elanor stood before him, still wrapped up in her crisp Seminary uniform, as was Ayr. Despite their proximity and shared attire, there had been no signals or hints from her that she was even remotely interested in him. Nonetheless, he could not ignore the fact that there was some tension growing between them. Why? All because he had a dragon that hers was promised to?

Ayr looked down at his uniform and patted it. "We're still wet. I don't think it would be a smart idea to sleep without drying off first.

Despite the brief respite of the walk, the dampness still clung to him, seeping through his Seminary uniform and chilling him to the core. Each step felt heavier as he trudged on, the weight of the wet fabric dragging him down. But he knew better than to voice any complaints, especially around this woman. This was just another test in the grand scheme of building character within the Seminary. A lesson in perseverance and resilience against the elements. If he resisted now, Elanor could fail him at any moment.

"I'm not opposed to sleeping in wet clothes. It'll keep me cool. Throw them over the fireplace if you have to. Unless that is you've got a problem with me seeing you naked." She cocked an eyebrow at him. "I can guarantee you that I've seen worse." Ayr hesitated for a moment. Elanor put her hands on his hips again, staring at him. "I thought you were wet."

"I am!"

Elanor pouted. "I'm waiting. Now hurry up."

The proverbial balls on this woman!

With no other options, Ayr reluctantly began to strip. His movements were tense and stiff, as if he was trying to hide his body from the watchful gaze of Elanor. He unbuckled his belt, carefully hanging the leather strip on a nearby vine that served as a makeshift clothesline. To his surprise, the flimsy-looking vine held the weight without breaking. Next, he unfastened the sheath of his sword and leaned it against the wall.

Ayr continued to undress, throwing his vest and undershirt over his head before kicking off his boots and shaking off any dirt from his pants. He hung them up on the line next to his belt, feeling exposed and vulnerable in only his undergarments.

As he turned back to face Elanor, he saw her eyes taking in every inch of his body. Her eyes moved with him, unnerving him further. No other woman he'd laid with made him feel like this. He felt self-conscious under her scrutiny while trying to maintain a confident posture. He'd been trained, but this was something different from the art of warfare. Ayr went to sit on the bed, but Elanor raised her hand to stop him. Her expression was unreadable, her eyes barely having moved from his groin in the last few seconds.

"What do you think you're doing?"

"Sitting down."

"Not with those, you're not." Elanor pointed to his waistline. "Take them off."

"I'll be naked in the presence of a lady."

Elanor raised an eyebrow. "So?"

"I don't have a choice, do I?" Ayr let out a loud sigh.

Elanor shook her head in amusement, a small smile playing on her lips. Without any hesitation as to not give her the satisfaction, Ayr bent down and carefully removed the last of his undergarments, revealing what was left of his tall and muscular frame. Elanor's eyes briefly flickered over him before she returned her attention to his face. A chill rose up from the ground as he placed the undergarments on the line with the rest of his clothes. He hoped that they would dry quickly, as he didn't want to spend too much time in his current state.

Ayr could not shake off the feeling of vulnerability as he stood exposed in front of Elanor, who seemed completely unfazed by his nakedness. Her gaze lingered once again over his groin and surrounds, and Elanor smirked again. Ayr was completely hairless, having shaved everything before arriving at the Seminary. The chill whistled through the gaps in the wooden logs once again, sending another shiver down Ayr's spine.

"Do you like what you see, my lady?"

Elanor's eyes didn't move. "I've seen better."

A dagger punched through Ayr's chest. He winced at the remark, but otherwise remained motionless. Elanor's upper lip curled, and she dropped to her knees. Ayr braced himself, but instead of anything happening between them, Elanor crawled towards the firepit. Whilst on both of her knees, Elanor cupped both of her hands together and whispered something inaudible into them. She spread them out in front of her and a spark shot from between them into the firepit. The spark caught and a small flame ignited in the pit. Ayr stepped back from it.

"How did you do that? I thought dragons were the magic ones."

Elanor stood up and grinned at him. "I'm glad that your father didn't tell you all of our secrets. He broke every other oath that he took. It's something that will happen when you bond with Azura."

Ayr ignored the comment about his father. "I can use magic?"

"Little bits. Never anything substantial without consent from your dragon first. Just make sure you keep your usage in check. Too much and you'll pull too much energy from your dragon, killing you both. The first rule of using magic is to be smart with it. It is not an infinite resource."

Did everything turn into a lesson with Elanor? "Right. So, what do you think?"

"About my cabin or about you?" She briefly glanced up and down at him. "I think you should sleep like you said you would."

"What are you going to do?"

"Join you."

"Oh."

Ayr could only watch in awe as Elanor began to undress before him. His mouth hung open; his eyes transfixed on her every move. Slowly and deliberately, she peeled off each wet article of clothing, revealing more and more of her delicate porcelain skin. Ayr could not tear his gaze away as she moved gracefully around the room, hanging each piece near the fire to dry. It was like watching a performance - not seductive, but mesmerizing nonetheless.

Elanor's movements were slow and purposeful, with no wasted motion. She glanced back at Ayr who now stood close to the door. The sound of fabric rustling, and the faint scent of damp earth filled the room as Elanor shed more layers, leaving a trail of discarded clothes in her wake. Ayr watched in amazement, entranced by the simple act of undressing that Elanor was performing. Her hands were performing art before him, her figure becoming more exposed the more she shimmed and removed.

She stood before him in nothing more than her undergarments. A tight white corset and short hose stockings that left little to the imagination. Ayr held his breath as Elanor popped the top of the corset open, her breasts spilling out in front of her. Whilst sizeable, they would not affect her combative prowess. Elanor continued to remove the corset and Ayr could feel himself going red in the face. There was something pulling at the back of his mind, like a tug that he couldn't get rid of.

Elanor glanced back over her shoulder at him. "How are you doing, Ashbourne? Do *you* like what you see?"

Ayr was stunned into silence, his mouth opening and closing soundlessly. The flickering flames of the fire cast a warm glow over Elanor's figure, complimenting the gentle curves that were otherwise hidden beneath the rough fabric of her Seminary uniform. She was taut, and even with the curves of her hips, had muscle throughout the rest of her body. Like Ayr, she was completely hairless below her head.

"I thought you said you were ok with being wet."

Elanor smiled at him, flashing all of her perfectly white teeth at him. Ayr was grateful for the distraction. He could not keep eye contact for long. "I lied. I wanted to see what you'd do first. It'd be stupid of me to stay in them. I know we're dragon riders and our dragons are nearby, but they can't keep us warm all the time."

"Your magic couldn't dry them?"

"What did I say before, Ashbourne?" Elanor could have whacked him over the head with a spoon and the delivery would have been the same. "Be smarter with your magic. Whilst Evor is fully grown, I still don't want to take that risk and kill us both. If I was closer to Evor, sure. I'm not going to waste that much energy when the fire is something that's easier to start and maintain. Now, are you going to get on the bed or just stand there like a stunned mullet?"

With his legs feeling like they were made of iron, Ayr took a step and collapsed onto the bed. It was more brittle than a normal bed, made from an odd mixture of materials - leaves that crumbled beneath his weight, dry and lifeless, and random objects scavenged from the forest floor. Wooden beams supported the makeshift bed, creaking slightly under Ayr's weight. It was a rough and uncomfortable resting place, but it would have to do for now in this unfamiliar and unforgiving environment.

Ayr carefully shifted over on the small, narrow bed, making room for Elanor to join him. The thought of being this close to her in such a confined space made his heart race and his palms sweat. He tried to ignore the heat rising in his cheeks as he lay down, leaving plenty of space for her to stretch out beside him. The leaves were rough against his skin, but it didn't matter. This was all about being close to her. Turning away from her, Ayr faced the wooden wall of the humble hut they shared, trying to steady his breathing and calm the butterflies in his stomach.

"What are you doing, Ashbourne?"

"Being polite."

Elanor laughed softly and she lowered herself onto the bed. It creaked again under the new weight, even though she would have only weighed a little more than half of what Ayr did. He could not hide anything now that they were both lying here, exposed and vulnerable. Everything would be laid bare in this tiny space, but if he wanted to stay warm whilst sleeping, it was the only option.

Elanor's delicate hand rested on his shoulder, sending a shiver down Ayr's spine. Her touch was like a spark, igniting his senses and causing his body to tense. With a deep breath, he turned to face her, the sharp scent of her filling his nostrils. As their eyes met, he knew that he couldn't look away. The strange sensation was back in the back of his head again.

"We're not going to get warm if we're not sharing heat. I don't know if you noticed, but I don't have blankets anywhere. Unfortunately, they weren't in great supply when I went through the Hungering."

Ayr's eyes dropped. He could see all of Elanor, exposed and naked beside him. Her pristine, and silky-smooth skin glowed in the firelight. Elanor's scent was intoxicating; being this close to her would not end up doing either of them any favours. Ayr let himself be taken by Elanor as she placed his hand over her stomach. Not that it'd do much to keep them warm, but it was better than nothing.

She grinned at him. "Just be glad this isn't a test."

"Why, am I failing or passing?"

"Both." Her shoulders shook as she laughed.

"This isn't normal. Why are you doing this? We shouldn't be doing this."

Ayr froze as he felt an icy cold finger press between his shoulder blades. Elanor's laughter was soft in his ear. "Feel free to put your clothes back on at any time. I didn't think you'd be complaining. Just don't try anything or you might find something stuck where you don't want it."

"I wouldn't dream of it."

"Good. I'm not sure how you'd look walking around with your sword stuck up your ass. Now go to sleep. You've got a big month ahead of you."

SIX

As Ayr slowly awoke, he noticed an odd sensation in his body. It took him a moment to realize that the events preceding his slumber were only a dream. But as he opened his eyes and felt the weight of Elanor resting against him, he knew that what had happened between them was real. They had both fallen asleep together, without any physical intimacy. Raising his head, Ayr looked over Elanor's figure, illuminated by soft rays of sunlight streaming through the window. She lay uncovered, her skin glowing in the afternoon light. Ayr pondered what to do next - should he wake her or let her sleep peacefully?

The firepit was still burning, allowing there to be enough light in the cabin. With Elanor cutting off his exit, Ayr slid forwards out of the bed. He placed his feet on the ground and stood up slowly, careful not to disturb Elanor. It wasn't until he was removing his clothing from the line that he heard her stirring. As Ayr turned, he realised that she was already awake. Her eyes burned with the reflection of the fire in them.

"What in Chilijo's name do you think you're doing?"

"What's it look like? You're not the one that has to survive out here for the next month. I'm making sure that I've got enough daylight to do everything that I need to do."

Elanor gracefully reclined on the bed; her long limbs stretched out in front of her. Ayr snuck a glance at her, his gaze quickly darting away as she caught him staring. Her musical laughter filled the room, sending shivers down his spine and making his heart skip a beat.

"You can look, you know. You're not still a virgin, are you, Ashbourne?" Ayr bit his lip. "Ashbourne, hello?"

Ayr shook his head and returned back to reality. "No, I don't know what would have given you that impression."

Elanor smirked and her eyes ran down his body. "Nothing at all." She then turned on the bed and peered out the doorway. "You're running out of daylight, you know."

"All the more reason for me to get moving sooner rather than later. What about the dragons?"

Elanor paused for a moment as if waiting on a response from him. "They're fine, but you're right. We should go back to them. I'd hate to keep them waiting, even though they wouldn't be missing us right now."

"Azura is still too small to do anything with Evor, isn't she?"

Elanor nodded. "At least you understand basic biology, Ashbourne. She is indeed. But like humans, they still need to connect. Azura has known Evor for thirty years, but she now has much catching up to do."

With a graceful leap, Elanor sprang from the bed and joined Ayr in removing her clothes from the line. The chilled breeze continued to filter through the hut. The firelight caressed her naked skin as she moved fluidly, a perfect picture of strength and femininity. She was every bit the fighter he had imagined, her broad shoulders and thin waist a testament to her physical prowess. There was no doubt in his mind that not only could she control the enormous dragon outside, but also confidently wield the sword that hung on her hip. It had already been at his throat enough.

The realisation hit Ayr like a splash of cold water. He needed to stop staring and get dressed. With a sense of urgency, he threw on his boots and sat on the edge of the bed to tie them. Elanor wasn't far behind him, her footsteps soft against the wooden floor. But Ayr wasted no time and quickly strode out of the cabin into the surrounding woods. The golden light of dusk was fading fast, casting shadows all around. He cursed himself for oversleeping - there were still so many things to be done before nightfall. A moment later, Elanor emerged from the cabin, her hair shining faintly in the last rays of sunlight.

"Ready to go?"

Elanor nodded with a smile. "Thought you'd never ask. Do you know the way back?"

Everywhere Ayr looked was just another path, covered by the thicket of trees. "I was hoping you might."

"Do you see that?" Elanor pointed towards one of the red oak trees directly in front of them. On it was a red circle no more than head height.

Ayr peered at the red circle, narrowing his eyes. "Looks like a directional marker. The forest looks the same no matter how you look at it."

She winked at him. "Good spot."

"So, what, it's going back towards the tunnel?"

Elanor shrugged. "One way to find out. I can't tell you anything, remember."

Ayr sighed and rolled his eyes at her. "Are you always like this? You know where we're going don't you?"

"Yes, of course I do. The best part about being a rider isn't our increased strength or durability. It is our connection with our dragons. When you reach the level that I am at with Evor, you will be able to sense where your dragon is at all times. Come on, let's go. Lead the way, Ashbourne."

Ayr laughed and he started in the direction of the red circle. What other choice did he have? Ayr's heart pounded in his chest as he quickened his pace, his feet tearing past the marked tree and into the dense forest. With each step, he broke through layers of fallen leaves, creating a satisfying crunch underfoot. Behind him, Elanor's footsteps echoed, her determination keeping her close on his heels.

Though Ayr was ahead of Elanor, she was not far behind; they both pushed their limits all the way to the edge of the island. The tall, swaying palm trees dominated Ayr's vision once again, their rustling leaves providing a soothing soundtrack to the otherwise tense atmosphere. And beyond them, the shimmering body of water that surrounded the island added to its ethereal beauty. Ayr's gaze shifted towards the tunnel where they had entered this place.

Elanor hit the water with a splash, the force of her entry sending ripples across the surface and causing nearby fish to scatter in all directions. Ayr followed suit, his body sinking into the cool depths. The water enveloped him, washing away the dirt and grime of their journey through the island. He kicked his legs and propelled himself towards the tunnel entrance, which was now just within reach. As he turned to check on Elanor, her head broke through the surface, her hair dripping with droplets of crystal-clear water.

"Ready to go under again?"

Ayr shook his head. "You first."

The return trip through the water tunnel felt like a blur compared to the journey there. With practiced kicks, Ayr effortlessly glided through the passage and emerged beside Elanor in a matter of moments. The clear waters surrounded them, but Ayr was prepared this time, and it was nowhere near as daunting as before. However, a new element greeted them on this side of the rock wall – Evor's piercing gaze as he stood waiting in the water. His dark eyes seemed to bore into their souls, questioning their every move.

"Did you enjoy your rest, riders?"

Elanor smiled up at him. "We did. Thank you for asking. Did you?"

Evor started to stretch out like a giant cat. "I did. This place brings back fond memories of where we first bonded. What are your plans for this evening, Elanor?"

"Sun's going down. It'd be a shame if we left the rookie rider here all by himself. Azura isn't overly ready to hunt on her own yet in such conditions, is she?"

Evor shook his head. "She is still far too small to hunt an elk. I will make things easier for her whilst she rests."

"I was going to go hunting. I have a sword. I can hunt for both of us." Ayr put his hand on his hip, grabbing at the hilt of his sword.

Elanor laughed softly. "It's sweet you're wanting to provide for her. A sword won't help you much hunting out here. You won't be able to out speed a deer, and you can't exactly throw your sword at a bird."

"I can try."

"You can." Elanor shrugged her shoulders and moved towards the shoreline of the creek. "But I doubt Azura would appreciate eating nothing more than a small bird. We can help you, off the record, of course. Do you intend on eating alone tonight?"

"As much as I'd just like the time with Azura, I'm sure we could do with the company."

"Good, don't complain then. Smoking water, Evor? Let's get onto the shoreline for your own safety, Ashbourne."

Evor's eyes glinted with a fierce purpose as he narrowed his gaze down at them. He bared his teeth in a silent challenge, waiting until both Elanor and Ayr had safely cleared the water before taking action. Elanor placed her arm across Ayr's chest, holding him back. If the dragon could have smiled, that would have been it. With a swift movement, Evor lowered his head to the surface of the water.

His mouth opened wide, revealing a raging inferno within. Flames surged forth, cascading into the water below. The once calm surface now erupted into chaos as the flames licked and devoured everything in their path. Ayr could feel the heat and pressure building inside Evor's chest as he held his breath for just a few moments longer. Finally, with a heavy exhale, he relented, and the flames quickly died out, leaving nothing but a thick cloud of smoke in their wake.

Evor crouched down at the edge of the crystal-clear water, his sharp claws extended. With another swift movement, he plunged them into the depths and emerged with half a dozen wriggling fish skewered on his talons. With a flick of his wrist, Evor brought his claws onto the shoreline, presenting his catch to Elanor. She reached up with nimble fingers and expertly plucked each of the half dozen fish off him. Most she let fall to the soft ground below, but one of the smallest she passed to Ayr, who eagerly accepted it with a grateful nod.

"Is this good to eat?"

The fish exuded a tantalizing aroma, as if it had been expertly seasoned and grilled over an open fire for just the right amount of time. The scent of charred wood mingled with hints of herbs and spices, making every mouthwatering bite even more irresistible. It was a dish fit for a king, worthy of being savoured slowly and enjoyed to the fullest.

Elanor smiled at him as she grabbed her own fish. "That's another benefit of having a dragon. Anything you want cooked will be instantly barbequed. Eat up, it's freshly cooked."

"What, with their scales still on?" Ayr looked down at the cooked fish in his hand. There'd be no way he was eating past the scales.

Elanor had already torn into her fish, chewing through the scales, with fish splattered all over her face. She looked up at him grinning. "What, don't you have a knife?"

"I have a sword. That won't do the job though."

Elanor grunted and slid her hand down her muscled leg, revealing a small, sturdy knife tucked into the folds of her boot. With a flick of her wrist, she sent the knife sailing through the air to Ayr. He barely caught the handle, his fingers grazing the sharp edge as it spun past. Ayr's stomach growled at the thought of finally tasting food. He wasted no time in scaling the fish with quick, precise movements. The warmth from the freshly caught meal radiated through his hands, signalling its readiness to be devoured.

Ayr eagerly tore a succulent chunk of flesh from the freshly caught fish and brought it to his lips. The salty flavour of the fish was just what he needed to satisfy his hunger. Elanor sat down beside him and wasted no time in continuing to dig into her own meal with equal enthusiasm. Together, they sat on the soft ground, surrounded by the peaceful sounds of nature. As they devoured their catch, Evor's deep bark could be heard echoing off the nearby outcrop. Azura emerged from the rocks, her sleek scales glistening in the fading light. With a joyful prance, she made her way down to join the group by the shoreline.

"Hello, rider."

Ayr's warm, genuine smile spread across his face as he chewed on a succulent piece of fish. As he looked at her, he realised how much she had grown since he had last seen her.

"Hello, Azura. Did you enjoy yourself whilst I was away?"

Azura's tongue flicked in and out of her mouth like a snake. "Very much so, thank you. Yes, Evor and I spent some quality time together. Something that has been rarity ever since he chose Elanor as his rider."

"Evor got you some dinner."

"Yes, I know he told me. But I am not hungry."

Evor grumbled as he lowered himself to the ground. "A young dragon must eat."

Even though he was now laying down, Azura still had to straighten her neck up to glare up at Evor. "I'm not young. We were hatchlings together if you could remember things correctly."

"Apologies. Lesser grown dragons."

"That's not much better." Azura scolded him like a wife would scold her husband for dragging mud on his boots through a freshly clean house. "Riderless dragons would be the correct term to use."

"That's changed now. I am looking forward to seeing how you grow. If our hatchling year was anything to go by, you will excel."

"As long as Ayr is looked after, that is all I care about. I can go days without food."

"She will do well." Elanor moved her eyes away from Azura and looked at Ayr. "Something gives me a feeling."

"I wonder what that could be."

Elanor smiled at him over the top of her fish. She was nearly finished her meal and held it out towards Azura. "I'm done. Do you want to take it?"

Azura's deep blue eyes glimmered with excitement as she eagerly took her place in front of Elanor. With a swift flick of her wrist, Elanor tossed the fish towards the dragon, who moved with lightning speed to catch it before it even reached its peak in the air. In a matter of seconds, all that was left of the once-lively fish was a few scattered scales and bones. Elanor brushed off her hands and gracefully rose from the ground, her auburn hair tousled. Evor noticed and placed his head over her.

"Are you finished, Elanor?"

"Just, Evor."

"Very well, Elanor, we'd best be off."

Elanor stretched out her back and sighed. "Well, good luck, Ashbourne, I'm sure you're going to need it. A lot can happen in the Hungering."

"What, you're not going to come back?" Ayr rose to his feet.

"You have to do it on your own. If anyone finds out I was in-volved here, that could terminate your time here at the Seminary. Even once you have completed your trials, everything you achieve could be thrown into question."

"You knew that you were involved here. You've booted a few re-cruits out already, what's stopping you from doing it to another one?"

Elanor shrugged. "If I was going to kick you out, I should do it based off the fact that you're Dalton's son, but I don't think I will. Maybe it's because I have a soft spot for Azura. I've never seen her choose anyone in my entire life. I thought that I'd be the rider for her, but it turns out that it was just a dream."

"So, you're putting yourself through all this for Azura? Why wouldn't you do it for Evor?"

"She's a special dragon." Evor rumbled behind Elanor, slowly bowing his head in agreeance. "When you spend some time with her, you'll find that out."

Azura nudged her head into Ayr's hand, emitting a low rumble of contentment. Her soft, white scales gleamed as Ayr gently scratched the top of her head. With each stroke, Azura pressed closer to him, her large body nuzzling against his thigh in a display of affection. As his hand trailed down her graceful neck, she let out a melodic coo and closed her eyes in bliss. Despite her size, the magnificent dragon seemed to melt into a puddle of joy at Ayr's touch.

"Don't stop doing that, even when she grows. All dragons like that."

"I'll keep that in mind, Elanor."

Elanor reached into one of the pockets on her sturdy, weathered uniform and unveiled a large piece of folded cloth. As she unfolded it, Ayr's eyes widened as he recognized the familiar red plume that had adorned Elanor's head when she wore the mask. With a swift motion, she pulled the mask over her head, concealing her features entirely. They were replaced by the black and white cloth. Her eyes looked fierce, the pattern around them replicating a hawk silhouette.

"Good luck recruit! May your dragon always breathe fire."

Ayr frowned. So, it wasn't just a family saying. "And may his wings carry you forward."

"So, you know our words. At least your father taught you something, Ashbourne."

"My father taught me many things."

The mask covered Elanor's face, making it impossible to decipher the woman's expression as she turned away from him. Evor lowered his neck, allowing Elanor to gracefully mount him. Considering Evor was larger than a house, Elanor took some time in climbing onto his back, scaling up his legs like a cat. As soon as she was settled on his back, Evor lifted his head and gazed upwards towards the open sky, ready to take off.

"Good luck, little one. I look forward to seeing your progress when you return to us."

"Thank you, Evor. I'm sure the rider will be able to show me a great deal."

Evor took a step forward, his wings unfolding with graceful ease. He scaled the rough rock face in one fluid motion, each powerful beat of his wings propelling him higher and higher into the sky. He flew up above the trees and within a manner of moments had vanished from view, leaving Ayr in awe.

"How long until you think we can do that?"

"I don't know, how long is going to take for us to get to know each other? I want to fly."

"You can't fly yet?"

Azura gracefully unfurled her wings. As Ayr watched, he could sense her disappointment. Her wings were small and stubby, barely reaching beyond her own height. They lacked the strength and power needed to lift her into the sky. It was a cruel reminder of her limitations, a constant weight she carried with her. Ayr felt sympathy for his winged companion. She deserved to soar freely like the birds above, but instead, she was confined to the ground, unable to reach her full potential.

"I would if I could. I can glide, but that's about it. My wings aren't big enough to hold my body in the air yet."

"Well, we need to change that then. What can I do to help?"

"Nothing. Just keep being you. The closer we grow together the more I will grow. I can feel that I have already grown slightly in the time that we have been here."

"Then let's work together. I want you big enough to ride by the time the Hungering is over."

Azura's mouth opened slightly, revealing her fangs. Ayr was beginning to learn that this was her way of smiling at him. "I'd like that."

SEVEN

As the days passed, it became increasingly evident that Ayr's constant presence by Azura's side was having a profound effect on her growth. At first, the changes were subtle, but now, there was clearly a significant difference in her size. Every morning, she would wake up nestled close to Ayr, her position shifted from the previous night as if seeking comfort and protection.

Today, as Ayr rubbed the sleep from his eyes and looked down at her, he could see that she had grown another head length since yesterday. Her once slender tail now bore a striking resemblance to Evor's, with small spines just starting to emerge along her back. As he ran his hand over them, he marvelled at how quickly she was growing and changing under his care; her once tiny form now too heavy for Ayr to lift. As he laid beside her, he could feel the warmth of her body because of the fire that burnt within her belly. Ayr could hear the steady rhythm of her breathing. His hand traced over her newly grown spines, marvelling at how they had multiplied in just six days. There were now at least half a dozen protruding from behind her neck, with another set beginning to form along her tail. Each one was a delicate yet powerful weapon, adding to Azura's already impressive stature.

The cool, crisp nights and mornings in the wilderness had become more bearable with Azura by his side. She was not only a source of warmth, but also a wonderful companion. As Ayr slowly woke from his slumber, the majestic white dragon stirred beside him. Her long body stretched out, easily twice as long as his own height. Letting out a low groan, she turned to face him, her large blue eyes locking onto his with affection and trust.

"Good morning, rider. How did you sleep?"

The dull ache at the back of his head had become a familiar sensation for Ayr. Each day, he scoured the pit and its surroundings for any materials to improve his living conditions, only to be met with more rocks and debris. In the end, he resigned himself to using his vest as a makeshift pillow against Azura's warm body, finding some solace in her presence as he settled down for the night. The ground was unforgiving, but the gentle sound of Azura's breathing and the faint rustling of leaves above provided comfort in this place.

"Good. How did you sleep? Are you ready for another day?"

Azura gracefully rose to her full height, towering over Ayr. It was remarkable how much she had grown in just a few short days. She sat back down and absently scratched at her hind leg, her underbelly rising and falling with each breath. The soft morning sun glinted off of her white scales, giving her a regal appearance. The air around them seemed to hum with the energy of her transformation, as if the natural world itself recognized her newfound stature.

"Fine! What did you want to do today?"

"You're not ready to fly yet, are you?"

"Not yet. I imagine it will only take a few more days and then I can start to learn. I feel like my wings are almost big enough."

She unfolded her massive wings and suddenly the once dimly lit cave was filled with Azura's formidable presence. Ayr felt grateful that he had been sitting on the ground to avoid being accidentally knocked over by her immense size. He could not believe how much she had grown since yesterday, her wings now sporting sharp spikes along the edges. As he took in every detail of her transformation, he wondered about the progress of the other recruits' dragons. Were they also experiencing such rapid growth, or were some surpassing others in size and strength? The unanswered questions added to his anticipation and curiosity about what lay ahead in the Hungering. Would they be discovered, and would they need to fight for their lives?

Although his father had trained him in techniques to defend against dragons, Ayr could not shake the fear of facing a creature as massive and powerful as Evor. None of the other recruit's dragons would be at his size yet, and having Azura with him would make other dragons easier to deal with.

"If you can't fly yet, we can still go for a hunt today. I imagine the deer in the forest are excited by your presence."

"We?" There was a hint of humour in Azura's voice. "I didn't know you were any good at hunting."

"I would be if I had the right parts for it. Unfortunately, just coming out here with a sword wasn't my best idea."

"That's true, not all of us can be this beautiful." Azura shook her long neck and stretched upwards. "Well, we'd better get you food. I know how fragile humans are."

Ayr frowned, offended. "Excuse me? We're not fragile."

"Brittle little bones, weak stomachs and a cough is enough to put you in bed for three days. Yes, Ayr, I think humans are fragile." Azura spoke with a tone that was all to matter of fact as if she'd had this conversation with other dragons before.

"When you put it like that, you have a point. What do dragons get?"

Azura frowned and pondered for a moment. "Nothing. We are removed from the sicknesses and concerns of lesser beings."

"That must be nice."

"You will benefit from it too, rider. Once we are bonded, my magic will flow through your veins. Whilst you won't be infallible, certain things will no longer affect your health and well-being."

"Excellent!"

Azura reached the edge of the rocky outcrop that served as their shelter, the jagged edges jutting out like teeth from a dragon's mouth. The warmth of the morning sun caressed her scales, highlighting the delicate curves and lines of her face. She hummed as she looked to the sky.

"Hmm. I know my wings aren't big enough yet but let me see if I can fly today."

With a daring leap off the ledge and over the babbling stream, she defied gravity without any regard for her own safety. It was a daily ritual, one that she did with fearless determination in an attempt to soar high. Ayr held his breath as he watched her drop, his heart pounding with both fear and awe. But just as she reached the lowest point, her wings unfolded and began beating furiously against the air. Azura let out a triumphant bark as she flew across the pit, her body gliding effortlessly through the open space. Her joy was palpable as she pulled herself up onto the opposite ledge and turned to face Ayr, her wings shimmering in the sunlight with each graceful stroke. Ayr beamed back at her, completely enchanted by her exhilarating flight.

"Azura! You did it!"

"If I flew any further, I would have lost control and crashed to the ground. You won't be able to ride me today."

"Can you try again? Practice makes perfect."

"Sure!"

Without hesitation, Azura leapt off the edge and put herself in the empty space above the stream once again. This time, rather than flying in a straight line, she turned, looking more comfortable the second time around. She banked to the left and then again to the right, making her way back towards Ayr, before finally setting herself down in front of him. Ayr took a few steps back, giving Azura the extra space she needed to land. Ayr clapped his hand together, applauding her.

"Well done! That was incredible, Azura. How do you feel?"

"Good! Maybe I can try with you on my back tomorrow. I'd hate for anything to happen to you if I couldn't support your weight."

A grin was spreading across Ayr's face. "Sounds good to me. I didn't think you'd be flying so quickly."

"I guess it helps when you have a good rider."

Ayr kicked at the ground. "I'm *not* a good rider. I still know nothing."

"You're taking care of me so far and are accelerating my growth. I can't really ask for anything more than that."

"I'm glad I could help."

"Now let me help you." Azura was stretching out her wings once again. "Stay here whilst I go get breakfast."

"Can you not burn them until after I've skinned mine?"

Azura playfully closed one eye and reopened it, giving Ayr a sly wink. "No promises."

Azura's graceful movements carried her towards the stream, her wings outstretched as she glided effortlessly through the air. With a powerful dive, she broke through the surface of the water and began to swim at lightning speed. The crystal-clear water was soon tinged with patches of red as Azura swiftly caught and devoured her prey. Her head breached the surface of the water, revealing well over half a dozen fish dangling from her jaws. Each one had a different shape and size, a testament to Azura's skill as a hunter. She was only getting better by the day and no fish was any match for a dragon.

With minimal effort, Azura shook her scales free of any water and shot up towards Ayr on the outcrop. She landed again, this time with a little more grace than before. Azura placed the fish on the ground at his feet.

"I got some good ones today."

"You did." Ayr beamed at her.

She had done well in catching their first meal for the day. The smallest offering was a simple whiting, but it was enough to make Ayr's stomach grumble with hunger. Skinning the fish with his sword took more effort than he would have liked, but with no other blade available, it was the only option. Over the past few days, Ayr had become quite skilled at using the tip of his blade to effortlessly remove the scales. Each movement was fluid and precise, a dance between man and weapon as he prepared their dinner in the fading light of day.

When he was finished, he held the fish up in the air in front of Azura's face. Taking her time and being careful not to burn him, she released a slow, steady stream of heat. The fish cooked in seconds before Ayr's eyes. He still wasn't used to the sensation of seeing it happen so quickly. Still holding onto the fish tail, Ayr lowered it onto his sword, the only thing that he had that could double as a plate, as he waited for it to cool.

As he waited, Ayr's eyes followed Azura in fascination as she threw her head back and deftly swallowed another fish whole with each gulp. The water around them shimmered with the sunlight filtering through the trees, creating a peaceful atmosphere in their secluded corner of paradise. Despite his curiosity to explore further, Ayr was content to stay in their small haven for now, especially since they were blessed with an abundance of delicious fish. Watching Azura enjoy her meal, he felt relaxed and humbled by this simple yet idyllic life they had created together. With her by his side, it seemed like a fever dream.

Between bites of succulent fish, Azura's head tilted back towards the sky, her eyes searching for something. She repeated this action five times before finally settling her gaze on a specific spot in the sky. The bright blue expanse above was dotted with fluffy white clouds and the occasional bird soaring gracefully through the air.

"Do you hear that, rider?"

Ayr shook his head, confused. "No, there's only the wind. What can you hear?"

"Someone's here." Azura's tongue flicked in and out of her mouth. "I can smell them."

"Where, Azura?"

With calculated grace, Azura lowered her lithe body to the ground, her belly barely an inch above the swaying blades of grass. Her sharp gaze scanned the ridgeline above them, searching for any signs of danger. Finally, her eyes settled on a particular spot straight ahead of them, hidden among the brush. Ayr narrowed his own eyes and followed her line of sight to see a snake-like head emerging from the foliage. The dragon's yellow eyes slowly revealed themselves as it crept out into the open. Its scales were a deep, dark green, blending seamlessly with its surroundings and making it nearly invisible in the forest shadows - a perfect camouflage for an ambush.

The morning sunlight cast a golden glow on the dragon's shimmering scales, blending them seamlessly with the trees and brush around it. Ayr's heart dropped as he watched the massive creature take each step, its powerful form stirring up the earth beneath its feet. This was not the sight he had hoped for. Just from the size of the dragon's head, he could see that it was already much larger than Azura. A smaller figure sat on top of the dragon's head. It was already big enough to ride.

The figure was a young male with a clump of blond hair that fell messily over his forehead. He was no older than Ayr himself, and he wore a Seminary uniform that was tattered and torn in several places. Some of the tears looked like they had been sword inflicted, whilst three identical cuts across his sternum appeared to have been dragon inflicted. This recruit had seen battle. Ayr recognised him from his first day at the Seminary, but had forgotten his name.

"So, this is the Ashbourne child you told me about, Heath. He doesn't look like much, but I do remember him from the day I met you. I'm surprised he got accepted. I'm also still very much surprised that you chose him to be your rider, Azura." The dragon spoke in a deep, calm tone that would have calmed Ayr if it currently was not unnerving him.

Ayr wasn't the only one unnerved. Azura slowly rose to her full height. "He's as good as any recruit that walked through those gates. What do you want, Grisham?"

Grisham gracefully rose onto his hind legs, showcasing his impressive height to Ayr. Despite still being in the early stages of development, Grisham towered over Azura, standing almost twice as tall as her. His powerful physique was accentuated by his long neck, which was at least twice as thick and twice as long as Azura's slender one.

"We wanted to see what the fuss what about. Didn't we, Heath? It was about time we found you. We've scoured the entire Garden of Chilijo. Nobody would tell us where you went."

Azura's eyes narrowed on the green dragon. "You've covered the entire garden in a week? I'll bet you made a lot of friends along the way. How many did you kill?"

"Some." With a practiced, fluid motion, Heath slid off Grisham's back, sliding down his neck until he reached the pit. Heath's boots landing softly on the ground below. Drawing his sword from its sheath with a metallic ring, he stood next to Grisham, both rider and dragon ready for battle. The cool breeze rustled through Heath's hair as they surveyed the landscape before them, their steely gazes taking in every detail of their surroundings. "And we're here now. I'm sure you know what for."

The hairs on the back of Ayr's neck stood up as Azura coiled her body around him. "You can't attack us. You're cheating if you're attacking riders and their dragons before the call is made."

"We made our own call." Grisham's eyes were now glowing with a fiery yellow energy. "There aren't many recruits left, you know."

"Is that how you got so large so quickly? By feasting on the bones of your fellow hatchlings?"

A deep bellow came from Grisham's chest. "That is why, in their infinite wisdom, the Obelisk chose to call it the Hungering. I can't understand why they'd allow an Ashbourne in the Obelisk, even if you are the nephew of the Overlord."

Ayr's hand hovered over the hilt of his sword. "Why can't I be here? I've done nothing to you."

"Your father's army torched my family's lands during the war. He also killed my cousins in cold blood. I haven't seen Dalton face any repercussions since then. What a way to come out of hiding. It's been years since the war, and he sends his son to the one place he is most likely to die."

Ayr's hands flew up in a defensive gesture, his palms facing outwards, as he tried to diffuse the tension. But standing before him was a dragon much larger than he could have ever imagined at this early stage of development. Azura, had only recently taken flight and was no match for their opponent. The odds were stacked against them, and Ayr knew that a fight would be futile.

"I don't want any trouble. You also don't want this fight."

Heath laughed and tightened his grip on his sword. "I don't want this fight? On the contrary, this is the one fight I've been waiting my whole life for."

"You know who my father was. Do you really think it's a good idea? His blood runs through mine. Dalton Ashbourne is the one man that didn't need a dragon to bring the Commonwealth to its knees."

"All the more reason for you to die before history has a chance to repeat itself, Ayr Ashbourne."

Grisham's deep growl rumbled beside Heath, sending shivers down Ayr's spine. The green dragon was still only half the size of Evor, but he could feel the tension in the air as Azura braced herself. Even with her newfound strength and skills, Ayr knew that she was no match for the ferocious beast before them. His massive size and sharp claws would surely overpower her in an instant. Ayr's hand instinctively went to his sword hilt again, preparing for an intense battle. The air crackled with energy as both sides stood their ground, waiting for the other to make the first move.

"I'm here to learn to be a rider." All Ayr wanted to do was diffuse the situation. Azura was outmatched.

"So was Dalton. This is part of the process. You'll either live or you'll die."

Grisham let loose a mighty roar that sent further shivers down Ayr's spine. Azura let loose a roar of her own that was nowhere near as deafening. She challenged him, but based on their roars alone, Ayr knew that they would both die. Maybe he could kill Heath before Grisham tore him to pieces and that would be enough. Heath walked towards him; his blade pointed at him. Ayr drew his own and raised it as he walked towards Heath. Heath's upper lip curled as he moved his sword in his hand, swinging it around in front of him.

The metallic clang of their blades meeting rang out through the training grounds as Ayr and Heath engaged in a fierce battle. Ayr's breaths came out in grunts as he struggled to hold his ground against Heath's relentless attacks. It reminded him of sparring with his father, but Heath was on a level above anything Dalton had ever been. As they continued to clash, Heath suddenly stepped back and lowered his sword. The dragons still had not come to blows yet, both circling each other like a pair of sharks.

"What are you waiting for Grisham! Kill her!"

The emerald dragon burst into motion, its powerful body lunging towards Azura with fierce determination. Azura, equally as nimble and quick, leapt back just in time to avoid the attack. Meanwhile, Heath had repositioned himself and charged at Ayr once again with his sword raised high. Ayr, ever perceptive, dodged Heath's blow and countered with a calculated thrust of his own. Dalton had tested Ayr with every possible scenario, drawing from past opponents and battles. The Commonwealth was renowned for its strategic methods in all aspects of life, including sword fighting.

Ayr leaned into it for now, duelling with Heath who was still holding his sword in only one hand. Knowing that he physically could not keep up with the other recruit's power, Ayr was forced to give ground.

He could see Azura and Grisham out of the corner of his eye, their dance matching the one that Ayr and Heath were having. The only difference were the growls, roars and the flashing of fangs and claws. Azura pounced on Grisham, flipping him onto his back. Ayr lost sight of them as Heath charged at him again.

He was skilled, and he controlled the tempo of the fight, forcing Ayr to question every decision he made. Heath continued to hack away, snarling and grunting with each thrust. Despite his best efforts, he had no way of breaking Ayr's defence. It was only a matter of time before he would. Ayr was beginning to tire, and the constant roaring that came from the dragon fight only made him nervous. The fighting continued back and forth between the two until Ayr turned and saw Azura create separation between her and Grisham. This was Ayr's chance.

He turned and fled, not waiting for Azura, or looking back over his shoulder. Heath's shout of surprise was enough to know that he had done the unexpected and imagined that the blond recruit was now streaking after him. What worried Ayr more was Grisham. Ayr quickly snapped over his shoulder. His sprint had seen him put distance on Heath, but Grisham was a different story. Both Azura and Grisham were bounding after him, closing the distance with ease.

Ayr kept back, focused on the tunnel ahead of him. Just maybe if he could make it to the water and swim under the cavern entrance, Grisham wouldn't be able to follow. He could feel the dragon's hot breath on his back as he dropped to the ground at the last second. The majority of Grisham's body passed overhead. Something caught the back of Ayr's leg, pushing it into the ground and tearing away at his flesh. Ayr screamed.

He lost what was happening around him as the ground rushed up to meet him. Ayr heard a human voice shouting, while the dragons roared. Ayr struggled to lift his head up. As he did, he was greeted by a cyclone of dust. A white tail, followed by a green tail flashed overhead, as another dragon roared. Azura was doing what she could to protect him. His stupidity had cost him. In what world was running away the best option?

Something whipped into his back, splitting both his uniform and skin open. Ayr shrieked again, as he tried to climb to his feet. Blinding pain shot through his right leg, and he collapsed to the ground. Everything from his knee down was on fire. With no other option, Ayr tried to climb to his feet once again, only to collapse once again. More pain shot up his leg, feeling as if it was on fire. His right leg wasn't working and had given out on him completely. He looked down, finding it nothing more than a bloodied mess. Blood streamed from at least two gaping wounds with portions of skin missing, cut down to the bone. Screaming, desperate to get away from the larger dragon and his angry rider, Ayr tried once more to bring himself back to a vertical base. Putting all of his weight onto his left leg almost got him standing but before he could balance, he felt something large scoop up underneath his arm.

"Stay with me, rider!"

He was suddenly hurtling forwards, moving faster than he could on his own. Ayr shot towards the cavern entrance and looked down at what was propping him up. His arm was wrapped around Azura's neck as she moved at a breakneck speed. The white dragon was focused on their destination with an intensity that Ayr had not yet seen from her.

"Hold your breath!"

Ayr did as he was told. Azura left the ground, as did his feet as she lunged forward into the air. He heard Grisham's jaws snap shut behind them a moment later as Azura dove and hit the water. It was like she was hunting fish. Azura shot through the water and quickly passed underneath the low tunnel.

When they breached the surface, Ayr gasped for his first fresh breath of air in about a minute. He checked over his shoulder, seeing no trace of the green dragon pushing his way through the rocks. His leg was still throbbing, and he clung onto Azura like his life depended on it. Azura kept her head above the water as she swam to the shore. Ayr tried to assist where he could, kicking with his good leg, but he accidentally kicked with his bad leg, a scream tearing from his lips.

Azura was panicked. "What's wrong?"

"I think I broke something,"

"You don't need to help rider! Rest. I will look at it when we get to shore."

EIGHT

Azura steered them towards the sandy beach hugging the shoreline of the island nestled in the heart of the cavern. The warm sun high in the sky flooded the cavern with light, illuminating every nook and cranny. The gentle lapping of waves against the shore and the distant cawing of seagulls were the only sounds as they approached their destination. But somewhere in the distance, a deep rumble echoed through the cavern walls - a sound that could only belong to Grisham.

Azura laid Ayr down onto the beach. Ayr sighed as he collapsed onto the sand, unable to stand fully on his one good leg. He finally let his sword go, allowing it to rest in the sand beside him. Laying underneath the dragon, he looked up into her big beautiful blue eyes. He could see his own reflection in them, and he looked pitiful. What other option did he have? There was no access to any medical facility here. Nor would any of the other recruits try to help him, if Heath's mentality was anything to go by.

"Can you cut a tree down?"

Azura nodded. "Yes, of course, however I am struggling to understand what the point of that would be."

"Well, if we get a decent enough branch, we could refine it and turn it into a crutch."

Azura tutted. "Don't be stupid. We don't need to do that."

"Why not?"

"My tears can heal you, rider."

"I'm sorry, what did you say?"

Azura nodded again, affirming what she had just said. "As long as the connection to the rider is strong enough, we can heal you. To me it looks like you've broken your leg. I can fix it."

"This is insane! I know you're a dragon, but is there anything you can't do?"

"I can't fly to the sun."

"How do you know? Have you ever tried?"

Azura snorted at him. "You're a funny human, Ayr. I knew I liked you. Now if you want your leg fixed, hold still."

With a gentle nudge of her foot, Azura carefully rolled Ayr onto his side. He let out a pained groan as his leg was twisted into an unnatural angle, far from how it had been when he first collapsed onto the soft sand. Azura's voice was filled with concern as she cooed at him, as if trying to ease the pain and apologize for causing it. Her touch was as tender as it could have been for a dragon of her size.

"It's fine!"

"No, it's not rider, you're in pain. Stay still!"

Laying face-down in the gritty sand, Ayr struggled to turn his head and see what Azura was doing. With delicate movements, she positioned his leg beneath her own head for support. He held still, allowing her to take care of him. As he glanced out of the corners of his eyes, he noticed tears welling up in hers, glistening like dewdrops. They then began to cascade down her cheeks, much like they would on a human's face.

As her tears fell, Ayr could feel each one land with a heavy splash on his exposed leg. The hole that Grisham's attack had left in his pants was now a wide gateway for the droplets to reach his skin. As they trickled down his leg, Ayr felt a chilling sensation spread through his body like ice water coursing through his veins. His leg trembled uncontrollably, as if he were experiencing a painful cramp in the middle of the night. There was no pain, only a sudden, rapid cooling of his skin.

A sharp, icy sensation jolted through Ayr's leg as Azura's foot connected with it. The cold was so intense, it felt like his leg had been submerged in a frozen lake. Just as suddenly as it came, the freezing effect dissipated, and his leg began to throb with warmth once again. As Azura lifted her foot from his leg, Ayr let out a groan and rolled onto his back, frantically rubbing at the spot where her foot had struck him. A red mark was already forming, evidence of the intense impact. The pain dissipated into nothingness.

"What did you do? It feels amazing!"

"What any good dragon would do. Taking care of my rider."

With a swift motion, Ayr hoisted himself up to his feet and encircled Azura in his arms. She melted into his embrace, basking in the warmth of his body against hers. Her head nestled comfortably against his chest. The scent of her skin enveloped him, calming his racing heart and grounding him in the present moment.

"I can't thank you enough."

"You don't have to, rider."

As they rested against each other, Ayr felt a subtle shift in movement. Azura's body remained still, but he could sense her pushing him away. She began to grow before his very eyes. It was only a few inches, but the sudden increase in height was undeniable. Though she was still far from being able to stand up to Grisham on her own, Ayr felt a surge of happiness at any growth at this stage. Grisham's growth seemed to be weeks ahead of them, and Ayr knew that every bit of progress counted if they wanted to succeed in the Seminary. He could not ignore the target that had been painted on his back, but he refused to let it slow their progress towards their goal.

Ayr broke their embrace and frowned at Azura. "There's a much bigger dragon out there. He broke the rules, didn't he?"

Azura nodded. "Indeed, there was no call. I remember your father's name and what he did to the Commonwealth. Still, what Grisham and his rider have done today prove that they should be removed from the Seminary. There is no excuse for breaking the Obelisk rules."

"What can we do? We can't tell anyone, can we? Who out here is going to help us?"

Azura shook her head. "That tunnel is the only way that I know out of this cavern. If that recruit and Grisham continue to stalk outside it, I don't see how we could get out of it."

"We could fly?" Ayr shrugged his shoulders. "I don't have any other idea."

"We could, but I don't know if I'd be able to evade Grisham in the air, even without you on my back."

"How much are you likely to grow in the next few days?" Ayr started to pace. "I don't want you getting trapped in here."

"With how much Evor grew in the time he was in here, there's no way he would have been able to get out from where we came in. There has to be another way."

Ayr threw his hands up in the air. "What do you mean he didn't tell you? According to Elanor this is where they spent most of their time."

"I know. There has to be a way that Evor got out of here."

"We need to find it before Heath and Grisham. I just don't know where it would be. I saw nothing here."

"Did Elanor show you the whole cavern?"

Ayr shook his head. "She only took me to the cabin."

"Hmm. I want to scout ahead, but I don't want to leave you by yourself."

"I could get on your back." It seemed like a reasonable suggestion to him.

Azura shook her head and took a step back. "Don't. I wouldn't be able to fly properly yet. And if I'm flying at speed, that uniform simply won't be enough to protect you from the damage that I'd do to you. We'd need to frequently stop to heal any wounds you'd sustain."

"I'm sure there's a technique so that I can ride you without a saddle."

Azura shook her head again. "There is, but I'm not the right being to teach you it. I'm not willing to endanger your wellbeing just so we can travel faster. We go together or not at all."

"If we don't find that second entrance, Grisham will get in here and finish what he started. I'm in danger either way."

Ayr could see the worry etched into every line on Azura's face. She knew he was right, and her expression betrayed her fear. Grisham and Heath were surely nearby. If there was a second entrance to this cavern, they were doomed. Azura turned away, her eyes scanning the rocky ceiling above them as if searching for a solution in its crevices. Ayr could feel the tension thickening in the air around them, like a heavy fog that obscured their thoughts and movements. This desperate situation seemed almost suffocating, but they had come too far to turn back now.

"If I leave you, I need you to stay here. Understood?"

Ayr nodded and knelt to pick up his sword. "I'm not defenceless you know. I know my way around a sword."

"You don't know your way around dragons. Hide in the trees and wait for my return, rider."

With a sudden burst of strength, Azura propelled herself into the vast expanse of the sky. Ayr watched in awe as her majestic wings shimmered against the faint light that filtered down into the cavern. With the grace and speed of a peregrine falcon, she soared across the cavern and disappeared into the thick canopy of trees in the forest beyond. Ayr stood still, taking in his surroundings. Unlike his last visit to this cave, he was completely alone now. He took a deep breath, savouring the cool and damp air that hung in the cavern. His stomach rumbled slightly. Thankfully, as he glanced around, Ayr found a berry bush nearby. Ayr moved to it and sat down beside it. He began plucking away at the berries.

His eyes remained fixed on the mouth of the cave, half expecting a raging Grisham to emerge from the dark waters at any moment. The deafening roars of the dragon still echoed through the cavern, but for now, his concern was appeased. However, as the silence settled in, Ayr felt a sense of unease creeping up his spine.

His hand gripped tightly around his sword, poised and ready for any potential threat. Each passing minute felt like an eternity, every second stretched out in agonizing slowness. After what seemed like an hour had passed, he caught sight of Azura's familiar white wings. She flew past Ayr on the far edge of the cavern before turning back towards the beach with purpose.

Ayr rose from his seated position as she got closer. "Did you find anything?"

Azura shook her head. "No, there is no other way into this cave."

"We haven't checked underwater yet. If one entrance is like that, what's to say the other isn't?"

"Nothing. But come, you'll need rest. Any healing from a dragon's tears will need a short period of time for you to recover properly. Once the magic sets in properly, you'll want to sleep, especially for such a major injury."

Grumbling, Ayr tried to push her away. "I feel fine."

Azura glowered at him. "Are you sure? You need rest."

As she spoke, Ayr's vision began to blur, and his head swam with dizziness. His legs threatened to give out beneath him, but Azura quickly swooped in, her strong neck providing support under his arm once more. Ayr clung to her instinctively, his senses dulled as he struggled to stay conscious.

The path they followed was familiar, having walked it with Elanor only days before. Azura expertly navigated through the trees until they reached the small cabin. With a gentle nudge, she guided Ayr to the door and pushed it open for him. Exhausted and weak, Ayr collapsed onto the bed inside.

"Stay here, rider. Rest. I'm going to go and scout the island to see what else is around."

Ayr muttered at Azura, his words slurred and muffled by the drowsiness that threatened to overtake him. He saw her tilt her head in concern before gracefully taking flight, leaving him alone in the stillness of the forest. The soft rustling of leaves and chirping of birds surrounded him, but Ayr's mind was consumed by the pressing danger lurking nearby. Despite his best efforts to resist, he could feel himself succumbing to sleep. Even as he drifted in and out of consciousness, his mind refused to find peace. Images and memories spun around him like a never-ending carousel, taunting him with their fleeting glimpses.

Like a pig being turned on a spit, Ayr tossed and turned on the bed. His body was restless, trapped in between the realms of sleep and wakefulness. With each rotation, he could feel the drowsiness slowly slipping away. Finally settling on his back, Ayr's eyes fluttered open to see a figure looming over him. The sudden jolt of adrenaline snapped him out of his drowsy state completely.

"You!"

With a sharp hiss, the sound of a sword being drawn pierced through the air. He saw the flash of steel - it hurtled down towards him. Ayr rolled out of the way, reaching for his own sword, but it was still in its sheath. Ayr hit the floor and sprung to his feet as the sword came down again. He felt the wind from the blow on his back. The hut was cramped, and he took a step back, trying to give himself more room.

Heath flew across the room, not allowing any separation to occur. Ayr had no choice but to throw his sword up, sheath included.

Heath's sword beat down upon Ayr's, cutting through the supple leather of the sheath. Ayr lashed back at Heath, kicking at his knee. Heath stepped back, but the back of his foot got caught on the bed. He stumbled and Ayr tried to press an advantage he didn't have.

Ayr stepped forward with his sword above his head. Heath reached out, grabbing Ayr to try and stabilise himself, but in the next moment, Ayr found himself travelling through the air. He landed a second later, back first, crashing against the wall of the cabin. The wood gave way and there was a rumbling thunder as the cabin started to come undone. Not wanting to get squashed by a falling log, Ayr scrambled out of the door and into the open space. Heath followed him, on his feet, ducking out of the cabin as the roof collapsed.

Ayr was on his back and the separation had given him enough time to draw his sword. Without a standing base, Ayr was outmatched in terms of power and manoeuvrability. Heath had all of the power behind him. Ayr was almost defenceless on the ground. He threw his sword up in a feeble attempt to block. Heath's sword swung down in a murderous arc, in a two-handed grip. Ayr grunted as he tried to push Heath away, but the other recruit was too powerful.

Heath beat down upon Ayr's sword thrice and Ayr felt it slipping from his grip. He retightened his grip on Heath's next downward strike and rolled to the side. Heath jolted forward, expecting his blade to hit something, and the opening allowed Ayr to dart forwards. Heath was waiting for Ayr to rise, lashing out with a kick that sent Ayr back to the ground. Ayr's head hit the ground, and his vision went temporarily black.

A commanding figure stood over him – it was not Heath. Ayr's vision adjusted again and as he looked down at the ground, he saw Heath laying at his feet. The figure stood behind Heath's crumpled body; their height accentuated by the low light that cast shadows across their form. The stark contrast of their white and black mask, adorned with a striking red plume, made them instantly recognizable. In one hand, she held a sword by its blade, the weapon still sheathed in its leather casing.

Ayr squinted trying to make out the figure. "Elanor?"

"Who else?" Elanor reattached her sword to her belt. "Geez, you're lucky I decided to come back and check on you. I know when the call is supposed to be sounding, and this recruit thought it'd be a good idea to attack you before it."

"You're not supposed to help me."

"No, but we still do regular checks to make sure you're still alive. If we get down to five recruits before the month is up, what's the point in continuing the challenge? I've long suspected that my Hungering wasn't the only one where foul play has occurred."

Ayr sat up slowly. "You were attacked as well?"

Elanor nodded in response. "I was. I gutted the recruit that thought he could get the better of Evor and I. Unlike you, Ashbourne."

"I was incapacitated."

"That's no excuse. What would you do if the call sounded now? You'd be dead and Azura would be without a rider."

Ayr frowned. There was no denying that fact. "So, what happens now? How many recruits are left in the Hungering?"

"With this one out of the mix? Five."

"Wait, do you mean it's over?" Ayr rubbed his head.

Elanor grunted as she glared down at Heath. "I'll take this piece of shit back to the Obelisk where we'll punish him and boot him out of the Seminary. It's a shame. Grisham is a good dragon He was waiting outside the entrance. I was hopeful his recruit would pass the trials. Sort yourself out and return to the entrance of the garden when you hear the next dragon roar. Then your real tests will begin. Well done, Ashbourne."

Despite the mask covering her face and her stoic demeanour, Ayr wanted to pull her close and kiss her. After weeks spent in isolation, with only Azura for company, they were finally safe. He grinned up at her, relieved to have someone by his side once again. He wanted to savour this moment of peace and safety, knowing that it would not last forever. For now, in this brief moment, everything was perfect.

"I don't know why you're smiling, Ashbourne. This is usually the easiest test if you don't do anything stupid. The real struggle will be getting through the rest of the trials."

"He tried to kill me twice. Haven't I been through enough?"

Elanor laughed loudly, both of her hands on her hips. "Are you serious? This is where it will get harder." She glanced down at the prone figure of Heath once again. "Probably should not have knocked him out. Will make it harder to get him through the tunnel."

"I can help you."

"You don't need to."

Guilt filled a pit in Ayr's stomach. "I insist. I'm the reason why you're both here."

Elanor crouched over Heath, her muscles straining as she positioned herself to lift him off the ground. She grunted with effort, and she used her body weight to gain control over his limp form. With a final push, she stood upright, supporting his weight effortlessly as if he were nothing more than a feather in her grasp.

"The day I ask for help from an Ashbourne will be the day I die."

A deafening roar echoed through the cavern and Ayr's head snapped upwards to see Azura returning to him. Her massive, pristine white wings beat at an incredible speed, carrying her back to them faster than he had ever seen before. As she angled herself for landing, the air around her seemed to shimmer with power. With a mighty thud, she landed heavily on the ground, her wings almost collapsing from the force of her momentum. The sound of her landing reverberated off the walls, causing the ground beneath their feet to tremble.

"Rider! Are you ok! I came as fast as I could."

"Yes, I'm fine. Thanks to Elanor." He glanced up at her with a smile. It was impossible to tell if she returned the gesture or not, her face still hidden underneath the mask.

"I saved him, Azura. You have nothing to worry about."

"And Grisham? What will he do once he sees that his rider has been incapacitated?"

"Grisham is speaking to Evor. He understands the rules of the Obelisk just as you do, Azura. There will be no further resistance from Grisham. As soon as the call sounds, please bring Ashbourne back to the entrance of the garden."

Like Ayr, Azura was generous. "Do you need help?"

"No, I'm fine. I can handle one ragtag misfit by myself. You two get ready to leave. You will have until sundown to return to us. Make sure there is no trace of you here once you depart."

NINE

Ayr perched on the bed as the minutes ticked by. Elanor had taken Heath and disappeared into the depths of the forest. The dense canopy above cast dappled shadows on the ground, creating a sense of secrecy and suspense. Ayr breathed in the earthy scent of moss and decaying leaves, feeling small and insignificant among the towering trees. The sound of rustling branches and distant birdcalls filled the air, adding to the tension of the moment. Finally, after what felt like an eternity, Azura raised her head to the sky.

"Wait, can you hear it?"

Ayr listened to the sounds in the environment, but nothing seemed out of the ordinary. "Hear what?"

"Listen, rider."

Ayr turned his head towards the sky as a low, slow rumbling filled the air. The sound grew in volume, booming into a deafening roar that sent shivers down Ayr's spine. It was a sound unlike anything he had ever heard before, one that seemed to shake the very ground beneath him. Whatever dragon had uttered the roar would have been gargantuan.

"What was that?"

"The call, rider. We're free of this place."

"We're not actually free, are we? We don't have to fight through anymore recruits?"

"Yes. Stay by my side and I will keep you safe, rider. I think it's time we left this place, don't you?"

"Elanor said not to leave a trace that we were here." Ayr shot up and picked up the first wooden log that was on the ground.

"You're forgetting I can fix that with ease. Stand back please, rider. In fact, it might be wise if you retreat to the water's edge, just in case."

"Why, what are you going to do?"

A thick, billowing plume of smoke spilled from Azura's mouth, engulfing her face in a swirling haze. Ayr realised what she intended to do. He stepped out from underneath what little of the hut remained and moved away. Azura stood before the ruined remains of the once sturdy cabin. Ayr watched in stunned silence as the smoke continued to rise from her. The acrid scent of burning wood lingered in the air, even though she hadn't begun burning it yet.

"Understandable. I'll see you soon, Azura."

Ayr made his way across the island, only stopping to look back when he was near the shore. A short while later, a fierce roar echoed through the air and Azura emerged from between the trees, her powerful wings propelling her forward as she quickly closed the distance between them.

"Come on, rider. It is time that we left this place. Get onto my back."

"Your back? For what purpose? You won't be able to fly with me on your back."

Azura flicked her wings in a display of force. "I'm not going to fly, but I can still carry you. It will make the journey back to Seminary easier, will it not?"

"I wouldn't say no. But I don't want you carrying all the burden."

"Carrying you is no burden, rider." Azura was insistent. "It is my job. I'm now big enough to carry you and thus I will do so. I don't want to hear any complaints from you, since you won't hear any from me. Now get on."

"You said I'd cut myself without a saddle."

"When flying, yes. Whilst on the ground and swimming, you'll only move with the motion of the ground and water. You can handle that can't you, rider?"

"Sure." What other choice did he have?

Azura gracefully lowered her body to the ground and landed softly beside him, her sleek scales brushing against his side. Ayr cautiously approached, taking careful steps as he surveyed her powerful form. He wondered where he should sit on her, unsure of how to mount such a magnificent creature with no saddle or reins to guide her. His heart raced with both excitement and fear, knowing that this was a once in a lifetime opportunity to ride a dragon.

"Just above the wings for now." Azura seemed to read Ayr's mind, answering his question before he had even asked it.

With a quick scramble, Ayr found his footing and deftly climbed onto Azura's back. She coiled slightly to the side, her muscles shifting under his weight as he settled in between two of the sharp spines on her back. As soon as he was secure, Azura stood up with a powerful thrust of her hind legs. The rush of movement caught Ayr off guard, almost sending him tumbling off, but he managed to steady himself with a firm grip on the spikes.

"Why aren't you hanging on, rider?"

Ayr's hands gripped tightly onto the smooth, curved spine in front of him as Azura shifted and began to move. The sensation was reminiscent of riding a horse, but with less swaying and a wider base for stability. Ayr had only ever ridden horses with saddles before, but even without one he found it impossible to imagine it being as painful as this experience on Azura's back. Every jostle sent sharp pains shooting through his body, causing him to clench his jaw and tighten his grip even more. There was no time for rookie errors, he needed to focus on staying balanced and secure until they reached their destination.

Azura gracefully glided through the calm, crystal-clear water. Ayr followed close behind, his arms wrapped tightly around her spines as they descended into the depths. The walls of the cavern loomed above them, their jagged edges casting eerie shadows on the ocean floor. Azura's sleek, powerful body propelled them forward effortlessly. As they approached the barrier that separated the underwater world from the surface, Azura dove down and swam beneath it with ease as Ayr clung to her back for dear life. Bubbles danced around them as they emerged into the sunlight once more, the warm rays casting a golden glow on their slick skin. Ayr let out a gasp of relief, grateful for the sun's warmth and the fire burning in Azura's belly that would dry him off in no time.

As Ayr clung to Azura's back, the raised scales on her body pressed uncomfortably against his pants. He winced, grateful that she wasn't airborne at the moment. Azura carried him towards the edge of the pit they had descended into weeks ago. Though they had managed to escape its depths, now there was a different kind of pressure - the looming threat of having to return in order to survive. The jagged, foreboding walls of the pit rose high above them. The air inside was thick and heavy, as if weighted down by burden that Ayr carried on his back. With each step closer to the edge, Ayr's heart pounded in his chest, unsure of what awaited them beyond.

"Hang on!"

Azura turned her head in annoyance. "What for? We have nothing left here and we need to be back at the entrance to the Garden by sundown. You heard Elanor."

"I did. But if you fly up the wall, you're going to cut me open."

"Lean forward as we go up. That should alleviate any danger to your legs."

Azura gracefully began her ascent up the walls and Ayr followed her instructions carefully. As he leaned forward, he could feel the gentle, swaying movement of her body beneath him, as if they were walking on solid ground. The rigid scales of her back rubbed against his legs, their ridges creating a sensation that was both foreign and exhilarating. With each step, he felt his heart race with anticipation as they climbed higher and higher. Moments later, Azura levelled out and they were out of the pit. Ayr took a sigh of relief as he looked around at their surroundings.

"Do you remember the way, Azura?"

Azura's sinuous neck coiled and twisted, her piercing left eye glaring up at Ayr with intense focus. "Do you still not trust me, rider?"

"I trust you. I just want to make sure."

"I know the way."

As they trekked through the dense forest, Ayr found himself lost in Azura's company. She continued to chatter away as she shifted underneath him. She moved with grace and determination, her claws crushing the underbrush beneath them. The trees eventually gave way to an open expanse of land that was the rest of the Garden of Chilijo.

Ayr could see dragons soaring in every direction, with riders perched on their backs or flying solo. It was impossible to see who was who until they drew closer to their destination. As they approached the top of the hill where they had left the other recruits weeks before, Ayr recognized them by their distinctively smaller dragons.

As Azura made her way up the steep hill, a looming shadow suddenly fell over them. An enormous, red-scaled dragon, nearly matching the size of Evor in its massive wingspan and powerful body, soared overhead. The beating of its fiery wings echoed through the air as it ascended towards the peak of the hill.

Ayr's mouth hung open, gawking at the size of the dragon. "That's not a recruit, is it?"

"It is. That dragon is Bersos. For him to get that big, he would have eaten other dragons."

"I hope we don't have to fight him."

Azura continued her ascent up the hill. After the tumultuous weeks he had just endured, Ayr could barely recall the names of the other recruits, let alone their accompanying dragons. Each face that greeted him was as unfamiliar as the day he first arrived. However, amidst the sea of strangers, there were two faces that stood out to him, waiting patiently for his return. Lucas and the woman who had saved his life. Elanor.

Elanor stood tall and commanding upon the crest of the hill, her arms folded across her chest. She wore the same uniform as Ayr, but hers was without any signs of wear or battle. It must have been nice to change frequently at the Obelisk. Her mask had been removed, revealing her sharp cheekbones and piercing blue eyes that glinted with determination. As she gazed out over the landscape, she exuded an air of strength and unwavering confidence.

Evor, the towering black dragon stood tall and imposing behind her. His stoic yellow eyes bore down on Ayr and Azura as they made their way up the steep hill. Ayr felt small in his presence and wanted to shrink away. With a powerful beat of its wings, the blue dragon touched down on the ground, sending a gust of wind and dust in all directions. Its scales glistened in the sunlight, reflecting hues of gold and emerald. Evor stood tall and steady as the majestic creature landed gracefully at his feet. A sense of excitement passed through Ayr, knowing that one day he and Azura would be able to do the same.

They finally reached the top of the steep hill. Elanor scanned the group with a critical eye, her expression cool and composed. Her gaze paused on Ayr, who felt a spark of excitement at gaining her attention. He quickly suppressed his smile, not wanting to draw any unwanted attention. His eyes darted over to Lucas, who stood tall and imposing with his arms crossed and a stern expression etched into his features. The tension in the air was palpable as they all waited for their next instructions, eager to prove themselves worthy of this prestigious training program. They had all made it past the first step.

"So, this is all that remains, is it?" Nods of affirmation answered her question. "Excellent, well I'd just like to congratulate you all on succeeding in your task. You may now all move onto the next phase."

Ayr's curiosity got the better of him. "What's involved in that?"

Elanor's eyes lingered on Ayr, and he felt a shudder run through him as he remembered their time spent in the cave. Despite her attempts to hide it, he could still see the playful woman who had teased him into removing his uniform with a mischievous glint in her eyes. The memory flooded back, bringing with it the feeling of her soft touch against his skin and the heat of their bodies pressed together in the dim light. His heart raced at the thought, even as he tried to push it away and focus on the present moment. Elanor's gaze held him captive, and he was glad that it was her turn to speak.

"More tests. We need to ensure that you can properly bond with your dragons. If you cannot, then you're of no use to us. Come with us, please."

Elanor gracefully turned her back, her movements fluid and precise. Lucas and Evor followed suit, their expressions unreadable. Intrigued by their actions, Ayr and the other recruits trailed behind wordlessly. They worked back along the path they had initially come upon the first time they had entered the Garden of Chilijo.

Instead of heading down the familiar path, Elanor steered them to the left and onto another open area. It was like the Garden of Chilijo, with wide open spaces and a sparse population of dragons and their riders. However, there was a noticeable difference here - most of the dragons seemed smaller in size compared to those in the Garden of

Chilijo. They appeared to be newer recruits, their dragons still in the process of growing like Azura.

A winding river flowed through the heart of the valley. Along its banks stood an aged stable, its wooden exterior weathered and worn by time and the elements. It sat behind the river, on the nearest bend that backed onto the base of a mountain. This stable, unlike any other Ayr had seen before, was as large as a castle and housed dragons instead of horses.

The sunlight peeked through broken windows and cracks in the walls as Elanor led them closer. Each step brought them closer to the abandoned structure, and Ayr noticed its complete state of disrepair. Moss clung to the roof tiles, weeds grew wildly in the surrounding area, and the wooden beams were rotting away. It was evident that this once grand stable had fallen into ruin over the years.

As they approached, Ayr's heart sank as Elanor stopped outside the stable. Perched atop the highest window was a large yellow dragon, one that made Azura look comically small in comparison. One half of the dragon rested comfortably inside the stable, while the other half basked in the warm sunlight. Its long tongue lolled out of its mouth in a contented manner. Despite their presence, the dragon seemed unbothered and gave them a lazy once-over with its large, golden eye. Turning back to face the five remaining recruits, Elanor raised her voice to be heard over the sound of chirping birds and rustling leaves surrounding them.

"Welcome to Zenender's Ranch!"

One of the recruits stepped forward, his eyebrows raised. "What's this?"

Elanor's head snapped to him. "This will be your new lodgings. This is where you will be housed until you have bonded with your dragon properly."

Another of the recruits whose name Ayr had forgotten stepped forward. "What do you mean! We're not going to be comfortable! My father paid good money to have me fed and sheltered here. You need to provide for us! That was part of the arrangement! I won't have this. First we survived the Hungering, and now this? This establishment is a joke!"

Lucas cleared his throat. "Owens, was it? You won't be receiving any of that until you have officially bonded with your dragon. That is when you become a rider and not before."

"When's the ceremony then? We've been through enough and it's clear to me that these dragons have at least taken a liking to us five. We should be going through the bonding process already."

Lucas had been polite for long enough and now he snapped. "Patience, child! We will complete the ceremony soon. You will be comfortable here, as it is a step up from the Garden of Chilijo."

"Then when do we begin the trials?"

"If you won't exercise patience, we will begin right now." Elanor cut across Lucas, glancing at him. "I assume that the bridge is ready?"

Lucas nodded at her. "Absolutely. If this recruit wishes to press us, then we will go there immediately. What do you say Owens?"

"We're ready! I'm ready now! Let's get this over and done with."

"Shut up, idiot!"

Ayr allowed his voice to carry, loud and unapologetic. He stood with his chest puffed out, ready to face any consequences that may come from his words. The other recruits turned their heads sharply, their eyes full of anger and disapproval as they fixated on him.

Owens turned with his hands on his hips. "Well, well, if it isn't the Ashbourne. How did you manage to survive the trial? Your father wouldn't have lasted a day in there."

Ayr glared back at Owens. "My father made it through the Seminary as the only one of his intake. If I was anything like him, you would have died in a raging fire weeks ago."

Elanor put her hands up. "Recruits! It appears to me that you are indeed well rested. We have another test for you."

"Yes. We have something else to show you."

Lucas turned to follow a well-worn path that cut through the thick forest, leading away from Zenender's Ranch. It was barely wide enough for a horse to pass through, let alone a full-grown dragon. The trees towered over them, their branches reaching out like spindly fingers towards the sky. As the recruits followed the path, their dragons walked beside them, their massive wings brushing against the low-hanging leaves and branches. Despite the tight squeeze, the dragons seemed to know exactly where they were going, their instincts guiding them forward. The group remained silent as they made their way closer to the mountains, the only sounds coming from the rustling of leaves and twigs underfoot and the occasional snort from one of the dragons.

As they neared the mountains, Ayr's heart raced with anticipation. In the distance, he could see a structure looming on the path ahead. Evor soared overhead and gracefully landed in front of it. The group followed behind, their feet crunching loudly on the rough ground. Ayr's once energetic footsteps were now sluggish and heavy, weighed down by the weariness accumulated from their long journey. Before them stood a giant archway, adorned with intricately carved dragon heads that were almost as large as Evor himself.

The pillars leading up to the archway were bejewelled with ornate designs and symbols, and the dragon heads hung from them at an angle, their fierce mouths gaping open. Despite his size and strength, Evor waited patiently for them to approach. A spike of fear raced down Ayr's spine under Evor's scrutinizing gaze. As the recruits climbed the final slope that brought them face to face with Evor and the archway, both Lucas and Elanor turned back to face them.

"Recruits, as some of you are aware, you need to complete more trials before we believe you can complete the Bonding. Evor!" Lucas gestured behind his body as Evor stepped out of the way. "Recruits! Welcome to the Catalyst."

As Evor moved aside, the ground seemed to split open, revealing a narrow chasm that pulsed with molten lava below. The intense heat radiated up towards Ayr as he cautiously approached the edge, mesmerized by the roiling of the fiery liquid. As his eyes adjusted to the brightness, he could make out a slim bridge made of charred wood stretching over the chasm and leading up towards the distant mountains.

It was a treacherous path, with only one visible way up and down. The air was thick with the acrid smell of sulphur and the sound of bubbling lava echoed through the rocky walls. There was a sense of both danger and awe at the sight before him.

"Typically, the last of you to finish the course would be eliminated, however considering you have completed the Hungering first, all you need to do is finish the course. Your dragons will not be able to provide you with any assistance. If they do, you will be eliminated. Due to the fact that you have come straight from the Hungering, we have opted to remove the time limit. However, just because we have removed the time limit does not mean this will be any easier on you. The Catalyst is a challenge, even for the most experienced riders. You will be finished when you reach the flag at the top of the mountain. We will be waiting. Good luck and don't die. You may begin when you are ready."

TEN

"What are you waiting for? Get going!"

Ayr jolted as Azura's voice entered his ear. Lucas was done speaking and stepped to the side of the path. Before the rest of the riders had even finished saying goodbye to their dragons, Ayr was tearing his way past the other recruits. Ayr was not the fastest by any stretch of the imagination, so he needed all the help that he could get.

The towering archway loomed on either side of the path, its intricately carved stone pillars reaching towards the sky. Ayr barely noticed it as he focused on his escape, his breath coming in ragged gasps. Behind him, he could hear the other recruits shouting and their dragons' roars echoing off the walls of the archway. Despite their pursuit, Ayr knew he was losing ground. As he neared the bridge, his heart sank at the sight before him. The wooden structure swayed dangerously over the deep ravine, its planks worn and splintered from years of use.

What made it worse, was the fact that it sagged in the middle, dipping dangerously low to the lava below. With five bodies on it, the bridge would sag even more than it already was. Needing to keep his head start, Ayr threw himself onto the bridge without hesitation. Even as he took his first step, he could feel the wood underfoot threatening to break. The next beam was no more secure, however the next was missing all together.

With each leap, Ayr's heart hammered against his chest as he soared over the gaps in the bridge. The flames from the lava below licked at his feet, threatening to consume him. His muscles ached from the intense exertion and beads of sweat dripped down his face and neck, merging with the already damp fabric of his vest. If he stopped, he'd die. He needed to keep moving, keep pushing forward. His eyes scanned the beams beneath him, searching for any sign of weakness or damage that could cost him his life. If he could somehow cause the entire bridge to collapse, it would buy him precious time and possibly save his own life. He knew his fellow recruits would do the same to him without hesitation in order to secure their own survival. It was a ruthless competition where only the strongest and most cunning would survive - and Ayr was determined to be one of them.

Ayr was nearing the edge of the bridge, now well and truly only the other side of it when he heard his name called. "Ashbourne!"

With gritted teeth, Ayr resisted the urge to turn and taunt his fellow recruits. He knew it would only bring about more tension and animosity between them. Instead, he pushed onward, exiting the bridge and following the winding dirt path that led towards the towering mountain ahead. The air grew colder and thinner as he ascended, each step bringing him closer to the unknown challenges that awaited them in this desolate place.

Above, Evor let out a deafening roar that reverberated off the side of the mountain, causing small rocks to shift beside Ayr's head. Evor flew with careless grace, his massive shadow casting a dark veil over the sun-drenched sky. Ayr felt a sense of awe and fear as he watched the other five dragons trail behind Evor in a perfect 'v' formation, as if preparing for battle.

The path that Ayr ran up was treacherously narrow, no wider than the length of his sword. Every step felt like a gamble as he teetered on the edge, the bubbling lava below seeming to seethe and rage in response to Evor's presence. Ayr's eyes stayed fixed on the ground beneath him, scanning for any potential hazards. He deftly dodged to the side as he spotted a crack in the rocky terrain. The soil crumbling away from the edges of the fissure was a tell-tale sign of its danger, one misstep could lead to a deadly plunge into the fiery depths below.

As Ayr made his way down the path, the constant heat and steam of the surrounding lava river finally began to dissipate. The narrow path widened, revealing a breathtaking view of the rolling hills and towering mountains in the distance. Ayr glanced back to see that the other recruits had successfully crossed the bridge and were now following his lead up the winding dirt path. Despite his initial head start, he could feel them gaining on him once again.

Up ahead on the path, Ayr could see the entrance to another cave. It was as wide and tall as the archway had been. Why were Elanor and Lucas sending them up here? Ayr continued to run, his feet pounding on the dirt as he neared the cave. There appeared to be no light source, nor was there any sign of any tools that he could use. He'd have to go in blind.

Ayr drew his sword and checked over his shoulder once again. The other recruits were still a short distance away. Ayr looked up at the cave, wondering if there were any easier pathways to the top of the mountain. This was a test after all. He spotted another cave entrance, high above his head, that came out onto a precarious looking ledge. Ayr saw no lava underneath it, but a fall from it would still result in his death. Not fearing what lay ahead in the darkness, Ayr charged inside the cave, eager to keep his lead on the other recruits.

He had no idea how he was going to navigate the cave without a source of light. He slowed as he entered the mouth of the cave. Darkness enshrouded him and Ayr quickly realised he was unable to see even far as the sword outstretched in his hand. He'd need to rely on his other senses. If only he'd had Azura with him. He was already missing her.

Ayr stumbled over a piece of rock and planted his sword in the ground to regain his footing. He took a moment to collect himself, drawing a deep breath before continuing. Ayr turned back and saw that the other recruits had now entered the cave, their silhouettes blacked out by the light behind them. Knowing his competition were still so close, Ayr took another step into the cave and heard a rumbling coming from somewhere above him.

The rumbling sounded like thunder, echoing throughout the cave. Ayr paused, trying to assess what it had come from. Was the mountain this cave was in a volcano? Ayr continued to walk into the darkness, holding his sword out in front of him, ensuring it scratched the ground like a blind man's cane. It would not do the sword's integrity any favours, but if for whatever reason the ground fell away in front of him, Ayr would not fall to his death.

After a few minutes of fumbling in the darkness, the sword hit a wall. Ayr stopped, examining the ground at his feet, before poking his sword out in front of him at different angles. He moved his sword on a horizontal line, listening to where the wall ran.

He placed his hand on the wall and returned his sword to the ground. Ayr turned to his right and kept walking towards where he hoped the exit would be. With no light available to him, he needed to move as quickly as possible, but he needed to ensure he stayed alive. Ayr could hear the other recruits somewhere behind him. Their whispers and footsteps followed him through the cavern as their sword points dragged along the ground.

Ayr started to climb in an upwards trajectory; he shortened his grip on his sword and took each step with a little more caution, knowing that stable footing was necessary to proceed. There'd be no use in beating the other recruits to his grave.

The ground beneath Ayr's boots trembled, a low rumbling that sent vibrations coursing through his body. It was like being caught in the clutches of an earthquake. As he turned to investigate, a blinding orange light illuminated the entire cave behind him, casting eerie shadows along its rough stone walls. The rumbling grew louder, almost deafening now, as if something massive and powerful was approaching. Ayr's heart began to race as he braced himself for whatever was coming.

"Humans... Why have you ventured into my lair?"

The deep, resonating voice sent a shiver down his spine and caused his hairs to stand at attention. The powerful sound seemed to emanate from all directions at once, filling the air with an overwhelming presence. As he looked around, there was no sign of anything or anyone nearby except for the vast expanse of the cave. It could only be the roar of a dragon, its immense power and strength echoing through the mountains and into his very core.

"I can smell you. There's five of you. Where are you, humans?"

Ayr kept silent, but he instinctively drew his sword closer to his body and stopped moving. If a dragon was that close with that loud a voice, he'd have heard it moving. Ayr didn't know how high the cave stretched above his head to the ceiling. Was the dragon hanging somewhere above him like a gargantuan bat? The glow grew brighter.

"I am Gorgon, the mountain guardian! You will burn in my fire!"

Ayr didn't stand around as the glow now illuminated his path forward. He was on the correct path, one that was rising up towards the outcrop that he had seen outside the mountain. The path ran wall to wall and Ayr had found his way to the far side.

Seeing that his path ahead was lit and unobstructed, Ayr started running up the slope, towards what he hoped would be freedom. The dragon roared from somewhere behind him. Now that he was no longer trying to ensure that he was no longer falling to his death, Ayr made good time in climbing the slope. With every step he took, he could see the small exit getting closer and closer above his head.

As the dragon roared again, the orange glow that filled the cave faded away until it was dark once again. The darkness was filled with a terrifying stomping that echoed off every wall. Even though he knew the dragon was nowhere near him, Ayr could still feel the ground shaking. The orange glow started to fill the cave again.

"Come here! You will not escape me!"

Gorgon's voice boomed in his ears, but the dragon was still far away. Ayr could only hope someone else was being chased by it. With the light illuminating his way again, Ayr made his way up towards the exit. Down beneath where he had just come from, he spotted two of the other recruits sprinting around the corner of the cave. Ayr paused for a moment to catch his breath, and when he saw the last two running for their lives, he turned away.

The exit was almost within reach and the cave shook around him, Ayr kept running; he did not stop until he burst out of the cave and into the late afternoon sunlight. He heard another roar from the dragon inside the cave, but considering there were still another four recruits it was chasing, Ayr felt a lot more secure. The ledge he was on was another tale, however. There was a steep drop off only a few meters in front of him.

With a decisive click, Ayr sheathed his sword and continued along the narrow ledge, carefully scanning the ground for any potential cracks or obstacles. He was grateful for the momentary break from the uphill sprint, but the powerful wind gusts blasting against him were less than ideal. His unkempt hair whipped around his face, obscuring his vision and causing him to struggle to remain upright. The winding path beckoned him further into the formidable mountains, a reminder that he still had a long way to go before reaching safety.

Ayr continued to follow the path as it wound around higher in the mountain. It wasn't long until he came across another entrance. There was no way down from here. He had one way forward. Sighing, Ayr drew his sword again and plummeted into the darkness of the cave. Ayr paused as he stepped into the darkness, assessing his surroundings. The wind ripped through this part of the tunnel and a short distance away, he could make out sunlight coming through another entrance.

As the dragon roared again and the orange glow started to fill the cave once again, Ayr saw his only way across to the next exit. There was a zigzagging path across an open chasm, no wider than a meter across. Normally this test of endurance and athleticism would be no problem for Ayr. But once again the orange glow started to fade away and Ayr was left staring at a dark open space, making this challenge all the more difficult. As the last of the light faded, Ayr set about memorising what he could of the layout of the path before him.

Placing his sword on the ground once again, Ayr took another step forward and hoped for the best. The start was simple, but with the shaking ground growing more unstable as the dragon continued to approach, Ayr needed to ensure every step was wide enough and secure. He took three steps forward, poking the ground in front of where he wanted to go with each step. On the fourth, his sword met nothing, sliding past where Ayr had felt it go into the ground before.

Ayr turned slowly, almost as if he was blindfolded. He dragged the sword slowly, in a circle around him. He knew roughly where the path was to his right, but he had to be sure. A jolt of excitement surged through his body as he found his next step. His sword caught the edge of the path, and he dragged it over it to ensure that he had the distance he required. Ayr took his next few steps, until the path straight ahead of him ran out. He repeated the process with his sword, dragging it around until he found where he could move safely to. It was a slow process, but he was making progress. *Better safe than dead.* There was nothing, apart from his own greed, that would stop him now. Ayr continued through the darkness alone, but with each step, drew closer to his goal. The light at the end of the tunnel continued to grow.

At last, Ayr was an arm's reach away from the exit. He looked down at what would be the final piece of path between him and safety. Ayr poked his sword directly in front of him but found nothing. He dragged the sword around, thinking there must be a mistake. Of course, the Commonwealth had no interest in making this challenge easy. There was only one way forward.

Ayr sighed and slid his sword back into its sheath. Taking a deep breath, he took a step back to where it was safe. Ayr bolted forward and pushed off with all of his strength. He launched through the air, flying just as easily as a dragon through the wind. Ayr stretched his arms forward, ready to grab the ledge if need be, but his jump was enough to carry him the distance.

With a wordless release of air from his chest, Ayr grinned. Relief washed over him like a wave as he cleared the ledge and now was on solid ground. The exit was no more than a step away and the path was illuminated by the sunlight that spilled in from outside. Once outside, however, he realised the challenge was not finished yet. The exit led onto an even smaller ledge and as he turned to looked at the path that was barely big enough for him to put one foot beside the other, Ayr saw footholds pickpocketed along the mountain side. He could walk and use them.

Ayr put his hand out into the first foothold and took a step. The small ledge was unstable, and thankfully the footholds were available to him. Slow progress was progress once again, the small ledge giving way to a sheer drop into the wilderness below. Ayr continued along the ledge, never looking down, grabbing foothold after foothold, praying that the narrow path would support his weight.

Finally, the path opened onto a wider berth, and Ayr could release his vice-like grip on the rocks. Standing up straight, he began to walk normally again, taking in the breathtaking view around him.

As he continued towards the summit of the mountain, he could hear faint voices talking. One of them sounded familiar, and his heart raced with excitement. He could sense her, presence, even though she was just out of sight.

"I hope they all make it out alive. It would be a shame to see any of their talent go to waste."

"If Chilijo allows it, it will be so." The voice was male and human. Lucas.

"May he be merciful today."

As Ayr crested the summit of the mountain, all eyes turned to him, but Azura's were the warmest, glowing with pure joy. Elanor's expression was hidden behind her mask, leaving an air of mystery around her. Before anyone could speak, Azura bounded towards him like an enormous puppy, her powerful wings beating against the wind as she closed the distance between them.

Ayr braced himself, but at the last second, Azura caught him in a tight embrace with her forelegs. The dragon's scales were warm and smooth against his skin, just as he remembered from their previous reunions. Being apart for this long had felt like a lifetime, and Ayr was overwhelmed with warmth and joy at finally being reunited.

"Ayr!" Azura snuggled into his chest and Ayr rubbed her head all over. He felt every single one of her scales underhand as they shared a moment together. "Congratulations. You beat the Catalyst."

"Nothing was going to keep me from you. Not even the darkness."

"Well, I'm glad you made it."

"Recruit Ashbourne!" Lucas's voice cracked like a whip interrupting them. "Get in line."

Ayr shot him a look with a raised eyebrow. "Get in line? There's nobody else here. I'm enjoying a moment with my dragon."

"Yes, clear the path for the other recruits to return." Lucas gestured beside him and the rest of the dragons. He gritted his teeth as he glared at Ayr. "I'd appreciate it."

"Apologies." Right now, he had no intentions of angering Lucas. Ayr glanced at Azura as he stepped away and she followed him.

"Thank you, recruit. Now we just need to wait for the others before we can begin the next part of your trials."

ELEVEN

Ayr turned away, ready to indulge in Azura's company, but Elanor interrupted any plans that he had in mind. "Kaiser! I'd have a word with the recruit if I could."

"Why would you do that, Lady Sunfire?"

"He is the first to complete the Catalyst. Surely that is worthy of celebration, is it not?"

Lucas' eyes narrowed as he stared in Ayr's direction. "If you insist. This is very unorthodox."

Elanor whirled around to face Ayr and Azura, her hair swirling dramatically behind her. With a flick of her wrist, she removed her intricately designed mask from her face, revealing a sly smile that played on her lips.

"Congratulations, Ashbourne. I thought you'd be the first to fail the Catalyst."

Ayr snorted and smirked. "Sorry to disappoint."

"Genuine congratulations are in order. But the Catalyst is not over yet."

"Not over? What do you mean?" Confusion seeped into Ayr's mind. "I completed the task."

"There is more to the trial than just evading Gorgon."

Ayr held up his hand in front of her. "Stop, you can't help me, remember."

Elanor's eyes flashed. "I'm the one that makes the rules here, Ashbourne."

"Leave me. I'd like to rest. I'll figure out the rest of the Catalyst once the others are here."

Elanor scoffed. "Okay, if you insist. I won't help you then."

"I appreciate the thought, but it's not needed."

Elanor stepped back towards Lucas and to where Evor was waiting for her. The mountain was now a place of hushed reverence, an unspoken agreement among the gathered parties to maintain silence. Thankfully, Ayr didn't have to wait long for the others to join him on the summit.

One by one, each recruit emerged from the Catalyst and was met with exuberant greetings from their dragons. As each recruit rose from the cavern, Lucas and Elanor greeted them by name. The first was Taven Taylor who was claimed by his purple dragon, Grithoss. He was quickly followed by Stephen Gable. The enormous red dragon that had flown back to the hill at the top of the garden claimed him.

As soon as Stephen was reunited with his dragon, Hussian emerged from the Catalyst and joined his bronze dragon. A tiny pang of disappointment entered Ayr's mind as he watched three of the four other recruits make it through the test unscathed. As they anxiously waited for the fifth and final recruit, Owens, to emerge from the cavern, Ayr's eyes flickered to Azura beside him. She stood tall and poised, her deep blue eyes scanning their surroundings with a keen intensity. She looked different upon closer inspection.

"You've grown again." Ayr ran his hand down her side, feeling her blunt scales underneath his hand. The size difference wasn't an absurd change, but it was still another few centimetres.

Azura turned her head to face him. "I've still got a long way to go yet, rider."

Ayr shuddered at the thought of her development and how far behind the others it was. "I really hope we don't have to fight these other dragons."

"They are males. All rage, with no technique. I'm older and more experienced. We will be fine."

After a short while, Owens emerged from the shadows, and his blue dragon bounded over to him with the same puppy like energy as the others had for their riders. Ayr hoped that his dragon would crush him. Lucas quickly suppressed any outward displays of affection. With all of the recruits now gathered in one place, he stood tall and intimidating, his dark gaze piercing each and every one of them. A hush fell over the group as they awaited his next move.

"Congratulations gentlemen, you've successfully beaten the second trial. I'd like to give you a moment to rest before taking on your final task."

As Lucas went to speak again, a deafening explosion shook the ground beneath Ayr's feet. He was knocked off balance and fell to the ground, along with everyone else around him. The force of the blast was so powerful that even Evor stumbled and swayed. Ayr's ears were ringing, making him dizzy, and he turned to see where it came from. His eyes widened in awe as he saw Gorgon, unfurling his massive wings and taking flight towards the clouds. The sun glinted off his dark scales.

Owens, as usual was the first to complain. "You put us in there with that monster?"

Lucas rose to his feet, pushing himself off one knee. "Gorgon was not going to hunt you. He was merely there to ensure that you were observant in the face of danger. Tell me the cave wouldn't have been that hard without a dragon in there. You are still being tested and we will continue to test you. Any questions?"

"How much more have we got to endure?" Ayr sniggered as Owens continued to complain. Was this really one of the best recruits in the group?

"As much as we tell you." Elanor's voice cut harshly through the darkening air. "Is it time, Lucas?"

Lucas glanced up at the sky. He smirked and nodded to Elanor who began to speak. "Sometimes, you won't be able to fly with your dragons. Sometimes, the only element strong enough to stop a dragon will come into play and sometimes you won't be able to get home. Your third task is simple. You survived the Hungering, but now you need to survive the Catalyst properly."

"That wasn't the Catalyst?" Finally, someone that wasn't Owens spoke up. The sandy-haired boy looked perplexed.

Lucas spun, infuriated. "Hussian! The more you ask stupid questions, the longer you're holding yourself from the Bonding. That was Gorgon's cave. You have one task remaining. Now let Lady Sunfire explain it."

"Storms around the Commonwealth are among the worst in the known world. Only the seas around Taagras are known to be more volatile, and therefore we cannot fly there. The top of this mountain is your only shelter from the storm tonight. The Catalyst will test the bond between you and your dragons. Survive until the morning, and we will come back for what's left of you. If you leave this summit and flee into the cave, we will know. You will surrender your dragon, should that be the case."

"You can't be serious! We have shelter that we can use!" Ayr rolled his eyes as Owens started to complain.

"Ah, so you want to accept your lodgings now, you ungrateful little shit?" Lucas snorted. He looked down his nose at Owens. "Only when it's convenient for you, how typical of your family."

"You can't do this!" Owens squealed with frustration. "It's inhumane."

"You're not undergoing these trials to be human. You're doing them to become a rider. Now get on with it! Lady Elanor, are we leaving?"

Elanor nodded eagerly. She lifted her arm high and Evor lowered his long neck to scoop her up in one fluid motion. Elanor made it look effortless as she climbed onto his back and slid down his neck with the grace of an acrobat. Lucas needed more assistance from both Evor and Elanor, but soon he was settled comfortably in the saddle that Ayr had grown accustomed to seeing Elanor ride in.

With a deafening roar, Evor spread his wings and launched into the air, soaring towards the east to escape the impending storm. Ayr watched them go, a pang of envy gnawing at his gut. If only he could have been up there with them, feeling the wind rush past and the thrill of flying on Azura's back. But for now, he remained rooted to the ground, watching wistfully as they disappeared into the darkening sky.

Azura nudged her nose under Ayr's arms once again. "Rider, we need to make preparations for tonight. You and I are not going to survive in a storm on top of this mountain without assistance. This is the final test we need to pass together, and then we can be bonded, properly."

"Ok. What help do we have?"

Ayr's gaze swept across the desolate landscape, taking in the vast expanse of bare terrain. The summit of the mountain loomed before him, its jagged edges stretching on for almost as far as the eye could see. Ayr wondered what lay beyond that edge - perhaps a steep drop-off that mirrored the one he had just climbed up. The wind howled around him, carrying with it the scent of pine and earth. A sense of isolation washed over him as he stood at this peak.

"Do you see where that first drop off is?" She slowly raised her tail. Ayr nodded. "There will be a tarp in there for us. That will help protect us from the storm."

"Is it an actual storm? Or is this just magic?

"Why would the Commonwealth lie to you?"

Ayr's jaw tightened. "They have before."

"Rider..." Azura warned.

"I'm going to get the tarp. Stay here. We'll ride this out."

The skies erupted with the deafening roar of thunder, shaking the ground beneath Ayr's feet. He quickened his pace towards the location Azura had directed him to. Amidst the chaos, he spotted a dark green tarp that she had described - it was large enough to cover both of them. As another thunderclap boomed above them, Ayr rushed back to Azura, his heart pounding in his chest. Was it truly just thunder, or was it the terrifying roar of Gorgon? Despite the uncertainty, Azura smiled at him reassuringly as he reached her with the tarp in hand.

"How are we going to secure it?" Azura pawed the ground, and Ayr felt a wave of stupidity wash over him. "Was there ever any doubt?"

"Quickly, rider! Throw it over me and I can use my wing as a shield. It will help protect you from the elements."

"What about you?"

Ayr looked up at the sky. "Lightning strikes frequent this place in these storms. The tarps are brought here for your survival. As long as I am somewhat covered, the magic in my body will dispel the rest of the energy."

"So, you're immune to it?"

Azura nodded. "Almost. Now hurry!"

The other recruits huddled close to their dragons, their eyes wide with confusion and fear. Ayr stood in the midst of them, determinedly unfolding a large tarp. His movements were precise and confident, causing some of the other recruits to protest his actions.

"Hey! What are you doing? Where did you get that?"

Hussian ran over towards him, but he was ultimately stopped by Azura. She stood up, bearing her fangs at him and snarling. Hussian didn't come any closer, opting to retreat to the relative safety of his own dragon. Moments later he was venturing across the desolate landscape with the other recruits, searching for a tarp of his own. Ayr flung his tarp over Azura's back just as the rain began. It was slow at first, little more than a drizzle. As Ayr pulled the tarp over all of Azura's body apart from her head, it grew steadily heavier.

Azura gracefully lifted her majestic wing, and Ayr eagerly took cover underneath it. Instantly, he felt a sense of warmth and protection from the elements that were raging outside. With Azura's powerful feet securely planted under the tarp, holding it in place, there was no chance of it being blown away by the intensifying wind. Ayr was grateful for her presence; without her, this would have been an absolute nightmare. He would have been drenched and miserable, shivering to his core.

Ayr rested comfortably in his shelter, watching with a mixture of amusement and sympathy as the other four recruits struggled to set up their own. The dragons attempted to help, but their sharp claws were not suited for the delicate task of unfolding tarps. As the wind picked up, Hussian's tarp was caught and whipped away from him.

He let out a frustrated howl towards the sky before being called over by Owens. With an extra set of hands, the two quickly worked together to secure their shelter, seeking refuge under one tarp and Bersos' protective wing. Hussian's dragon also joined them, wrapping its massive body around the group for added warmth and protection against the elements. Ayr admired the creatures' loyalty and strength as he settled in for the night.

The deafening roar of thunder continued to reverberate through the air, rattling Ayr to his very core. He sought refuge in the warmth of

Azura's body, huddled close against her as the storm raged on outside. Amidst the chaos, Ayr could hear the muffled voices of the other recruits, drowned out by the intense crashes of thunder above. The rain pounded relentlessly against the roof, creating a deafening symphony with nature's powerful display.

"Azura, can you hear what they're saying?"

Azura nodded. "Yes, and none of it is good."

"What's it about?"

"It's about you, rider. They're disrespecting you."

"I need to sort this out, once and for all." Ayr sighed and rose from his laid-out position on the ground. As he rose, the other nearby dragons all turned their heads to look at him, their eyes like beacons in the darkening stormy sky. A shiver ran down Ayr's spine as the dragons maintained their stare.

"If they get involved, I can fight them for you, rider."

"You can't fight three dragons, Azura. I can handle this. I have to. As long as their riders don't invite them into the fight, I can take them on."

Azura went to stand, shifting the tarp. "Whilst I'm not bonded to you, I still feel an overwhelming desire to put your life before mine. I will fight with you."

"This isn't your fight, Azura. I can handle it." Ayr raised his hand, trying to stop her. "This is my family's fight, one that has been raging since before I was born."

"I'm part of your family now. The moment you complete the trial, and we complete the Bonding, we will be one."

Ayr gazed deeply into her big, beautiful eyes, searching for any sign of emotion. Behind their dazzling depths, there seemed to be a hint of sadness. He was drawn to her, his head instinctively tilting towards hers in a gesture of closeness and understanding. In response, she emitted a soft cooing sound, echoing the same emotion that he felt.

The moment hung between them, suspended in time like a treasured memory.

"You ask me to trust you. Now I need you to trust me, Azura."

Azura bowed her head, giving him her blessing. "I do, rider."

With a deep breath, Ayr stepped out from underneath the safety of Azura's large wing and the tarp that provided some shelter from the relentless rain. The water poured down in sheets, drenching him within seconds. Every drop felt like a bucket of ice-cold water, and he shivered as he trudged through the muddy ground under his feet.

Each step was a struggle against the force of the storm, but he marched on determinedly towards where the other four recruits were camped. The rain pounded against his skin and soaked through his clothes, making him feel like he was wading through a river rather than walking on solid land. Ayr didn't let it deter him. He had a mission to complete and nothing, not even this fierce tempest, could stop him.

Owens was crouched underneath his tarp, speaking to both Gable and Hussian. "It's his fault as to why they're doing this to us. My brother is a rider. This isn't normal. He told us all about it. They only changed the challenges when they realised who he is."

"I didn't have anything to do with this." Ayr raised his arms beside his head. "I am not my father, and I won't follow his path."

"You won't have the choice." Owens stood up from where he crouched. His eyes narrowed as he realised it was Ayr walking towards him. "Gable, get him, bring him here. It's time we ended this."

Hussian raised his hand, putting it in front of Owens. "Wait, Owens. What are you doing this for? We can deal with him when we get back to the Ranch. We can't fight him here. We need every hand we can get to see us through the storms."

Owens pushed Hussian's hand away. "You might want to deal with him later, but now is the time to get rid of him! He wouldn't be the first recruit to fall to his death from this mountain."

The shortest and stockiest recruit crawled out from underneath his makeshift shelter, his movements slow and deliberate to avoid slipping on the damp ground. It was just Ayr's luck that he also happened to be the most well-built recruit. As he approached Ayr, each step was carefully calculated, his gaze locked on his target. Gable reached out to grab at Ayr, but Ayr evaded his grasp with a swift sidestep. In response, Ayr gently pushed him back, causing Gable to stumble backward. The furrow of frustration deepened on Gable's face as the sky lit up with a sudden flash of lightning, momentarily illuminating the summit of the mountain.

"Don't make this any harder than it needs to be. Your father killed my uncle in the war and took his dragon."

Ayr laughed and smirked. "Your uncle must have been a poor excuse for a rider if my father, who wasn't a rider, was able to kill him."

"How dare you insult my family!" Gable's hand flew to his sword that rested on his hip.

Another blinding flash of lightning tore through the darkened sky, illuminating the landscape in a brilliant white light. The deafening boom of thunder shook the ground as Ayr crouched low, shielding his eyes from the intense brightness. He could feel the intense heat radiating from the bolt as it struck just to his left.

Through squinted eyes, he saw Gable's silhouette against the sky, his sword raised high and with a fierce roar, Gable charged forward, swinging his weapon down towards Ayr. Ayr drew his own blade and met Gable's with a resounding clash, the sound of metal against metal echoing through the air.

Ayr beat Gable's sword away as another lightning bolt struck the ground on the other side of them. If one directly hit either of them, with their swords in hand acting as conductors, it would go straight through them. Ayr needed to end the fight quickly. He backed away from Gable. The summit was large enough for all of the dragons to roost comfortably on it, but Ayr needed to go near the edge. His retreat from Gable was with purpose.

They danced between the lightning strikes that continued to belt the barren summit. Ayr was moving his body into position, feigning weakness to goad Gable into continually attacking. It was a tactic his father had taught him, using his opponent's greed and overconfidence against him. As they neared the edge, Ayr was no longer with his back completely to it. Consumed by his anger, Gable had only been focused on beating Ayr within an inch of his life.

Ayr checked over his shoulder, ensuring he was near enough to the edge to enact his plan. Gable came at him again and Ayr thrust his sword into his path once again. With the swords locked, Ayr did not pull away this time. Instead, he reached out with one hand, forcing weight away from his blade that allowed Gable to come forward. Gable stumbled and Ayr took advantage of him faltering. With nothing more than a quick tug, Ayr spun to the side, ripping Gable over the edge of the mountain.

A deafening silence enveloped the air as Gable vanished into the churning storm clouds below. The wind roared and thrashed around Ayr, but he pushed forward towards Azura, determined not to falter. Gable's dragon, Onoss, rose from his resting spot. The tarp that had been covering his broad back fluttered away in the fierce gusts of wind, exposing his gleaming red scales. His wide eyes widened even further in shock at the abrupt disappearance of its rider. The dragon let out a snort, sensing danger.

Onoss started to howl mournfully. There was no chance that with the height of the mountain that Gable would have survived. The dragon launched into the air and Ayr ducked thinking that the dragon was coming for him. The dragon's claws almost scraped the top of Ayr's head as he ducked. As Ayr stood, he saw the dragon swoop over the edge of the mountain as lightning crackled around it. In an instant, the dragon was swallowed by the storm, never to be seen again.

Ayr turned back towards where the other recruits were still camped. Owens and Hussian, were both on their feet, their mouths agape in surprise. The third surviving recruit, Taven was nowhere to be seen. Ayr paid them no attention as they went to step out from underneath their makeshift tarps, their faces contorted with confusion and anger at what they had just witnessed.

Owens' hand hovered over his hilt but thought against removing it from its scabbard. "You'll pay for that, Ashbourne! He was one of us."

Ayr snorted. "Yeah? I'd like to see you try."

TWELVE

Ayr didn't dare close his eyes for the rest of the night. He listened intently to the pounding rain and booming thunder above, every muscle in his body tensed for any sign of danger lurking beneath his flimsy tarp shelter. Even Azura, lying next to him, seemed to be on high alert as they weathered the storm on this desolate mountain. Sleep was impossible in these conditions, with nature unleashing its fury upon them. As dawn approached, Ayr eagerly awaited the light that would signal the end of this turbulent night. The storm began to slowly recede, giving way to a breathtaking sunrise painting the horizon in hues of pink and orange.

Ayr remained underneath the tarp until the storm had well and truly passed, the last of the lightning now well off to the north away from them. He glanced out from underneath the tarp, none of the other last three remaining recruits had made any movements to kill either him or Azura. Azura stirred beside him. With the storm now far off in the distance, Azura shrugged the tarp off her back, and it slid down to cover Ayr. He wriggled out from underneath it and stood up.

"Good morning." Ayr surveyed the surrounding mountain top. It was even more desolate than it had been the night before, the ground scorched with even more lightning strikes.

Azura opened her mouth into a yawn that could have engulfed Ayr. "Good morning, rider. It appears that we are the first awake."

Ayr groaned. "I didn't sleep."

"I know." Azura yawned again.

Ayr rubbed his forehead, remembering the events of the night before. "I killed someone. Wouldn't that keep you up all night as well?"

Azura rolled her eye over to look at him. She wore an almost sad expression on her face. "When your life is in danger, rider, no, it would not. If you were to be the one thrown over the edge there, I would have done exactly what Onoss did. I am surprised that he did not return to scorn you."

"Do you not wonder where they've gone?"

Azura's face was blank. "Wherever Onoss took that recruit's body is not my concern. When a rider dies before their dragon, the chances are the dragon will go mad. Whilst they're not bonded it is more unpredictable, but dragons are emotional beings. We feel just as much as humans do, if not more. Onoss will be in mourning."

"Can I make amends with him?"

"If you ever see Onoss again, yes. You had best pray that he finds a new rider quickly. However, I would not worry about that now. We have more important things to concern ourselves with."

As he turned his head, Ayr's heart leapt in his chest. Flying towards them, rising up from the ground was none other than Evor. The sunlight danced off of his shimmering scales, casting dark shadows across the sky. Ayr could see two figures riding on his back, their silhouettes clearly visible against the bright blue canvas above. It was Elanor and Lucas, both sitting comfortably in adjoining saddles attached to Evor's enormous body. The sound of heavy wings filled the air as he gracefully approached their group. Behind Ayr, he heard movement and saw the other recruits slowly waking up.

Evor ascended swiftly, effortlessly reaching the summit of the mountain as the other recruits struggled to uncover their dragons from the heavy tarps. With Evor's heavy wings bearing down on the mountainside, Ayr struggled to maintain his feet, feeling like he was going to get swept over the side. Evor landed and lowered his neck with a graceful motion towards the ground. This allowed Elanor and Lucas to dismount safely onto the rocky terrain below.

Elanor removed her plumed mask as soon as she hit the ground, flicking her hair out behind her, catching the early rays of the morning sun. She cast her gaze over Ayr before it quickly flicked to the other three remaining recruits. With a small shake of her head, Elanor approached them. Her uniform was newly pressed, with no evidence it was the same as yesterday. Lucas followed a step behind her, his hands folded behind his back.

"I see we lost one overnight. Lady Elanor it would appear that you were wrong."

Elanor's gaze hardened. "Not who I thought it would be either. What happened?"

Owens' hand shot up with lightning speed, pointing a finger in Ayr's direction. Ayr shook his head in disbelief and scowled at him. The tension between them crackled like electricity in the air, mirroring the storm that had raged through the night before. Owens' eyes gleamed with determination as he made his accusation.

"It was him! It was Ashbourne! He threw Gable off the side of the mountain!"

Ayr glared a hole in him. "If you'd told him to leave it, nothing would have happened."

"What happened?" Elanor sighed and stepped between them. "Obviously Gable, was not strong enough to stand among you."

"Gable came at me with his sword so I threw him off the edge of the mountain."

He didn't stutter, or blink. He half expected Elanor to reach across the gap between him and slap him or discipline him, but the motion never came. Instead, Elanor barely registered what he'd said and moved in between the two distinct camps. She looked again at the other recruits, holding her hands by her side. Owens began to voice his complaint.

"He killed Gable in cold blood! Gable did nothing to him."

Elanor cut Owens off. "Where is Onoss?"

"I'm not sure. He flew off once Gable had gone over the edge."

"Then he is in mourning. It is a shame, but there is nothing we can do for a dragon like that. Despite our relationship with them, dragons are skilled creatures with minds of their own." Lucas glanced around at the dragons on the mountaintop. "No offence meant."

Evor spoke for the dragons. "We know what you mean, Kaiser. None taken."

"Well, if this is all that's left, we'd best push on with the final stages." Elanor clapped her hands together with a smile. "Your third test is simple. Using your dragons, you need to fly down from here."

"Wait!" Owens screamed across the plateau again. "What are you going to do about Ashbourne? He fucking killed a recruit! The call hadn't sounded."

Lucas had heard enough. "Recruit Owens! Your father paid for you to attend the rider's preselection course, did he not?" Owens nodded slowly in response. "As you would have been instructed, the call was only valid during the Hungering. As a result, recruit Ashbourne has broken no rules. Now stop complaining and let's get on with it! Apologies, Lady Sunfire. As you were saying?"

"Yes, you and your dragons will need to fly."

Ayr couldn't believe what he was hearing. Everything else to this point had been incredibly challenging. Why was this so different? "Is that it? What if our dragon isn't big enough yet?"

Elanor smirked at him. "If you don't fly your dragon down to the Seminary then you will fail and be removed from the program. I don't think I can be any clearer. If you haven't bonded with your dragons enough by now, you *will* fail."

"I can't wait to get off this hill." Hussian puffed out his lips. "When can we start?"

"Now. There will be a punishment for the last one to arrive. Your dragons will know the way home. They will fly you to the Obelisk."

"Wait! The Obelisk?" The small, soft-spoken boy named Taven that stood next to the purple dragon finally spoke up. "We shouldn't be going there yet, should we?"

"Do you want to complete the Bonding? Recruits, the Flight has already started. Get moving!"

"Quickly, rider!"

Ayr didn't need any further encouragement. His heart racing, he turned and spun towards Azura, eyes wide with anticipation. Azura stood still, her body tense as she waited for Ayr to join her on her back. As soon as he was settled, she wasted no time running towards the edge of the mountain and leaping into the air with all her might.

Her wings, spread out from her back like a pair of dazzling white sails catching the wind. With every powerful beat, they lifted higher and higher into the sky, carrying Ayr along for the ride. He clung onto Azura's neck tightly, his knuckles turning white as he prayed that she would stay airborne. The rush of wind in his ears and the breathtaking view below took his breath away, but there was no time to enjoy the spectacle.

Despite Azura's compact size, she managed to keep them both airborne as Ayr lay heavily on her back. The pound of their wings echoed through the air as they ascended higher into the sky. Behind them, Ayr could see the other dragons finally taking flight as well. In comparison to Azura, they were much larger and faster, their powerful strokes propelling them closer with each passing moment. Determined to push Azura to her limits, Ayr leaned down over her head and urged her onward through the crisp, cool air. The rush of wind and the distant roar of the other dragons filled his senses as they raced towards their destination.

"Can you go any faster?"

Azura didn't respond and started to dip into a dive. Azura was gathering an incredible amount of speed as she stepped into a deep dive. Ayr felt like the skin was going to pull off his face. He could do nothing but hang on and enjoy the ride that Azura was taking him on. Ayr didn't dare to turn his neck either, fearing the strength of the wind would make him permanently face that way.

The ground shot up at them, but Azura was in control. He could tell minute by minute she grew more confident and comfortable in the air. Slowly, Azura began to flatten out, beating her wings to make her go even faster. They were shooting across the Garden of Chilijo at breakneck speed, the features of the ground simply nothing more than a blur to Ayr. They were approaching Zenender's Ranch, but Azura made a sharp left turn. Ayr almost jolted off her back but maintained his grip on one of her spines.

Within moments, Ayr could make out something that he had never seen before. It was the one place of the Seminary of Fire that had been shrouded in mystery, kept from him until now. Every person who aspired to become a rider knew about it, revering it as the source of their power.

The Obelisk stood tall and imposing, its form stretching towards the sky like a silent sentinel. A city had grown around it, sprawling and bustling with life. This was no ordinary city - it was built for strength and resilience above all else. Ayr had travelled far and wide in his young life, never staying in one place for too long as a result of Dalton's paranoia. Yet, he had never seen anything quite like this.

Intricate fortifications lined the perimeter of the city, protecting its inhabitants from any threat that may come their way. At the epicentre of the bustling metropolis stood the imposing Obelisk, emanating a palpable aura of dominance and significance. The tall, bulky structure towered over the surrounding buildings, casting a deep shadow over the city below. Its sharp edges jutted into the sky, casting a looming shadow over half of the city that was not yet touched by the golden rays of the sun. The Obelisk was a gargantuan, mushroom shaped structure, a symbol of power and supremacy over all who gazed upon it.

The Obelisk was vast, with enough space for the serpentine creatures that soared gracefully through the air. Dragons of all sizes and colours filled the sky, some circling around the clearing while others approached and departed from various points. Their magnificent wings cast shadows on the ground below, creating a mesmerizing dance of light and darkness. The air was alive with the sound of their powerful wings beating against the wind, creating a symphony of thunderous roars and echoes.

Ayr turned his head back to ensure that the other recruits were behind them. To his surprise, they were. Evor was bringing up the rear, not travelling at his full speed.

"You did well." Ayr rubbed his hand on the side of Azura's neck and she cooed at him.

"Are we still in front of the rest?"

"By a long shot. Thank you."

"My pleasure." Azura rumbled underneath his hand.

"Do you know where we're supposed to be going?"

"Of course, rider."

Ayr shifted in his saddle, leaning back to take in the sights and sounds of the Obelisk even more. The bustling city streets were filled with dragons of all sizes, their wingspans casting shadows on the cobblestone below. Some flew gracefully through the air while others walked leisurely with their riders, as if they had nowhere to be.

Out of nowhere, Azura rose higher into the sky, catching Ayr off guard and nearly unseating him. He tightened his grip on her scaly neck as she gradually slowed down, revealing their destination. Before them, at the centre of the Obelisk, stood a colossal tower, its height dwarfing even the largest dragons or buildings around it. This was the heart of the Commonwealth, where all important decisions were made and where their power resided. The tower seemed to radiate an aura of authority and grandeur, looming over everything in its dominion.

Azura soared into an expansive open space, vast enough to accommodate even the mightiest of dragons. Ayr's heart raced as they flew deeper inside, the dark walls reminiscent of Gorgon's cave. In the distance, a regal purple dragon and its rider stood waiting for them on a platform near a large open door. The wind howled around them, whipping through Ayr's hair and against the sleek curves of the chamber walls.

Fiery braziers lined the walls, the flames casting long shadows as they flickered in the darkness. Even though this was the Commonwealth's centre of power and control, Ayr still felt uneasy. There was a clear square area in front of the main door to this open area, that would allow Azura and the other dragons space to land on. It hung out over the empty void, easily holding any dragon that would land on it.

Azura headed directly for the landing area. The purple dragon took several steps back from the landing pad as Azura swooped in and landed. Ayr patted her gently on the side and she lowered her neck, allowing him to get down easier. Within moments, the other recruits were entering the harboured section of the enormous tower. Azura nudged Ayr towards the purple dragon and its rider, who had his arms crossed as Ayr approached.

"Recruit Ashbourne!"

The closer Ayr got to the rider; he could see just how large he was. He was dwarfed by his dragon. His impeccable uniform strained against his bulging muscles, as if they were desperate to break free from the tight confines of his vest. The rider's cropped black hair was sprinkled with flecks of white, giving him a distinguished ruggedness. His piercing green eyes glared disapprovingly, adding to the intensity of his presence. Every inch of him exuded strength and authority, a formidable figure in the midst of chaos.

"Major Kaladin and his dragon, Gundrag. They're heroes of the war with your father." Azura whispered into Ayr's ear. "Be respectful."

"Sir, yes sir!"

Kaladin folded his bulky arms across his chest. "What do you think you're doing here? You should have died out in the Hungering,"

"Sir, I am here to continue with my trials."

Kaladin scoffed, looking down his nose at Ayr. "Yes, Elanor told me. As far as I'm concerned, no Ashbourne should be able to partake, especially after what happened during the war."

"That is none of my concern. I am here to become a rider."

Kaladin's upper lip curled, and his right arm stiffened. "Not if I have anything to say about it, you won't. Did Azura choose you or did you have to con her into it?"

"It was my choice. I can see his potential." Azura glowered at Ayr, rushing to his defence.

Gundrag leered down at Azura. "All that time and you chose this runt? I'm disappointed, Azura."

Kaladin nodded with approval. "Who knew you'd grow into such a fast flyer, Azura. I look forward to seeing what your future holds with this Ashbourne runt. I would break him in two."

Azura puffed her chest out which resulted in a snort from Gundrag. "Not without going through me first."

The steady, rhythmic beating of wings filled the air behind them, announcing the arrival of the other recruits. One by one, they gracefully landed on the smooth stone landing pad, their powerful wings propelling them to a perfect stop. Evor landed last with a thunderous crash that shook the platform and the Obelisk with it. Elanor slid down from his neck with practiced ease and marched confidently towards Kaladin.

Kaladin opened his arms wide. "Ah, Lady Sunfire. Good to see you had some recruits survive the night. I didn't believe you at first, but can you tell me why are you humouring the son of Dalton Ashbourne? He should be dead, along with his father."

Elanor didn't reciprocate Kaladin's gesture. Instead, she was closed off and to the point. "Are you the patron of admission? You've been around here for a lot longer than I have. Do you forget who the recruit's uncle is? Are you going to go against the Overlord?"

"I'm not going to question Anton Ashbourne. But you surely aren't going to allow him to drink from Chilijo's chalice, are you?"

Elanor's gaze hardened, matching Kaladin's for intensity. "He's bonded with a dragon. If the Bonding does not reject him, then there is no reason to."

Kaladin took a step back and snorted. "Fine. Don't blame me when he turns out the same way as the last Ashbourne and tries to destroy us."

"And how do you know he won't, Major? I've had enough of this discussion. Are you going to join us or not?"

Kaladin's entire body stiffened as he drew in a deep breath. Behind him, Gundrag made the same motion. "I don't have a choice, do I?"

Elanor smiled up at him. "No, you do not. Either Ashbourne gets his chance at bonding with Azura, or none of the recruits do. I don't think Anton would approve, do you?"

Kaladin shook his head in response and turned with a grunt. "Recruits, dragons. If you could follow me, please. I will take you to the Bonding ritual."

One by one, the recruits and their dragons fell in line behind Elanor. Lucas who remained on Evor's back as the large black dragon took flight. He heard Azura pine beside him and flicked his eyes to her as her head turned to follow Evor out of the safety of the landing bay and out into the sky.

"Where are they going?" Ayr frowned wondering why Evor was leaving Elanor behind, but she didn't seem at all concerned by it.

"You'll see, Ashbourne."

THIRTEEN

Elanor ushered them through the first open space and deeper into the Obelisk. Ayr was in awe. He turned his head from side to side, trying to take in every detail of the impressive structure. The sleek, modern design of the Obelisk matched that of the Union Tower that lay far to the north, with its sharp edges and monochromatic colour scheme.

As they stepped deeper inside, it was like entering a world of darkness - every surface was painted black, giving an illusion of endless depths. Despite the intimidating atmosphere, Ayr felt drawn in by the mysterious allure of the Obelisk. The recruits' accompanying dragons only added to the grandeur of the Obelisk, their size hopelessly dwarfed by the vastness of the halls around them.

Strips of light filtered through a glass ceiling above, illuminating the halls with a soft glow. And yet, even with this natural light source, at least half a dozen braziers were still lit and scattered throughout each hall Elanor led them through, casting flickering shadows on the walls and floors. Ayr wondered what secrets and mysteries lay hidden within these dark halls. Had Dalton made it this far inside the Obelisk before he had been outed by the Seminary?

The Obelisk was like a maze, with twisting hallways and staircases that seemed to lead in endless circles. Ayr followed Elanor and the dragons, grateful that they knew the way through this labyrinth of stone. After a long walk, they ascended one final staircase, and Ayr could see the bright blue sky above them. The sound of beating wings grew louder as they neared the top, and Ayr's heart raced with anticipation. As they reached the summit of the stairs, Ayr's jaw dropped in awe. This magnificent sight had not been visible during their flight in.

He found himself trapped in a colossal pit, larger than the one he had shared with Azura during the Hungering. The jet black walls that towered over him were easily ten times the height of Evor. No matter which way he looked, the pit seemed to stretch on endlessly, except for the empty space behind him that provided a glimpse of the outside world. It was as if the entire Obelisk had been encompassed by this formidable pit. The air inside was heavy and stifling, suffocating any hopes of escape.

Around the top of the structure, sheets of metal jutted out, providing some semblance of shelter from the elements above. Half a dozen dragons were suspended from the ceiling, their massive bodies hanging in mid-air. Some peered curiously down at the recruits below, while others remained aloft, their wingspan spread wide. A powerful bronze dragon turned its head and descended from its perch, landing with a deafening thud just inches in front of the startled recruits. The ground trembled beneath its weight as it gazed down at them with fierce intensity.

"Lady Elanor! Are these the recruits for the ritual?"

Elanor nodded promptly. "Indeed, they are Lord Chairman!"

The imposing figure of the dragon's rider loomed over its head, casting a shadow that seemed to engulf them. The Lord Chairman, was adorned in his own mask and, stared down at them with a blank expression. His mask was adorned with a dark blue plume, in stark contrast to Elanor's vibrant and colourful red. "Bring them forward, then. You are past time."

Elanor bowed her head. "Yes, Lord Chairman. Recruits! With me!"

Ayr's gaze was drawn to the raised platform at the centre of the room. It stood high off the floor, imposing and regal, with two sweeping staircases leading up to it from either side. The stairs met in the middle, creating a small gap that seemed minuscule compared to the grandeur of the entire structure.

Atop the podium stood a tall stand, holding a gleaming chalice in its centre. Lucas dressed in regal red and golden robes, was leaning against the podium with an air of authority. Behind him stood eleven highbacked chairs, each designed with the same material as the ornate walls surrounding them.

The room was filled with an air of authority and power as three men, all resembling Kaladin in their hardened demeanour and years of experience, occupied only a fraction of the available seats. Their presence alone made it clear that their positions were indisputable. They had traversed the depths and heights of the world, experiencing all that it had to offer. Which of them had fought against Dalton in the war?

The Lord Chairman took his seat in the second row on the left, where he could observe and guide from a position of power. His dragon launched itself back into the air, shooting up with incredible speed towards the ceiling, coiling around the edge like a colossal snake.

With a confident stride, Elanor led the recruits forward to the grand podium. Each step was deliberate and purposeful, her head held high, and her gaze fixed ahead. She ascended the stairs without missing a beat. At the summit, she turned to face the recruits and their dragons, beckoning them forward with a graceful gesture of her hand.

"Dragons, you know what is required of you. Please join us, so that you may become one with your riders."

Silently, the dragons followed her up the grand marble staircase and arranged themselves in a single file line behind the ornate podium. Their powerful presence filled the room as they stood at attention, their long tails swishing back and forth in anticipation. Lucas took a deep breath, his eyes scanning the imposing creatures before him, before finally turning back to face the recruits. The silence was palpable, broken only by the soft rustle of wings and the occasional rumble from one of the dragons.

Lucas gave a satisfied nod. "This looks like everyone."

Elanor gracefully lowered herself into the chair to the left of the Chairman, who glared at her presence. She extended a hand towards him, and he reluctantly clasped it in a tense exchange. The Chairman leaned in and whispered something in her ear, prompting a rare smile to cross Elanor's face. Ayr kept his gaze on her, observing every subtle movement she made. Suddenly, their eyes met, and Elanor caught him studying her. A sly smirk tugged at the corner of her lip as she playfully challenged him with her gaze.

Lucas cleared his throat and began to address the recruits. "It is my great honour to welcome you to the Bonding! You have passed all of the trials we have put in front of you. We brought you here today so that you could bond with your dragons."

A low murmur of anticipation rippled through the gathered recruits. Lucas raised the shimmering chalice high above his head, its golden surface reflecting the warm rays of the sun and casting a magical glow upon the surrounding faces. As he held it aloft for all to see, a hush fell over the group, each recruit eagerly awaiting what was to come next.

"I present to you, the chalice of Chilijo. This chalice was forged when the pact between the humans and the dragons was made. In his infinite wisdom, Chilijo sought to bind us. Rider to dragon, dragon to rider. This is the *true* test of what it is to be a rider. With Chilijo's chalice, we will decide if you are worthy of your dragons. Recruit Hussian, you're first. Step forward, please."

With a determined stride, Hussian made his way towards the podium. As Hussian was walking up to the podium, Lucas moved to stand beside Nokam, the bronze dragon that had claimed Hussian. The dragon extended his long neck and rested it beside Lucas. Nokam grunted and let out another snort as Lucas raised the chalice to his neck.

"Nokam. May I have your blood?"

"You may have my blood."

Lucas' hand instinctively went to his hip, where he grasped the cool hilt of a curved dagger. The handle was adorned with a red gemstone that glimmered in the dim light, mirroring the stone on the chalice they were after. With anger in his eyes, Lucas drove the knife into Nokam's flesh just above the shoulder, eliciting a guttural growl of pain from the bronze dragon. Blood oozed from the wound; Lucas withdrew the dagger and pressed the chalice against it, collecting the crimson liquid within its ancient vessel. Once satisfied with the amount, he wiped the wound clean and held up the chalice triumphantly, a smug grin spreading across his face.

He turned and held the chalice out in front of Hussian. "Drink!"

With shaking hands, Hussian took hold of the ornate chalice and lifted it to his lips. He pressed the cool metal against his parched mouth and took a slow sip. Lucas, standing beside him, could not wait any longer. He reached out and placed his fingers under the base of the chalice, tilting it upwards to help the liquid flow into Hussian's mouth.

As Hussian drank more, his eyes slowly opened wider and wider, revealing a hint of panic. He attempted to pull away from the chalice, but Lucas held him firmly in place, making sure every last drop was consumed. As he continued to drink, the corners of Hussian's mouth began to bubble. Hussian's eyes continued to widen, and blood started to trickle from the bubbles.

The red gemstone on the chalice began to glow, a dark red that matched the colour of the blood spilling from it. At last, Hussian let go of the chalice and it clattered to the floor with a loud metallic clang. A moment later, Hussian followed the chalice, falling to the floor, his body convulsing as more blood spilled from his mouth. Silence fell over the podium as Lucas continued to watch on.

"That is a shame. He was talented. I would have liked to see him go all the way."

Nokam lowered his massive head, letting out a low, mournful moan that echoed through the chamber. Elanor rose from her chair and approached him, her hand outstretched to gently stroke the scales on the dragon's side. Nokam's eyes flickered open and he turned his head towards her, a glint of gratitude and trust shining in his deep golden irises.

Elanor reached out and stroked the dragon's face. "You will find another rider."

Lucas was unphased. "Your connection with your dragon *will* assist you, but ultimately, as long as your dragon chose well, there will be no adverse effects. Recruit Owens! Get up here!"

With a trembling hand, Owens cautiously approached the podium. Ayr could see the nerves in his face, even from his distance. Lucas took the same careful steps with Bersos, Owens' dragon, smoothly communicating with him through touch and whispered words. The dragon rumbled in acceptance as Lucas asked for its consent to share its blood. With a mighty roar of pain, the dragon offered its sacrifice willingly. The sound echoed through the chamber, followed by a moment of reverent silence as the chalice was filled with the crimson liquid of dragon's blood.

Lucas thrust the chalice towards him. "Drink."

Owens took the cup in both hands. He glanced over the lip at Lucas. "I'm not going to end up like that am I?"

"You have nothing to fear, rider." Bersos rumbled beside him. "You are strong. Do as Kaiser commands and let us finish formalizing this process."

Owens brought the chalice to his lips and tilted it back, the liquid inside glimmering. As Ayr observed, he noticed no visible change in Owens' demeanour. He drained the cup down to the last drop, the gemstone embedded in its base began to radiate a blinding light. Handing the chalice back to Lucas, Owens wore a wide grin on his face, his eyes shining with excitement.

"I feel incredible!"

"Well done, Owens."

With a gracious gesture, Lucas extended his hand, and Owens reverently handed over the chalice. As he stepped back, his head hung low and his pale face contorted in discomfort, as if on the verge of sickness. He composed himself and moved to stand by the midnight blue dragon. Bending his large, scaly head down, the dragon accepted Owens' presence with a gentle breath. Owens' hand moved in a slow rhythm as he scratched behind Bersos' horned ears.

"Well done, rider."

"Recruit Taven Taylor! Your turn!"

Taven ascended to the podium, his steps slow and calculated. Was he emboldened by Owens' recent success? The body of Hussian still lay at their feet, a grim reminder of the dangers that lurked within the chalice. Taven stood tall, his chin held high as he turned to face the purple marvel, Grithoss that stood waiting for him with a glint of excitement and happiness in his eye. Lucas stood beside Grithoss, dagger in hand.

"Grithoss. May I take your blood?"

Grithoss bowed his head and rumbled. "Yes, Kaiser. Be done with it!"

Lucas pressed the chalice against Grithoss' side and cut into his scales. Lucas thrust the chalice in front of Taven, who took it and drunk it in a single motion. Taven opened his mouth, displaying the contents to Lucas.

"Show some decorum, recruit!"

Taven shut his mouth. The chalice glowed in his hand as he handed it back to Lucas. Lucas took the chalice, shaking his head as Taven joined Grithoss with the rest of the recruits behind the podium. Now it was Ayr's turn, the final recruit left standing. As Ayr gulped, he made his way up the steps towards the podium. Would he too become like Owens and Taven, celebrated and revered? Or would he meet the same fate as Hussian, a bloodied mess left behind on the ground?

"Ashbourne! Get up here!"

Azura's gaze locked onto him, her intense blue eyes following his every step as he ascended the stairs. The weight of expectation hung in the air, not just from the humans gathered around, but also from the dragons. Ayr strode confidently onto the podium, his presence commanding attention from all sides. He joined Lucas and Azura, standing tall and proud at their side.

"Azura, may I have your blood?"

"Yes, Kaiser. You may have my blood."

The glint of the ornate knife caught the light as Lucas raised it high above his head. With a swift, brutal motion, he brought it down into Azura's side, eliciting a piercing howl that deafened Ayr in his right ear. He gritted his teeth and instinctively covered his ear with his hand, but his focus remained on soothing Azura's pain. Within moments, the howling ceased and Azura's breathing became ragged. As Ayr looked up again, Lucas was standing before him with a chalice in hand, a victorious smirk gracing his face. The metallic tang of blood mixed with the earthy scent of sweat and fear filled the air around them.

Lucas glowered at him, holding the chalice in front of him. "Drink, son of a traitor. Do what your father could not do."

Ayr's eyes glared daggers at the man in front of him, but with a sigh, he reluctantly took the ornate chalice. His gaze flickered between Elanor and Azura. With a deep breath, he brought the cup to his lips and peered down into its contents. The deep crimson liquid, Azura's very blood, filled the chalice and seemed to pulse with a life of its own. Ayr closed his eyes, his mind racing with conflicting emotions and thoughts about what he was about to do.

"Good luck, rider." Azura's voice was a calming presence.

Without needing any prompting from Lucas, Ayr tentatively opened his mouth and swallowed some of the contents of the chalice. The blood was cold, colder than ice, sending a shiver down Ayr's spine. It felt as if he had plunged headfirst into an icy lake, the shock overwhelming his senses.

He struggled to keep going, to continue drinking despite the biting chill that threatened to freeze him from within. He refused to give up, not with Azura standing by his side. With each swallow, Ayr could feel the ancient power of the blood coursing through him, filling him with a sense of invincibility and purpose.

Ayr groaned and pushed through the freeze. He threw his head back a little further, tipping the chalice one last time until all of the blood had run into his mouth. Ayr dropped the chalice and fell forward onto all fours. He spluttered, but desperate to keep the blood in his system, kept his mouth shut. Ayr digested for a moment as he felt a surge of icy energy surge through him. A howl escaped his lips, one that sounded like a small dragon.

Ayr's energy surged through him as he stood up and turned to face Lucas. His muscles felt invigorated, coiled with strength and ready for any challenge. He stood taller, his shoulders broad and squared, exuding a sense of confidence and power. If someone were to swing a sword at him now, he was certain he could stop it with just his hand.

"Have I passed your test, Kaiser?"

Lucas struggled to suppress a smirk as he gestured to the side. "Yes. Take your place, Ashbourne."

Ayr swiftly turned on his heel, his footsteps crunching against the ground as he fell into line beside Azura. She nuzzled him with her snout and nestled her head under his arm, a gesture of comfort and love. In that moment, a wave of warmth and familiarity washed over Ayr as he felt Azura's voice fill his mind like a gentle whisper in his ear.

Well done. I'm proud of you.

Ayr almost jumped into the air. *You can hear me?*

Yes, rider. I can hear you. We have completed the Bonding. Now listen.

"Congratulations on completing the Bonding!" Lucas stood in front of the line with his hands behind his back. "These dragons will continue to undergo their transformation. As will you. Now that they are bonded to you, they will be able to hear your thoughts, share your secrets and the two of you will be able to communicate with each other through your minds. This is a special bond, do not squander it." Lucas's eyes passed over Ayr. "As some of you know, we are not afraid to strip dragons from careless riders."

Ayr clenched his fist, but otherwise did nothing. He was still reeling from the injection of dragon's blood. He could feel it seeping into every vein in his body, like an ice-cold liquid. He wondered what had gone so wrong with Hussian.

"Now that you have passed the trials, you will be assigned a master. It is with them that you will learn the finer arts of becoming a rider. We leave it up to them to choose their novice rider. If you don't like who has chosen you, then tough. Much like the rest of this selection process, you won't get another choice. Pray the right master for you picks you. Face front! The floor is yours, masters."

Ayr and the other recruits, along with their dragons all turned in unison to face the masters, who rose from their chairs as one, their imposing figures casting long shadows in the dimly lit room. The only sound was the soft rustle of fabric as they made their way towards the waiting recruits and their beasts. Each master would leave with a new apprentice.

Ayr stood tall, his arms at his sides, trying to exude confidence in the presence of these powerful masters. One by one, each master carefully inspected the recruits and their dragons, their sharp eyes scanning every inch of them. Ayr felt that he was being overlooked by most of the masters, save for one who seemed to show particular interest in him and Azura. Elanor was the exception. She knew exactly what she wanted. It was almost as if she was standing off to the side, twirling her hair at him. Ayr remained frozen to the spot as she approached him.

Stay calm. Azura's voice entered his mind again. *I can see everything you're thinking.*

I'm not thinking about anything.

A vivid image flashed through Ayr's mind, encapsulating his first glimpse of Elanor. It was a moment ingrained in his memory, as if it were yesterday. He could see her now, standing in front of the seminary with a graceful poise, removing her mask from her head. The sunlight danced off her golden hair and highlighted the delicate curves of her face, drawing him towards her like a magnet. It was a sight he would never forget.

I'm going to have to get used to this.

Yes, you are. Azura's reply was instantaneous. *I know how you feel. Remain focused, here she comes. Just remember that I am yours now. I am here to help you.*

Elanor stood no more than half a foot away from him. Now she was taking the time to properly assess him. "Ayr Ashbourne. Son of Dalton. Why did you come to the Seminary of Fire?"

Ayr's eyes remained locked on hers; he had to remain focused otherwise he'd lose himself in them. "To learn how to become a dragon rider." Ayr gritted his teeth and continued. It wasn't the answer that she was looking for. "To correct the mistakes of my father."

This was said loud enough for the other recruits to hear. A brief smile came to Elanor's lips as the other recruit's heads snapped around to ogle at him. Elanor continued with her questions.

"Do you, Ayr Ashbourne, swear to uphold the values and the good name of the Commonwealth."

Ayr didn't hesitate. "I do."

"Very well. May your dragon always breathe fire."

"And may his wings carry you forward." Ayr completed the proverb without drawing an extra breath.

"Very good." Elanor turned towards Lucas. "Lord Chairman! Kaiser! I've made my selection. Ayr Ashbourne will be my student."

As Ayr's name was called, the other two masters were wrapping up their interrogations. Their stern faces bore down on each candidate, searching for any hint of weakness or deceit. The room was heavy with tension and the air seemed to thicken with every passing moment.

The man with a heavyset figure and the thickest grey beard spoke firmly, his voice carrying authority. "From this day forth, recruit Bradley Owens will be my student."

The other master stood forward. "Recruit Taven Taylor will be my student."

Each master stood proudly beside their recruit, their chests puffed out and shoulders squared. Elanor positioned herself to the right of Ayr, giving him a clear view of Azura without obstructing their connection. Lucas nonchalantly leaned against the podium, exuding an air of confidence and authority.

"You're all predictable, aren't you? I'm glad that this has gone according to our discussion. It will make the paperwork a lot easier. You may present the riders with their saddles."

Elanor kept her expression carefully composed as she turned away from Ayr and sauntered back towards the chairs. Ayr stole a glance, watching her graceful movements as she knelt down to retrieve a package from beside them. Elanor glided back to Ayr's side, her hair swaying gently with each step, and presented him with the saddle she had retrieved.

"Have you ever put one of these on?"

Ayr took it in both hands. "Not on a dragon."

"Let me help you."

Elanor's smile was warm and reassuring as Azura lowered her head to allow them to saddle her. With practiced movements, Elanor guided Ayr, and they worked together to secure the saddle into place, just behind Azura's powerful neck. Elanor made sure everything was securely fastened before giving a gentle tug on the saddle to test its stability. The other recruits were also receiving help from their masters, each one focused on the task of saddling their dragon mounts.

With the saddle now mounted in place, Ayr climbed onto Azura's back, and already felt more comfortable. The saddle was broad and allowed him more movement across her back without feeling like he'd fall off. As he inspected the now secure saddle, he noticed that unlike horses, this saddle had two holes in it near where his hands would usually rest.

"What's this for?"

"That'll allow me to do manoeuvres without a fear of you falling off."

"Awesome!"

Elanor's fingers traced the curve of Azura's shoulder, a swell of pride shining in her eyes. Ayr tensed up, even though he wasn't the one being touched.

"Are you all set?"

Ayr nodded with enthusiasm. "Absolutely."

Lucas cleared his throat again. "Recruits, now that you have passed the trials, I'd recommend using the rest of today to bond further with your dragons. Get used to the saddles while you still can. "Your true test will begin tomorrow!"

Azura cooed as she turned her neck again. "I hope you're ready for this, rider. Let's fly."

FOURTEEN

Ayr patted Azura's neck gently. "I'm always ready when you are."

"If you say so, rider."

As soon as the words left her lips, Azura's body tensed, and she burst into action. With a powerful leap, she thrust herself violently into the air, causing Ayr to grip onto his saddle for dear life. Her movements were no longer graceful and controlled, but wild and erratic. The sound of her wings beating against the air was deafening, their force rocking Ayr's eardrums. As they ascended above the walls of the Obelisk, rays of sunlight began to streak across Ayr's face. He instinctively raised his arm to shield himself from the blinding light, but it was a futile effort against the intense brightness.

Bersos and Grithoss rose with them, their shimmering scales reflecting the sunlight like a sea of midnight blue and purple diamonds. A sense of excitement and anticipation filled the air as they soared higher and higher. Ayr wondered what the rules were now that they were airborne. Would they engage in a chase after Ayr and Azura, or would they allow them to continue their flight undisturbed? Before he could dwell on it any longer, Azura's voice broke through his thoughts, bringing him back to the present moment.

"Rider, where do you want to go? We are safe. We can do whatever we please."

Ayr shrugged. "I don't know. This is your home, not mine. What can you show me?"

Azura laughed gently at him. "Yes, this is my home, but would it surprise you if I said I had not seen a lot of it with my own two eyes?"

"Because you haven't been able to fly?"

"Yes. I am grateful that the others were able to share their experiences with me. But there are many things that I wish to experience with my own eyes."

"Where are you going to take me then?"

"Somewhere special."

The wind whipped through Ayr's hair as the dragons soared high above the Obelisk. The other two riders, and their majestic beasts had disappeared from view, lost somewhere in the vast expanse of sky. Now it was just Azura and Ayr, alone in the endless blue expanse. Azura angled them towards the south, her keen eyes plotting their course away from the blinding sun. Ayr shrugged, unbothered by their movements. Could she still sense his emotions, even at this height? As they glided through the clouds, the world below looked like a miniature painting spread out beneath them.

"Are you hungry yet, Azura?"

"We will eat when we land. I can catch something there, if the others are correct."

The saddle was a welcome barrier between himself and Azura, but Ayr found himself fidgeting in it. After spending most of his time riding Azura bareback, the added cushion was a new sensation. He knew it would be more beneficial in the future, sparing both his legs and his rear end from the strain of long rides. The leather creaked under his weight as he adjusted his position, feeling the new grooves that had formed in the short time he had been in it.

"Is something troubling you, rider?"

Ayr fidgeted in the saddle again. "No, I just need to get used to the saddle."

"Do you need me to land?"

"No, keep flying." Ayr yanked on one of the saddle straps around his legs. It tightened ever so slightly, and he felt more comfortable. "Don't stop until you've reached wherever it is that you want to go."

"Strap in then, rider."

Ayr leaned further forward into the saddle, locking himself in place at Azura's warning. He clasped his hands around the spokes that were inside the saddle. He leaned forward and feeling that Ayr was secured, Azura lurched forward as well. The dive was deeper than what they had done on their last flight, Ayr could only hang on helplessly. He was completely at the mercy of Azura.

Azura pulled out of the dive and if he had not been strapped in with the saddle, Ayr probably would have gone flying with nothing underneath him. Azura shot through the air faster than an arrow and the ground passed beneath Ayr in a blur. He hung on for dear life, not knowing where Azura was taking him. After a while she started to slow down and Ayr finally felt like he could relax again.

He looked over her head as he released his hands from the saddle. Ayr sat back, taking in a deep breath, trying to regain everything that he'd lost. With all of the excitement and exhilaration that riding on Azura brought, it was equally as terrifying. What was not terrifying, however, was where Azura had brought him. Much to his surprise, they were far away from the Obelisk, near where they had stayed in the pit. Ayr thought he could see it as they flew overhead, spotting the familiar creek and rocky outcrop as something that stood out from the surrounding landscape. Azura kept moving over it however, heading towards the nearby mountains. Azura didn't stop until she had reached them.

As they flew ahead Azura had spotted a plateau that seemed to be her destination. She gradually decreased their speed and carefully adjusted her angle to prepare for the landing. Her wings flapped rhythmically on each side of Ayr as she gracefully descended towards the ground. The landing was gentle, aided by the thick layer of leaves and foliage that blanketed the surface below. Lowering her head, Azura provided Ayr with a smooth dismount from her back onto the ground below. The scene around them was like something out of a fairy tale, with trees adorned in vibrant autumn colours and sunlight streaming through the canopy above.

An explosion of wildflowers in a rainbow of colours surrounded Ayr, blurring together into a vibrant sea of petals. He could not discern the boundaries between each plant, their stems and leaves intertwined in a gorgeous display of nature's artistry. What truly captured Ayr's attention was the abundance of wildlife, something he had sorely missed in the barren pit where he had spent the last month of his life.

Azura, with her keen senses and feline grace, was already on the hunt. She leapt after the rabbits that darted in every direction, her magnificent body propelling through the air like a living projectile. Some were too slow to escape her reach and Azura pounced upon them with all the ferocity and playfulness of an oversized puppy.

Ayr would have never been able to catch them on his own and he was thankful for her assistance. The rabbits squealed as they were caught under Azura's claws. One would be enough to satisfy Ayr, but how many would Azura need? She continued to hunt the rabbits like a bloodhound, flushing some out of burrows with her flame, before poking a claw into the ground, scooping the lifeless body of the rabbit out. Finally, Azura had gathered enough of them and returned to Ayr.

"Hungry?"

"Just a little bit." Ayr drew his sword and poked one rabbit with it, skewering it through the middle. "Any chance I can use the oven?"

Azura's face lit up with a mischievous grin, if she were capable of such an expression. She watched intently as Ayr held his sword out, waiting for the perfect moment to unleash her powerful breath. The air around them crackled with energy as Azura released a controlled stream of heat from her mouth, precisely aimed at the raw rabbit on the blade. The smell of sizzling meat filled the air as Ayr turned his sword, cooking the rabbit to perfection in one full rotation. Impressed by her abilities, Ayr took a bite of the now-cooled rabbit. It wasn't until he had finished chewing that he realised the hair was still on the rabbit, causing him to cringe in disgust.

Azura laughed at him, chuckling, amused. "Kaiser did say you would undergo a transformation."

"I don't think that was what he had in mind. Surely it was something more to do with our bond."

Azura rolled her shoulders as she gulped another rabbit down. "We will see, little rider. I fully expect you will change me as well."

As they ate their simple meal of dried meat, an orange and black butterfly landed lightly on Ayr's shoulder. It flitted around his head, then disappeared from view. Curious, Ayr raised his eyes from his food and was met with a mesmerizing sight. A multitude of butterflies, in varying shades of bright orange and deep black, floated gracefully through the air around him.

Their delicate wings caught the sunlight in a dazzling display, creating a kaleidoscope of colours that danced before his eyes. Enthralled by the enchanting scene, Ayr slowly lowered himself to the ground and leaned back against a nearby boulder. The swarm of butterflies continued their journey, fluttering over the edge of the cliff and disappearing from sight. For a moment, all was still except for the gentle rustle of leaves and the occasional chirp of a bird. Ayr felt at peace in this momentary oasis that was unlike anything the pit had ever offered him.

"This is beautiful."

"It is, rider. Just one of many privileges that we get to indulge in here at the Seminary. The joy this brings me is akin to that of when I found out who I was promised to."

Out of nowhere, Ayr's mind was flooded with the image of a dragon. Slowly, more detail seeped into Ayr's mind, more colour and a more defined outline of the dragon in question. As the image formed, questions slipped from Ayr's mouth. Azura had clearly pushed the image into his mind. The dragon in question was Evor.

"For the last thirty years I have been waiting for a rider that could claim me. Evor and I were only hatchlings when we were promised to each other. Now that I have my rider, there's every chance that our connection will grow stronger, not just physically between us, but also mentally between our riders."

"I'm going to get connected to Elanor?"

Azura blinked at him. "When a male and female rider are bonded with dragons that are promised to each other, you could say that there are the changing of feelings. As our relationship grows, so will yours. You are going to become more like me, remember."

"So, you're saying that Elanor and I will end up together? That doesn't seem right. She hates my guts."

"Who are you to question the whims of fate, rider? These pacts are older and more magically powerful than the dragons themselves. What's to say that in a year's time a meteor doesn't strike the Obelisk and knock it from the sky?"

"But she's my master. That would affect *everything* between us."

"Everything happens in this world for a reason. We'll go to your first lesson with Elanor tomorrow and she will be able to teach you more about being a rider. That *is* why you're here, is it not?"

"I can't do that if we're going to have some magical connection."

"Do you not want to? It was my understanding that humans paired together, just like dragons do. You meet, you become close, you mate, you die. It is the circle of life."

Ayr shook his head. "I can't be with her. She wouldn't allow it. Since we completed the Bonding I've felt more drawn towards her, but that's to do with you isn't it?"

Azura nodded in response. "Your bond may yet take years to bloom like one of the wildflowers. For now, cast your thoughts aside. We have company."

Ayr lifted his gaze towards the sky, straining to see what had captured Azura's attention. The bright sunlight made it difficult for him to make out anything at first, but as he squinted and shielded his eyes, a small speck on the horizon began to take shape. It grew larger with each passing moment, until Ayr could see that it was a creature flying towards them. He recognized it immediately: Evor. There was a wave of happiness that washed over him, but it did not come from him. It had come from Azura.

Ayr cautiously stepped back from the edge of the steep mountain, creating a small clearing for Evor to land on. As the majestic creature descended, Elanor's bright red plume stood out against the backdrop of green foliage. The air around them seemed to swirl and dance with excitement as Evor gracefully touched down on the rocky terrain, much to the delight of Azura who eagerly awaited their arrival.

"Evor!"

"Hello little one."

Ayr's gaze was locked onto Elanor, his only focus in the world. She slid down the enormous black dragon with ease, as she had done countless times before. With a swift movement, she removed her mask and tucked it into her belt, revealing her striking features to Ayr's eager eyes. Her piercing gaze met his, sending a shiver of anticipation down Ayr's spine. Everything else blurred as he stood transfixed by her presence, unable to tear his gaze away from the alluring woman before him.

"Thought we might find you here, Ashbourne."

"How did you know?" Ayr glanced over her shoulder. Azura and Evor were already becoming acquainted. That had not taken long.

"Funny feeling." Elanor grinned at him. "Those two will always know how to find each other. Walk with me. We'd be wise to give them space."

She pivoted away from Ayr and the dragons with her gaze fixated on the gentle curve of the creek. Ayr started walking after her, quickening his pace so that he could remain by her side. The sky above was alive with the chatter of birds, their melodic chirps harmonizing with the soothing rush of water as they strolled along the tranquil stream. The air was crisp, carrying with it the earthy scent of moss and wet stones. The peaceful atmosphere enveloped them, offering a momentary respite from the Seminary.

Ayr raised an eyebrow. "What do you mean? They can't know those things about each other."

"They're promised to each other. They have been since birth. Promised dragons have an incredibly intimate connection with each other, one that is only eclipsed by dragons and their riders."

"Yeah, Azura told me. I don't understand. Is it magic?"

Elanor rolled her eyes at him. "Everything is magic here, Ashbourne. Haven't you learnt that yet. We have a special place in this world. The connections we share with the dragons, the duty we have to protecting the Commonwealth - it all plays a big part in how the world operates."

"So, what's my end goal?"

"You don't know what your goal here is? Why did you even apply to be a part of the Seminary then?"

"I wanted to do something good for the world. What easier way than to come here?" Ayr shrugged.

Elanor laughed, shaking her head. "What easier way indeed. You're not going to do anything good up here. Was it her idea?"

Ayr nodded. "She wanted to show me this place now that she can fly with me on her back."

Elanor turned and smirked at him. They had not travelled far down the creek, but Elanor grabbed his wrist, turning him back the way they came. "Of course. Who are we to question the whims of our dragons? Even hatchlings are more knowledgeable than the wisest humans."

"How does that work? Surely humans that have lived a lifetime know more than dragons fresh out of the egg."

Elanor smirked and shook her head at him. "Dragons can communicate in many ways yet unknown to us. Some say their eggs pass down lessons of their ancestors."

"Do you believe that?"

"Evor has alluded to it, but there is only so much he can tell me. He doesn't know the full extent of their magic either. Anyway, that doesn't matter right now. I'm here to show you to your lodgings. Do you know where you're going to rest your head tonight?"

"I'm guessing we'll be at Zenender's Ranch, won't we? The place that Owens was so ungrateful for if we needed to stay there."

"You'd be right. Whilst he might try and bribe Kaiser and Scherr, unfortunately for you, my recruit isn't so lucky."

"Why aren't I so lucky? I could bribe you if I knew what you wanted."

"You're an Ashbourne. The only thing that I'd consider as a bribe would be something that you would consider a punishment. I'm sure both you and Azura don't want that, do you?"

"Not necessarily. Perhaps you could give me some leniency."

"No. You're an Ashbourne."

Ayr let out a loud sigh. "Well, it was worth a try."

Elanor chuckled, and a wave of relief washed over Ayr. "It was. Now come on. I'll take you and Azura back to the ranch before it gets dark."

FIFTEEN

As the sun began to dip below the horizon, Elanor stayed true to her promise and brought Ayr to the ranch. Evor soared gracefully beside Azura, providing her with companionship and a barrier of safety during their journey. Ayr did not trust that Owens and Taven would not attack them.

Ayr sat tall in his saddle, mounted on Azura's strong back, stealing glances at Elanor whenever he thought she was not looking. With her mask concealing her face, it was difficult to decipher her thoughts and emotions. The vibrant pink and orange colours of the sky painted a beautiful backdrop for their ride towards the ranch with the comforting sounds of wings against the wind guiding them forward.

Careful. Azura was in his mind again.

What?

She's still your master at this point. You don't want that affecting your relationship whilst you're still learning, do you?

You need to keep away from Evor then. If we're so connected because of the two of you, you aren't doing me any favours. How long will I be under her guidance for then?

That will depend solely on you. It may take a few years for me to be fully grown and for you to know everything you need to know about being a rider. It's more than just survival techniques and sword play.

A couple of years! If you keep going at the rate you're going with Evor, I'm going to be in serious trouble.

Discipline is a skill that needs to be fostered and grown, not a natural given ability.

Maybe you should practice what you preach.

Azura started to cough audibly mid-flight. Evidently, she had found what Ayr had said humorous. Evor heard the laughter and glanced over.

"Is everything okay, little one?"

"Yes, everything is fine. My rider just makes me laugh."

Evor scowled at Ayr. "Good, just as long as it remains that way."

"We won't have any issues, Evor. All I want is for Azura to be happy." The last thing he wanted to was draw the ire of the enormous black dragon.

"Good. I will accept no mistreatment of my promised."

Humans are more susceptible to make mistakes than dragons are.

Don't paint us all with one brush, Azura. You've seen inside my head. You know what I'm capable of.

Can you keep yourself sane around Elanor?

Azura. You know me.

I will not be held responsible if you can't keep your relationship with Elanor to a level that is befitting of master and student. My bond with Evor is undeniable and nothing will compromise that.

She hates me. She's only taking me under her guidance so she can ensure I don't turn out like my father.

That doesn't mean she hates you.

Has it been done before? Has a promised dragon's rider hated the other?

More often than not.

So, what can I do about it?

Don't fight fate. You forget that I have influence over Evor, and he in turn over Elanor. If you are so concerned with her hating you, you need to ferry it from your mind.

You'd do that for me?

I'd do anything for you, rider.

Ayr leaned back in his saddle as he closed off his conversation with Azura. The descent towards the ranch had already begun; Ayr could feel the rush of air against his skin as they dove downwards. As they neared the ranch, Ayr caught sight of a brown spotted dragon sprawled lazily across the roof, basking in the afternoon sunlight with its belly to the sky. Its head tilted ever so slightly, curious eyes glancing up at the approaching dragons before returning to its relaxed state. The other dragons paid it no mind as they landed gracefully beside the ranch, their powerful wings beating against the air as they came to a stop. Ayr slid from the saddle, while Elanor remained on Evor's back.

"It looks like we're first, Ashbourne."

Ayr glanced around, half expecting to see the other recruits appear. "Great. So, what am I supposed to do until they get here?"

"Make yourself comfortable. I'll come and get you in the morning for your first lesson."

"You're not going to stay?"

Elanor shook her head. "Why would I? I've done my time here. You're a big boy, aren't you?" She lifted her mask only to poke her tongue out at him.

"Yeah, and I've got Azura. I just worry about what the other recruits will do to me."

"You survived last night, didn't you?" Elanor laughed at him softly. "You'll be fine. Kill them if you have to."

"I'm allowed to?"

Elanor shrugged. "If you have to, Ashbourne."

"Thanks for the vote of confidence."

Azura nestled over Ayr's shoulder. "Come, rider. Zenender's Ranch is one of the easiest parts of what we will do together as dragon and rider. It will only get harder from here."

Elanor smiled at her. "Azura is right. This the easiest step on your path to becoming a rider. Rest well tonight and I will see you at first light."

"First light? That's a bit early, isn't it?"

"Do you want to get a foot up on the other recruits?"

Ayr shrugged. "Don't see why not."

"Excellent, see you tomorrow. Evor!"

With a mighty exhalation of air, Evor sprang into the sky with effortless grace, his form rapidly shrinking in size. Beside Ayr, Azura let out a deep sigh as she watched her promised soar off into the distance once again. There was a pain in Ayr's chest. Azura's heart was heavy with longing and anticipation for their inevitable reunion.

"I can't wait until we're finished training."

"I bet you can't." Ayr rolled his eyes. "I can see what you're thinking too."

Azura huffed beside him. "Don't question me for it. Evor is my promised. Should we go and see what our new home looks like?"

"Sure. It doesn't look like much."

Zenender's Ranch was no castle or lofty manor. Upon closer inspection, Ayr realised that they would not be any better protected than they had been during the Catalyst. The crumbling walls and rusted support beams of the old building offered little defence against any potential dangers. It was a surprise to Ayr that a structure in such disrepair could withstand the weight of a roosting dragon, despite its size. As they approached, he noticed an open double door, its wooden frame warped and worn by time and weather. Azura easily fit underneath with her large wings tucked close to her body.

Everywhere Ayr looked, there were gaping holes in the once sturdy ranch. The wooden beams were splintered and broken; the straw strewn about haphazardly. As they ventured inside, Ayr's eyes took in the sight of dragons, alongside their riders. The ranch was a bustling hub of activity, with riders caring for their loyal companions. Some glanced at Ayr with indifference, while others observed him with curiosity. He could sense a range of ages amongst them, from older teenagers like himself to seasoned adults. Azura's gaze also swept over the dragons, a look of understanding passing between them. They all knew who she was.

Zenender's Ranch seemed to stretch on endlessly, with stalls opening up as they delved further into the depths. Each stall was like its own miniature world, decorated with unique trinkets and personal touches. The smell of hay and musk filled the air, mingling with the sound of rustling wings and low growls from the dragons. As they made their way through the maze-like ranch, Ayr felt a sense of awe and wonder at this hidden world of dragon riders. He had to cut his own path in it.

"Pick a place where you want to roost, rider. We're all the same here. No rider is better than any other."

Ayr looked up and down the walkway. "Where are all the other riders?"

"Zenender's Ranch is used by many as a place to get away from the Obelisk. If you're ever in need of a quieter space, this is the place to be."

"None of these other riders lodge here?"

"Very few are permanent. We'll remain here until your master deems you ready to become a fully-fledged rider."

Ayr stopped in front of one of the open lodgings and inspected it. Despite its size, it appeared that Azura would not fit comfortably inside. "How will I know when that is?"

"When she tells you."

"You've been here for how many years? Why aren't you telling me more?"

"It's all part of the process for the riders to figure out. I can only guide you so far. Truth be told, most of the process has been kept secret from me."

"How? You've been alive for thirty years."

Azura sighed. "The Commonwealth excel at keeping secrets. I wouldn't be the first dragon to *not* know the ins and outs of the world around them."

"Then why do we serve them?"

"We do what we must, rider."

"Right." Ayr flicked the next wooden beam he came across with his finger. He was surprised that it didn't fall to pieces. "Ok, so then do you have a preference about where we should lodge ourselves for the foreseeable future? Everywhere looks like it's the same. Full of holes and hardly any more shelter than the Catalyst."

"I have no preference. But we should avoid the back of the ranch."

"Why?"

"Can you not hear him?"

Ayr's ears strained against the silence, trying to catch any hint of what had caught Azura's attention. As they cautiously took a few more steps forward, Ayr's feet felt the vibrations before his ears registered the sound. It was a low rumbling, like a giant snoring in its sleep and making the ground tremble with each breath. Ayr paused and turned to Azura, raising an eyebrow in curiosity. The stillness of the ranch was broken by this mysterious rumbling, adding an uneasy tension to their surroundings.

"What is that?"

"Do you remember your friend from the Catalyst?"

"Gorgon?" A pit deepened in Ayr's stomach. The less time he had to spend near the terrifyingly large dragon, the better. "But how does he fit in here? There isn't enough room to shelter him. We would have seen him as we flew in."

"Go a little further and we will stumble upon Gorgon's pit. A tunnel runs under the river. Here will do."

Azura turned as she faced the commotion coming from deeper within the ranch. Ayr followed her gaze and took in the vast expanse of the wooden structure, stretching upwards to a pointed ceiling. The scent of hay and what could have been dragon sweat filled his nostrils as he surveyed their surroundings. Azura had found a suitable spot for them to rest, but Ayr felt a tinge of disappointment in their temporary shelter. He tilted his head back and gazed up at the rough wooden beams supporting the roof, imagining all the stories that must have unfolded beneath them. Sighing, he turned to join Azura in their chosen spot.

"This will have to do."

"Don't be so disheartened. This is still a roof over your head. Every rider faces this challenge."

"There's no privacy either."

"I don't recall you having a problem with it when Elanor was sharing space with you." Azura chuckled at him.

Ayr felt a burning heat spread across his cheeks as he recalled the intimate moment he and Elanor had shared in the murky depths of the pit. The memory had been pushed to the back of his mind, and was now back with full force. Azura visibly shuddered and pulled away from him, her eyes wide with shock and disgust.

"Rider!"

Ayr jolted as well, quickly realising what he had done. "Sorry."

"You know I can see *exactly* what is going on in your mind, don't you?"

"Yes, I still need to get used to it."

"It's fine. I just wasn't ready for that. I didn't realise that's what the two of you had gotten up to in the cave."

"Nothing happened!" Ayr jumped up, defensive.

"I know. Otherwise, it wouldn't have been so awkward for you."

"So, is this what it's going to be like from here on out? I won't have a moment to myself?"

"I won't have a moment to myself either." Azura nodded at him. "Come on, don't worry about it. One day you and I will essentially be the same living entity. We simply will not be able to function without the other nearby."

"Come on, let's try up here then."

With a powerful leap, Azura launched herself into the air and gracefully landed on the loft above the ground. A collection of wooden plants was laid out, perfectly positioned for Ayr to use as climbing aids. Azura slithered her way up the beams, using her strong body to propel herself forward and upward. The wood creaked under her weight, but none of the beams gave way. Ayr followed closely behind, his agile movements allowing him to easily vault up into the loft. As he joined Azura in the cramped space, he admired her strength and gracefulness. Despite the limited area, it was more than enough for both of them to fit comfortably.

Ayr's gaze swept over their new home, taking in every detail. The ceiling was low and rough, a reminder of their humble beginnings. In one corner of the room was a small bed that looked as though it had been hastily thrown together. Ayr chuckled at its size. It barely seemed big enough to accommodate his lanky frame.

He could already imagine his feet hanging over the edge, scraping against the hard floor below. As he approached the bed, he noticed a new and pristine purple blanket resting on top. Curiosity piqued, Ayr picked it up and brought it to his nose, inhaling deeply. The sweet scent of lavender tickled his senses, bringing a sense of comfort and calmness to his mind.

"That belonged to another recruit."

Ayr turned. "Did you just get into my head again?"

Azura hummed gently. "I never leave it."

"Still going to take some serious getting used to. Why would someone leave that here?"

"Perhaps they are coming back.

"I wouldn't leave something that nice here by accident."

Azura blinked her enormous eyes and smiled at him again. She laid down, curling herself into a ball. Darkness was quickly starting to enshroud them, the sun slipping from sight. Ayr returned the purple blanket to the bed and then sat down upon it. He glanced over at Azura who had now closed her eyes. She was breathing deeply in time with the sounds of breaths from Gorgon.

With the last rays of sunlight, Ayr could see that rain clouds were forming once more. It would rain again tonight. He sighed. Just what he wanted. Hopefully the poorly patched roof would provide sufficient shelter from the rain.

"Why can't I hear Gorgon?"

The rhythmic, thunderous breaths of the enormous dragon had filled Ayr's ears ever since Azura had pointed out the sound. But now, there was a sudden and eerie silence that permeated the stables. It felt as if the world itself had lost its heartbeat.

"Well, he's not there all the time, is he? Just be grateful we'll be able to get some rest whilst he's not here."

"Where does he go?"

"To the mountain, rider. Recruits are being brought to the Seminary of Fire all the time. Gorgon is also so old he gets bored and confused easily. He wants a change of scenery every so often."

"I see." Ayr stifled a yawn in his hand. "Truth be told, I'm feeling a bit tired after today's events."

"That will be the Bonding still having effects on you. I'm grateful I don't have to go through the transformation that riders do."

"Should we sleep then? If we're both exhausted, I don't see there being any reason for us to keep wasting energy."

Azura let out a deep breath. "Yes, rider. If I know Elanor like I think I do, you'll be for it in the morning. Goodnight."

"Goodnight, Azura." Ayr slumped back onto the bed as the first drops of rain began to fall from the sky.

Despite his fatigue, Ayr could not get to sleep. He remained on his back, staring up at the ceiling, letting the rain fall on his face. Azura had shifted several times to cover him, but eventually, her body had fallen to the side, pressing against the far wall. Ayr wasn't game enough to wake her. She was in a deep sleep. The rain was not the only issue he was having, however. As he lay there, able to shift properly on this unsupportive bed, Ayr could feel his blood freezing.

He wanted to scratch it and tear at his skin, but what good would it do? It felt like there was a ball rushing through his bloodstream, down his arm and into his hand. It spread out into each of his fingers. Ayr flexed his hand, trying to ascertain where the weird sensation was coming from. As he continued to examine the weird sensation, it ran back up out of his fingers, along his arm and then into his shoulder. Ayr let out a gasp.

Azura raised her head. "Remain calm rider. That is the magic testing your body, making sure you are a suitable host. Hussian's test occurred a lot earlier than most. It would appear that he failed. Your test will be ongoing."

"For how long?"

"However long it takes. Every rider is different."

Ayr threw his head back in frustration. "You can't say it all depends on me."

"I have the skills and magic required. It's up to you to unlock your potential."

Ayr sighed. "Great."

"If it brings you any pain you will just have to fight through it. There is no stopping my blood once it has been injected into your blood stream." Azura lowered her head back to the ground.

"Should not you already know if we're a suitable rider? You're the ones that chose us after all."

Azura chuckled softly and she closed her eyes again. "Try not to let it bother you. Sleep, rider."

As if a spell had been cast upon him by her mere command, Ayr could feel the weight of sleep settling over his body. He lay back on the mattress, his eyelids growing heavy as a wave of drowsiness washed over him. Every inch of his being fought against the enchantment, his arm stubbornly refusing to succumb to its effects even as he drifted into slumber. Restlessness plagued him in his sleep, until a voice suddenly cut through the fog of drowsiness and brought him back to consciousness.

"Hey!" Ayr jolted properly awake. "Hey!"

The voice was feminine and definitely human. Ayr sat up, before another boot nudged into his ribs. He jolted to the side, falling off the bed and hitting the floor with a thud. He groaned in pain as the wooden floorboards shuddered underneath his sudden weight. Ayr heard the sound of metal on leather, and his hand flew to his own hip, but his sword was nowhere to be seen. Instead, he raised his hands, crying out.

"Wait! I'm with the Commonwealth! I'm a rider!"

"Ooft! New recruit?"

"Yeah. We came up here because we thought it was abandoned."

"Well, it's not. Why did you take my roost? Who said that you could come in here? You're lucky I didn't split your throat open." The voice was definitely female.

"Uh, my dragon."

"What is it? Your first day here or something?"

"Yeah. I only completed the Bonding today." The darkness was crippling. If only he knew a spell that could break through the night.

"Oh, well that explains why you're so exhausted and why Azura hasn't woken up yet."

"You know my dragon?" Ayr was dumbfounded.

"Everyone that's been at the Seminary for more than five minutes knows Azura. It's all anyone has been talking about as well. After all these years, she's finally found a rider."

"Sorry to disappoint."

"Sorry? Don't be sorry." She stuck out her hand in the dark. "The name's Bonnie."

Ayr slowly stretched his hand forward, half expecting it to be cut off by a blade in the dark. Instead of meeting steel, Ayr found himself wrapped up in Bonnie's hand. As Ayr went to pull away, she yanked him towards her. Ayr was back on the bed in a heartbeat, and in the next motion, Bonnie pushed him back. He was exhausted enough as it was, he did not need anything more.

"I feel like I need to welcome you to the Seminary with a gift."

Ayr saw no point in resisting. "Go for it."

With all her weight bearing down on him, Bonnie nestled herself on top of Ayr's chest, her muscles taut and compact. He could feel the strength in her arms as she pinned him down, half expecting her to begin choking him. She was a force to be reckoned with, defying any preconceived notions of fragility. In this vulnerable position, Ayr had limited capacity to fight back, his body at her mercy.

Instead of forcing his hands back like he had anticipated, Bonnie guided them towards her hips, wordlessly inviting him to participate in her movement. As she began grinding her hips into his, Ayr struggled to make sense of the situation.

Bonnie's physical prowess was undeniable as she continued to dominate him, removing whatever clothing impeded their connection. She was far too strong to be human, this had to be a dream. Yet it didn't feel like one. Her movements became frenzied and desperate, each one eliciting a deep groan from her and a corresponding reaction from Ayr. He wanted to pull away, he wanted to escape, but he was trapped.

Amidst all of this wild passion, Azura remained sound asleep beside them while Ayr's exhaustion weighed heavily on his mind and body. He continued to ride the wave, indulging in each of Bonnie's high-pitched moans as she continued to straddle him. Bonnie's moans reached a climax, and she shuddered as she dug her finger nails into Ayr's chest.

Ayr lay still, his body frozen with a mixture of shock and anticipation. Bonnie, who had just been on top of him moments ago, now scrambled off and hastily began putting her clothes back on.

This time, it felt different. The air hung heavy with the scent of sweat and desire, their bodies still humming with the intensity of their recent encounter. Ayr's heart thudded against his chest as he held his breath, waiting for Bonnie's next move. It was both thrilling and terrifying, not knowing what she was thinking or feeling. Time seemed to stand still as they both caught their breath, unsure of where to go from here.

"Enjoy your night." Bonnie clambered up from the bed in a hurry. "I'll find somewhere else to sleep tonight."

Ayr blinked and Bonnie had vanished without a trace.

SIXTEEN

The sun rose quickly, casting a warm, golden glow over Zenender's Ranch. Ayr rose with the sun and scanned the area, his eyes searching for any sign of Bonnie. He strained his ears, hoping to catch the sound of her voice or laughter, but there was only silence that greeted him from other riders. The sound of Gorgon's booming breaths filled the ranch once again, reverberating through the beams like distant rolling thunder.

Ayr felt a sense of unease as he continued his search for Bonnie, a knot forming in his stomach as time ticked by. Azura was by his side, also searching for Bonnie. By the time other riders were rising, they had already completed an entire circuit of the ranch and had found no trace of her. Azura was starting to have her doubts.

"Are you positive it wasn't a dream?"

"I'm positive."

"I don't sleep that deeply. I would have known."

"How can I show you, my memories? Will you believe me then?"

"You need to gather all of the detail of the memory in a ball. The way that Evor described it to me from the human perspective was that you act like you're throwing a ball to me. Then I will be able to see all of the information."

Ayr raised his eyebrow. "Just like that?"

Azura nodded slowly. "Just like that."

Ayr concentrated on recalling every detail of the previous night, his mind working like a puzzle to piece together the events. He opened his mind and extended it towards Azura, who glided into his thoughts as gracefully as she flew through the sky. With a gentle touch, she devoured the memory he had offered her, savouring it like a succulent meal. As she finished, she turned back to Ayr with a glint in her eyes, as if she had just unlocked a secret treasure trove of information.

"I believe you, rider. There was no spectre in a dream. That voice is familiar to me, and I'm sorry that it happened to you."

"Why are you sorry? Once I was over the initial shock I enjoyed it."

"I can see that. I'd advise staying away from this woman. If not for your own safety and sanity, but also mine. Bonnie is a mature student here at the Seminary."

"Why? What's screwing a more established student going to do to you?"

"You need to remember that we are bonded now. Any action either of us takes will affect the other. I already have my promised dragon; I don't need something complicating that connection. Are you done with your search now? I imagine Elanor will be waiting for us. Evor is nearby." Before Ayr could speak, Azura answered the question for him. "Outside. Come on."

With Azura as his guide, Ayr ventured through the slowly awakening ranch and emerged on the other side, where they had entered last night. As they approached the exit, Ayr could make out Evor. His tree trunk sized legs waited for them in the early morning sunlight. Ayr shielded his eyes with a hand as they stepped out into the blinding rays.

Elanor was perched on top of Evor's head her identity still concealed by her mask. Her uniform was freshly pressed and pristine. Behind her stood two other dragons, belonging to the masters of Owens and Taven. The air was thick with the scent of hay and leather, mixed with an unmistakable hint of excitement and anticipation for the day ahead.

With a gentle tap from Elanor, Evor let loose a vicious roar that resonated through the stables and beyond, causing birds to scatter from their perches in the nearby trees. The echo of his powerful voice lingered in the air as he lowered his head, allowing Elanor to dismount gracefully without breaking her rhythm. She straightened herself up and removed her mask, revealing her striking features underneath. As she shook out her long hair, it cascaded over her shoulders like a waterfall behind her. Ayr and Azura were captivated by her charm as she smiled at them with bright eyes full of life and adventure.

"Good morning. I'm so happy to see your smiling faces."

Ayr felt Azura stretch out behind him. "Good morning. What did you have in plan for us today?"

"Did you eat? Chances are you'll want your strength today."

"No, I didn't. Should I have?"

Elanor tutted and reached into the folds of her uniform. Her hand reappeared and something flung through the air at Ayr. He snatched it mid-flight to find that it was a large piece of jerky. "Excellent, you'll eat now then. When you're ready, come with me."

"Where are we going?"

"Not too far. Don't worry, you won't need anything today."

Elanor turned and Ayr went to follow her but was distracted by the sound of beating wings in the air. Ayr looked up as two new dragons were landing on either side of Evor. One of them was Grithoss, Taven's purple dragon, which meant the midnight blue dragon beside him could only be Bersos. Ayr rolled his eyes as Owens made himself known.

"I hate everything about this. We've completed the Bonding and yet they still make us hunt for own our food."

Bersos grumbled his agreement. "Yes, I agree, rider. We should be fed."

"And we should be able to rest our heads in a comfortable place. My father would not stand for this." It was clear Owens had not stopped complaining throughout the entire night about every little detail that upset him. Ayr smirked in his direction.

"I thought it was better than camping out in the wild. We actually had a semi decent shelter for once. I at least had a bed."

Owens' eyes found Ayr and they narrowed at him. "Shut it, Ashbourne!"

Ayr still had not taken the smirk off his face. "Or what? You saw what I did to Gable."

"I won't let that happen to me so easily. I'm a different fighter all together."

"Hey!" Elanor snapped. "There won't be any of that whilst I'm here."

Owens scowled at her. "You're not my master."

Elanor puffed out her chest and made herself taller in front of Owens. He still sat on the back of Bersos and was a sight to behold in his own right. Beside Elanor, Evor let out a low snarl. "No, I'm not. But guess who can still make your worthless life a living misery? Now if you're done complaining, I will take Ashbourne to our lesson for the day. Don't you have somewhere to be, recruit?"

Elanor ignored anything further that Owens had to say and beckoned to Ayr. Without another word he followed her, not wanting to antagonize the situation further. Elanor was still on foot, looking unimpressed as they walked away. Evor turned as well, shadowing Ayr from Owens and Bersos. Elanor led Ayr towards the forested area that surrounded Zenender's Ranch. Once they were a reasonable distance away, Evor stopped.

"Come little one, the riders don't need us for their lesson today."

"They don't?" Azura barked with surprise.

Evor smiled at her. "No, little one. I have much to teach you."

Azura's exuberant barks filled the air as Evor launched himself upwards. Her tail wagged excitedly as she circled around Ayr, urging him to join in the fun. With a fond smile, Ayr waved her off and watched as she shot up into the sky after Evor. The two soared higher and higher, their dark silhouettes quickly disappearing into the bright blue sky towards the radiant sun. Ayr felt a twinge of envy at their freedom and ability to fly with such ease.

Elanor sighed beside him. "I swear, recruits like Owens are getting lippier by the intake. Back when I joined, it was yes sir, no sir."

Ayr shrugged. "I don't like him either."

"You'd be doing the Commonwealth a favour if you shut his mouth."

Ayr's eyes widened. Yes, he had killed Gable, but that was under duress. "I can't kill him in cold blood. Isn't that against Seminary rules?"

The corners of Elanor's mouth curled. "I didn't say anything. You can do whatever you like now that you have completed the Bonding. The Commonwealth might have something to say about it, but you'd only get in trouble if you got caught."

"It sounds like you're pushing me to do something dangerous. I can't lose Azura."

"No, you're right. It was foolish of me to suggest. Do you have any more questions?"

"Yeah, I do actually. Do you know a Bonnie?"

Elanor's eyes narrowed upon hearing the name. "Why?"

"She approached me last night. I thought I was dreaming."

"What did she do when she approached you?" Ayr hesitated with his answer and Elanor seized upon it. "When she comes calling again, you're going to refuse her."

"Why would I do that?"

"Because you're my student. It's your job to comply with all reasonable requests that your master gives you."

"That includes my love life, does it?"

Elanor laughed softly. "I'm going to tell you now, Ashbourne. A night with Bonnie doesn't constitute a love life."

"That sounds like you're jealous to me."

Elanor's laughter increased in volume. "Oh, Ashbourne! I have welcomed many men into my arms over the years. I'm sure as you have figured out by now that I do not go wanting for male attention."

"Then why are you telling me what I can and can't do?"

"As your master, it is up to me to decide what behaviour is acceptable or not within the Seminary. Just because you thought it would be appropriate to let her advance on you, doesn't mean this is normal behaviour that goes on in the Commonwealth. Every intake, your new friend Bonnie, does her best to get with a recruit. Male or female, it does not matter. Unfortunately, she's worked out how to do so without getting caught. We can't prosecute on a he said, she said basis."

"Why is it so bad if she's sleeping with new riders?"

Elanor glared at him. "Because they die. I'm personally sick of it."

"Is there any guarantee that she will come back. The way she acted led me to believe that it would be a one-night affair."

Elanor shook her head. "It probably won't be. If you don't want it to happen again, pray that your side effects from the Bonding are over. That is the only time she strikes."

Ayr glanced down at his hand and flexed his wrist. The ice-cold pain was still there, but it was only a fraction of what it had been last night. "She was stronger than me? How is that possible?"

"When you go through what we call the aftershock, you are weak. Your dragon is impaired, and you lose some motor function. Hopefully it doesn't last too long for you, Ashbourne. The lessons after today will only get harsher."

"Plenty to look forward to then."

Elanor chuckled in response. "I'm glad I chose you, Ashbourne. It's dull when you pick a recruit that doesn't have a sense of humour."

"Great, so where are we going today? We don't have our dragons to take us anywhere substantial."

"Here will do. I just wanted to get away from the ranch a little."

"I see. What's today's lesson then?"

"Remember the magic I conjured in the pit?"

Ayr nodded his head slowly. "Yeah. You're not going to make me do some today, are you?"

Elanor frowned and pursed her lips at him. "Hmm. Probably not today. Your bond with Azura is still new, but this lesson is a good introduction into how to produce magic. Are you ready?"

"Yep!"

"You'll probably want to sit down then." She pushed down on his shoulder, forcing him towards the ground. Ayr went willingly. "Most recruits find this taxing at the best of times. First, get comfortable. You need to be in complete control when you're learning magic."

Ayr settled onto the soft grass, his legs crossed and back straight, mimicking Elanor's poised posture. She perched beside him, pushing her chin outwards in determination. With a gentle nod, she motioned for Ayr to follow suit. He mirrored her movements, feeling a sense of calm washing over him. As he leaned back and closed his eyes, the warmth of the sun on his face brought a contented sigh to his lips. The bright rays danced through his eyelids, casting a warm glow on their peaceful setting.

"You don't need to do that, Ashbourne. Relaxing is great, but what if you need to do magic in the heat of battle. What then?"

"I'll be used to it by then."

Elanor laughed at him again. "You'll be given no tasks within the first few months unless absolutely necessary. Your magic *may* start to foster in that time frame, if you're lucky."

"If I'm not lucky?"

"Don't be mistaken and think that these skills develop overnight? Our magic is not something that is natural. We weren't gifted by the Ancients from birth like others in the world. I've seen the wizards from the western regions that have the given talent. Ours comes from the dragons, and will only grow as the bond does. You'll be lucky if you can create a simple locking spell in six months."

"A locking spell?" Ayr's mind was spinning.

"Yes, something to create locks on doors and chests amongst other things. Because our magic is forged through the dragon, it takes us longer to generate the energy needed to create the spells. In a few years you might be able to replicate what I can do."

"So, what do I need to do to make it work?"

"Today's lesson is simple. You're going to sit here and meditate."

"And do what exactly?"

Elanor shook her head and folded her arms. "Nothing. Evor has taken Azura a considerable distance away. The aim of your meditation is to reach out and connect with her. Now that you're getting the aftershock, you will be able to increase the connection between the two of you. The only way to do that is practice. Control yourself, Ashbourne. Be better than your father."

"I *am* better."

"Then prove it to me, Ashbourne. Call to Azura, draw on her power, and feel the blood of the dragon inside you. Relax." She closed her eyes and took a deep breath in. "Listen."

A moment later an echoing roar flowed over the hills that surrounded them. Ayr glanced up at the sky. "Evor?"

Elanor nodded. "This is the connection. I call to him, and he responds. He calls to me, and I respond. To become a rider is to become a singular being with your dragon. Now grow. You want to be able to project your voice to her anywhere. It is a bond, part of the magic that you had put in your body yesterday."

Ayr closed his eyes, shutting out the world around him as he focused all of his senses on Azura. He took a deep breath, filling his lungs with the crisp, clean air that surrounded them. In his mind, he visualized every detail of his dragon: her iridescent scales that shimmered in the sunlight, the elegant curves of her body, and her piercing blue eyes that seemed to hold infinite wisdom.

With each exhale, he called out to her, hoping she would hear him. Ayr's heart raced with anticipation as he waited for a response, but all he was met with was silence. The aftershock still pulsed through his arm, sending a tingling sensation throughout his body. Though it was more of a nuisance than pain now, he wondered if it would continue to affect him negatively. The sensation continued to ebb and flow, almost like a heartbeat in his arm.

"What do you see? Has she called back to you yet?"

"Nothing. Should I be able to see something?"

"Clearly your connection is not strong enough yet. Stay here, continue to meditate. I will come and find you when I believe you have had enough. Move from this spot and I won't be impressed."

Ayr nodded. "Got it."

He heard her move away, the grass crunching under her feet until there was the sound of silence in his ears. Nothing moved until he had been acclimatised to the area for quite some time. Birds slowly began to come out, chirping away and Ayr listened to their sounds. They were truly distracting. Ayr sighed and realigned his focus. He focused on Azura, wondering where she could be and what she was doing with

Evor. He was truly getting into a new zone of focus with the sounds slowly no longer bothering him.

Ayr was searching, and his voice was projecting in every direction. There was an emptiness that reverberated back to him. He continued to search until he could feel the heat of the day slipping away, and Ayr wasn't hungry despite the fact that daylight was beginning to fade. A squirrel, or some other small rodent squeaked nearby, and Ayr jolted upright. He'd heard something from her. It was faint, but there was a sound. He repeated his cries, but then they fell on deaf ears. Ayr continued his search, desperate to find Azura, but nothing more came from her.

There was no giving up until he felt a hand on his back. A voice cut through the silence. "Did you find anything?"

As if he was waking himself from a deep sleep, Ayr broke his meditation and opened his eyes slowly. He let out one final deep breath, staring straight ahead at the thick oak tree directly in front of him.

"I only heard her once. It was faint."

Elanor moved in front of him and crouched down. "Good. That means there is a connection there. If you'd told me you'd gotten more, I would have called you out for speaking shit. One call on the first day is still a remarkable achievement."

"How long will it take?"

"As long as it takes." Elanor echoed Azura. "You cannot rush this. For some riders the process can take weeks, while others can take months. As long as the dragon has faith that they can build the connection with the rider, then we will keep them here."

"Who was the fastest?" He already full well knew what the answer was. He wanted to hear it from her.

"Dalton Ashbourne. Called his dragon in three days. Some say that he didn't eat or sleep in that time. I'm sure you know the truth."

"I'm going to break his record. Keep Evor and Azura where they are."

Elanor's eyes widened with fear. "You *will* comply with any reasonable request that your master gives you."

"Do you not want me to excel, master?"

"I won't have you follow the same path as your father!"

"I'm going to prove to you that I will not. I've heard the stories, all my life. I wonder, did you ever think to question what caused Dalton to go mad?"

"My father would never lie to me."

"Neither would mine." Ayr met her glare. "Let me meditate and beat his record. Azura and I will bond faster. How many years did she wait for a rider? Let me help her."

Elanor hesitated; her judgement conflicted. "Do you always make life harder for yourself, Ashbourne?"

Ayr laughed at her, shaking his head. "No, but this isn't about me. This is about Azura."

"I understand. But how is your aftershock?"

Despite the persistent aftershock that had been coursing through his arm all day, Ayr let a small smile curl at the corners of his mouth. The sensation was now more like tiny electric shocks pulsing through his veins, causing him to clench and unclench his fist in an attempt to ease the discomfort. But despite the pain, he couldn't help but feel a sense of satisfaction and accomplishment, knowing what result it could bring so quickly.

"It's been fine. I haven't felt it all day."

Elanor narrowed her eyes at him. "Are you sure?"

Ayr nodded. "Why would I lie to you?"

"You're an Ashbourne."

"I wouldn't lie about this. Not to you. Can you just leave me here. I'll be able to do it."

"What if the wolves come hunting? You've got nothing but your sword."

"I don't care. I'm going to break the record one way or another. Watch me if you have to. That's my compromise."

"Fine. But the moment I hear anything that I don't like the sound of, I'm pulling you out of here."

Ayr nodded and closed his eyes again. He sunk deep back into his meditation. There was no time to waste. Ayr went to work, calling out for Azura at every step that he took. He could not part his way through the cloud that was in front of him. He kept searching for Azura regardless of how much time passed. Ayr was committed.

Rider?

Azura's voice finally burst through the veil, coming back to him as clear as day. It was as if they were standing next to each other in an open room.

Where are you? Evor told me you were trying something ridiculous and to be patient. But this isn't possible. It's too early! Nobody has ever communicated with their dragon in less than two days.

No, it's not. I've been here for two days. I am committed to you!

Rider! You're not supposed to do that! Dalton was the first and last to forge a proper connection in under three days and for good reason. It's dangerous! Stay right there, I'm coming to get you.

How do you know where I am?

I will find you, rider.

Ayr was the first to break the communication. Slowly, he pried open his eyes and found himself enveloped in impenetrable darkness. The only sound that reached his ears was the symphony of crickets chirping around him, their melodies blending into one another. He smiled as he leaned back, relishing in the comfort of what he had just accomplished. A haunting howl echoed through the air, followed by a chorus of wolves joining in from a distance. The hair on the back of his neck stood on end, but he felt a thrill at the primal call of the wild. Azura was making her way to him, and he would be safe.

SEVENTEEN

Rider!

Ayr jolted awake, muscles tight and senses on high alert as the familiar voice of Azura echoed in his mind. His hand flew to the hilt of his sword; always within reach, even in his sleep. With a sharp intake of breath, he forced his eyes open and quickly assessed the situation. The dim sunlight revealed their familiar surroundings - the cozy roost tucked inside the ranch walls. A small sigh escaped his lips as he realised there was no immediate danger. The tension in his body eased slightly, but Ayr remained vigilant, knowing that danger could come at any moment.

"I still can't believe you. I still don't know how you did it."

It was two days on from the event and Ayr had not stopped hearing about his achievement from Azura. The other riders in Zenender's Ranch also did not receive the news well. Word had spread about who Azura's rider was; more so now than ever, Ayr was drawing an eerie eye from the rest of the riders and their dragons. As a result, the riders had stayed far from him and Azura had taken to keeping Ayr in their roost.

"What do you mean? I had to. The next stage about becoming a rider was all about our connection."

"But you, you did that for me? You put your life on the line..."

"I did it for you. I want us to grow stronger together."

Ayr groaned, still feeling the aftershock, throughout his body. He knew that Azura could feel his pain, sharing it with him. Perhaps he had done the wrong thing in pushing through so hastily. Maybe he should have waited, and this was now his punishment for being so overzealous.

For two long days, Elanor had granted him a respite after completing the gruelling task. Azura remained on high alert during this time, keenly aware of the lurking dangers surrounding them at the ranch. Hour by hour it seemed like their connection deepened. Every rustle in the leaves or creak of a door set Ayr's heart racing, anticipating the arrival of the elusive Bonnie. He could see it all through Azura's eyes.

"I know. Your master wants to see you again today. Do you think you've recovered enough?"

Ayr nodded, clenching one fist. "Absolutely."

Azura lowered her head, her eyes staring into his. "Don't lie to me."

"I'm fine."

"Ayr, if you can't be honest with me, all of the work you did two days ago will be undone. I haven't waited thirty years for my rider, only to be abandoned after such a short time. It's the aftershock. Isn't it?"

Ayr bobbed his head in slow agreement. He reached for the bowl sitting beside his bed and retrieved the spoon from the thick mixture within. It had been brought to him last night by Elanor. Bringing it to his lips, he took a hesitant slurp, fighting against his natural aversion to the taste and texture. The goop coated his tongue and slid down his throat, a reminder of his current situation. Ayr pushed through, determined to nourish himself even if it meant forcing down this unappetizing substance.

"Did you lie to Elanor?"

"Yes." He flexed his arm again. "I can *still* feel it."

"I would have thought it stopped by now. I apologise that I cannot do anything to ease the pain."

"You don't have to." Ayr took another quick scoop from his bowl. "I need to bear it."

"Would you like me to go catch you something, rider?"

Ayr shrugged as he shovelled another spoonful into his mouth. "Be my guest. When does Elanor want to see us?"

Azura nodded. "And soon."

"Will I have time to eat?"

"I will have a hot meal to you in minutes. Tend to your aftershock. I never truly leave your side, rider."

Ayr lowered the bowl of goop beside the bed and tensed his arm once more. The aftershock was rampant, almost as bad as it had been for the past few days. Ayr grit his teeth together, trying to hide the pain from Azura as she took off, shooting out of the broken wall that made up their shelter. She soared out into the open sky and quickly became nothing more than a speck on the horizon. Ayr didn't take his eyes off her until she had vanished from view. He continued to clench his fist, the aftershock still radiating up to his shoulder.

Ayr had hoped that Elanor or Azura would have some kind of ointment or treatment for the aftershock, but so far, they had not mentioned anything. How long would this pain last? It had been days. Now without Azura near him it was only growing. Cold ran down his spine, like fear as it overwhelmed him.

Unable to hold back any longer, Ayr threw his head back in a mixture of agony and frustration, letting out a guttural scream that seemed to echo through the empty room. The aftershock continued to course through his arm, causing him to clench his muscles in a futile attempt to find relief. The burning sensation was almost unbearable.

Rider!

He felt Azura already turning away from her hunt. In his hunger, Ayr urged her to stay on her course.

It's nothing! It's fine! Just get me some food. I'll be ok.

I don't want you in pain.

There's nothing you can do about it. Please just get me some food.

Rider...

I know, you don't want me in pain. I will get through this, like every rider and my father before me.

This time it was Azura who cut the communication. Due to their bond, however, Ayr could still feel her, like she was an extension of his arm, just out of his reach. Whatever she felt, he felt. Whilst he had no control over it, Ayr felt like his arms were also wings, rising and falling with each beat that Azura made. He did not want to envision what his aftershock felt like to her. If only there were a way he could spare her the pain.

He felt Azura dive through the air, falling upon what Ayr could only imagine was a deer. He felt her mouth open, and slam shut around the poor creature. It was almost like he was crunching the bones in his own mouth.

It felt odd, half devouring a creature out of reach, but it was going to be something he had to get used to if he wanted to be a rider. Moments later he heard the sounds of Azura's wings as she returned to him. She carried half of a deer's carcass in her mouth as she came into land. Azura took another mouthful of deer, which left only one hind leg for Ayr. She dropped it into his hands, and he went to work with his sword, cutting away some of the unneeded flesh. Azura lapped it up quickly before Ayr had all he needed. He held it out, and Azura obliged, her hot breath running over the leg.

Ayr smiled at her. "Thank you for that."

"Anything for you, rider."

Ayr bit heartedly into the leg, the only thing taking his mind away from the pain caused by the aftershock. He began gnawing away at the cooked flesh. Anything he did not finish would disappear quickly down Azura's throat. An entire leg was too much for him, and Azura was eyeing the slab of venison hungrily. Ayr held it out towards her and Azura jolted forward with a surge of speed, snatching it from his hand.

Ayr jolted forwards as he felt like Azura was ripping his arm from the socket.

"Hey! Gentle!"

Azura immediately looked apologetic. "I'm sorry, rider. Sometimes I don't know my own strength. I am still growing after all."

"It's ok. Maybe I should just leave my leftovers on the ground from here on out."

"That may be wise, rider. Should we go see Elanor? I saw her arriving as I returned."

"Sounds like a plan."

She was not saddled today; Ayr opting to keep the saddle in the relative shelter of the stable. They had not gone riding since Ayr's aftershock kept flaring up, Azura opting to let Ayr rest. With his arm aching, Ayr pulled himself up onto Azura's neck and wrapped his arms around her. She had grown substantially in the past few days. Whilst still nowhere near the gargantuan size of Evor or Gorgon, she would easily swallow Ayr whole now.

She turned, her tail smacking against the opposite run-down wall that made up their shelter. The wall didn't move, but Ayr heard the collision, thinking it was enough to do some damage. Azura launched herself into the air. As she emerged, Ayr felt the strong sunlight against his skin, basking in it. Azura landed outside the ranch, as Evor was lowering himself to the ground with a thud that eclipsed any sound that Azura made.

On top of Evor's head, Ayr saw Elanor as she removed her mask and smiled down at him.

"Hey you! How's your aftershock?"

"Manageable."

Don't lie.

Ayr winced and scratched the back of his head. "Not great. It's gotten worse in the last few days."

"Do you think it was wise to do what you did during your meditation?"

Ayr nodded. "Absolutely. I'd do anything for Azura."

Azura turned her head, her eyes sparkling with admiration as they met Ayr's gaze. In that moment, their emotions intertwined and a current of electricity pulsed between them. Even without words, they understood each other completely, their emotions mirroring one another's in an intricate Sauriaan dance.

"Right, well, if that's the case, I'm going to assume that you're ready?"

"Ready for what?"

Elanor's face broke into a wide grin as she gracefully dismounted from her saddle, her feet landing softly on the ground. She beckoned for Ayr to do the same, and he followed suit, carefully sliding down from Azura's back. Elanor looked up at the two magnificent dragons towering over them, their scales shimmering in the sunlight.

"Have you two got somewhere to be?"

Evor snorted as he flapped his wings. "We do, Elanor. How long till you be?"

Elanor patted the giant's leg. "We're not doing anything crazy today. Give us until mid-morning."

"As you wish. Come little one."

The two dragons stretched their powerful wings, launching themselves into the air with a booming burst of wind. Ayr felt as though he was being pummelled by the force of Evor's powerful gusts; still, he was unable to resist grinning at Elanor, who smiled back at him with equal exhilaration. Once Evor and Azura were gone, quiet returned to the front of the ranch. Elanor turned to Ayr.

"Hey Ashbourne. I've got something to show you."

"What is it?"

Elanor held up her mask. "I wanted to go through a simple lesson with you today. We need to make you one of these. You can do whatever you want to it, but I imagine that riding around on Azura having bugs and Chilijo knows what else in your face isn't a pleasant experience."

"How did you know?"

Elanor shrugged with a grin. "Some call it intuition."

Ayr rolled his eyes and grinned back at her. Even just being in her presence was something else entirely now. Was it an effect of Azura's and Evor's relationship? It was like a switch. One minute Elanor was just like anyone else, the next she was one of the few people that mattered to him in the world. Was it Azura's doing? If so how could he stop it affecting him like this? The last thing he needed was more distractions. Elanor could prove to be the biggest.

"So, what's the process then? I could do with one."

Elanor smirked at him. "Glad you admitted that I'm right."

"I never said you were. What do we need? Some sort of clever material?"

"That's exactly what we need."

Elanor reached into her pocket, her fingers deftly retrieving a small black cloth. As she unfolded it before Ayr's eyes, he could see that it was no larger than his own head. He took it from her outstretched hand and examined it closely, turning it over to inspect its every corner. The fabric was smooth and unadorned. Despite its plain appearance, Ayr felt drawn to the cloth in his hands, wondering what secrets it may hold within its folds.

"What's this?"

"Dragoncloth. It's stronger and a bit more breathable than your normal run of the mill cloths."

Ayr rolled his eyes. "Are you serious? That's a very original name. So, what do we do with it?"

"Do you know what a weave is?"

"What, like a spell?"

Elanor nodded her head and pulled the cloth gently from Ayr's hand until just the end of it was brushing against his palm. He went to pull at it, but Elanor raised her forefinger.

"Dragoncloth has been embedded by the dragons to be malleable to our will. With a little bit of magic, you will be able to direct it to conform to your will. I'm going to show you." Elanor clasped the dragoncloth between both of her hands and raised it to her face. "Now that you're bonded to Azura properly, your magic will be stronger than it was before. Use her presence and forge the dragoncloth as to how you want it to be. Create an image in your mind of what it should look like, if you want you can change it later."

Wanting to stand out from the crowd, yet remain true to Azura, an image popped into Ayr's mind. He would use the white and black design, much like Elanor's. Elanor passed the dragoncloth to him and Ayr took it in both his hands like she had. He looked up at her inquisitively.

"Speak to it. Use the magic in you. Mold it to how you want it to be. This is your canvas to paint on."

Ayr looked at her and then peered back at the cloth. He raised it in front of his face and started to envision what he wanted it to look like. He started to speak, as if giving the cloth directions. As he started to speak, he could feel it and see it already changing in his hands. A warm sensation filled his stomach as his vision began to materialize on the cloth before him. There was no rhyme or pattern to it, but soon, the cloth was more white than black.

Unhappy with it, Ayr furrowed his brow and went about giving the pattern more detail. The streaks in the mask became more solid, now finally representing what Ayr was hoping for. He kept whispering to the cloth until he was finally happy with it. It was a wolf's face, bearing its fangs.

Elanor stood over him. "Do you want a plume? Just run your hand along the top so the magic knows where to go."

It was something that Ayr had not thought about. He liked Elanor's plume and wanted one of his own. It gave the mask a sense of prestige and regality. He did as Elanor had instructed, keeping on theme with the rest of the mask. A blue plume began to spring to life. It was the same blue of Azura's eyes. Now that it was complete, Ayr looked at it with confidence. He could feel the magic now fading away and his body relaxed.

As he was staring at the mask, a wave of exhaustion came over him. He felt drained, suddenly. Ayr keeled over, lowering the mask, resting it against his knees. He coughed and looked up at Elanor weakly. His arm still pulsed, the pain of the aftershock still having not faded.

"What's happening to me?"

"The mask is extensive. Was this the first spell you've cast with Azura's assistance?"

"Yes. I haven't done anything since the last time I saw you."

"How do you feel? You look awful."

Ayr planted his knee on the ground, and he looked up at Elanor. "Should this be normal?"

"Call Azura back and she will give you the strength you require. There's somebody else that I want you to meet today."

"Where are we going?"

Elanor smiled at him as she held out her hand. "We're going to the Obelisk."

Seeing no reason to refuse her, Ayr called out in his mind. *Azura! I need you!*

EIGHTEEN

As Azura and Evor returned to them, Ayr felt a wave of revitalizing energy wash over him, as if she were transferring her own vitality to him through their unseen connection. He remained on one knee as she landed gracefully before him, her eyes filled with concern for his well-being. The intense blue of her irises shimmered in the sunlight. Without a word, she raced towards him, her movements fluid and graceful like a dancer's, radiating love and support for her companion.

"What did you do to him, Elanor? Was this the weave?"

Elanor nodded. "Didn't you feel the energy transference?"

"I did. I was wondering what you were doing."

With a grunt, Ayr pushed himself up from the dusty ground. His palms were coated in dirt and sweat; he wiped them off on his tattered trousers before reaching for the mask in his left hand. As he rose to his full height, he held the mask out towards Azura with a mixture of pride and hesitation.

A grin spread across Ayr's face. "I am sorry for the worry I caused you, but this is what we created, together."

Azura noticed the mask and looked down at it with approval. "Well done, rider. I see that you kept my colours too."

"What else would I do?"

Azura closed her eyes in content bliss as Ayr's fingers gently scratched behind her ear. Her elegant neck arched gracefully, allowing

Ayr to reach every spot that brought her pleasure. A low, rumbling sound echoed through the air, filling it with a soothing warmth, like a cat purring but amplified to the size of a small house. Ayr looked over at Elanor, who stood with her hands confidently planted on her hips and a mischievous smile playing on her lips.

"Right, are you two done? We have places to be?"

"Sorry." He stopped patting Azura, much to her disapproval.

"You're forgiven. You shouldn't need your saddle; we're not doing any crazy flying today. You're progressing much faster than the other recruits. Most recruits take months to create the bond you have with your dragon, so it's time that you met our watcher."

"Watcher? Has someone been looking at me the entire time I've been here?"

Elanor laughed softly, bringing her hands up to her chest. "No, the watchers work for the riders. They are magic users, gifted with the power of foresight. We are summoned if they have a vision about us. Then we're given a task. Are you coming, Ashbourne?"

Ayr nodded. "Sure. Give me a moment."

Ayr raised his mask to his face, relishing the cool touch of the smooth material against his skin. He pulled it over his head, feeling as it settled snugly into place. To his surprise, the mask was nearly transparent, allowing him a clear view of his surroundings.

Azura already had her neck low enough for Ayr to step over. He easily climbed onto her and then slid into position along her back just before the first spine. Evor lifted Elanor into the air and stretched his neck out towards the sun. Evor let out a loud bellow that echoed around the hills. At Elanor's call, Evor lifted off from the ground, Azura not a moment behind them. The two dragons soared through the air side by side, Azura far enough away from Evor to avoid being hit by his enormous wings.

As they neared the Obelisk a flight of dragons could be seen departing from its peak. As they took to the sky, their powerful wings created a deafening roar. At first, it was just a few dragons leaving, but as time passed, the number grew until the sky was filled with their majestic forms. Ayr's eyes searched for any sign of concern on Elanor's face, but her mask concealed all emotion.

No. Azura answered his question before he had had a chance to ask it. *This is not normal. With this many dragons scrambling, the watchers must have seen something.*

On today of all days? Why couldn't it be happening when we were in the pit?

Be grateful that it didn't. You are more prepared today than you were two weeks ago. We can both fight.

The dragons larger and more agile than Evor and Azura soared past them without a care in the world. Their vibrant colours and varying sizes painted a mesmerizing picture against the clear blue sky. Ayr glanced back at Elanor as they flew towards the Obelisk, but she remained unresponsive. He could do nothing but wait until they landed. Azura positioned herself behind Evor, trusting his lead as they flew into the underbelly of the Obelisk. The structure's shadow grew over them as they approached the first landing pad.

Elanor had climbed down from Evor before Azura had even landed. Ayr made sure he was quick with his dismounting as well. Elanor pat Evor's leg. "Stay here, will you? Keep an eye on Azura."

Evor bowed his head. "Of course."

"Hurry up, Ashbourne!"

"What's wrong? What were all those dragons doing."

Elanor seemed dumbstruck. "The watchers must have seen something. I've never seen this many dragons scramble."

"Why not? What happened the last time that this many dragons were scrambled?"

Elanor shrugged. "It could be anything. There are threats con-stantly evolving all across the world. It is our job to neutralise any that can have world threatening consequences."

"But a threat that it needs that many dragons going after it? Surely that can't be good."

"No, but we're equipped to handle most things. The watchers have clearly seen something. Are you coming?"

With a nod of understanding, Ayr followed Elanor through the winding corridors and staircases. The walls were adorned with intricate tapestries depicting scenes of ancient battles and mystical creatures that weren't just limited to dragons. Elanor moved swiftly, her long hair trailing behind her as she led Ayr deeper into the maze-like struc-ture.

Ayr felt disoriented in this unfamiliar place, like he was making his way back towards the Bonding. The walls seemed to shift and morph as they passed, making it even harder for him to keep track of their path. He relied solely on Elanor's guidance, knowing that if she left him now, he would be hopelessly lost. Despite the uncertainty, Ayr marvelled at the grandeur of the Obelisk and its endless secrets waiting to be discovered. Where was she taking him?

The pair of riders passed by others, some walking alone and other walking in pairs. Each rider wore their uniform proudly, their chests puffed out as they went about their business. Others looked appre-hensive as they walked past. Ayr was curious about their state of mind. Despite the distance between the two, he could still hear Azura in his mind.

They're nervous. I wonder what we've missed. Evor has not told me anything yet.

I'm sure he would if he knew something.

Elanor turned down another corridor, the flickering torches cast-ing shadows along the stone walls. They walked for what felt like ages until they reached a heavy wooden door adorned with a bold red x. The door stood tall and imposing, hinting at secrets and mysteries that lay beyond its threshold. Despite his nerves, Ayr felt a thrill of excitement at the unknown possibilities waiting on the other side. Ayr raised an eyebrow in curiosity, but before he could speak a word, Azura's voice entered his mind once again.

The Observatory. It's where the watchers do their work.

Elanor interrupted Azura's conversation with Ayr. "Welcome to the Observatory. When you go inside, make sure you're careful not to touch anything."

"Is it dangerous?"

"That's one way to describe the future. Only truly bonded riders can open this door."

They approached the door and Ayr stretched out his hands to push against it, however there was no movement. Ayr grunted and pushed on the door with both hands now. It was still unmoveable.

"Harder than it looks, right?"

With ease, she pressed her hand against the door, and it swung open effortlessly. Ayr stood there staring at her in disbelief. Her strength and ease left him speechless, wondering about the true extent of her abilities.

Ayr took a step back, his hand instinctively reaching for the hilt of his sword as the door creaked open. This area was unlike any other part of the Obelisk he had explored. While darkened corridors with windowless walls had been the norm, this wall was lined with wide windows that flooded the space with brilliant sunlight. The rays danced across the polished floors and illuminated every corner of the corridor, stretching from one end to the other in a golden embrace. Ayr's eyes widened in awe at the sight before him, wondering what secrets this place held and why it seemed so different from the rest of the mysterious Obelisk.

As Ayr followed Elanor out into the corridor, he glanced down, thinking he was stepping out into open air. Instead, there was glass underneath his feet, giving him a view of the city beneath him. They were approximately halfway up the Obelisk, the corridor extending far into the distance.

"Hurry up, Ashbourne. You don't want to keep her waiting."

Everywhere he looked, there was something new in this corridor. It was as if this had been an afterthought, added on once the rest of the Obelisk had been completed. Ayr ducked as a green dragon rocketed overhead, completely oblivious to the glass ceiling that its claws scraped over. There were stairs up ahead dipping down and Ayr could only see the ceiling of the room ahead. It was about as large as the landing pad and completely circular. There was nothing flashy about it, being this far down in the bowels of the Obelisk.

Elanor started her descent and Ayr quickly followed. This room was made of glass in every direction, every ceiling and every piece of furniture appeared to be opaque. Elanor went to step into the room when she was approached by an older woman - she was the first-person Ayr had seen in the Obelisk *not* in uniform. This woman wore a hooded burgundy robe. Her feet were bare against the glass underneath them.

The remnants of her eyes were now nothing but empty sockets, the skin around them withered and wrinkled. No longer did she possess the ability to control their movements, as they bounced aimlessly within their hollowed spaces. Her eyes darted back and forth with a catatonic frenzy, like a marionette, displaying no signs of consciousness or awareness.

"Elanor? Is that you?"

"Yes, mother. I want you to meet someone. Ashbourne, I want you to meet my mother, Grace ..."

"Is this the rider that was chosen by Azura?"

Grace stretched out her hand, fingers splayed as if searching for something. Ayr watched curiously as she reached out towards him. Elanor gently took hold of his hand and guided the two of them together. Grace's touch was soft but firm as she explored Ayr's arm, moving up towards his face with a sense of familiarity. Ayr was unsure whether to embrace this strange elderly woman or retreat from her touch, but there was a warmth and gentleness in her actions that put him at ease. Grace's hands were like embers against his skin, radiating a comforting heat as she caressed his face.

"It is, mother. This is Ayr Ashbourne."

"Whose son, is he?" Grace's voice deepened.

"I'm Dalton's. I'm sorry if you have a problem with that, but you aren't going to be the last person in this academy to have a problem with my lineage."

Grace let out a shriek and threw her hands up in the air. Elanor moved to comfort her immediately. Grace froze and started to mutter under her breath.

"Black wings, white wings, when they come together the world will burn. Golden flames, golden fire. Ash will be reborn!"

As if a spell had been lifted, Grace's laboured breathing returned to a steady rhythm and her eyes regained their usual manic movements. With a furrowed brow, she glanced back at Elanor, her expression one of confusion and uncertainty. She was still blind.

"Adventure lies in your future, my love. You'd best be careful going forward. Danger lies around every corner."

Elanor placed her hand gently on Grace's shoulder and started to turn her away. "Ok she's had her vision now. Thank you, mother, for all that you do."

"Are you leaving so soon?" Grace sounded hurt. "I haven't even given you a task yet."

Elanor was frowning deeply. "No, I just came to introduce you to the Ashbourne."

"Ashbourne? Ashbourne who?" It was clear that she was confused. This woman who had so confidently made several bold predictions now seemed like she didn't know which way was up.

"My new student. You didn't predict anything. We'll come back when you summon us again."

Grace smiled warmly. "Very well. You know where to find me if you need me." She turned away and went back inside the room.

Ayr blew out his lips. "Well, that was interesting. That was your mother?"

Elanor was still frowning. "Indeed, it was. So, she had nothing for us, only a premonition."

"Is that normal?"

"For some watchers, but not all. If my mother has had a premonition about us, we need to be careful. I'm not sure what any of it means exactly."

"Don't worry about it. We'll do it together."

"That's exactly why I'm worried. But since she didn't have anything for us. I suppose I'd best show you and Azura around the Obelisk. Come on."

NINETEEN

Elanor's steps quickened as she led Ayr away from the Observatory and deeper into the Obelisk. As they walked, Ayr noticed the confident strides of the other riders passing them by. Some were deep in conversation while others carried themselves with purpose and determination. Every now and then, a dragon no larger than Azura would amble past.

"Are they hatchlings? How many dragons are yet to find their riders?"

"At any given time, you can expect at least two dozen hatchlings to be around the Obelisk. As soon as one group of recruits is put through the Catalyst, another is on the way. Sometimes I grow concerned if the Commonwealth has become complacent because there is nobody to test the skill of recruits. I just need to remember that the dragons are the great neutraliser."

Ayr shook his head "All dragons aren't the same."

"No, they aren't. It's our hope that when a dragon chooses its rider that it can be paired with someone who will help balance it. Some riders will be much better at fighting than others, while others will rely on their dragons more for it."

They neared the end of the glass corridor and Ayr was curious. "So, what's our goal? Do riders just sit around waiting until the watchers find something for us to chase down? I thought becoming a rider meant that I would be preserving peace and protecting the world."

"The directive of the Commonwealth is that the riders will enforce peace across the world."

"By sitting here waiting for your mother to give you a premonition?" Ayr stopped as Elanor did, her fist curling into a ball by her side. Ayr smirked at her. "Stop me when I'm telling lies."

"If the watchers deem it appropriate, we will go out. The known world cannot have us solve all of its issues for it. It is far too expansive for us to govern the entirety of it. That's why the watchers send us on our tasks."

"If there's a problem somewhere, we should help."

"You don't have to like the way it is. You just need to accept it. You're a sworn member of our order now."

"I am for now. What if I don't like it and choose to leave. Azura will come with me."

Elanor's lip curled into that all too familiar wicked smile. "Then we'll have to hunt down and kill another Ashbourne."

"Remind me what happened last time that happened."

Elanor's mouth snapped shut and she turned her head away from Ayr, her eyes flickering with an inner turmoil. Ayr let a small smile play at the corner of his lips, but he quickly masked it when he caught Elanor's gaze. She led Ayr confidently through the bustling Obelisk, the sounds of their boots echoing against the stone walls.

As they made their way back towards their starting point, Ayr realised that they were passing familiar sights. Just as he began to think he had a grasp on their route, Elanor abruptly turned down a side alley and guided him into a vast, circular room. One entire wall was absent, revealing an opening large enough for even the mightiest dragons to gracefully descend upon. Like the observatory, this space was situated beneath the Obelisk, but instead of a dome, it boasted an open ceiling. Ayr's gaze travelled upwards, taking in the dizzying heights above him.

He could also sense Azura approaching, her presence no longer hindered by the solid walls of the Obelisk.

She rounded the bend and came into view, with the much larger Evor right behind her. Ayr laughed to himself, imaging the bigger dragon chasing her down. Thankfully, they were friends and promised to each other. Within moments, the dragons were coming into land, Evor taking much longer on this new platform than Azura. Elanor smiled up at Evor and rubbed his leg, unspoken words passing between them, before she turned towards Ayr.

"The one thing we haven't tested yet is your swordcraft. I know you've killed at least one other recruit, but I want to know how well you stand up in a fight on your own with nothing but your sword. We have jousts here at the Seminary. If you can manage to impress someone like the Overlord, you may very well see yourself elevated to a higher position within the Commonwealth."

"Do we joust on the backs of our dragons?"

"Not usually no. Makes it seem a little more fun and means that we need to rely on our own skill. Whilst recruits will die all the time, now that you're a rider, we want to protect you at all costs. That means nobody should be dying during what we consider sport."

Ayr frowned. "I see. Has any rider ever died during a joust?"

Elanor shrugged and laughed. "If they're not good enough, sure. Now come on, are you an Ashbourne or a coward? Draw your sword and show me what you're made of."

Elanor slowly drew her sword, and she pointed it at the ground in front of him. Ayr put his hand on his hilt and didn't draw his. He waited until Elanor took a step. The hesitation would have cost him if it was a real fight. Elanor was quick on her feet, faster than Ayr would have liked. The only person he had faced who could match her speed was his father. Elanor skipped towards him, thrusting her sword towards his hip.

Ayr had to react, stepping backwards. The blade only missed his hip by an inch. Ayr spun out of the way of the next stabbing motion, finally pulling his own sword from its sheath. Elanor was as fast as a striking serpent. Ayr was outmatched.

He looked for an opening but found none. Elanor's blade was everywhere, cutting through the air around him, forcing Ayr to be even more defensive. She was toying with him. Ayr's many fights against his father had taught him that. Dalton had always seemed to have time to pull his blows away in time to ensure that Ayr was not struck.

If he parried, Elanor would have another two strikes on his blade before he had stepped away. There would be no combating her like this. Sweat began to drip on Ayr's brow as he parried another heavy-handed strike from her. How was she this powerful? Elanor hit with all the force of a small giant, her sword seemingly more like a club than an actual sword.

Don't give up.

Azura's words were comforting, but Ayr was being beaten into submission. Any offence he tried to hit back at Elanor with was countered, thrust aside like he was a petulant child, swinging aimlessly. Ayr's breath came in ragged gasps now, but Elanor seemed as fresh as ever. She continued to attack him, and Ayr parried with one last desperate attempt. Their swords crossed, and they stared into each other's eyes, before Ayr tried to pull away.

He was caught. Elanor was fluid with her movements and there was nothing Ayr could do. She wrenched his sword away, using her own as leverage. Ayr was powerless as his sword left his hands and a boot from Elanor forced him to the ground. Ayr stumbled as he fell flat onto his back. He glared up at her in shock.

Be humble. Learn from this experience please.

Ayr pulled himself into a seated position, defeated. He ignored his sword on the ground in front of him and shook his head. "You're something else. How are you so strong?"

Elanor put her hands on her hips and laughed. "Come on, Ashbourne. Just because you were beaten by someone better, doesn't mean you have to sulk. Your father would not have done that."

"Do you actually know anything about my father?" Ayr's eyes narrowed. "Or do you just spout the same bull shit that the Commonwealth has told you about him?"

"Do I know anything about Dalton Ashbourne? I think you'll find I do."

"I said the stories don't count!" Ayr's hand curled into a ball.

Rider! Don't do something that you'll regret. She is still your master!

"Dalton Ashbourne tried to court my mother when she was betrothed to my father. He killed my uncle and nearly killed my parents as well. He's a scoundrel, someone I'm glad that they kicked out of the Commonwealth. Did your beloved father ever tell you why the war started in the first place?"

"You took his dragon from him without reason. He didn't do anything. That's why he tried to court your mother. As a way to get back at your father."

"How dare you!" Elanor's face contorted into an ugly twisted version of itself. She went to raise her hand, but Ayr ducked away from her. "After everything I've done for you, *this* is how you speak to me?"

"I won't stand for having my family insulted!"

"History is written by the victors, and your family lost the war. At least I'm willing to tell you the truth. These words aren't from my family either."

"I don't need to hear *your* truth!"

Rider!

She started it.

I don't care. She is your master.

"The negative perception of Dalton Ashbourne comes from your uncle."

The thunderous roar of Evor shook the ground beneath them. His massive form loomed overhead, his yellow eyes burning with anger as they glared down at Ayr. Elanor stood tall and fierce, her sword raised and aimed directly at Ayr's throat, ready to defend against any attack.

"Go on, say something stupid. I won't hesitate to end the Ashbourne line before its heir has another chance to get out of hand."

Ayr put his hand up to block the sword coming any closer. Not that it would do him much good. Elanor would push her sword through his hand all the way to his throat. There would be nothing to save him, not even Azura.

Rider! Stop!

He could sense the intensity of Elanor's desire. Every fibre of Ayr's being longed to stand and take the punishment from Elanor. As he reached out, he felt a powerful wave of resistance from Azura, a further unspoken plea for him to stop. Like a smaller dragon being snarled at by a larger one, Ayr backed down.

"Did she talk to you?" Ayr nodded in response. "Good, it's about time that someone talked some sense into you. At least one of you has restraint in the relationship. Azura, I want you take him back to Zenender's Ranch tonight. I'm going to need to reconsider Ashbourne's place in the Obelisk. A display like that is not befitting of a rider. You need to be able to control your emotions."

"You're sending me back there. I thought I was done with it? After everything I've worked for? After the connection that Azura and I have built?"

"Just be grateful that's all I'm doing, Ashbourne. I could very well have you booted out of the Seminary all together. This is not your birthright."

Just accept it Ayr. I know you want to fight right now, but neither you nor I are strong enough to win. Evor would crush us both, even without Elanor's help.

You want to fight them?

My will is linked to yours. Neither of us can deny that. I want to fight, but you need to wait.

What about your promise?

Evor and I will always be promised to each other. Dragons can forgive each other, particularly a promised pair, something that humans cannot so easily. If there is a quarrel between a promised dragon's riders it will eventually sort itself out. Do not act now whilst you are still heightened. It will not end well for you.

Won't end well for me? She has no idea what I'm capable of.

Let's not show her yet. It's far too early for that.

"Ahem! Are the two of you finished yet? There are other beings in the room, you know."

Elanor cut across their internal conversation, interjecting herself before Ayr could even open his mouth to respond. He suddenly became aware that he must have been frozen in place on the ground in front of her, like a statue caught mid-movement. His words to Azura were left hanging, suspended in the air like forgotten promises.

"We'll do as you have asked."

With a graceful bend at the waist, Elanor tossed Ayr's sword back towards him. The weapon spun through the air, glinting in the sunlight before it reached his outstretched hand. He caught it by the hilt with a deft movement, bringing it to a stop just inches from his face.

"Good. I want you to think about this before I see you again. Remain in the ranch until I summon you or arrive to collect you."

Defeated, Ayr clambered to his feet. Elanor turned her back to him and made her way over to Evor. The giant black dragon lowered his head, allowing Elanor to climb on him with ease. Once Elanor was seated in her saddle, Evor bowed his head again, this time towards Azura.

"Goodbye, little one. Good luck with this interloper. Perhaps you will be able to talk some sense into him. I will miss you."

"I will miss you too, Evor."

Evor kicked off from the ground and his wingbeats filled the void underneath the Obelisk as he rose into the sky. Ayr raised his head as he watched him go and he felt Azura snuggle in beside him. He raised his hand to her neck and began to stroke her scales.

"I don't want to be held back by her."

"Be careful not to overstep, rider. We will have our day."

TWENTY

The isolation that he was enduring would have been unbearable for Ayr if not for Azura. She stayed by his side day and night, her sleek white scales providing a warm comfort against the cold wooden walls. When she left to hunt, the loneliness crept in like an unwelcome guest, but thankfully her returns were swift.

One day quickly turned into two and two quickly turned into a week, each day blending in the dim lighting of Zenender's Ranch. Without Elanor's presence, there was little for Ayr and Azura to do except pass the time with mundane activities. Ayr found solace in exercising just below their roost, rarely speaking to anyone, or engaging in idle gossip. He was content to mind his own business and focus on caring for Azura and himself amidst the sparsely populated ranch. This was a punishment he had not expected. Why was Elanor taking so long to return?

No matter what Ayr tried, there was no leaving Azura's presence. She lingered in his mind like a persistent dream, her voice always ringing in his ears. Every night they slept side by side, and he noticed how much she had grown. Inch by inch, she seemed to stretch and expand, like a flame steadily growing brighter. Her warmth enveloped him, but in the back of his mind, he wondered what it would be like at the Obelisk.

"It's just as good as you'd expect it to be."

"I've only briefly seen the inside of it. Are we going to get there soon? I grow tired of this ranch." Ayr sighed and shook his head.

"Elanor will come back to you. I've never known her to hold a grudge for long. Despite her hostile exterior, what you'll find underneath is a kind and warm person."

"You wouldn't know it. I thought because you were promised to Evor, it would have made the whole process easier. Didn't you say you'd speak to him on the matter?"

"Conflict is natural in a human's life. It's all that you seem to strive for. Once you've finished fighting someone, you then pick up your sword and go and find someone else to fight."

"It's not in *my* nature."

Azura scoffed at him. "Yes, you are special, I wouldn't have chosen you as my rider if you weren't, but you cannot fight humanity at your core."

Ayr shifted beside Azura, pressing his back more into her. "Then why become a dragon in servitude?"

"I believed that I could make you better."

"What if I make *you* worse?"

Azura's chest heaved with a deep, shuddering breath before she released it with a sigh. The sound rumbled from within her, like a distant thunderstorm brewing on the horizon. Ayr could almost feel the weight of her emotions through the vibrations in the air.

"You are my rider. Your will is my command. I will try and guide you, but I can only do so much."

"I understand. I don't want to lead you astray."

"And you won't, little one." Azura's voice carried warmth.

"Should we sleep then?"

Azura bowed her head. "We should. Goodnight, rider."

"Goodnight."

He rolled over, huddling beside Azura, her fire keeping him warm as it had done for so many nights in the pit. Once Ayr was tucked in and falling asleep, he shifted moving closer to Azura's side. Her warmth enveloped him like a protective shield. The wooden boards of the ranch were broken and splintered, offering minimal coverage from the harsh elements outside. Still, it was still a step up from their previous makeshift shelter considering he at least had a bed.

He kept himself close to her, trying to stay warm. Hopefully tonight, there would be no aftershock and that if Bonnie came searching again, that Azura would be able to keep him safe. As Ayr drifted off to sleep, he thought he heard a noise. He sat up, his eyes darting across the small space that they inhabited. Just as he went to stand, the pain of the aftershock returned.

Ayr groaned as it started to take hold of his arm entirely. This time was different to the last time, however. Rather than just being a pins and needles in his arm, the aftershock was more gripping. It tightened along the entire length of his forearm as though it was in the grip of a giant. The aftershock was testing him more than ever. He groaned internally, doing whatever he could to not wake Azura. The pain kept escalating, shooting up and down his arm. As he tried to flex it and remain silent it worsened and Ayr finally let out a cry of pain.

Azura jolted awake. "What is it, rider? The aftershock?"

Ayr desperately tried to flex his arm, but it retained its rigidity. He tried to move his arm with his left and found the result much the same. The pain was radiating throughout his entire body, and he felt entirely locked up as he felt the pain shooting past his shoulder and into his chest. Azura's calming voice tried to fill Ayr's mind, but was drowned out by the sharpness of the pain.

Rider! Take some of my strength!

Ayr continued to contort for a few more seconds, which felt like a lifetime. Azura's misery echoed in his ears until the pain finally started to subside. Ayr's faculties returned, and he began gasping for air as he lay recovering from the pain.

"Are you ok, rider?"

"That felt... different." Ayr between gasped breaths.

Azura lowered her head in an attempt to comfort him. "It's testing you."

"It's almost like it knows what I'm going through. I can feel it eating away at me."

"That's very convenient. I've never heard a rider describe the after-shock to me like that."

"How long can you stay awake, Azura?"

Azura groaned as she stretched out. "However long you need me to."

"Stay awake tonight. I don't want anything to happen to me."

"As you wish, rider."

Ayr reclined beside Azura, his eyes closed, and his senses attuned to the distant rumble of thunder. Thunderstorms were a common occurrence for Ayr, but after his time in the Catalyst and with only a flimsy shelter to protect them in the ranch, he felt on edge. Azura's touch reached out to him once more, soothing his troubled mind. Ayr reached behind him, his hand brushing against Azura's scales. "Thank you for being with me."

Azura cooed softly. "There's no place I'd rather be."

Ayr's heavy eyelids drooped as he listened to Azura's gentle lullaby, a sweet rumbling that emanated from deep within her chest. The sound of it was like a warm embrace, lulling him into a peaceful slumber. As he was about to drift off, a sudden jolt startled him awake. He strained his ears and heard an unfamiliar noise intruding upon their tranquil space. With a surge of adrenaline, Ayr's eyes flew open to see a mysterious figure looming over him in the dim moonlight.

"I thought you'd be asleep by now!" It was Bonnie. "No matter. You'll still be weak from the aftershock."

Azura!

Ayr's cry for help was stifled by Bonnie as she pounced on top of him, the weight of her body knocking the breath out of his lungs. The reaction was almost instantaneous. Azura reacted instantaneously, rumbling to life and standing protectively over them. Ayr heard a high-pitched squeak coming from above, like that of a frightened mouse, a sound that was coupled with a sharp snarl from Azura. The weight that had been pressing down on him was suddenly gone, leaving only himself and Azura in their roost. He could see Azura's muscles tense over him, ready to defend against any further threats.

"It appears you had a visitor, rider. Do you want me to chase her down?"

"Yes! Quick, she could kill me. Come on!"

With a swift leap, Ayr pushed himself up from his seat and raced after Azura as she dashed out of the ranch. They both had the same destination in mind, and Ayr knew that if Bonnie stayed within the walls of the ranch, he might have a chance to catch her. He descended the makeshift ladder of crates and boxes that he had carefully assembled over the past few weeks.

In the distance, faint flickers of light could be seen from the fires of other recruits still awake in their roosts within the ranch. As Ayr reached the ground, he realised that Bonnie was already too far ahead. He refused to give up. Determined, he bolted after her, his heart pounding with adrenaline. Azura would surely catch Bonnie, but Ayr was determined to close the gap as much as possible. It was not until they were nearing the entrance that Ayr's focus was broken by another noise, causing him to momentarily lose track of his surroundings.

"Stop!"

A shadowy figure emerged from the dark recesses of the ranch, just as Bonnie was about to make her exit. With a swift movement, the figure thrust out their arm, forcefully knocking Bonnie off her feet. She landed on her back with a jarring thud, the air knocked out of her lungs.

The figure loomed over Bonnie and delivered a cruel kick, sending her sprawling back into the dirt. Ayr chuckled at the sight of the Bonnie hitting the floor as he ran towards the scene. As he drew closer, he could make out the features of the figure. She was all too familiar to him. Elanor.

"Just what do you think you're doing here, Bonnie? Zenender's Ranch is for new recruits."

"I came to visit one of them! That is my right, isn't it?"

"Didn't you just listen to a word I said? New recruits only." Elanor looked up at Ayr and winked. "Thanks Ashbourne. Knew you'd be useful."

"Wait! What?! Ugh!" Bonnie was abhorred. "I laid with an Ashbourne! Why didn't you tell me that was his name!"

The corners of Elanor's lips curled. "More than what you bargained for? Maybe you should do some research first, rather than just going for someone who has the aftershock coursing through their veins."

"Let me go!" Bonnie struggled against the strength of Elanor's boot weighing down upon her chest. "You can't hold me here! Let me go!"

"I think I can. Either you stay here with me in silence or if you decide to flee, Evor is waiting outside. He will not hesitate to swallow you whole."

Bonnie whimpered. "But you can't! I've done nothing wrong?"

"Considering that you've engaged in activities with my student, I dare say it is well within my jurisdiction to decide what is right and wrong when it comes to him."

With a hasty motion, Elanor jerked her boot away from Bonnie's chest. She stood up and without a word, darted towards the open door. Her movements were quick and fluid, like a wild animal escaping its captors. Elanor watched with folded arms as Bonnie disappeared into the night. She let out an amused laugh at the girl's reckless nature. Ayr heard a snapping of a giant jaw from somewhere above. He saw the shadow of Evor moving, and Bonnie had vanished into the darkness in a split second, leaving only the echo of her footsteps behind. The shadowy figure of Evor emerged from the inky blackness outside, his head laying on the ground just inside the doorway. His long snout extended into the ranch, twitching.

"How did she taste, Evor?"

Evor grunted and snapped his jaws together. "Hollow. It's almost as if I ate nothing."

Elanor narrowed her eyes. "I don't think this is the last we've seen of Bonnie. You'd best keep watch, Ashbourne."

"Why? She got eaten, didn't she?"

"Not if she was a witch."

Ayr frowned at Elanor. "A witch? I thought they were extinct within the Commonwealth?"

"It would appear not."

"I don't want her coming back. I'll be sleeping with my sword."

"You should have been anyway. I'm glad you lied to me about the aftershock because without you I would not have caught her. I'm surprised we didn't think about this sooner. But with that little vanishing act, I'll need to report her to the other masters."

"Have you had a recruit lie to you about the aftershock recently?"

Even in the shadow created by the fire light, Ayr could see Elanor scowling at him. "No. But now that Bonnie's been flushed out, there should be less threat to other recruits."

"So, what now? Am I going to come back and train with you?"

"Are you going to lie to me again? I can't train someone that I can't trust."

"Why did you take so long to come back to me? I don't want to train under someone that will cast me aside."

Elanor scowled at him again. "You weren't cast aside. You did yourself a great disservice the last time we stood in the Obelisk. If you weren't an Ashbourne, I would have thrown you out by now."

"I thought that would be grounds for me to get removed."

"Dalton wasn't the only Ashbourne to come through the Seminary. Your uncle, the Overlord, has taken an apparent interest in your training."

"Anton? He hasn't seen me since I was a child."

"He still takes an interest in you. It's now within my best interests to make sure you succeed. I'll ask you again, Ashbourne. Are you going to lie to me again?"

Ayr shook his head. "I want us to have a good relationship. One between master and student."

"Good. Then we can start tomorrow. I want to investigate the aftershock a little more and see what Bonnie was *really* up to. If she was sneaking around here, laying a curse on all of the new recruits, then I want to know. We'd find some dead in the ranch with their blood drained from their corpses."

"That doesn't sound like a witch to me, are you sure she's not something more nefarious?"

Elanor shrugged. "I don't care. Next time I will get Evor to shower her in flames."

"That sounds like a great plan. But if you don't have the after-shock, how are you going to lure her out?"

"That's for me to figure out, Ashbourne." Elanor clenched at her wrist and flexed her hand as if to pump blood to her arm. "I've been aftershock free for quite some time now."

"I could help."

Elanor shook her head with displeasure. "No, you've done enough. Now get some rest. We will watch over you tonight. Tomorrow, we'll begin your next phase of training in earnest."

TWENTY-ONE

Weeks passed in a blur of relentless training. Elanor proved herself the more skilled warrior time and time again. She pushed Ayr to his limits each day, leaving him with numerous cuts and bruises that throbbed with pain. Each night, Azura's gentle touch and healing magic eased his suffering. But even her powerful abilities were unable to take away the constant ache that seeped into his bones.

As they lay together in their shared room, Ayr could see that Azura's body bore as many bruises as his. Evor's training was just as hard as Elanor's. She claimed it was for her own betterment, but Ayr could see the toll it took on her each day. Despite the physical and emotional challenges, they continued to support each other, knowing that this gruelling training would ultimately prepare them for whatever dangers lay ahead in their journey towards becoming a proper rider and dragon themselves.

Despite her small stature for a dragon, Azura was still rapidly growing. In just three short weeks, she had increased her size by a third, making the roost they shared feel increasingly cramped. Ayr could feel the tightness of the room pressing in on them, and he yearned for Elanor to broach the subject of finding them a more suitable home.

As he sat sharpening his sword, beads of sweat formed on his forehead from the intense sparring session he had just finished with Elanor. The sound of metal against stone echoed through the quiet ranch, a constant reminder of their constant need for readiness in this uncertain world.

Despite swinging his blade with all his might, Ayr's best attacks proved useless against her guarded defences. He knew he would need a new sword soon, one that could withstand the strength and ferocity of his opponent's blows. Perhaps the Commonwealth would be able to provide him with a suitable replacement.

With each swipe of his dulled sword, Ayr could feel his frustration grow. The sound of powerful wingbeats caught his attention, and he stood up just in time to see Azura swoop down into the ranch, gracefully landing before him. In her talons was a freshly killed deer.

She pinned the deer to the floor and using one talon, parted the deer with one of its hindlegs. Azura picked the leg up and then she gently deposited into Ayr's outstretched hands. As he thanked her with a grateful smile, Ayr marvelled at her efforts. Ayr held the deer leg out, as had become one of their traditions. Moments later the deer leg was cooked and Azura was busy devouring the rest of the carcass.

Ayr smiled at her. "Do you ever get tired of this?"

"As long as you are happy as my rider, I don't care for too much. I think you've discovered that dragons are a little more resilient than humans."

Ayr scoffed as he took a bite from his deer leg. "You're not wrong about that. What do you think our masters have in store for us today?"

"More of the same. We are still learning what it means to be a dragon and rider."

"You say that, but you're getting far too big for this place. I barely have room to move anymore."

"It's a good problem to have. Would you prefer that I am still but a hatchling, unable to defend you? I can feel myself growing to my near full potential."

Ayr smiled up at her. "I can't wait to see that."

"I won't be as large as Evor."

"I don't see how that will be a problem. I've never been the biggest either."

"Are you nearly finished? I dare say that Elanor and Evor are waiting for us."

Ayr tore into the succulent deer leg, juices dripping down his fingers as he devoured it with frightening speed. His stomach growled loudly, reminding him of the weeks spent surviving on meagre rations from the Obelisk and scraps provided by Elanor. Despite being well-fed now, his first meal of the day was always a primal experience, reminiscent of a rabid dog ravaging its prey.

"Just, rider."

Azura nodded at him and stood up, her long legs unfolding gracefully beneath her. She towered over Ayr, smiling down at him. Ayr had to jump in order to climb onto her back, even with her neck being lowered to the ground. The muscles on Azura's sleek body rippled under his touch as he settled onto her; their bond was palpable even before they took flight.

The small ranch room could not contain them any longer. With a burst of energy Azura launched them into the sky. Ayr quickly retrieved his mask from his pocket, pulling it over his face as Azura soared higher. He felt the rush of wind against his skin, his heart racing with exhilaration as they left the ground behind. Any time he got to spend in the air with Azura was always time that he relished.

Azura's back was bare, the old saddle having been outgrown weeks ago. It now hung at the leatherworker's, being outfitted with new straps to accommodate Azura's rapid growth. Ayr could sense her eagerness and impatience through their bond as they flew together, but he knew she would not push him beyond his limits. Since the saddle had been taken away for alterations, Azura had been flying at a more leisurely pace, constantly checking in with Ayr to make sure he was comfortable.

This was just another day in their routine. As they flew over the horizon, Ayr could see the familiar silhouette of Evor drawing closer. Without hesitation, Azura began to slow down as she sensed the presence of their mentors approaching. Evor drew nearer and slowed down as well. Elanor waved at them when they drew level with each other, both dragons beating their wings slowly to maintain their elevation.

"Good morning, Ashbourne! I see you're up early."

"Why wait, Elanor? You said there would be lots to do."

"You're correct. Glad you chose not to waste time. Follow us."

Ayr found himself slipping and Azura paused for long enough to ensure that he had enough time to regain his balance. Once Ayr was safely on her back once again, Azura darted through the sky in the pursuit of Evor. Just being near him made Azura happier. Ayr could feel every sense of feeling radiating through her body. The emotions flowed into him as well and Ayr could not take his mind off Elanor.

The figure of Elanor was mostly hidden, her petite frame obscured by the formidable bulk of Evor. Azura increased her speed, easily catching up to Evor and flying alongside him. As they flew, Evor's massive head turned, and his jaws opened wide as a small bird darted in front of him. In a blink, Ayr watched as the bird disappeared into Evor's mouth, swallowed whole in one swift motion. Ayr chuckled at this display, having grown accustomed to seeing Azura do the same with smaller creatures in an instant. The scene was both awe-inspiring and slightly unsettling as the group continued their flight through the sky.

The dragons soon came into land in the Obelisk. Azura took her time, landing softly behind Evor. They were near what Ayr had begun to call the sparring room, although Elanor was yet to share its name. Elanor was the first rider to dismount. She removed her mask and slid down from Evor. Ayr did the same and met her between the two dragons.

"So, what have you got in store for me today?"

"Sword!"

In a swift, fluid motion, she unsheathed her sword and Ayr quickly followed suit. The past few weeks of training with Elanor had strengthened him immensely. Her relentless physical trials pushed him to his limits and beyond. When Ayr had first arrived, he was not unskilled in combat, but Elanor's prowess was on another level entirely. Each strike from her carried the full force of Evor behind it, but now Ayr was able to withstand her blows with more ease. He clenched his jaw as their blades met in a resounding clash that echoed through the training room.

With a grunt of her own, Elanor withdrew from him and smiled. "Good, you've improved. If I'd launched at you like that a few days ago, you still would have buckled."

"I haven't had a choice. Azura makes me stronger."

Elanor smiled again. "Let's see if that holds true."

She swung at him again, and this time, Ayr was even more prepared. Rather than shrinking away from her strike, Ayr stepped into it, going on the offensive. Now it was Elanor's turn to struggle against him. She moved away as Ayr swung his sword around again. If Elanor had not managed to get her blade up in time, it would have cleaved her head in two. The dance between them had truly commenced.

The last few weeks had given Ayr all the tools he needed to defeat Elanor. She wielded her sword in her right hand, much like him. Her power and speed exceeded any opponent he had fought before as a result of her bond with Evor. If he cheated Elanor, there would be consequences. They danced around one another, Ayr using his half sword in both hands. The slightly longer hilt allowed him to wield it like a great sword with none of the drawbacks.

Elanor flicked her blade up at him, hoping to catch him off guard. Ayr wasn't able to reverse his grip in time to bring his guard down. Elanor's steel grazed off his hilt, just as it struck his forearm. Ayr hissed and took a step backwards. There was no time for him to lose focus on the wound. It was glancing and nothing more. Already, Ayr could feel the hot blood trickling down towards his elbow, but he still had full use of his arm.

He swung again, wanting nothing more than to give Elanor one of her own back. She was due. Using his sword's longer reach, Ayr swung wildly. One uppercut was followed by a fast overhand strike. Both were blocked and Elanor attacked him again. Ayr managed to quickly cover himself ensuring that his own sword was a wall against Elanor's.

"Hmm." Elanor nodded. She took a step back and lowered her sword. Ayr paused, expecting another attack, but none came. "You're improving. It's slow, but you're already picking up what we expect of riders. I'm finally going to file your paperwork. Your connection with Azura proves that you're ready for the next phase of your training."

"I'm going to move into here? After the last few weeks?"

"You need to relax, Ashbourne. Most recruits are still months behind where you have progressed to at this stage."

"I want to be the fastest to become a fully-fledged rider."

"I like your ambition. But you could just tell me that you're sick of me if you want."

"I'm not sick of you. Our dragons are promised to each other. I feel like even if I were to leave the Commonwealth that I'd still be drawn back here because of Azura."

"She is a special dragon. And not just to me."

Ayr grinned as he agreed. "She certainly is."

You're too kind. Azura had been listening. She stood over them, her neck swaying over them like a tall tree. *You should be grateful of the invitation. Not every rider makes it to the Obelisk to live amongst those that have passed the trials.*

Ayr bowed his head. "Thank you. Do you have any further lessons for me today?"

"No. I have a room in mind for you. You two should come with me."

"What about Evor?"

"Oh, there's more to the Obelisk that you haven't seen yet, Ashbourne. Do you realise just how big this place is?"

"No, I've only seen what you've showed me."

"Riders are at their best when they have their dragons with them. The only dragon that I've seen that can't fit inside the Obelisk is Gorgon. Only he or an elder dragon wouldn't fit, but there's a very good reason for that."

Ayr was unfamiliar with the term. "Elder dragons? They sound wise, why wouldn't you want them nearby?"

There was a loud chortling that encompassed the air around him. Ayr looked up at Evor who was spluttering in a coughing fit. "Elder dragons are the furthest thing from wise, Ashbourne. 'Elder' is a name used for the rabid beasts that refused Chilijo. They came up with it to give themselves a sense of importance. They roam the world unchecked and can grow to enormous sizes. Those that are hundreds, if not thousands of years old can outgrow Gorgon. They are not to be trifled with, even by experienced dragons and their riders."

"So, what, are they hunted by the Obelisk or the Commonwealth. I've never heard of them before."

Evor stared down at him. "They are hunted. We don't advertise the fact that rogue dragons are outside of our control. Elanor and I have personally slain one with the help of a dozen other riders. They are savages."

"And what's Gorgon? What do you classify him as?"

"Gorgon is still a lesser dragon."

Ayr snorted and laughed. "I don't think there's anything lesser about him."

Elanor shrugged casually. "Yet he still had a rider once, thousands of years ago. A man known as Tal'davin in the first great war."

"And he now just spends his days hiding under the Catalyst, living a life to scare the new recruits to the Seminary?"

Elanor chuckled. "You're quite right. Now, if you'd follow me, Ashbourne, I'll show you to your quarters."

Elanor started to walk away, and Ayr quickly followed her. "So, what are the other differences with the elder dragons and lesser dragons?"

"Since they are not shackled to riders, elder dragons are considerably more powerful with almost no restrictions to what they can do."

Elanor led him deeper into the Obelisk, the corridors here both wide and tall enough to comfortably fit Evor side by side. Whilst Evor was one of the largest dragons that Ayr had seen, there was still more than ample space between his head and the ceiling, implying that there were bigger dragons that walked these halls as well. Ayr felt engulfed, and as Elanor took another right, he found himself looking down a dead end. It was clear that their destination was along here.

A fierce, red dragon's head emerged from one of the rooms near the far end of the corridor, its sharp, golden eyes scanning the surroundings. Its powerful, scaled body stood tall and proud, towering in between the heights both Evor and Azura. On its back sat a woman with fiery strawberry hair pulled back into a high ponytail, her Commonwealth uniform pristine and pressed. She wore a confident smile as Elanor and Ayr approached, her intense gaze meeting theirs with determination and strength. The air around them buzzed with excitement and anticipation, the dragon's hot breath mingling with the scent of leather and smoke.

"Elanor, it's good to see you again! Who's this?"

Elanor smiled warmly at her in response. "Victoria, this is Ayr. He is my new student."

Victoria dipped into a shallow curtsy and her dragon dipped its head as well. "Well, it's always nice to meet a student of Elanor's. I'm sure she picked extremely well. This is Baramir."

"Pleasure." Baramir's voice was almost as deep and rolling as Evor's.

"So, I take it this was the new neighbour you were telling me about? Shame about the last name though. It's been awfully quiet here without the two of you."

Ayr raised an eyebrow. "The two of you?"

"Yes, this used to be my old room." Elanor smiled at Ayr before turning back to Victoria. "I'm sure Ayr and Azura will make it up to you,"

"Azura?" Victoria's eyes flicked to her, and a wave of pride washed over her face. "It's so good to see you growing."

"It is a relief to me as well, I can assure you."

"Well, Baramir and I had best be on our way. We've got the time trials to complete today. Araxis wants to see if we can complete the course in under a minute."

"Under a minute? That's a tall order! But you can do it, Victoria!"

"Thanks." Victoria bowed her head and smiled. "Enjoy your stay here, Ayr. I hope you and Azura are happy together."

Azura wagged her tail. "We are. Best of luck with your trial."

With a swift and graceful stride, Victoria and Baramir glided past Ayr and Azura, disappearing down the dimly lit corridor. Elanor lingered for a moment before stopping at the closed door, her gaze following the fading sound of their footsteps. The air seemed to still in their absence, leaving only a faint trace of their presence behind.

"Well, here we are."

Ayr glanced up and down at the door. "This is where we're going to be stationed now?"

Elanor nodded. "Yes. If you have any problems, I will be directly above you."

"There's no getting away from you then?"

Elanor smiled at him. "No, there will not be. Anything in this room is also for you. The last owner was very generous."

"Way to toot your own trumpet."

With a gentle push, Elanor pushed open the heavy wooden door. The rusty hinges groaned in protest as the door reluctantly gave way to reveal a vast and spacious room beyond. A stale, musty scent greeted them as they stepped inside, mingling with the faint smell of old wood and forgotten memories. The floor was covered in polished tiles, which looked worn down from years of use. Despite its age, the room still held an air of grandeur, capable of housing even the largest of creatures. Azura would have no problem finding comfort in these walls.

The room was dominated by a deep pit, its floor covered in a thick layer of golden straw. It seemed to stretch for miles, easily able to accommodate the lithe form of Evor and still have ample space left over. Azura's eyes sparkled with glee as she darted towards the pit and pushed open the opposite door with all her might. With a burst of energy, she leapt into the air and landed gracefully in the centre of the straw, sending it swirling in every direction like a flurry of glittering confetti. Her laughter echoed through the room, filling it with joy and light.

Ayr was still taking in the rest of what would be his and her new quarters, feeling the pure joy of Azura radiating through his entire body. She dove in and out of the straw like a child, happy to be playing in sand at the beach. Azura continued to frolic for a while longer before she paused and put her head up.

"Thank you, Elanor."

Ayr agreed with her. "Yes, thank you, Elanor."

"Don't worry about it. You're making progress. Have the rest of the day off getting comfortable. Head to the mess hall when you're hungry and they'll serve you. Tomorrow, I'll give you more lessons."

"How many more lessons do we have to go?"

"Has your magic developed properly yet?" Ayr knew that Elanor knew the answer.

She cast her gaze down her nose at him and raised an eyebrow.

"I didn't think so. I'll see you tomorrow, Ashbourne."

TWENTY-TWO

yr and Azura leisurely explored their new quarters, taking in the sights and sounds with wonder and awe. The room was expansive - far bigger than Ayr could have ever imagined within the confines of the Obelisk. Azura had not moved often from the comfortable bed of straw that was at her disposal. She stretched out like a cat, her spiked tail curling in the air behind her.

"Are you enjoying yourself?"

"Very much so, rider. Does it look like I am?" Azura laughed gently. "Whilst I am a dragon, and I'm not estranged to rough conditions like what we had in the pit and during the Catalyst, this is where I am most happy. Inside this room, we don't have to worry about anything, as long as you lock the door."

"Why, who's going to disturb us if I don't? I can't imagine Bonnie would be a threat anymore. Do other riders move about much here?"

"Yes, riders will constantly move around in the halls here. There are strange things that we will need to overcome in this place."

"Like what?"

"Despite the dragon's best efforts, along with the riders, there are small creatures that we can't get rid of. They are small and are incredibly clever. They don't come out if someone is looking in their direction."

Azura continued to bask in the warmth of the sun filtering through the windows as Ayr continued to inspect the room. A thick pipe, resembling a chimney, caught Ayr's attention. While it was large enough for Azura to stick her entire head into it, this chimney was designed with much larger dragons in mind, like Evor, who resided here before them. Ayr walked over to the chimney and inspected it. Instead of smoke and ash billowing from its opening, there was a large button beside it which was large enough to have a dragon hit it with their tail or to have it pushed in with a claw.

Curious, Ayr stretched out his hand and pushed the button in with his fist. Nothing happened straight away. As he tried to press the button again, Ayr heard a clanking noise from somewhere behind the metal wall of the chimney. A few seconds passed and more clanking filled his ears. Then out from the right-hand side of the chimney, a large deer carcass appeared. It was already prepared with even some of its fur removed. It was clear that someone somewhere was preparing the carcasses before sending them down what could only be a conveyor belt. This was a place for the dragons to be fed without needing to leave the Obelisk.

Ayr jumped up with excitement. "Azura! Look at this!"

"Yes, that comes straight from the kitchens."

"Are you going to come and eat then?"

"I am hungry. And I suppose you need to make use of the oven."

Ayr smiled and stepped back from the chimney, allowing Azura to put her head in through it and grab the carcass out. She prepared the deer quickly and began to eat. With Azura being fed and happy, Ayr had nothing else to do. He had explored the giant room enough and for the first time in what seemed like years, was completely comfortable and warm.

One edge of the room housed enormous windows that would allow Azura to come and go as she chose. Ayr tended to his sword, using a whetstone that was on the workbench in the room. He sat in the leather high back chair beside the straw pit that Azura spread out in. This was the first time he had seen her like this.

Ayr watched her for a short while before he leant back in the chair. Ayr carried on with the whetstone, sliding it methodically from hilt to tip in a repetitive, metallic song. The afternoon sun finally started to filter in through the windows and Ayr was finished with his sword. He'd returned the sword back to its former glory. Ayr inspected the sword, holding it up to the light, ensuring that there were no markings on the blade. Satisfied, he returned the sword to its sheath and settled back into the chair.

Ayr closed his eyes and savoured the peacefulness of the moment with Azura. The soft rustling of straw beneath them was the only sound in the large well-lit room. Azura lay still beside him, her breathing slow and steady. Every so often, she would shift and roll over, but remained in a state of quietude. Ayr's eyes grew heavy as he began to drift into slumber, but just as he felt himself slipping away, a loud knock jolted him awake. He sat up quickly, his heart pounding in his chest. Azura stirred lazily next to him, her eyes slowly turning towards the source of the noise - the door.

"I don't imagine that's Elanor. Evor is nowhere near us."

"Who else would it be?"

Azura slowly rose to her feet. "I'll be right behind you, rider. I can't open that door unless I want to break it."

Ayr rose to his feet as well, drawing his sword from its sheath. Ayr had taken his boots off; his bare feet glided across the tiles in silence. As he reached the door, another knock came from it. Ayr glanced back at Azura who was standing over him and nodded. With another breath, Ayr pushed the door open. He half expected to see another dragon staring back at him - it was only Elanor.

"Good evening, Ashbourne." Elanor's eyes glanced over his sword that was pointed at her throat. "I'd put that away before you take someone's eye out."

Ayr lowered his sword. "You can never be too careful. Azura was just telling me about the creatures that roam these halls at night."

"Ah, of course." Elanor smiled at him. "You can't plan for them. Don't worry about it. There are more pressing matters at hand. Evor is calling you, Azura?"

"I can sense him."

"Go to him. I have another lesson for Ashbourne tonight."

Azura bowed her head slowly. "As you wish, Lady Sunfire." She exited the room, stepping over both Ayr and Elanor before slinking out the door.

"Another one? I thought you said to rest."

Elanor nodded. "I did. I hope you've eaten."

"I went exploring and sharpened my sword. What else was I supposed to do?"

"Rest and eat, Ashbourne. Follow the instructions I give you. I hope you didn't think you were getting off that easily. I have more magic to teach you. I'm not having my student become lacking in that department. Our magic paired with our dragon's strength is what ensures that we can police the world safely. It is our advantage over most other things."

Elanor slowly freed her hands from behind her back, revealing a massive leather-bound book. The book was so large that she had to hold it with both hands, cradling it like a precious treasure. Its cover was worn and creased, evidence of its age and importance. She ran her fingers over the embossed blank space where the title should have been, savouring the texture and weight of the ancient tome in her grasp.

"I've got a present for you."

Ayr's fingers trembled slightly as he stepped forward, his hand reaching out to touch the cover of the book. The soft leather beneath his fingertips felt warm and inviting, almost as if it were alive. He ran his thumb along the embossed blank space, studying the intricate details with a curious gaze.

"It's for you. You're not going to be able to remember every bit of magic I teach you straight away."

"So, I have to carry around this tome?"

Elanor retracted and pouted at him. "If you don't want it, I can take it back."

"No, it looks amazing. Thank you, Elanor."

The book slipped from Elanor's hands as if it had a mind of its own, falling into Ayr's grasp with an almost audible thud. He turned it over, his fingers tracing the edges of the worn cover. With curiosity piqued, he began to flip through the pages, only to find them all blank.

At first, he thought it must have been intentionally left that way, but as he searched further, not a single word or illustration appeared. Ayr's expression shifted into a perplexed look as he raised his gaze to meet Elanor's, who seemed to know exactly what he was thinking before he even asked the question. Azura was meant to be the one that he was bonded to, not Elanor.

"It's a blank tome for you to start recording any magic you encounter or use in. Every rider gets one. You underestimate how hard magic is when you're first starting out."

"I set a record in bonding with Azura. What's to say I can't master magic quickly? The bond that a rider has with their dragon will have some effect on the magic?"

"It does. I am yet to master my magic in the years that I've been with Evor."

"Did my father ever get this far?"

Elanor shook her head. "He was already gone by this point."

"Ok, so where do we begin?"

"I have an idea. Come with me."

With confident strides, Elanor passed by Ayr and approached the straw bed where Azura had rested just moments ago. Her eyes scanned the area, taking in the open hole where Azura had retrieved her food from. A glimmer of curiosity sparked in her gaze as she leaned forward to inspect the opening before pressing the button. Slowly but surely, the track behind the wall began to whirl and a fresh carcass emerged, its scent filling the air with a mix of blood and raw meat.

"You can read and write I assume? I'm sure Dalton would have taught you that much."

"I'm not uneducated. What are you going to show me?"

"Do you remember the spell I used to make the fire in the cave?"

Ayr shook his head in response. "I know you created a fire, but if you asked me to recreate it, I wouldn't have a clue."

"Good thing we're covering this first then. Did you manage to find the quills in here?"

"Yes, I'm not an idiot." Ayr rolled his eyes.

"Never said you were. Go get one, quickly."

With a determined stride, Ayr made his way to the desk at the corner of the room. He opened the top drawer and sifted through it until he found a sturdy quill with its feathers still intact. Next to it was a small tub of ink, which he also retrieved before making his way back to Elanor's side. The rich, dark liquid sloshed gently against the sides of the container as he walked back to Elanor.

"What am I learning about today?"

"You're going to create fire. It's a simple enough spell, one that doesn't take a whole lot of energy to do. Magic is complicated, no matter how you go about it. You will need to devise something that works for you."

Ayr frowned as he glanced down at the quill in his hand. "I thought you were supposed to be teaching me."

"It's not an exact science. You'll also learn shortcuts as you go through and are able to control your will even more. I haven't done this in a while, so please, bear with me. All that matters when you're first starting out is your technique. I don't need you trying to over complicate things and having you blow yourself up."

"That wasn't my goal anyway."

"Watch and you might learn something."

Elanor's eyes were fixed on the carcass in front of her, an intense concentration etched onto her features. She sucked in a deep breath of air, expanding her chest and lifting herself up to her full height. She exhaled and placed her hands down over the metal plate nestled in the hole.

Ayr stood by, watching every movement of Elanor's agile wrists as she flicked them forward with precision and purpose. It took longer than the first time she had done it back in the pit. As sparks began to fly, Elanor pulled her hands away, observing as they danced and crackled against the carcass. She allowed them to ignite for a few seconds before waving her hand over the flames, controlling their intensity until they were extinguished completely.

"It's easy enough if you have an ounce of focus."

"Can I try?"

Elanor smiled at him. "Do you remember the motions?"

"Yes." He was focused on the task at hand.

"Here, Ashbourne, let me help you."

She placed her hand over Ayr's, almost touching skin on skin. A shiver ran down Ayr's spine and he tried to readjust. He did not want to give into her. Ayr looked into her eyes as Azura crept into his mind.

Rider! Are you okay? Evor just told me that you're going to perform some magic. Do you need assistance?

Ayr breathed an audible sigh of relief, grateful for the distraction. His shudder was enough for Elanor's hand to slip off his.

Yes. I need your power.

It is yours to take, Ayr. Do you need my guidance?

Watch me.

With a grimace, Ayr leaned closer to the carcass, his nostrils filled with the pungent stench of raw meat. The flesh was slick and cold under his fingers, and he wondered how long it had been dead. Azura, always curious and probing, lingered in his mind as he prepared to cast his spell. Her power surged through him, tingling at the tips of his fingers as he gathered his energy for the invocation. Despite the smell and discomfort, Ayr's determination remained unwavering. He would master this spell and prove himself worthy of Elanor's approval.

With a focused mind, Ayr visualized the flames that Elanor had created just moments before. He could feel Azura's energy aiding his will as he summoned the sparks into existence. Mimicking Elanor's hand movements, Ayr watched as the sparks grew and danced in front of him.

Excitement bubbled up inside him as Elanor let out a cheerful chirp, egging him on. With a surge of determination, Ayr willed the sparks to transform into brilliant flames within a blink of an eye. They shot up higher than Elanor's had, fuelled by his intentions. As they grew, Ayr urged them to engulf the dead meat in their fiery embrace. With a simple wave of his hand, Ayr dismissed the flames and turned to give Elanor a triumphant smirk, revelling in his newfound power.

"So, what did you think? How did I do?"

Elanor scoffed. "How do you think you did? I have never seen someone be able to do that so quickly and efficiently. Beginner's luck, Ashbourne. Show me again."

"Why have I got to show you again? I just proved that I could do it, didn't I?"

"I can't go back to the masters with just one piece of evidence. The Overlord in particular will be most curious. How did you feel after your first piece of magic?"

"Accomplished." Ayr bowed his head to stare at where the flames he had summoned had been. "I feel like I could take on the world."

Elanor gestured with her hand towards the carcass. "Show me then. If you feel like you can handle it, show me more power then."

"More power?"

Elanor nodded. "If you're so confident. I can't remember the last proficient magic user we had here. I told you Azura is a special dragon."

"I believe it more and more every day. She means more to me than anything else in the world."

Elanor gestured towards where the carcass lay, waiting for him to do something to it. Ayr looked back down to where he would cast his spell next. He could not look Elanor in the eyes. If only the source of his power was only coming from Azura, then he might have been able to be honest with her. He refocused on his magic, determined to make the spell grander than the last had been.

TWENTY-THREE

As the days passed and Ayr continued his training with Azura, he found himself growing more confident in both her powers and his own abilities. Elanor would often give them space to work on their skills, occasionally setting up a designated meeting spot for them to reconvene. As a newcomer to the Obelisk, Ayr still struggled to find his way through the intricate pathways and secret passages. But with Azura's keen senses and knowledge of the place, she acted as his guiding light amidst the labyrinth of halls and chambers. After living here for over three decades, she knew every twist and turn like the back of her hand.

What she could not help him with were the constant glares and stares that he would receive from his fellow riders. Word had spread amongst them by now that an Ashbourne was a rider. And not just any Ashbourne, Ayr Ashbourne, the son of Dalton. The mad rider who had led a rebellion against the Commonwealth. The glares quickly picked up steam, becoming verbal insults. They were nothing more than small jabs as riders passed him in the hallways.

"You're going to die here, Ashbourne!"

"Your father will pay for what he did to us!"

Unable to do anything without being reprimanded, Ayr kept his head down as he moved about the Obelisk. Azura did what she could to comfort him, picking up on his sadness the moment an insult was hurled his way. They were frequent to the point where at least once every corridor, someone would hurl one at him. Ayr did his best to ignore them, Azura comforting him as they went.

Just ignore them rider. They don't know you.

I am an Ashbourne, they are right. My father did betray the Commonwealth.

Yet your uncle serves as Overlord. You can choose your own path.

Ayr's stomach growled, a constant reminder of his struggle against his increased metabolism since bonding with Azura. Despite the increase in muscle mass and tone from his time there, he knew it wasn't solely due to a healthy diet and good eating habits. He entered the mess hall once again, accompanied by Azura.

The hall was one of the largest spaces in the upper levels of the Obelisk, spanning from end to end with ample room for even the largest dragons to move freely. As they made their way through, Ayr noticed a dozen riders scattered amongst the strategically placed benches, leaving enough space for dragons to pass without incident. The aroma of freshly cooked food filled the air, tempting Ayr's senses as he searched for a place to sit and eat.

Most of the riders were accompanied by their dragons. Many dragons refused to dine in the mess hall with their riders, often opting for the open skies and the beasts that roamed the plains around the Obelisk as a more suitable feast. Ayr cast his gaze around the mess hall. Most riders averted their gaze, too busy occupied with their full plates in front of them. One rider, however, near the edge of the hall stood up. Ayr recognised him instantly and his heart plummeted in his chest. Owens had finally made it to the Obelisk.

"Ashbourne! I can't believe they let a piece of shit like you in here. Your master hasn't killed you yet?"

"Unfortunately for you, no." Ayr was checking each corner of the room for Owens' dragon. Was this a trap? "I see they finally let you in here though. Does Bersos finally like you enough? I didn't think that worms would be able to bond properly with dragons?"

"Very funny. I don't know what you did to con your dragon. Or did you get special treatment considering your uncle is the Overlord?"

"There's no need for special treatment when your dragon believes in you. Azura and I have a fine connection. One that grows stronger every day."

Owens was getting closer. He had his hand on the hilt of his sword, his face twisted and contorted. "I haven't forgotten what you did to Gable."

"Killing other recruits was allowed as part of the Catalyst. He would have done the same to me in a heartbeat."

With a swift, fluid motion, Owens' sword appeared in his hand, the sharp steel ringing as it slipped out of its leather sheath. All eyes snapped towards the two men. Ayr stood still, his muscles tense and ready for whatever move Owens might make next.

"Fuck you Ashbourne! I'm going to finish what Gable started! You should have been the one to fall from that cliff that night! I'm going to gut you like a fucking fish!"

Rider!

Azura had seen the sword first, but Ayr knew that it was on the way. He was prepared. Owens moved slowly, the pace that his sword moved through the air seemed to be only half of what Elanor's was. Ayr did not bother drawing his sword as he stepped back, allowing Owens' sword to go past his shoulder. Ayr moved in, cutting off the space that Owens had to work with. Owens brought his sword around his body with an overhand strike, but Ayr moved past the strike once again and lashed out with a shallow front kick aimed at Owens shin. Owens tried to block the kick, but only resulted in him stumbling as Ayr's foot connected. His sword hit the floor and Ayr kicked it away.

Owens fell onto his back as Ayr pushed him over. Owens grunted as his head hit the tiles with a meaty smack. Ayr was incensed. He scrambled on top of Owens, keeping his head back. Owens was still out of it, but as he felt the weight on top of him, he started to kick and buck. Ayr did what he could to keep Owens pinned. One fist hit Ayr in the side and he grunted in pain, but continued to push onwards. Ayr stretched one hand out and grabbed Owens' throat.

"Get! Off! Me!" Owens words came out forced. Ayr continued to apply pressure to his windpipe. There was nothing else Ayr wanted more than to feel Owens stop moving beneath him.

Ayr ignored Owens' fists as they continued to strike him in the side. Owens' eyes were beginning to bulge from the downward pressure that Ayr was putting on his neck. He was struggling and Ayr could feel his neck straining against his hands. Another strike hit Ayr and he shifted his weight, bringing his knees up to try and crush Owens' arms. He missed and received an elbow into his quad for his trouble.

"Rider! What the fuck are you doing?"

Ayr had no time to register the voice behind him before a violent force yanked his head back. It felt like he was being lifted into the air by a giant hand, helpless and small. He was flung away from Owens and hit the ground with sudden force. Ayr tried quickly to regain his footing but was met with a black boot, kicking him in the stomach. Ayr's only option was to recoil as he looked up at the one who had booted him. The long pant covered leg ran up to a familiar face, her hair falling around her shoulders as she looked down at him with disgust. Ayr could see the rage of Evor radiating through Elanor.

"Ashbourne! I should have known it was you! What the fuck do you think you're doing?"

Ayr's body was still trembling with the shock of what had just happened. Adrenaline surged through his veins, making him feel almost invincible. But even as he tried to push himself up from the ground,

Elanor's boot pressed firmly against his chest, keeping him down. His gaze locked onto Owens, who was now sitting up slowly and rubbing at his neck and throat.

"Ashbourne!"

"What!"

"Get up!"

Elanor removed her boot from his chest, and Ayr rose to his feet, defeated.

"You're a moron! On today of *all* days, you decide to brawl with another rider in the mess hall. What have you got to say for yourself?"

"I wish I could have had fifteen more seconds to finish the job."

"Ha! That sounds like Dalton!" An unfamiliar voice rang across the mess hall.

Ayr turned his head and saw two heavyset men marching down the mess hall towards him. Ayr recognised the first as Major Kaladin, the man who had *welcomed* him into the Obelisk. The equally broad purple dragon, Gundrag walking behind him was also another giveaway as to who he was. The man beside him, however, was a mystery.

He stood at the same height as Kaladin, his presence just as imposing. There was no dragon behind him, yet he seemed to fill the room. The man was adorned in opulent red robes that draped his entire figure, hinting at the wealth and power he possessed. Like Kaladin, his face was hidden beneath a thick beard, but what was visible was heavily marked by scars, a testament to the battles he had faced. Underneath the beard, Ayr could make out an all too familiar face. It was more worn and ragged, but Ayr recognised it as Dalton's. There was a difference of about a decade between Dalton and this man, but that decade made him all the more dangerous. Tales of his escapades were rife throughout the Commonwealth and beyond.

"Hello, uncle."

The piercing yellow eye of Anton Ashbourne gleamed fiercely, seemingly independent from his calm blue one, as he towered over Ayr. Despite Ayr's already impressive height, Anton easily stood a head taller, and his broad shoulders and muscular frame made Ayr feel like he was being pressed against a wall. The weight of Anton's presence loomed over him, making Ayr suddenly aware of his own smallness in comparison.

"Uncle?" Anton scoffed. "That's something you've never called me, Ayr."

"I've come to the Seminary to become a rider."

Anton scoffed again, shaking his head. "Under the direction of Dalton, no doubt."

"Uncle, I came to serve."

Anton placed his hands on his hips and let out a hearty laugh. "And I rode Chilijo in the first war! Lady Sunfire, you've certainly got an entertaining one on your hands. How did he pass the Bonding?"

Elanor shrugged with a neutral expression. "Azura chose him. Nobody else had any say in it."

"Hmm. This is the dragon that couldn't choose a rider for thirty years. I wouldn't put any faith into her judgement."

"She's a good dragon. I would trust her judgement before most others here. That sounds to me like Drementhol is speaking through your lips."

Anton nodded and his voice deepened. "He is. Drementhol never leaves me."

"Does he roost on the Obelisk?"

"He does. He's not here to seek quarrel with Azura. Nor am I here to seek quarrel with my *nephew*."

"That's something I wish that most of the other riders had in common with you, my Lord. Has this visit sated your curiosity?"

"It has. If the boy has bonded with the unbonded, then perhaps you were right to allow his continuation in the Seminary."

Elanor bowed her head. "Thank you, my Lord. I assume that you will now conduct your business here."

"Yes. Kaladin, take me to the Lord Chairman's chambers. It is most unfortunate with what happened to Lord Cuthbert."

"It is indeed sir. Dead in the middle of the night. So tragic for such a young rider to be elevated to such a position. Please, come with me." Kaladin bowed his head.

The two men, along with the colossal purple dragon all turned and began walking back in the direction they had come. Anton had only taken a handful of steps when he paused. Slowly, he pivoted on his heel and glared back at Ayr with a fierce intensity. Ayr felt the temperature in the room rise as Anton's angry gaze was fixed upon him.

"Oh, and Lady Sunfire?"

"Yes, Overlord?"

Anton pointed a finger towards Ayr. "Punish him. I won't have the guttershite get away for defiling the mess hall. It is clear that he needs to learn some manners. Feel free to get creative. He's not my son."

Elanor dipped her head again. "Yes, my Lord."

Anton's heavy boots echoed loudly against the stone floors, slowly fading away along with the louder steps of Kaladin and Gundrag. The once lively mess hall fell into a heavy silence as they made their way out of the long room. The air hung thick with tension and anticipation, each person holding their breath as they watched the three figures disappear from sight.

"Get up!" Ayr's attention focused back on Elanor. She stood over him, still unmoving. Azura stood over her shoulder in kind, unwilling to move. "I have half a mind to flog you here in front of everyone, Ashbourne."

"You wouldn't." Ayr groaned. He had not recovered properly from hitting his head.

"You're right, I wouldn't. But that's only because our watcher has found something that you'd ought to see."

Whispers, like a swarm of bees, started to buzz and hum around Ayr. Their voices were hushed and uneasy, filled with an underlying fear. Everyone avoided speaking near Elanor, afraid that she might hear their words. Ayr looked up at her, his eyes wide and clouded with confusion, not understanding the hushed conversations swirling around him. His mind reeled with questions as he tried to piece together what was happening.

"The watcher? Your mother?"

"Yes. That's the only thing that's saved you. I think it's very convenient. I'm somewhat disappointed that Azura didn't stop you."

Azura flicked her tongue out of her head and blinked. "I serve my rider. I too have my own problems with the rider who offended him, Elanor."

Elanor's eyes narrowed. "I hope you haven't corrupted her."

"I can assure you, Elanor, that I am still as pure of heart when Ayr and I met. Whilst my goals are slowly aligning with the rider more day by day, I am still the same dragon."

"Hmm, I hope so. We will need it. Are you coming or not?"

"Yes, give me a moment." Ayr nodded as he tried to push himself off the ground.

She remained standing, not offering Ayr a hand as he stood up. Elanor's unwavering gaze swept around the room, taking in the expressions of the other riders and their dragons.

"What do you want? Get back to your meals!"

There was an uneasy silence around the mess hall as the dozen riders all went back to their meals. Their dragons stood over them like silent sentries, all of them undoubtedly having conversations with each other between dragon and rider. By the time that Ayr was solidly on his feet, Elanor was already making her way out of the hall. Ayr shot one final glance at Owens who looked up at him with distain.

"Fuck you!" Owens' voice was returning to normal.

"Ignore him, Ashbourne."

Ayr wanted to go back and kick him whilst he was down one final time, but under Elanor's instructions, Ayr resisted the temptation. He followed her, with Azura only a few of her larger steps behind him.

I thought you handled that well. That could have been worse.

Been worse? Ayr laughed out loud. *Azura, I almost strangled him to death.*

That is the dragon's true nature coming out in you. You will need to try and control it where possible.

What does that mean?

I'm beginning to think that between your aftershock, magic and now this, that you might not be a normal rider. Riders often only suffer from the aftershock for a little while and those that do aren't affected by the dragon's rage.

Am I sick?

I'm not sure. We will need to investigate. Keep acting like everything is normal. I do not want Elanor becoming suspicious until we have at least been to the library and done some research. Go with Elanor to the observatory. We can make plans to go to the library later.

Elanor cut across their conversation. "Is something wrong? Do the two of you want to share something with me?"

"Nothing is wrong. We were just having a quiet moment between rider and dragon. I'm sure you can understand that, Lady Sunfire."

"That was more than a quiet moment."

Ayr spoke up. "Azura was just congratulating me on a job well done."

He had no time to get any further words out. Elanor spun on her heel, her open palm finding the side of his face. Ayr recoiled from the hit, wondering how she had been so accurate with it.

"I *knew* something was going to happen! I followed Owens today to make sure you two didn't cross paths."

"Why lie?"

"I didn't lie. My mother would still very much like to see us in the observatory. There is something that she has come across, but luckily, I don't believe we have to action it straight away."

"Is this just a precursor? Telling us that something is on the way?"

Elanor nodded. "Yes, it gives us time to prepare. The watchers are considerate like that. I know of some places that have similar systems in place and their watchers didn't give them the warning until the very last minute."

"What happened to them then?"

"They died. The Commonwealth is not willing to follow in their footsteps. Azura, if you wouldn't mind going and visiting Evor, he's waiting outside."

Azura nodded towards Elanor and backed away, turning down one of the last corridors that they had come from. It was the quickest way to the outside.

I will see you shortly, rider.

With Azura fading from his mind, silence filled the Obelisk. Elanor started marching towards the observatory and the sound of her boots were the only thing that occupied Ayr's ears.

Ayr could not contain his curiosity anymore. "What is my uncle doing here?"

"Going about his business, just as you should." Elanor was blunt.

"If the Overlord of the entire Commonwealth is here on official business, it's something worth noting isn't it?"

"If the Overlord is here looking for a council replacement, it isn't good news for anyone."

"Why not? Men die every day, especially in their sleep."

Elanor shook her head. "Not dragon riders. Especially not young dragon riders. Their magic is powerful and affects our bodies. You will learn this in time. Something is amiss, but don't worry about it, Ashbourne. There are far more powerful men than you dealing with it. Now come with me."

TWENTY-FOUR

Ayr trailed behind Elanor through the winding corridors, their boots echoing off the tiles. They eventually reached a familiar pathway that led to the observatory. Unlike last time, when Elanor had slowed down to cautiously approach her mother's domain, she now strode ahead with determination. A sense of unease crept over Ayr as they neared the door to the observatory. Would Elanor's mother still be in the grips of madness, or would she have regained her senses? With a slow and deliberate motion, Elanor pushed open the door to reveal the well-lit interior of the observatory.

A palpable, eerie silence hung in the air of the room. Though it seemed more populated compared to Ayr's previous visit, there were no sudden movements or hurried whispers among the watchers scattered throughout the space. Dozens upon dozens of watchers sat at desks, their heads bowed and quills scratching away at unseen pieces of parchment in front of them.

Their collective concentration gave the impression of a hive mind, all working towards some unknown goal. The only sound was the soft scrape of quills against paper and the occasional whisper of pages turning. A chill ran down Ayr's spine as he took in the scene, feeling like an outsider intruding on some secret society.

One watcher, an elderly gentleman with a bald head came up to them. "Ah, Lady Sunfire. I assume you are here to see your mother?"

"Yes, I am, Alfred. I can't see her anywhere. Where is she?"

Alfred glanced behind him. "That'll be because she is currently on a break. Would you like me to fetch her for you?"

"Yes." Elanor impatiently stamped her foot. "That's why I am here. It was *your* messenger that summoned me. How can you *not* be prepared?"

"Apologies, Lady Sunfire. But you know what your mother is like. She needs all the rest she can get in her old age. Watchers as you know are not the most resilient of people."

"This is very true. Shall I wait here?"

"This is a large premonition. You may want to head to her table."

Ayr watched as Elanor shivered. "A large premonition? What does she have in store for us? Follow me, Ashbourne."

Alfred bowed deeply, his lanky frame nearly touching the ground as he stepped back to give them room. Elanor gracefully led the way into the observatory. The sound of rustling parchment and murmured conversations echoed throughout the room as they passed by rows of desks occupied by greying watchers, their faces illuminated by the warm sunlight coming through the glass. Beyond them, a group of young riders were deep in discussion with their watcher, pouring over a piece of parchment with intense focus.

Elanor marched forward, her footsteps echoing off the tiled floors. She slammed her fist onto an unoccupied desk, causing the parchment on it to rustle and stray inkwells to wobble precariously. A few moments later, Elanor's mother, Grace appeared from a side room deeper within the observatory. Her face lit up with delight at the sight of her daughter's unexpected visit, adding a warm glow to the already well-lit space.

The elderly woman scurried along, her feet shuffling rapidly as she passed by rows of tables, heading towards where Elanor and Ayr were patiently waiting. With a heavy sigh, she finally plopped herself down into the chair at the desk, her frail body nearly collapsing from exhaustion.

"Elanor! I'm glad you came so quickly!"

"What have you got to show me? Does it involve both of us?"

Grace nodded with an unusual eagerness. "It does. I've seen something, and it worries me. You may need more riders to help you through this quest."

"Are you going to tell us or just keep rambling? Every second is paramount to our preparation."

Grace's face contorted into something less than lady-like. "Fine. Here then! Take it!"

With a sudden burst of energy, Grace slammed her hand down on the desk, causing a stained and crinkled piece of parchment to slide across the smooth surface. The yellowed paper was covered in messy handwriting, as if the writer had hurriedly scribbled down their thoughts. It was clear that Grace had written it in a frenzy, her emotions evident in the rushed quill strokes and smudged ink.

"Read it! Read it!"

Elanor raised her hand like she was fending off a fly. "Just wait!" Elanor scanned over the parchment, her mouth opening ever so slightly as she read through it. "You can't be serious..."

Grace peered over the top of her glasses with a blank expression on her face. "I wouldn't have had this premonition if it wasn't true. You will face an elder dragon."

A chill shot down Ayr's spine. "I'm sorry? You mean just, Elanor, don't you?"

"No, both of you will face the elder dragon. That is why you are both here."

"When? Where?"

"I will show you. Take my hand."

With a gentle but determined gesture, Grace extended both of her hands. Ayr took her hand cautiously, mindful not to harm the frail woman with any sudden or forceful movements. As his fingers intertwined with hers, he felt a surprising strength emanating from her grip. Ayr could not have pulled away even if he tried. Grace's eyes rolled back into her head and a flash of light enveloped them.

A hazy, blue tint now clouded his vision, and he realised that they were no longer in the familiar surroundings of the Obelisk. Grace had transported them to a distant place. To his left, Elanor stood beside him, her features bathed in the ethereal blue light. He reached out to touch her, but she turned her head away and pulled her arm out of his grasp. The air around them felt heavy and unfamiliar, filled with an otherworldly energy that crackled and hummed beneath their feet. How had Grace gained such incredible power?

Azura! Are you nearby? I need you! No answer came to him immediately. *Azura! Where are you?*

"What are you doing, Ashbourne?" Elanor's voice sounded like it was far away, as if coming to him from the other end of a long tube. "Azura can't hear you here."

"Why not? Where are we?"

"This isn't real, we're not actually here. We're in my mother's vision. This is where we need to come to deal with the elder dragon."

Ayr blinked, his vision slowly clearing as if a layer of thick fog was being lifted by the sun's rays. And before him, a vast expanse of emerald grass stretched out in all directions, leading up to a mountain range that seemed to touch the sky. The sunlight danced and played on the rolling hills, casting a warm glow over the landscape.

As Ayr's eyes adjusted to the light, he noticed an unremarkable cliff face directly in front of them; as more of the fog dissipated, he could see something much more intriguing - a massive chasm carved into the earth. It was the size of an entire fiefdom, bigger than the Seminary

– the perfect place for an elder dragon to hide. A sense of dread and fear filled Ayr as he gazed upon this breathtaking sight, not wanting to explore and discover what secrets this place might hold. If the elder dragon was inside, there was every chance that both he and Azura were not going to come out alive.

Ayr cast a glance to the side at Elanor again. She frowned, furrowing her brow. "This looks vaguely familiar. I feel like I've been here before."

"It's too obvious, isn't it? This is obviously a trap, right? Where is it?"

"To the east." Grace's voice floated through the vision distorted and unclear. "Take your dragons north, until you see the morning sun rise, and then follow it until you are under the peak of it. There you will find this cave."

"Trap or not we need to go. Once watchers have shown us a vision, it is within our best interests to follow it until its completion. Thank you, mother. We will make our preparations and leave when we are able."

"I will not rise until you are gone from the vision. Best of luck to you, daughter. May your dragon always breathe fire..."

"And may his wings carry you forward."

Just as suddenly as he had been taken in by Grace's vision, Ayr was thrown back into his own body with a jolt. His mind reeled, trying to adjust to the sudden shift from one realm to another. Dazed and disoriented, he struggled to keep his balance as the room around him spun.

After a few moments, he realised that he had not even left his seat and let out a long sigh of relief. However, the sensation of being forcefully pulled back still lingered within him, leaving him feeling winded and dishevelled. In front of him, Grace remained motionless, her eyes still distant and lost in the depths of the vision. Her hand remained wrapped around his; as Ayr moved, Grace's fingers slipped away. Her hands hit the table with a gentle thud, yet she still didn't move. She stared straight ahead as if concussed.

Elanor jolted back to reality as well. It was clear that she was more accustomed to it, having gone through the experience multiple times before. Ignoring Grace's presence completely, Elanor turned to Ayr. Her eyes searched his face, taking in every detail as if trying to memorize every inch of him.

"Don't worry about her, she'll be fine. We need to prepare. An elder dragon isn't a threat we can take lightly."

Another shiver of fear shot down Ayr's spine like an arrow. "Is anyone else going to come with us?"

"The two of us should suffice. She didn't say whether I had to kill it or not. If she only shared the vision with the two of us, then we are the only riders that should take part in it."

"But you and Evor have killed an elder dragon. Didn't you say you'd taken a dozen other riders with you?"

"We did, but they had all seen the vision. This has me worried."

"What if it kills us? She's mad!"

"We have to do what was shown to us in the vision. There was nobody else present." Elanor frowned at him. "Failure to do so could have catastrophic consequences. We need to leave."

Elanor grabbed his wrist and stood up, pulling Ayr along with her. He was still unaccustomed to her strength. It was evident that she was being helped by Evor. She tucked her chair under her desk and beckoned for Ayr to do the same. He complied, and they made their way out of the observatory. There was an eerie silence as they exited - those eyes that had been watching them going back to their work. The watchers were a strange bunch, but now Ayr had to figure out how they were going to kill an elder dragon. If there were only two of them and their dragons, would it be enough?

With his wrist still in Elanor's grasp, Ayr was hurtled through the observatory at a faster pace than he had entered it. Elanor didn't speak to anyone, including Alfred on the way out. She stormed ahead of Ayr and burst into the corridor. Elanor kept walking and Ayr didn't want to start a dialogue with her. The moment the doors shut with a loud clunk, Elanor rounded on him, pushing him against the wall by his chest.

"My mother isn't mad, you piece of shit!"

"She's sending us into the potential lair of an elder dragon with no assistance. How is that not mad?"

"My mother is our watcher! As riders, it is our duty to serve them."

"If this is what my life will entail, I do not want to serve!" Ayr tried to push back but she was too strong.

"I don't think you ever did!" Elanor was mere inches from his face. "You're nothing but your father's son. Lazy, weak and pathetic!"

"Don't you dare!"

"Don't I dare? No, Ashbourne, don't *you* dare! You came in here and stole the one dragon that was incorruptible. Azura was as good as the rest of them. She needed a strong rider, someone that could do great things with her. Instead, she got you. A coward." Elanor took a step back and looked him up and down. "You're not a rider. I never should have chosen to mentor you. Fuck! Evor! Don't make me do that again."

"What?"

Elanor turned away from Ayr, her shoulders sagging in defeat and her eyes glistening with unshed tears and her voice trembled with frustration. Her steps started to echo throughout the hallway. Ayr shook his head. It wasn't enough, he had not said enough. He pushed back against Azura who was probing his mind. Now was not the time.

"Sunfire! Don't you walk away from me!"

Elanor whipped around, her long hair trailing behind her like a flag in the wind. With determination etched into her features and her hand balled into a tight fist, she stormed towards him, each step filled with purpose and fiery anger.

"Don't you ever call me that again. You don't have that right!"

"You can call me Ashbourne. Why is it not a two-way street?"

"What am I to you?" Fire burned behind her eyes.

"Many things." Ayr sneered at her. "Master."

Elanor raised an eyebrow. "An equal is not among them. Yes, you have a dragon, but may I remind you that Evor, for the lack of a better term, is twice the dragon that Azura is. Yes, they are promised together, but Evor has decades of combat experience that Azura simply does not. Yes, she will learn with time, but for now, Azura is nothing more than a pup."

"You're disrespecting us. I won't tolerate that."

"No, I speak the truth. Azura could not stand up to Evor."

"Are you implying that I couldn't stand up to you?"

"You're inexperienced and weak, Ashbourne." Elanor took a step closer to him.

The auburn locks of Elanor cascaded in front of his eyes, temporarily obstructing his vision. Ayr scoffed at her, the frustration and anger bubbling within him. Despite the urge to ball up his fist and ram it into her. It would be a receipt for all the hard lessons she had bestowed on him, but now was not the time to indulge in a dragon's rage. Instead, Azura's calming presence started to flood his mind.

Ayr resisted his initial temptation and instead slowly uncurled it, bringing his open hand up towards her face. He had to listen. It was Azura's magic, but he was powerless against it. Elanor's face started to soften as well. Was she being just as influenced by Evor?

Their bodies were mere inches apart, and he could feel the warmth radiating from her chest as she pressed against him. The scent of lavender filled his nostrils as he leaned in closer, their breaths mingling in the small space between them. He could see the faint freckles dusting her cheeks and the soft curve of her lips as she tilted her head back, challenging him with her fierce gaze.

Her pupils were dilating, and Ayr felt a sharp lump forming in his throat. A sharp, sudden pain shot through his body as something gripped at his pants just below the belt. With a yelp, Ayr stumbled back and tried to twist away from the pain. A wave of nausea came over him as the pressure on his groin was released. Tears threatened to spill from his eyes as he tried to regain his composure.

"You'll let me know when you're more of a man, won't you, Ashbourne?" Her voice was sweet like honey, but it was coated in venom. "Based off what I saw in the pit, I wasn't very impressed. I would have thought that the time you'd spent with Azura and myself that they would have grown. It seems that I was mistaken. I expect you ready tomorrow morning, or I will leave without you and Azura."

TWENTY-FIVE

Ayr and Elanor ascended through the winding corridors and staircases of the Obelisk, until they finally arrived at Ayr's room. The pair had not said a word to each other since Elanor had grabbed him. Ayr only stayed with her, unable to find his way back through the Obelisk without her assistance. As they entered the room, Ayr saw that Azura was already curled up in the straw bed, with Evor half out of it, his head resting protectively over her body.

The dragons lifted their heads, their piercing eyes locked onto them. With a graceful movement, they rose to their feet, the rustle of their wings echoing in the chamber. Ayr shrunk away, feeling like he was being judged by both Azura and Evor.

"So, you return, riders." Evor started to chuckle. "I'm glad to see that you've spoken to each other since we last saw you."

Elanor had her arms folded. "You saw the vision, didn't you, Evor?" The black dragon nodded his affirmation. "We're going after an elder dragon. Do you think you'd be able to handle one alone?"

Evor shook his mighty head. "No, rider. I do not. I'm not sure what your mother is thinking of sending the two of us alone. When do we depart?"

"As soon as I've gotten Ashbourne ready."

"Well, I'm not. I need some assurance, Elanor."

Elanor puffed out her chest. "Evor and I have killed an elder dragon before."

"So, you keep telling us. We get it, you've experienced it. But perhaps considering there will be so few riders going after it this time around, maybe we should take the night to study what we're up against?"

"Is that what you really think? It sounded like a lot more than that outside of the observatory." Elanor scoffed and shook her head at him.

I don't think you should lie about this.

What if she already knows.

Then it won't make the situation any worse. She could help us in our search you know. I won't be permitted to go into the library with you. Unfortunately, I won't fit.

How will I know what I'm looking for?

I can still guide you, rider.

"Yes, that's it. I just want the night. I need to learn more and know more about our assignment. Do you think it's wise for us to be riding out of here under the cover of night? We need to know where we're going."

Elanor glared at him. "I hope you're not trying to make more excuses."

Azura lowered her head between them. "He's not. I'd also genuinely like more information regarding the creatures. I have never faced such power before."

"Fine, we'll leave you two to it. I expect you to be ready at first light, Ashbourne. "Any later and I'll kick you out of the Obelisk."

With a sharp turn on her heel, Elanor headed towards the exit of the room. Evor rose from his seat and gently pressed his forehead against Azura's in a silent reassurance. He made his way towards the back of the room and the large double windows that were open for him. With one final glance over his shoulder at Azura, Evor took a deep breath and let himself fall from sight, surrendering to the pull of gravity. With their visitors gone, Ayr finally felt comfortable for the first time since he had been pulled into Grace's vision.

"I thought they'd never leave."

Azura glowered at him. "You should have let me handle that more. What were you thinking?"

"It's an elder dragon, Azura. What are we going to do against it?"

"We have to do as the watchers command, rider."

"It's not sustainable. I don't want to lose you."

"Well, I'm not scared." Azura began closing the distance between her and Ayr. "Why are you? We will do what is required of us as dragon and rider."

Ayr stretched out his hand and brushed it against Azura's neck. "I'm glad you're with me."

"I wouldn't want to be anywhere else." She nuzzled into hand, as much as her large body would allow. "Are you going to set off for the library now? You don't have much time if you want to find out about both elder dragons and the aftershock."

"Hmm, I probably should. Can you guide me?"

"Get on, rider."

Azura gracefully lowered her long, slender neck as Ayr stepped up to her. He hooked his arm over her neck and with a swift motion, she lifted him onto her back. Ayr's feet found purchase on her smooth scales, now large enough that he could no longer accidentally snag himself on them. The door to their chamber stood open and Azura confidently strode through it, her powerful legs propelling them into the grand hallways of the Obelisk.

The echoes of her footsteps rang out in the vast space as Azura hummed contentedly. Ayr kept a hand on her back, stroking her gently, his heart swelled with gratitude for his loyal companion as she led them down the corridors at a pace even faster than he could have run.

The journey was brief, the library appearing to be only a stone's throw away from their doorstep. If Ayr had not been familiar with its location, he would have easily missed it within the hustle and bustle of the Obelisk. Above the entrance, a sign adorned with an open book symbol hung proudly on the blackened, charred wood. The scent of old books and ink wafted from the area, enveloping Ayr in a comforting embrace before he even stepped foot inside.

"This is where I leave you, rider."

"Thank you, Azura."

He stepped down from Azura and dusted his uniform off. Azura cooed as he patted her one final time, before turning her tail and heading back towards their chamber. The library was one of the few places that did not have a doorway tall enough for most dragons to fit through. It was barely any higher than Ayr's head, like a tunnel dug into the side of the Obelisk. Upon stepping inside, Ayr found himself blown away.

A seemingly endless sea of books stretched out before him, with shelves soaring upwards towards the ceiling that resembled the height of the rest of the Obelisk. The musty smell of old paper and leather drifted through the air, beckoning him deeper into the overwhelming labyrinth of knowledge. Some shelves were stacked so high that even Evor, could not reach the top without leaving the ground. *Where would he start?*

"Are you lost, rider?"

Ayr's body tensed as a voice called out from behind him. He spun around, his hand instinctively reaching for the hilt of his sword that hung at his hip. Behind him stood a tall, gaunt figure, draped in a flowing white robe with a high collar around his neck. Perched upon his shoulder was a small green dragon, its coils wrapped tightly around the man like a serpent. The dragon's emerald eyes glinted with intelligence and curiosity as it gazed at Ayr. It was no bigger than a cat, yet it had all of the ferocity of Azura. The man's weathered face held an air of mystery, and Ayr felt a sense of unease in his presence.

"Can I help you?"

"Yes, who are you?"

His eyes narrowed as if he was trying to remember where Ayr was from. "I'm the librarian. It is my duty to guard this knowledge and distribute it to those searching for it. What are you looking for?"

"I'm looking for information regarding the aftershock and elder dragons."

"The aftershock? You're an integrated rider, are you not? What use could you have of that information?"

"I wish to study it, just like the elder dragon. Can you point me in the right direction or not?"

A soft gasp escaped Ayr's lips as he noticed the librarian's shortened arm, a stark contrast to his neatly pressed robes. But it was the missing fingers on that hand that drew most of his attention, until he looked closer and saw that the left arm was entirely absent from the shoulder down. The sight caused a pang of sympathy in Ayr's chest for the challenges this man must face every day.

"Head straight down this row, at the end you will find information about elder dragons. For the aftershock, however, you will need to the furthest left corner of the library."

"Thank you, do I need to be finished by any particular time?"

"No, but if you need assistance with getting a book down from the shelves, call for Davari. He will aid you and remove the book from the shelf. Once you are finished, he will return it."

"Thank you for your assistance, sir."

"Do not take any books outside of these walls. I would hate for another rider to be attacked by my flock."

Ayr bowed deeply, his heart racing as he backed away from the imposing figure of the strange man. He turned and hurried down the lengthy corridor, feeling as if he were being swallowed up by the endless rows of shelves that lined either side. Each step seemed to bring him deeper into a maze of towering books and artifacts. It was like walking through a dense forest, with no clear path and no end in sight. Ayr's hand reached out instinctively, seeking the comfort and guidance of Azura's reassuring presence, still within range despite their physical distance apart.

What's wrong with the librarian?

He used to be a dragon keeper. A hatchling once upon a time took his arm. He wasn't suited for keeping.

That's unfortunate.

Are you getting close?

Yes. I'm here now.

Ayr came to a halt at the end of the long row of shelves. Before him lay an endless expanse of books, their spines lined up in perfect symmetry. The dim lighting cast shadows over the leather-bound titles, making them seem almost magical. He knew he had to find the one that held the key to defeating an elder dragon, but which one?

Some boasted elaborate illustrations of dragons and their anatomy, while others promised ancient secrets and spells. But which one held the answers he so desperately sought? How could he discern the subtle differences between an elder dragon and a regular one? Ayr's mind raced as he stood amidst this vast library of knowledge, feeling overwhelmed.

"Davari!"

Ayr's eyes scanned the ceiling, searching for any signs of movement. Suddenly, a flash of midnight blue caught his attention against the backdrop of wooden shelves and ancient tomes. In the next moment, a small dragon tumbled from above and landed gracefully in front of him. Its wings softly beating the air as it floated at chest height, its size no larger than the green dragon that had been perched on the librarian's shoulder earlier.

"How can I assist you, rider?"

"Are you Davari?"

The dragon nodded. "Yes. Are you looking for a book on elder dragons? Is there anything in particular that you're looking for?"

"Yes, how to kill them."

"Wait one moment, please feel free to take a seat."

As Davari disappeared into thin air, Ayr's gaze shifted to the tables and chairs that dotted the walkway outside the rows of towering shelves. He pulled out a chair from the nearest table and sank into it with a soft sigh. Suddenly, a large, leather-bound book hurtled through the air towards him, landing with a thud on the wooden surface in front of his waiting hands. Its cover was worn and faded, but Ayr could make out the silhouette of a dragon on the front.

"Enjoy. Reach out if you need anything else, rider."

With a sharp flick of his wrist, Ayr opened the heavy cover of the book, its pages rustling with anticipation. He leaned in closer to the table, his eye scanning over the words and illustrations on the first few pages. It held promise - a map of uncharted lands along with an elaborate diagram that showed the anatomy of an elder dragon.

Ayr eagerly delved into the book, absorbing every word like a parched desert soaking up rain. Every diagram gave him more knowledge about what to expect. He was completely absorbed in the text, his eyes tracing each word with fervour. The minutes melted away into hours as other riders passed by, their numbers dwindling with each passing moment. The sun gradually dipped lower in the sky, casting a warm golden light across the pages of the book. Eventually it gave way to moonlight, which had prompted the librarian to provide him with a candle.

The gaunt, robed man had walked between the rows of books holding the candle afloat. He stood over Ayr, peering at the contents of the book. "Is everything to your satisfaction, rider?"

"Yes, thank you."

"Might I suggest you research your other topic of interest before you rest. There is plenty of knowledge available on the subject."

Ayr's tired eyes slowly closed as he let out a sigh and finally closed the book that had consumed his attention for hours. He reached up and rubbed his weary eyes before stretching his sore muscles. With a grateful smile, he handed the well-worn book back to the librarian.

"Thank you, I should probably start. Where did you say that books on the aftershock were again?"

The librarian held out his mutilated arm again and pointed towards another area of the library. "Furthest back left corner. Davari will attend you."

Ayr nodded and rose from the chair before making his way to the area that the librarian had designated. It was even quieter back here, without any riders in sight. Ayr slowed down, checking the corner of each row of shelves for any mention of the aftershock. He held the candle above his head and kept searching. He was ready to call out to Davari again, when he heard an all too familiar and unwelcome voice.

"Ashbourne! What in Chilijo are you doing here?"

Ayr spun around, a frown marring his features as he caught sight of Owens. The man was leaning casually against the nearest bookshelf, his figure shrouded in the shadows. Only the faint glimmer of light illuminated his form, leaving most of it concealed and mysterious. He stood just a few meters away, just far enough for Ayr to make out the general features of his face.

"I heard about your argument with your master outside of the observatory."

"So?"

Owens smirked at him. "Sounds like she'll kick you out of the Obelisk. You'll make your father proud. Keeping up the family tradition."

"I'm not my father."

"No, you're not. You're just on your way to becoming him."

Ayr's hands trembled as he clenched his fists, the muscles in his arms bulging with tension. His breaths came out in sharp, ragged gasps as he took a menacing step closer to Owens. In the dim light of the room, Ayr could finally make out his features, most noticeably, the chiselled jawline that had been beaten by Ayr, earlier in the day. The moonlight filtering in from outside cast a pale glow on Owens' skin, making him seem almost ethereal in the moment. Owens took a step forward towards him and Ayr recoiled.

"You need to be stopped. First it was getting a dragon that wasn't yours. Then it was murdering Gable on the Catalyst." Owens stopped and pointed at his face. "Then there's the matter of what you did to me."

"You did it to yourself. My hands were merely the tool that delivered you to that deserved fate."

"Just because your uncle is the Overlord, it doesn't mean that you're untouchable. It's time someone taught you a lesson!"

"And that's going to be you is it? You looked very much alone, Owens. Didn't anyone ever tell you not to fuck with an Ashbourne?"

"You'll pay for what you've done!"

Owens let out an incensed scream and launched himself at Ayr, who had been waiting for the other rider to attack him. He dropped the candle at his feet as Owens crashed into him. Owens' was heavy, hitting Ayr square in the middle. They fell backwards, and the air was driven out of Ayr. He raised his fists, attempting to turn Owens in mid-flight. Both riders landed on their side on the tiled floor. Ayr's head touched the tiles, but without any significant force. He needed to get to his feet, but Owen's arms were clasped like iron around him.

Despite being the stronger of the two, Owens was not immune to pain. Ayr struggled against his restraints, unable to free his arms, but he refused to give up. With a surge of adrenaline, Ayr lashed out with his head, the impact causing Owens to cry out in agony and finally breaking their bodies apart. Taking advantage of the brief reprieve, Ayr kicked at Owens' knee with all his might, creating enough space for him to spring back onto his feet like a panther on the prowl.

Ayr was fast, striking Owens before he could even get off the ground. His fist connected with Owens' face; he stumbled back towards the ground, clutching his nose, Ayr closed in again, this time driving his knee into his opponent's abdomen with a sickening thud.

Ayr fell with Owens, putting all of his weight through his knee strike. Owens coughed up a splatter of blood as Ayr slammed into him. In a desperate attempt to defend himself, Owens reached for anything within his grasp as he screamed in agony. But Ayr was relentless, grabbing him by the hair and forcefully slamming his head against the cold, unforgiving tiles.

With one hand, Ayr silenced Owens' screams by firmly pressing down on his lips. There was no soothing presence from Azura during this brutal encounter; instead, Ayr was consumed by an overwhelming surge of primal rage. Despite Owens' feeble attempts to fight back, Ayr remained in control, refusing to let go until he had exacted his revenge.

Ayr slammed Owens' head into the cold, unforgiving tiles once more. The sound of flesh meeting stone echoed through the room, and this time Owens' body went limp. Slowly, Ayr lifted his head to survey the damage he had inflicted. He could not help but smirk at the sight of dark blood pooling at the point of impact, proof of his strength and dominance. Without hesitation, he thrust Owens' head towards the floor again, revelling in the satisfying crunch of bone against unyielding ground. The scent of iron filled the air as blood trickled from Owens' wounds.

"Fuck you!"

A deafening silence filled the air as Owens remained motionless. The gaping cavity in the back of his head and the steady stream of blood pouring from it made it clear that any chance of a response was now non-existent. The metallic tang of blood hung heavy in the air. Ayr finally let go of Owens' head. He sat back and took in a deep breath of air. He started to laugh softly.

A solitary dragon's roar echoed in the distance, a haunting and mournful cry that pierced through the stillness of the night. The deep rumble reverberated through Ayr's bones, sending shivers down his spine as he finally began to comprehend the gravity of his actions.

TWENTY-SIX

The thick, dark liquid continued to spill out from under Owens' prone body as Ayr revelled in the sensation. The metallic scent of blood filled his nostrils, intoxicating him with its primal allure. This was one of his greatest victories - a tormentor from his days in the Seminary now lay lifeless beneath him. Ayr couldn't contain his maniacal laughter, relishing in the sweet revenge. Ayr savoured the solitude, basking in the glory of his triumph over his past oppressor.

Following a moment of respite, Ayr finally managed to crawl off the mangled form of Owens. As he collapsed to the side, he noticed the pool of blood that continued to steadily expand around them. The metallic scent was overpowering, and Ayr found himself tracing the intricate pattern it formed on the tiles as it crept closer to him. Each droplet seemed to hold a story, a memory, and Ayr's mind wandered into the depths of each one as they gathered in a macabre display.

Whatever sense of bloodlust had come over him was now fading from existence. It felt like a bad mood, but it felt so good. Had it come from Azura? Ayr rolled and went to stand, as he heard footsteps approaching. The dragon continued to roar in the distance, but the footsteps were smaller, more human. He didn't know what to do, so Ayr backed himself against the bookshelf and grabbed his sword from his sheath.

The rhythmic thud of approaching footsteps grew louder with each passing second, causing Ayr to tense and raise his sword in preparation. He gritted his teeth, the metallic tang of fear filling his mouth as he pressed his palm onto the blade, creating a deep cut. Blood welled from the wound in hot spurts, dripping down his hand and staining the blade of the weapon. With a quick swipe against his leg, he hastily wiped away the evidence just as the footsteps drew dangerously close, only a few rows away now.

A single lantern cast its flickering light through the narrow gaps of the towering bookshelves, painting the musty air with a soft yellow glow. As he followed its movements, his gaze drifted down to the floor, where shadows danced and stretched out like elongated fingers in the dim light.

"Who's there?" The voice was familiar. Elanor.

Ayr turned his head and gazed up at her, his pained and pleading expression. Her returning stare was hard at first, filled with suspicion and disbelief, but then softened as she took in the scene before her. The lantern, its wick burning low, cast its dim yellow light over the mangled body of Owens, his eyes still open in a frozen look of terror. More blood pooled around him, staining the ground beneath him. Ayr's breath caught in his throat as he struggled to find words to explain what had happened.

Elanor put her hand over her forehead and exhaled heavily. "Oh, for fuck's sake, Ashbourne. At least you had the sense to do this out of sight."

Seeing the funny side to the situation, Ayr smirked down at the fresh blood on his hands. "You're welcome."

"No, not you're welcome! I'm still going to have to clean this shit up! We can't just hide this. Good thing the book dragons have their heads up in the clouds. They won't come down until they are summoned by a rider or the librarian."

"What about other riders?"

"You're lucky. There's nobody else here except for the librarian."

"Then what do we do?" Panic was now beginning to set in. "This isn't the Catalyst."

"No, it's not." Elanor sighed again. "I can't keep doing this. I can't keep protecting you. You've broken the rules again. If this gets discovered, you'll be on trial for murder. It doesn't get any simpler than that."

Ayr finally stood up. "You're not going to let that happen, are you? You know what he did to me and how he tried to have me killed. We can spin it, tell everyone that he attacked me first."

"We could, but you're forgetting who you are. Do you think anyone, including your own family within the Commonwealth would believe you? Dalton murdered recruits from his intake as well."

"Is there anything you think that my father didn't do? It's a surprise he didn't overthrow the Commonwealth on his own."

"You know he almost did. We don't have time for this, Ashbourne. Are you going to help me move the body or do you want to get executed?"

"No, I don't, but I don't have any idea how I can hide it."

Rider... I can protect you. Bring the body to me.

You'll do what with it?

Hide it for you. Bring it to me and I will see all of your troubled thoughts flee your mind.

Thank you, Azura.

Ayr broke the communication and looked at Elanor. "Elanor. Can we get the body back to my room?"

Elanor's mouth opened into a wide 'o' shape. "Azura isn't going to eat it, is she? That's sacrilege."

"Do you have any better suggestions? Nobody can know about this. What are people going to say if they discovered you helped me try and hide the body?"

"I know... We just need to do something." Elanor frowned down at the body.

"Then help me take him to her."

"Ashbourne, what about Owens' dragon? I heard a cry just before. He'll be able to figure out what happened to Owens' body."

"There's no evidence. And is anyone here going to accuse Azura of wrongdoing? We might get it from the Commonwealth, but is anyone outside Anton going to take it up the chain? Would he even bother dealing with allegations?"

Elanor shook her head. "No, but we're not stupid. If Bersos figures out what we've done before we can work out a way to silence him, Azura will get examined."

"Let them. With how brittle boned Owens was I wouldn't be surprised if there was nothing inside her stomach after a couple of hours. She digests her food quickly."

Elanor smirked at him. "Ok, you make a good point. It's our best option at this stage. Bersos will have to be a problem for tomorrow. We just need to get past the librarian."

"Is there any magic that you can use?"

"Now that you mention it, yes there is. The oldest magic in the world. Get the body and get ready to run. You'd best hope there's nobody patrolling the halls this late at night, Ashbourne. Wait!"

"What?"

"You had to make a bloody mess, didn't you? We can't transport it without leaving a trail." Elanor tutted and flung her jacket from her shoulders. She lifted the body of Owens up and placed the jacket underneath it. Instantly the thick black fabric was soaked by the enormous blood pool. Even the jacket wasn't enough to cover Owens' bleeding wounds entirely, but it was enough to stem the flow completely. It would have to do.

Elanor passed Owens' lifeless form to Ayr who remained frozen to the spot. He raised an eyebrow at her. "What do you expect me to do with this?"

"Well, I'm not going to be the one carrying it. You're the one that has to shoulder this burden."

"So that's it? What about when we get out of here?"

"I'll meet you back at your chambers, Ashbourne. Just go straight down this row and then turn left once you reach the end. You'll be able to see the entrance from there, I imagine. Now get going and good luck!"

With a graceful bend, Elanor scooped the lantern up from the cold floor. Her lithe form turned on a dime and disappeared into the shadows. The warm light of the lantern illuminated her determined face as she moved with purpose, only to quickly fade from view. Ayr watched, heart racing, knowing they were running out of precious time before his fatal deed would be discovered.

He turned as well and found the library completely dark in front of his face. Owens' body was slowly getting heavier the longer he carried it. If only Azura could have flown in from the ceiling to devour it out of his arms. Ayr started down the corridor at a brisk walk, desperately trying not to lose control of the body. He could feel more blood leaking into Elanor's jacket.

Don't go too far. I will come to you, rider.

You'll arouse suspicions.

I'll arouse suspicions? I'm a dragon merely attending to her rider. How do you think that you will look carrying a body back here, dripping blood throughout the Obelisk? No, take it to the library entrance. I will have to finish it off there. The less time that body is out in the open, the better it is for everyone.

Are you serious? We will be exposed and in the open.

Just how long do you think it will take me to swallow a human?

You have a large mouth.

Azura chuckled inside his head. *Yes, and humans aren't the largest of creatures, now are you?*

Can you do it without making any mess?

Of course, what do you take me for, rider?

Ayr was making good progress through the library. He kept his head on a swivel, checking for the signs of any other riders that may or may not have been reading at nearby tables. So far, he saw none, but that could have changed in a moment. At last, after a minute of walking, he saw light coming from what he could only presume was the entrance that he'd walked through all those hours ago.

Laughter broke through the otherwise silent night air, making Ayr jolt. It was coming from ahead of him and he ducked into the nearest row of shelves. The laughter continued and as Ayr listened, he identified it as Elanor. Ayr peered through the gaps of the bookshelves, pulling one book out so that he could see what was going on. It took some shifting, but his eyes quickly found their way to Elanor.

Elanor was in a compromised position. She was on her back, facing towards the door. Ayr craned his neck to see further into the open space that was the library entrance. The reason for Elanor's laughter was evident. The librarian stood over Elanor, a childlike grin on his face. Elanor had positioned herself so that his back was to the entrance. Realising that this was his opportunity, Ayr made a great effort to soften his footsteps so that he wasn't heard. He closed the distance between him and the door, keeping an eye on Elanor and the librarian with every step.

His heart raced, if the librarian's attention was diverted, even for a second, there'd be nothing concealing Ayr and the body he carried. Considering that the dragon that rested on the librarian's shoulder was also distracted, Ayr thought he was home free. Without looking back at the librarian and Elanor again, Ayr slipped out of the library entrance and into the hallways of the Obelisk.

This time at night meant that most of the torches that lined the Obelisk's walls were no longer lit. Ayr continued to carry the body back towards his room. Azura had told him not to go far, but what other option did he have?

Ayr froze as he saw a dragon's shadow moving towards him from one of the linking corridors. Did it have a rider with it? Ayr turned his body to try and conceal some of Owens. Ayr let out a heavy, audible sigh of relief as Azura emerged from around the corner. The flickering firelight cast a warm glow upon her pristine, white scales, making her appear even more majestic. As her sharp gaze fell upon Ayr, she seemed to be burdened with an immense sorrow that radiated from her very being.

Rider. What are you doing? Come here!

Oh, thank Chilijo. It's you.

Who else did you think it would be? Zenender himself?

I was hoping it was just you.

Come on, rider. We need to see this finished sooner rather than later. Hurry up!

Don't worry. Can we just get this over with?

Yes, hold the body out for me.

With a grimace, Ayr obeyed Azura's command and struggled to move the lifeless body. His muscles strained against the weight, and his hands were slick with sweat. Azura hovered over him, her piercing gaze never leaving his every move. Finally, Ayr managed to put enough distance between himself and the corpse. In one swift motion, Azura extended her long neck and opened her mouth wide, revealing rows of sharp, glistening teeth. The stench of death and decay wafted from within her gaping maw, making Ayr recoil in disgust.

What have you eaten? You need to clean your teeth.

Not now, rider. Give me the body.

Ayr offered Owens up to Azura and her jaw closed around his upper torso. She lifted the body into the air and threw her head back. The rest of Owens body was devoured, gone from sight in a moment. He'd seen her do it countless times before, devouring the carcasses of dear and other beasts that inhabited the lands surrounding the Obelisk, but the gruesome scene of her eating a human was both terrifying and mesmerizing to behold.

It is done, rider.

Thank you. We should go now.

Yes, yes we should.

With a graceful dip of her neck, Azura lowered herself and extended her spines for Ayr to hold onto. She then lifted herself up, allowing Ayr to climb onto her back and straddle just behind her head. With Ayr in place, Azura moved quickly, covering the distance between the library and their chambers in a matter of minutes. Ayr saw no other riders or dragons until they entered the chambers.

A large black shadow was waiting as they entered the chamber. Evor raised his head and grumbled. Azura lowered her neck, allowing Ayr to slide off as they walked into the room. As she stepped into the room, Azura raised her head again and unleashed a stream of fiery breath at the chandelier high above their heads. The room immediately became filled with light as the flames took hold.

"What have you done, Ashbourne?" Evor's tone matched Elanor's.

"None of your concern, Evor."

Evor's eyes flashed with an angry glare. "Anything that affects Elanor is my concern. Do not think for a moment..."

Ayr's head jerked to the side as he heard hurried footsteps approaching from behind. He turned to see Elanor emerging from the doorway, her usually immaculate hair now dishevelled and tangled.

Her eyes held a hazy glint, as though she had just emerged from a deep slumber or a vivid dream.

"Evor. Ashbourne knows what he's done. There is no further need to berate him for it."

Evor narrowed his eyes. "I know what you did as well, Elanor. This is not a smart decision on your behalf."

"It doesn't matter." Elanor turned and shut the chamber door behind her. "It is done. Now, we all have somewhere to be tomorrow. We should rest. Don't you agree?"

With another loud grumble, Evor turned away from the others and retreated to the centre of the room. He curled up like a snake in the straw bed, his muscles tensed and ready to strike out at any perceived threat.

"Join me, little one."

"Yes, Evor."

Ayr shuddered as he felt something tussling in his hair. He jolted forward and spun, seeing that it was Elanor's hand in his hair. Realizing what it was, Ayr leant back as Elanor continued to play. The hairs on the back of his neck were on edge. It was what he wished Azura could do in moments to comfort him, but considering Azura was in her straw bed, there was little comfort she could offer him. Her presence nearby would be more than enough to keep him calm.

"You should sleep, Ashbourne. Tomorrow, we seek out the elder dragon."

"Are you going to stay with me, Elanor?"

Elanor laughed softly and pressed her body closer to his. Ayr involuntarily took a step towards the bed. "Do you need me to?"

"Your company is bringing both Azura and I great comfort. Perhaps you should."

"Then we should sleep Ashbourne. Tomorrow is a new day, and that bed has more than enough room for the two of us."

TWENTY-SEVEN

" Are you scared, Ashbourne?"

Ayr raised his head; a questioning look in his eyes as he lifted it from his meal. Evor, always the early riser, had already called for food to be sent down the conveyor belt. Elanor had busied herself with preparing a hearty meal for them before they set off on their journey. The aroma of sizzling meat and savory herbs filled the air despite the food being all but gone.

"No. I have Azura."

Elanor smirked at him. "I'm still scared. I've faced the terrors of an elder dragon before."

Ayr stood up, dusting his hands free of any crumbs. "Yet you've lived to tell the tale. What do I need?"

"You'll need your saddle, and I personally wouldn't recommend wearing your uniform."

"It's comfortable enough." Ayr shrugged.

Elanor was headed towards one of the cupboards at the end of the room. "If we need to venture into a town or something, sometimes being subtle is the best course of action."

"What would you recommend then? It's not like you've had such a great variety of options in here."

Elanor reefed the cupboard open, and a smile spread across her face. "We're going north. I'm glad you've worn a variety of clothes."

"I'm wearing this. What else do I need?"

"Even wearing your uniform seven days of the week will get boring. Have you tried getting a little bit of personality?"

"I thought it was all we could wear."

Elanor laughed. "Clearly you haven't looked around. Yes, it's great to know who's who, but it gets to a point where you need to change it up. Anyway, try this on. I'm glad I left it all here."

Emerging from the shadows of the cramped cupboard, Elanor hurled a dark, hooded cloak at him, the heavy fabric landing with a resounding thud on his chest. He felt its weight and texture in his hands, tracing the intricate stitching that ran along the edges. Meanwhile, Elanor continued to dig through the scattered shelves, her fingers swiftly sifting through the jumbled mess of objects.

A moment later, a pair of fitted riding trousers were also thrown at him. Ayr furrowed his brow in confusion as he examined the garments. This was Elanor's old room, he thought, sizing her up and realizing she was similar in stature to himself. Suddenly, Elanor turned around and put her hands on her hips.

"Come on, you haven't had any problems with it before. Strip."

"These aren't for me. What am I going to get changed into?"

"Stop being ridiculous, Ashbourne. They're your size. Now put them on. We don't have all day."

Ayr rolled his eyes at her playfully, a small smile tugging at the corners of his lips. He began to peel off his uniform, revealing the toned muscles and scars that adorned his body. Azura's admiring gaze was expected, but the added pressure of Elanor and Evor's watchful eyes made him self-conscious.

The room suddenly felt too small, the air thick with anticipation as he stripped down to his bare skin. It was as if every movement was magnified under their scrutiny, and Ayr felt a twinge of discomfort. He pushed it aside and focused on changing into more comfortable clothes, determined not to let their presence affect him.

He removed the Seminary jacket and pants and left them on the floor beside his boots. He took one look at the vest and sighed, throwing it over his shoulders. To his surprise, the vest was his size as he tightened it up, weaving the laces through the holes that bound it together. He quickly pulled on the black pants that Elanor had given him before finally stuffing his feet into his boots. Ayr collected his sword and fastened it to his waist.

"That wasn't so bad, was it, Ashbourne?"

Ayr shook his head. "No, but I could have just worn what I had."

"No, you couldn't have." Elanor tossed another item out of the cupboard at him. "That'll keep you warm."

With anticipation, Ayr reached for the next gift as Elanor watched with a satisfied smile. He could already feel the warmth radiating from it before he even unwrapped it. It was a simple but elegant grey travelling cloak, one that would easily fit over his vest. As Elanor rummaged through the cupboard, she pulled out a small leather bag and tossed it to Ayr. The bag was just the right size to hang comfortably over his shoulder, perfectly suited for carrying any necessary belongings on their journey.

"Do I need anything else? I was under the assumption this was going to be a hard and fast mission."

"Do you want to fall asleep in the saddle?"

"Not particularly, but I didn't think we'd be that long."

"Well, there's a blanket and some bedding in there in case we need it."

Ayr frowned at her. "Just one bit of bedding?"

"I don't remember you complaining after the last two times that we've laid beside each other."

"The first time was different. That was to stay warm."

"So is this." Elanor had the slightest hint of sarcasm in her voice. "We're going to the north. It will be cold."

"You've sure thought of everything."

"When you've done this for as many years as I have, you tend to prepare since you know what you're going to be getting yourself into. At least this time I'll have someone to carry the bag."

Ayr rolled his eyes. "Is that all I'm good for?"

"Your assistance is going to be very helpful. You can almost wield a sword as well as I can, and your other skills certainly aren't lacking either."

"Well, that was a backhanded compliment if I've ever heard one."

"Better than an insult, right?" Elanor laughed at him.

"I suppose. Let me saddle Azura."

The ornate mantle, its polished finished adorned with intricate carvings, stood proudly against the wall behind the main desk. An elaborate timepiece hung overhead, its hands ticking away the seconds of the day. What truly caught Ayr's attention on the mantle were two items that held great significance to him - Azura's saddle and his own mask.

The saddle, suspended by long straps that brushed against the floor, seemed to beckon to him. And beside it, resting upon a head mannequin, was his sleek mask. Ayr approached the mantle and carefully removed both items from their rightful place. He tucked the mask into his pocket before cradling the saddle in his hands, feeling its familiar weight and comfort

It was heavy, mainly due to its size and not from the materials it was made of. Azura stood up and walked over to him, lowering herself so he could get the saddle mounted on her. Ayr quickly worked under her neck and secured the saddle to her chest. With the final checks all completed, they were ready.

Elanor turned her mask over in her hands before lowering it over her face. "Just remember, you have to do anything I tell you to do when we're out there. It could be the difference between life and death."

As Ayr approached her, Azura's gaze fell upon him, her serpentine head turning to meet his gaze. The intensity of her blue eyes seemed to bore into his very soul. Each small scale on her skin caught the light, reflecting an iridescent white that glimmered in the morning sun that filled their chambers.

Are you ready, rider?

No, but if this has to be done it has to be done.

If you are worried about dying, don't be. I will take care of you.

I won't have you sacrifice yourself for me.

That's what a dragon will do for their rider if necessary. That's what we were made for.

A chill ran down Ayr's spine. The thought of losing Azura ate away at him like the aftershock. It would not be an option. He would do whatever he could to ensure that she stayed alive. Azura was much a part of Ayr as he was. Azura lined up beside Evor and the two dragons exchanged a glance.

"By all means, after you. Are you ready for your first mission Ashbourne?"

Ayr shook his head. "Haven't had a chance to be any less ready."

"Are you ready, little one?"

Azura barked up at Evor. "I was born for this. Let's fly."

Evor nodded slowly at her. "You know where we are going. Stay close to me. We fly north. If there is an elder dragon, we will destroy it. Understood?"

"Yes, Evor."

With a graceful stretch of his front legs, Evor took a final step forward and put his head out the window. Ayr, donning his mask and adjusting his posture in his saddle, took a deep breath. Elanor was now in her own saddle on Evor's back and turned to nod at Ayr. He nodded back. Evor took another step forward and as gravity overtook him, he slipped from view.

When you're ready, Azura.

I thought you'd never ask.

Let us fly then.

Azura followed Evor's steps, mirroring his fall from the platform. He quickly shoved his arms into the saddle, securing himself as they fell. Ayr was glad he had his mask already on as the air rushed towards his face. He could hear it on either side of his mask as it rushed past. The mask, despite the covering of his face, was still somewhat see-through and Ayr took in all that he could. This could be the last time he was seeing the outside of the Obelisk.

There was no need to check on Azura. Ayr could feel the happiness radiating out from her body, and in turn it radiated through him as well. Azura was in a free fall until she pulled herself upright and levelled out. Azura quickly caught up to Evor who seemed like he was waiting for her. Once she had caught up with him, Ayr felt like they were outstripping the larger dragon.

Elanor's face was impossible to make out underneath her mask, but he hoped that she was enjoying the flight as much as he would. They quickly left the Obelisk and the Seminary behind them, soaring over the several thousand rooftops that all belonged under the watchful eye of the Commonwealth. He breathed in a deep sigh of relief as they started to chase the morning sun. As they flew through the air, Azura began to hum. The sounds of her music took Ayr's mind off the task ahead and allowed him to relax as they flew.

TWENTY-EIGHT

As the sun began to dip below the horizon, its golden orange rays stretched across the open plains, casting long shadows in their wake. They had been chasing the sun as it made its journey to the north. With every passing moment, the sun faded more rapidly, until it was only a sliver of light on the edge of the earth's rim. Ayr squinted behind his mask, allowing himself to fully take in the beauty of this fleeting moment before them. The sky was painted in hues of pink and purple, giving way to a deep navy blue as nightfall approached. It felt as though they were riding into a painting, one that would disappear with every passing mile. But for now, they were here, riding together towards the last remnants of sunlight.

Can you see any better than I can? Is that what I think it is?

It's just a mountain range. You're seeing things that you want to see.

I think we should rest there for the night. It seems safe.

Azura's laugh echoed inside his head. *Have you ever been this far north, rider? So many creatures call that mountain range home. But, yes, if we are to rest tonight, that will be an ideal place. We will be able to easily protect you there.*

With a fierce and commanding presence, Azura released a deafening roar into the air. The sound reverberated through the surrounding landscape, causing birds to scatter from their perches and smaller creatures to scurry for cover. Evor, with his massive black head, turned towards Azura in response and let out a primal roar of his own, a show of strength and unity between the two powerful beasts.

"Evor! The rider wants to rest in the mountains tonight!"

"That is not a good idea, little one."

"That's what I told him!"

"I'm sure it can be done; we can watch over the riders whilst they sleep. We will land at the base of the mountains."

With a graceful shift of his wings, Evor adjusted his flight towards the looming mountains, and Azura followed closely behind. As they neared their destination, she overshot him and landed first at the base of the jagged peaks. With precise control, she gently touched down only meters away from Evor's careful descent. Ayr gracefully slid from Azura's back and Elanor alighted from Evor's sturdy form. The sky above them was darkening, casting an ethereal glow over the rugged landscape. The air was crisp and cool, carrying the scent of pine and earth. As he stood on solid ground once again, Evor looked up at the towering mountains.

"I do not believe there will be any storms tonight. We should be safe here."

Elanor nodded her agreement. "I imagine with any luck we will be able to find our destination by mid-morning."

"So soon?"

"Dragons can cover a lot of ground in full flight. These mountain ranges mark the very edge of our usual territory that we control. If these mountain ranges are here, that cave will not be far."

Despite his feet being on the ground, Ayr was no more secure. Azura was in his head, doing what she could to calm him, sending her energy towards him. The thought of facing the elder dragon was gnawing at the back of his mind. Nothing had prepared him for this. Ayr handed the bag that he carried over to Elanor who took it and crouched down.

"Come little one, we will hunt for the riders."

With a graceful movement, Evor spread his impressive wings to their full span and launched himself into the air. The powerful beats of his wings created a gust of wind that hit Ayr like a hurricane, almost knocking him off balance. Azura waited for Evor to gain altitude before following suit, her own wings stretching out in a fluid motion. Ayr and Elanor observed from below, with little to do but watch the two dragons take flight. As they ascended, Elanor unzipped the bag and started removing items one by one.

She handed Ayr the water skin he had been drinking from all day. It was only half empty, with plenty of liquid left inside it. Elanor spread the bed out at her feet. It was nothing more than a layer that would separate them from the rocky ground underneath. Ayr didn't like his chances of getting much sleep tonight. If he tossed and turned he'd find rocks poking into his back and side. It would be like being back on the Catalyst.

"Well, are you going to get a firepit sorted, Ashbourne?"

Ayr stood still, his mind racing. He was struck with disbelief and confusion as he looked at Elanor and then up at the dragons. How could he have forgotten such a fundamental aspect of survival in this new land? His thoughts turned to gathering wood for a fire, but as he surveyed his surroundings, it seemed that this place was scarce in natural resources.

The ground was barren and rocky, with only a few sparse trees dotting the landscape. A sense of urgency filled him as he realised the importance of finding a source of wood before the dark of the night. He had to think fast and find a solution to this problem if they were going to survive in this unfamiliar territory.

"Have you looked around?"

Elanor nodded up at him. "I have. You wanted to camp here."

"Can your magic sustain a fire without fuel?"

Elanor laughed throwing her head back. "Did you listen to anything I taught you? Despite what you may think, the fire will still need something to sustain it. I told you this weeks ago."

"Well if we don't have firewood, how are we going to make a fire?"

"Maybe next time you'll think. Call Azura back, we'll move deeper into the range."

Azura, I need you!

Yes, rider.

Moments later, Azura was returning to him, her white wings were barely visible against the darkening sky. She landed beside him and turned her head as Ayr climbed up her shoulder. Once he was secure in the saddle, Azura launched herself into the sky once again. Ayr pulled his mask down onto his face, protecting it. Evor and Elanor joined them moments later.

Where are we going, rider?

Up towards the trees.

Azura followed his request, and she landed again, further up the mountain. Ayr was much happier with this area. Whilst not as open as the base of the mountains, here was lusher, with a little bit of tree cover. Ayr patted Azura and slid down her side again, landing in a thin patch of grass that covered the surrounding area. Evor landed beside them and Elanor hit the ground a moment later.

"Is this what you wanted? Something a bit more protected, precious?"

"Yes, this will be fine. I can make a fire now."

Elanor reached up, scratching underneath Evor's chin. "Sorry to bother you, Evor."

"It is fine, Elanor. Sometimes lesser humans don't know what they want."

"What are you doing tonight, Evor?"

"If our luck has it, there will be a full moon tonight. Since Azura is now of a proper size, we may be able to begin to fulfil our promise to each other." Evor turned his attention to Azura who had not taken her eyes off him.

Elanor sighed. "I hope you're not going to do it anywhere near us."

"No, we will give you space. I know humans like their privacy."

"Have a good evening then, Evor."

"We won't venture too far away. We will bring you food shortly as well." Evor glanced sideways at Azura. "Call us if you need us. Come, little one."

Without another word, both Evor and Azura rose into the sky once again and quickly vanished from sight. With nothing to distract them, Ayr turned back to Elanor.

"If you don't mind, I'm going to go and get some firewood."

Elanor shrugged, unbothered. "Fine by me. Do what you have to do."

Ayr walked away from her, headed towards the shadows of the trees that bordered the base of the mountain. Ayr set about kicking his feet in the grass, his boots finding the first sticks that would make for perfect kindling. It was hard to see in the low light, but at least it was now, rather than in a few hours' time. Once both of his hands were full of kindling, he returned to where he had left Elanor alone to find the bedding stretched out on the ground once again.

"Took you long enough, Ashbourne. Have you got anything to control the fire with? We don't want it burning out of control."

"I just need a little fuel to keep it going. I'm going to use my magic to control it."

Elanor shook her head. "That's not something that I'd be wasting magical energy on."

"It's only a small fire. It won't take that much to control it."

"I know I've seen your ability, but do you really think that's wise to use that energy when chances are we're facing an elder dragon tomorrow?"

"It will only be whilst the dragons aren't here. What are they doing anyway? Fulfilling the promise to each other?" Ayr gestured to the sky towards where Evor and Azura had vanished.

"When dragons are promised to each other, it means they're promising to continue their species with each other. If you haven't worked it out by now, Evor and Azura are very much in love. They have both waited their entire lives for this night."

"Why now? They could have had heaps of time together in the Seminary?"

"Contrary to popular belief, dragons having sex isn't the quietest or most room conscious activity."

"Alright, well if you don't have any objections, I'm going to get this fire started."

Elanor gestured to the area in front of them. "Be my guest, Ashbourne."

Ayr tossed the kindling on the ground in front of him, not even bothering to arrange it properly. As long as he controlled the spell, he could ensure that the flames did not get out of hand. Ayr knelt down beside the twigs, hunching over them to ensure protection from the wind until his magic started to work. He completed the simple hand gestures that he had committed to memory. Waving one over the other was enough to cause the kindling to spark, and a few seconds later, a small fire flickered to life in front of him.

Now all he needed to do was ensure that the fire stayed alive. The night breeze was beginning to pick up, and this high in the mountains, it was doing what it could to cut through his clothes. Even with the cloak, he still felt the wind chill. The fire would at least give them a little something to stay warmer with. Holding his hand out so that the fire stayed alive, Ayr stood up and walked towards the edge of the cliff. It looked out over a seemingly endless darkness to the south where they had just come from, with not a light in sight.

Ayr tucked into his cloak more; he was receiving feedback from Azura, a higher emotional sense than what he was used to coming from her. Slowly the images began leaking into his mind, Evor surrounded her, keeping his body pressed against hers. It was vivid, and any attempts that Ayr made to reach her went unfounded. They were too closely bonded, as Ayr did his best to try and force the images from his mind. He heard a roar, echoing over the mountain ranges, one that could have only belonged to Evor.

"Come and sit with me, Ashbourne." Elanor was somewhere behind him, somewhere near the fire. "It's been a while since I've had the opportunity to just sit and talk with someone outside the Obelisk."

Ayr's gaze darted around, trying to appear nonchalant. The sound of cicadas in the background made it impossible for him to ignore her words for long. The constant buzz and hum of the insects seemed to seep into his very being, their presence almost overwhelming. It was as if they were trying to drown out all other senses and thoughts, including Azura's vision that clouded his mind.

"Ashbourne!"

"Sorry. I was... distracted."

"Was it Azura? They haven't started the deed yet."

"No, they haven't. But I'm sure you can feel it as much as I can."

"I would argue my connection with Evor is stronger than the one you have with Azura. Only if it is for the time that we've spent together."

"If our connection gets much stronger, I wonder how I'm going to be able to tell myself apart from her. She will be all consuming."

Elanor looked up at him. He could see her eyes glowing in the firelight beside her. In the firelight, their normal blue colour was turned a reddish yellow, matching that of Evor. She was curled under her cloak as well, not wanting to be scorned by the cold air around them. Ayr gave in. It was a reasonable request. Ayr let out a heavy sigh as he collapsed beside Elanor.

"What troubles you, Ashbourne?"

Ayr paused, caught off guard by the question. There were a dozen things on his mind, all of them worrying him to some degree: Azura, Evor, the elder dragon, and what reception would await him when he returned to the Obelisk. He didn't know where to begin, and just how honest he should be.

"Many a thing, Elanor."

Elanor scoffed at him. "You and me both. Do you want to be more specific?"

Ayr shuffled where he sat, trying to collect his thoughts. He could feel Azura somewhere away from them in the valley and he started to feel emotional. Was it as a result of what she was going through? Either way he opened up.

"Sometimes I wonder what will become of my name. I wonder if I'll ever be a footnote in history, but truth be told, nobody gives a shit. I'll die like a mortal man. The world won't weep, the heavens won't open and I will be lost to time."

Elanor gripped his arm. A flame burned behind her eyes. "You're an Ashbourne. Regardless of what you do, your name is etched throughout history forever. You can do nothing, and your family's legacy will live on forever. But what you do is up to you. You can change that and make it your own. I for one would not complain if the new wave of Ashbourne's became heroes in their own right."

Ayr stared deeply into her eyes. "You know just when to say the right things. You've been a good master. I'm not sure if I'd have survived the Catalyst without your guidance."

"It wasn't all just me. You had Azura."

"We wouldn't have stood a chance against Grisham and Heath if it wasn't for you."

Elanor shrugged. "You did most of that yourself. I just helped."

"I placed too much stress on Azura, and I shouldn't have."

"She's your dragon. She gladly shares your burdens with you."

Ayr nodded, looking at the ground. "I just want her to be happy."

"We all want our dragons to be happy. It's a strange relationship that us riders have with our dragons, but I wouldn't change it for the world. Evor is everything to me as I am to him. They want us to be happy too."

"You know, even though I've had months with her, I'm still not used to it."

"I don't think we ever truly are. Despite the dragons being the ones that help control and filter our emotions. You just need to remember that you're still young as is Azura."

Ayr looked up at Elanor and frowned. "You don't look that much older than me. How long have you and Evor been together?"

Elanor chuckled. "It's rude to ask a lady for her age. Just how old do you think I am?"

"I don't know. You've been with Evor for how long now? A couple of years. You can't be any older than twenty."

"Twenty?" Elanor chuckled again. "You know Ashbourne, I'd say you're correct normally, but no you are decades off."

"Decades?" Ayr could feel his heart sinking in his chest.

"Yes, I'm forty-three. I was a teenager when I came to the Commonwealth. Evor and Azura were both hatchlings by the time I came along. I wanted Azura but ended up with Evor instead."

"I don't know why Azura chose me, I'm not that special."

"Azura wouldn't have chosen you if she didn't think you were worthy. I have known Azura for most of my life." Elanor assured.

"When I'm not with her, I feel like I don't even know myself half the time."

"You're the son of Dalton Ashbourne. I find it odd that he'd send his son here, especially after what he did to us."

"He's a changed man now. He only wants the best for us."

Elanor threw back her head and laughed. Her long straight auburn hair was like a glowing mane in the firelight. "And I'm the Queen of Shalanty."

"I've been to Shalanty and have seen the queen there. You stand head and shoulders above her."

Elanor's face softened and the slightest shade of pink rushed to her cheeks. "Flattery will only get you so far, Ashbourne. I know we're nowhere near the Obelisk, but we can't just go developing feelings for each other for no good reason. I'm still your master after all."

As their faces drew nearer, Azura let out a loud pining that could be heard over the valley that separated the dragons and their riders. Ayr grinned, ignoring Azura. He could feel everything that Evor was doing to her, and he longed for Elanor's touch. Their lips drew nearer, and Elanor put her hand up to his face, touching his cheek lightly. Ayr's hand wrapped around the base of her neck and he pulled her closer. He closed his eyes as their lips met, and there was a surge between both him and Azura.

Azura!

Worry about yourself, rider!

"Ayr!" Elanor clicked her fingers in front of his face. Ayr shook his head, dazed. That was the first time she'd ever called him by his name. "First time that's ever happened to you, huh?"

"What?"

"Hello! Are you still with us? Clearly your connection with Azura is more powerful than I thought."

"I can feel everything."

"Good. Then feel everything with me."

"Wait! I thought you said we shouldn't."

Elanor leaned in, her eyes sparkling with both excitement and a hint of fear. Ayr hesitated for a moment, but he could feel Azura's guidance urging him forward. He followed the tugging sensation in his chest and closed the distance between them. As his hand brushed against Elanor's neck, he felt a surge of warmth spread through his body. There was no turning back now. This desire that had been simmering between them since they first met had finally reached its boiling point. It was like a wildfire burning within him, consuming all rational thought and leaving only a raw need for her touch.

Their lips met, and Ayr felt like the world had ignited. Two dragons roared in the distance, not in anger, but passion. Another shockwave of emotion from Azura hit him like a tsunami, washing over him, encompassing every part of his body. Ayr leaned into the kiss more, pressing harder against Elanor. She matched him and neither party wanted to be the first to split away.

Ayr could feel something rising in his sternum, desperate to get out. Feeling a surge of strength, he used his free hand and gently pushed Elanor back. She went with the push, laying back against the ground. She laughed, pulling him down with her as they continued their embrace. The dragon roars filled Ayr's ears and as the night grew longer, he only grew closer to Elanor.

TWENTY-NINE

The morning arrived; gentle rays of the sun crept slowly over the towering cliffs. The valley below basked in its warm, golden light, rousing Ayr from his slumber. As he opened his eyes, he was greeted with a tangle of fiery auburn hair resting against his face. Leaning back, he saw Elanor, her delicate features illuminated by the soft morning glow. They had drifted off together by the dwindling fire, their bodies pressed tightly against each other for warmth as the flames eventually flickered out.

Ayr gently brushed strands of Elanor's hair away from his face, careful not to disturb her as she slept peacefully next to him. Azura and Evor had returned to their side, taking their place in a semi-circle around them like guardian statues. The dragons lay sleeping, their scales gleaming in the glow of the morning light. In this makeshift circle of protection, Ayr felt safe and at peace with his beloved by his side.

As he rubbed the sleep from his eyes, he heard Azura stir behind him. She cooed softly before she opened her eyes, staring back into his.

Good morning rider. I hope you slept well.

Ayr stretched his hand out, scratching near her soft belly. Azura hummed peacefully, opening her mouth slightly like a dog, excited for the attention.

I did, and you?

Wonderfully. Ayr could hear the enthusiasm in her thought. He full well knew why. Despite Ayr being distracted by Elanor, Azura's emotions had been too much to control to any degree. She had been waiting for last night to happen since she was a hatchling.

You need sustenance. I will return shortly.

True to her word, Azura swiftly rose from beside him and unfurled her magnificent wings. The sun glinted off of her shimmering scales as she gracefully soared through the sky, her keen eyes scanning the forest below. In a matter of moments, she descended and grasped a small doe in her talons before returning to their campsite with ease.

Elanor and Evor yawned and stretched as Azura landed, the fresh kill dangling from her claws. Elanor emerged from the warmth of the bedding and stood up, while Ayr hungrily devoured the tender meat of the animal that Azura had provided for them. The aroma of cooked game filled the air.

Elanor smiled up at him. Her waking from her slumber was an entirely different experience. Gone was the hard exterior; it would not be long before that came back.

"Have you got some of that for us?"

"I didn't know you wanted any."

"Well, you didn't ask."

Evor stood overhead. "I will get us something on the journey, Elanor. In fact..."

He kicked into the dirt and shot down into the gulley in a gust of wind. There was a sudden squeal from a creature below and Evor shot back up to their camp in another moment. He was busy ripping another doe limb from limb, presenting Elanor with only the finest piece. She set it out on the ground and Evor controlled his breath, allowing the leg to cook within moments. He stepped on the ground around the now cooked leg, stamping out any further flames that still lingered.

Elanor tore into the deer's flesh with ferocious hunger, her teeth making quick work of it. She devoured it like a hungry wolf, relishing in the rich taste of the meat. Meanwhile, Evor gracefully finished off any leftovers, his large form barely registering the small prey as it passed through his cavernous throat. Even a single doe was not enough to fully sustain a dragon of his size.

"Today's the day we find ourselves an elder dragon. Ready, Ashbourne?"

"What happened to calling me Ayr?"

Elanor laughed and Evor echoed her sentiments. Azura gracefully lowered her neck, her muscles rippling under the weight of her rider. Ayr climbed into the saddle and settled onto Azura's broad shoulders, feeling a rush of excitement course through him. Elanor turned Evor towards the edge of the cliff and together they descended into the valley below. With each flap of Azura's powerful wings, Ayr felt the wind whipping against his face. They followed Elanor towards the east, Azura expertly tracking Evor's tail as they soared over forests and rivers below.

The morning hours flew by, the sun's rays quickly reaching their peak in the northern sky. The mountain ranges stretched out below like a vast ocean, each peak rising from the earth with jagged edges and dark, earthy tones. Ayr scanned the landscape eagerly, searching for any sign of the vision that Grace had shared with them. With every passing minute, his apprehension grew. The image had been so vivid, but was it just a fruitless pursuit? The afternoon sun was beginning to get lower in the sky on the horizon and that's when Ayr heard a shout from Elanor.

"Look!"

She was waving, further towards the east, directly ahead of her. As Evor's wings moved in and out of Ayr's vision, he saw what Elanor was waving at. It was what had been shown to him in Grace's vision. The mountain was massive, rising high into the sky, further than the rest. Its height was not its only distinguishing feature, however. The gaping maw of the cave mouth caught Ayr's attention. Six of Evor would have been able to stand on each other's shoulders like humans and still not have touched the ceiling. Whatever was inside it, was truly massive.

Evor started to descend down towards ground level and Azura followed him, encouraged by Ayr. The closer they got to the ground, the more Ayr felt a knot tying in his stomach. Azura touched down on the ground beside Evor and now both riders and their dragons were looking up at the cave in front of them. Ayr fumbled as he checked his belt, wanting to ensure that his sword was readily available.

Elanor raised her mask above her face. "Well, that's the cave that my mother showed us. That looks exactly like it was in the vision."

"It certainly looks like an elder dragon would fit inside it. Are you sure it's the right one?" Elanor just rolled her eyes at him. "You weren't serious, were you?"

"About killing it? Come on Ashbourne, I didn't know you were a coward after what you did last night."

"I've never faced anything like an elder dragon before."

"Many men have said that before. Yet, you have done what many could not."

"I'm not saying that I can't complete the task. I would argue that you're a little different to an elder dragon. One of the two things aren't looking to rip my head off."

"When the watchers give us a task, it is within our best interests to complete it as soon as possible. They only get flashes as to where and how to direct us. The last time that a rider failed in their mission, war broke out."

"What happened the last time a rider failed their mission?"

Elanor took a deep breath. "My father failed to kill your father upon him leaving the Commonwealth. You know the rest of the story."

"Well, no, nobody ever really told me."

Elanor scoffed. "Not even your father? I find that hard to believe."

"We didn't speak much when I was growing up. He trained me, and that was it."

"Hmm. It shows. Now that you're developing nicely and you have a dragon of your own, I can see the potential."

Ayr questioned her response with a raised eyebrow. "Thank you?"

"It was a compliment, Ashbourne. I'll be most disappointed if your father didn't pass his knowledge along, however. Are you coming or not?"

"We don't have a choice, do we?"

Elanor shook her head. "Unfortunately, not. Let's go."

Azura nodded and opened her wings on either side of her for what could be the final time. As Ayr stared at the cave in front of them, he thought he could hear a rumbling from within. He shuddered, half expecting to see an enormous dragon head coming out from it. Azura tried to comfort him, and Ayr reciprocated the feelings towards her. She took flight, stepping off the cliff, diving down into the valley below.

Ayr leaned into the saddle, clinging on as Azura continued to pick up speed. She was barrelling towards the ground, but already, Ayr could feel her starting to level out. He caught his stomach in his mouth, grateful for his mask as a giant bug flew up, smacking him in the face. Ayr recoiled, flicking it away as Azura continued to now gain altitude. She soared up towards the tops of the cave, covering the distance over the ground quickly.

As they neared the cave, Ayr immediately felt colder in the shadow of the looming mountain. They were still several hundred meters from the entrance when the sun above was blotted out. Another shiver rocketed down Ayr's spine - there was no turning back now. With Evor right beside them, Ayr felt dwarfed as usual, but even his size was no comparison to the cave.

Azura flew into the jaws of the mountain, with nothing but empty air around her. The cave immediately started to dip down and both Azura and Evor followed the path laid out before them. There was still just enough light for Ayr to see where they were going, his head constantly on a swivel, waiting for a much larger dragon to come swooping out of the darkness towards him. Aside from passing stalagmites and the cave dipping further down, nothing changed. On all sides of him was solid rock, seemingly untouched by any creature in years.

They had flown for what seemed like an age, when finally, the cave started to level out. There was a large hook in the cave and the dragons followed the bend as it then started to open up onto large circular arena. The term arena was putting it lightly. It stretched as far as the eye could see. Heading the arena was a tall cliff, one that ran approximately halfway as high as the cave. As they flew in, Ayr could see an ant sized cloaked figure standing, looking over the overwhelming area.

"Ashbourne! Look!"

Elanor yelled over the sound of the dragon's wingbeats and pointed down towards where the figure was standing. As they flew over the jagged cliff, Ayr's eyes caught sight of a humble tent nestled beneath a rocky ledge. The fabric was worn and patched, but it stood strong against the elements. Beside the tent sat a small fire pit, its edges etched into the earth by a ring of carefully arranged rocks.

Ayr nodded his understanding at Elanor's shout. Azura followed Evor in his descent. They swooped over the figure and then landed behind them, towards the back of the slope that was more or less centred in the middle of the cave. The figure had not turned, their back still to them. Ayr peered over at Elanor.

"What do you want to do?"

Elanor went to move her hand to her mask, but then suddenly removed her hand. She peered down at the mysterious figure. She also went to slide down Evor but rethought her decision.

"Wait here, Ashbourne."

"Why? It's just a person, they can't be that dangerous."

"You don't know some of the men that roam this world."

"According to you, my father was one."

The figure cocked their head and started to turn. Evor and Azura braced themselves, ready for any sign of hostility. Slowly, the hooded cloak was pulled back to reveal a man in his early forties. His short-cropped hair hugged his skull on both sides, emphasizing the sharp angles of his face. Ayr blinked in surprise as he recognized the familiar features of the man. The man's deep green eyes sparkled mischievously as he grinned up at Ayr. His voice held a hint of nostalgia as he greeted them warmly.

"Hello, Ayr. Who's this you've brought to me?"

"Father."

Elanor drew breath beside him. "Dalton Ashbourne, what in Chilijo's name are you doing here? I thought you were out in the wastelands somewhere, still mulling over your defeat."

Dalton's eyes flashed and he grinned the boyish grin that Ayr was all too familiar with. "Was that what my son told you was it? I'm glad the Commonwealth thinks that I am defeated."

"You were. My father all but pushed you out into the ocean."

"Your father? You're a Sunfire?" Dalton paused as if trying to remember the answer to a challenging riddle. "Ah, Elanor. You were but a child the last time I saw you."

Elanor stuck her chin out in defiance. "Don't speak my name. My father ended the war. You shouldn't be here."

"Yet here I stand before you, in the flesh. Sorry to disappoint." Dalton stooped into a graceful low bow. "If you're going to try to drown a man, I'd suggest tying an anchor around his feet to make sure he doesn't resurface."

"There's supposed to be an elder dragon here."

"Heh. And that was my son's first mission, was it? He was tasked by your watchers to take down an elder dragon? I'm glad they wanted him to succeed. Who was the watcher that assigned the task?" Dalton leaned back and drew in a deep breath of air. He closed his eyes and exhaled. "It was Grace Sunfire, wasn't it?"

"That's none of your concern!"

"Answer me, boy!" Ayr nodded slowly in response. "I thought as much. And you've got a dragon too. You've passed your test. What's her name?"

"Azura."

"And do you care for each other?" Dalton sneered up at him.

"We do."

"That's a shame. You have felt the one thing that I was unfortunate to miss out on during my life. The one thing that they took from me. The one thing that I would deny every other rider in the Commonwealth."

"Dalton Ashbourne! I'm taking you back to the Commonwealth so you can answer for your crimes against them. It is well overdue that you faced the Overlord and the Council for what you have done."

"I don't think so, Lady Sunfire. I'll be staying right here. You may go back there absent a dragon, however."

Elanor sat back in her saddle and laughed. "I'm sorry. I'm the one with a dragon. Evor is the veteran of a hundred battles. What are you going to do? There's nothing that will stop this from happening."

Dalton slowly turned his head, his muscles tensed as if he were listening for something behind him. Ayr held his breath, waiting in the stillness of the cave. It was not his imagination - there was a distinct rumbling, like the sound of heavy breathing emanating from deep within the cavern's walls. Ayr had grown accustomed to sleeping next to Azura, and even her loudest snores could not compare to this thunderous noise. It filled the cave and echoed off the walls, making it seem as if some great beast was lurking just out of sight.

Dalton's smirk had not left his face. "Sinibad! Rise! I have guests for you! You are hungry, are you not?"

The rumbling continued, until it formed into words. "You dare disturb my sleep, Ashbourne?"

"The watcher has found you. The riders have come!"

The rumbling turned into a loud snort that sounded like an explosion. "So, they have. I will uphold my end of the bargain."

The deep rumbling was suddenly replaced by a deafening crash that reverberated through the ground beneath Evor and Azura's feet. The dragon's eyes met, and Ayr felt a shockwave of fear shoot down Azura's spine. The scent of smoke and fire filled Ayr's nostrils as he began scanning their surroundings for the source of the disturbance.

What is it?

Rider, we came here looking for an elder dragon. This one is going to be more than we can possibly handle. I can smell him. He would swallow Evor whole. We need to go!

It was a trap?

Yes!

"Elanor! We need to go!"

Elanor remained stoic and drew her sword. "I'm going to kill the man that brought the Commonwealth to its knees. Dalton Ashbourne needs to die!"

"No!"

The sound of crashing water echoed through the cave, growing louder with each passing moment. Ayr strained to see in the darkness, his eyes scanning the cavern for any sign of life. A gargantuan figure emerged from the shadows, its massive size causing Ayr to gasp in disbelief. Its head alone was four times larger than Evor's entire body, filling up the majority of the space around them.

If Evor shook the ground as he walked, this dragon splintered it. If Evor blotted out the sun as he flew overhead, this dragon would send the world into an eternal darkness. As it moved closer, creeping further into the light, the elder dragon was illuminated by a golden glow that radiated from its massive body. It was both mesmerising and terrifying to behold, a fierce dragon with power radiating from every inch of its being.

"Azura!"

"Yes, rider!"

"We need to go now! Evor!"

The golden dragon continued to draw closer as both Evor and Azura took flight, their movements frantic as they tried to escape. Azura's heart raced beneath Ayr, her panicked breathing filling his ears. He desperately tried to soothe her, but the sight of the looming dragon was enough to send anyone into a frenzy. Ayr could feel his own heart pounding as they continued to flee from their pursuer.

Dalton's voice boomed over the sounds of Evor and Azura's wing beats. He had magic. Had he or Sinibad amplified it?

"Flee riders! Tell them that Dalton Ashbourne is served by Sinibad! Tell them that he comes for the Obelisk and all of the Commonwealth! Tell them that their empire will burn!"

TO BE CONTINUED...

ACKNOWLEDGEMENTS

Ah dear. Another book, another daunting acknowledgement page to fill out. I hope you all really enjoyed this one. It was a little bit different from my usual, but it was still very fun to write. I cannot wait for RAGE OF THE DRAGON (working title). In fact, if this book goes off, I may or may not be adjusting my future release schedule to have it come out sooner.

I think you'll really like it. The world of the Commonwealth will be expanding, and we will be getting into the head of a new character (it's Elanor and Evor). Needless to say, with the foreshadowing and events of this one, Rage is going to be explosive to say the least. I feel like the action in the spice department will get turned up a notch as well. You'll have to wait and see.

For those of you who know me, you know I don't like doing this page. It's almost as hard as the blurb. So here goes.

Firstly, if you are reading this book, thank you. I wouldn't and couldn't be doing this without you. Your support means a lot and I hope you really enjoyed this book. Hopefully this is not the last of my works you read and we can go on many more fun adventures together and you stick around for the ride.

Then of course, I have to shoutout my most dedicated. There's Ellie, Ajay, Samantha, John, Rachel and the big bad editor himself, Mr. William. All of these people are there to support me and it's phenomenal having a little team that all help me along the way. Couldn't do it without you! If there's anyone else I've forgotten, apologies, I did not mean to. There's a lot going on.

Anyway, that is all for now. I hope you stick around for the next one! I am really looking forward to it. May your dragon always breathe fire.

ABOUT THE AUTHOR

Matt Mememaro has a loose understanding of what the word finesse means. Matt is a workaholic when it comes to his books. For the foreseeable future, Matt intends to release at least four books a year. He is a very busy man. He intends to continue to release fantasy books into the foreseeable future. They will be coming thick and fast. He wants to have a stack of books as tall as he is before he dies.

You can find Matt everywhere, all you need to do is search for him. Alternatively, you can leave nice reviews for him and he'll come searching for you to cry at your feet. He is also amazed that you are reading this.

If you have enjoyed reading this book, please consider keeping up with Matt across his media outlets by scanning the QR code below. He would very much appreciate it. This is the best way to stay in touch with Matt and keep up to date on all of his future releases.